Bastard Verdict
By James McCrone

ISBN—978-0-9991377-4-1 (paperback)
ISBN—978-0-9991377-5-8 (ebook)

Cover Art Design, Mark Swan

Proofreading provided by the Hyper-Speller at wordrefiner.com

As always, for Lisa

I am deeply grateful to the following people for their support, insight and kind, critical eye during the preparation of this book: Alan McMunnigall, editor; Professor Gerald Carruthers, Professor Neil Walker, Professor Richard Johnson; Judy Aks, my family - Lisa, Fiona & Brad, Annie and Jake, Don & Carole; the Table 25 Group - Matty Dalrymple, Jane Gorman, Lisa Regan and Jane Kelly.

To all of you, thank you.

'But facts are chiels that winna ding,/An downa be disputed'
-Robert Burns, *A Dream* (1786)

BASTARD VERDICT

James McCrone

1

Anyone with the temerity to look upward into the rain that night on campus would have witnessed a kind of negotiated settlement between light and dark, as the wet Glasgow night held the pale glow from the Adam Smith Building's top floor close in a murky halo. One man did look up, before sullenly returning to the meager shelter of a young birch tree outside the west entrance to the building. He mopped his face and dabbed his bald head with a handkerchief as he settled back against the tree trunk.

Inside those high windows, brightness reigned, the lecture theatre dazzlingly arid and contemporary. Though it was chilly for all that. Not that Imogen noticed. Within her slow-burn, imposter syndrome panic, she felt flushed, anxious as she began taking questions.

FBI Agent Imogen Trager had finished her first lecture as the Alma Guthrie Visiting Research Fellow in the School of Social and Political Sciences at University of Glasgow. Twenty-five scholars, professors and graduate students sat bunched toward the front of a large lecture room in broad, curving rows of steeply raked seats. Each had listened with that cultivated, scholarly air of bored attentiveness to her inaugural lecture, meant as an introduction and discussion of her research interests for the coming year. Rain pattered against the windows, a discomfiting susurration that swelled and hissed during the agonizing moments of silence before questions and comments began.

The Head of School, David Reidy, sat next to her at a table beside the lectern in what felt like a well at the front of the room. He was himself cultivated, though administration had groomed him in its image. While most of his colleagues affected a smart-casual, anorak diffidence, he radiated trim-suited, camera-ready gravitas. To her immense relief, the gathered academics began to ask questions: regarding methodology, about the role and effects of policing in urban environments; two extended offers of help in research design methods.

As Reidy sensed that things were coming to an end, he asked a question of his own to wrap up.

"Thank you, Dr. Trager. Most enlightening and well presented," he said from the bottom of their shared well space. "You've given us insight into your research agenda for this year," he continued. "But I'm sure we'd all like to understand, as an FBI Special Agent, if you'd care to discuss how you *begin* your investigations. What's the catalyst?"

Even at the bottom of a well, Imogen stood out, long-limbed, a sharp bearing, with striking red hair and green eyes. "As I mentioned, my special brief is voting integrity," she began. "It's said that the difference between voting in North Korea and Texas is that in North Korea, if you vote, you're dead: whereas in Texas, if you're dead, you vote."

That won the chuckle she had hoped for, and she relaxed a little. She had a doctorate in political science but hadn't made a presentation to a group of academics in years. She was pleased that her proposal to investigate how voting security was processed in another country had met with some measure of approval and interest and pleased to now be on the firmer ground of criminal inquiries.

"Both of those methods, by the way," she added, "intimidation and fraudulent voting, fall under my group's purview, and we would investigate...though obviously not in North Korea. We're a *domestic* agency, after all."

Of course, she thought dismally, she wasn't part of that group any longer. Whatever praise the FBI bosses accorded her publicly, it was given through gritted teeth and rictus smiles. Most of the higher-ups at the Bureau still regarded her as a pariah. They were thrilled that she was taking her leave out of the country in the great abroad. The cowards.

"You've no doubt heard the braying about fraudulent voting in the U.S," she continued, looking out at the gathered academics. "But despite my little quip about Texas, in the U.S., like here, voter fraud is exceedingly rare and hasn't been a determining factor in an election in decades. But *electoral* fraud—manipulating, suppressing or outright disenfranchising voters—remains a danger. In each case, the fraud is an attempt to undermine or outright destroy the right of the people to determine their future.

"So typically," she continued, tapping the mental brakes lest her newfound calm erupt into indignant anger, "an investigation begins when someone at the Federal Election Commission, a State Attorney General or some other official files a complaint. Having determined that there's a case, and that it falls under federal jurisdiction, we open an inquiry and then I, or someone in my group, will be tasked with investigating. But we're also meant to be entrepreneurial, actively looking for potential cases."

Of course, she thought, it was the entrepreneurial part that seemed to land her in trouble. Then, because she couldn't help herself, she added, "And there's sometimes an infuriatingly myopic interpretation of the line between what's deemed to have violated the law, and that which is just morally unacceptable."

"I assume," ventured a small man with a knotty thatch of iron hair seated in the front row, "that you're aware Scotland may yet have its second referendum on independence from the UK some time this year or next, and—"

"—I knew you'd bring that up!" Reidy yelled. He looked at Imogen with embarrassed exasperation, then shook his head mournfully.

"And so," the second man continued, his eyes bearing into Imogen as though much depended on her answer, "how could we ensure that the next referendum isn't stolen?"

"Give it a rest, Frankie!" a scholar at the back of the room called out.

"I've read that Scottish Parliament wants a second referendum," she began, "and that they ran on it in the most recent election, but I wasn't aware there were irregularities in the one held in 2014—"

"Right," said a professor sitting next to Frankie, "that's because the irregularities're only in Wee Frankie's mind."

"See you!" Frankie began, turning to the man as uncomfortable laughter stirred through the room.

"Well, I..." Imogen murmured into the growing noise. "This may not be the place to talk about it. I don't know as much as most of you must about British politics, and irrespective of whether there was tampering the first time..."

Here the room erupted in passionate debate. By the look of things, the lecture hall could well have been parliament, with parties divided to left and right across the aisle. For a moment, she wondered whether she was cast as Speaker, and should be shouting "Order!" or whether that task fell to Reidy.

"HOWEVER!" she continued, as if taking the first role. "To answer the substance of your question: in my investigations, I make historical comparisons with similar elections, and I'm guided by events that don't conform. Anomalies don't always indicate malfeasance, but they're a good place to start digging."

"Aye, well there were anomalies aplenty!" Frankie interjected.

"The problem," she continued, "is that referendum votes are such rare events that there's not really a history to compare." She let that sink in. "How do you know something's an anomaly? Prior to 2014, there'd never been a referendum on independence, so what do you compare it to? Where do you look?"

She ended her presentation there, thanking all who had come as Reidy shook her hand and congratulated her. "Well," he said, "that was a little more robust than the previous lectures."

That was true, she thought. As a visiting fellow, she had attended the two previous lectures in the series, "Determination and consequences of the recognition of education among immigrants in Germany" and "(Un)settling epistemologies using digital tools." There hadn't been much controversy during the questions after those.

Reidy smiled. "What do you do for an encore?"

As the final cluster of scholars filed out of the room and Imogen began packing away her laptop, a man who had been sitting on his own near the back came forward. He was one of the few who hadn't entered the fracas. He had stood out, though. Handsome, well-groomed, with soft, boyish features on a man's slender body. Crisper, and with sharper angles—sharper elbows, too, by the look of him—than the graduate students and professors who had made up the bulk of the audience, he seemed more like a confident advertising agent. The department head nodded to him.

"Dr. Imogen Trager," he said, "this is Ian Ross, Special Adviser to the First Minister." He looked pointedly at Ross and made to leave. Imogen registered the look but didn't know what it meant. "You'll both be at the dinner?"

Ross nodded and the department head left them alone.

Holding out his manicured hand to shake hers, Ross said, "Wee Frankie's concerns—"

"—I'm sorry," she interrupted, "is that what you call the eminent Political Philosopher, Francis McDougal?"

"Yes."

"And he's Wee Frankie to everyone?"

"Not to the students, no. Not to his face, anyway," he added, with a mischievous grin. "Reidy misspoke just now. I report to Janette Ritchie, Chief of Staff to the First Minister of Scotland, not to the FM directly." The smile dimmed. "The chief of staff is aware that you can't establish a norm in a referendum like this, but it might nevertheless be useful to note and explore potential points of difficulty or weakness in the system, don't you think? Wasn't that part of your analysis of what happened in the Electoral College?"

"Indeed," Imogen responded. "But I would hope that if there's an open inquiry the Scottish or UK Election Committee is doing just that." She reached down for the UK-US plug adapter.

"Yes," he said nebulously. "Maybe *you* might look at it as well? Unofficially, of course. Because irrespective of what's been said publicly, a number of us are pretty convinced it *was* stolen last time. And if this referendum does go forward, we want to make sure it isn't stolen again."

2

He'd felt it for a day or two already, a presence watching him from across a street, or the someone who turned a corner just as he looked round. The previous day he'd noticed a figure sitting alone in a car. The engine started, and it pulled away when the driver saw that he'd been noticed. So, he was being watched, followed. But by whom? And why? He'd had a good look at his shadow the previous day when he started the car and pulled away, and the clues only raised more questions. It wasn't a Serious Organized Crime Command operation. He'd more than likely have been tipped off about something like that. And even so, he'd have been able to tell, would have seen them working in pairs and noted the "handoffs" from one officer to another. This seemed to be solitary, possibly the same man each time. Which was a worry.

Buff Lindsey was head of the Madmen crime syndicate in Dundee, itself part of a larger criminal enterprise throughout the UK and abroad. He referred to himself as the Dundee "shop steward." Whoever was watching him didn't seem to come from management. The Madmen used foreign outsiders for this kind of work, and the shadow, based on what Lindsey had seen of the man's clothes, his face and build, was local, loutish. British. And not the police.

A rival gang? he wondered as he sauntered alone that night out the alley leading from the collision centre chop-shop where one of his offices was located. Reaching the main street, he looked up and down it, noted someone waiting in the passenger seat of a car across the road to his right. Lindsey turned left. He had no rival in Dundee, he mused, and any potential usurper would know that his death would only goad the larger syndicate into scorched earth retaliation.

A dismal night. The air seemed smothered in gray baize. Light seeped from the few working streetlamps, registered in large, greasy pools along the pavement and the road. As Lindsey walked down the empty street between derelict warehouses and shuttered shops, he heard whoever it was get out of the car and fall into step some thirty or forty yards behind him. Could it be someone who wanted revenge? This last seemed the most likely, and the most worrisome. Such men were unpredictable.

Buff was taking a chance being out alone on the streets like this, but he needed to turn the tables and put an end to whatever this was. He had chosen to face this problem alone because if he was wrong and it *was* his bosses looking to clean house, his favored, right-hand man Alec would likely be part of the scheme. "Ye don't get tae be heid, alive and fifty-seven all at the same time," he thought, "without a healthy dose a paranoia."

There was a pub ahead, at the near corner marking a tentative hipster foray across the boundary road between the Madmen's playground and an up-and-coming district. In the boozer, it was all beards, tattoos and grim Spotify playlists, but the owners knew the score, and Lindsey enjoyed dropping in from time to time, was pleased to find that part of the hipster ethos was keeping on tap some of the brews he liked and remembered from earlier days.

"Liam," he roared at the barman as he entered. "A pint of heavy, if ye've no objection." He put a five pound note at an empty spot on the bar and indicated that he was heading for the Gents. The barman nodded as he drew the pint.

Lindsey slipped out the back door.

A narrow service alley for deliveries and rubbish collection ran along the back of the building. Lindsey crept toward the street, stepping carefully in the darkness between puddles and grease. He was approaching the corner where the alley met the road when his shadow arrived. The stalker moved cautiously but his eyes were fixed on the pub's doorway at the corner. *"Definitely an amateur,"* Lindsey thought. *"No even a glance down this way."* His follower was a big lad, a head taller than Lindsey and outweighing him by two stone. Now, barely six steps from him but still focused on the pub door at the corner, Lindsey saw him slow and touch a bulge in his jacket. Gun.

At 57, Lindsey might not have been as spry as in earlier days, but he still knew his business—and someone carrying a gun had to be subdued. Quickly. Lindsey's knife was out. The shadow registered him too late as he struck from the darkness. He slammed the butt of the hilt into the man's left eye and again at his temple. As the man recoiled, Lindsey stamped viciously into the man's left knee. Then a swift kick in the groin.

The big man's bulk collapsed in sputtering, breathless agony. A hand fumbled inside his jacket toward the gun. Lindsey stabbed this time, slicing him across the hand and wrist. With one hand he stuck the point of his blade into the man's fleshy neck and with the other grabbed him under the jaw and hauled him deeper into the alley behind the bins.

"Who sent you?" Lindsey hissed, when he was sure they were out of view of the street.

"Fuck off!" the man sputtered, as he sat in one of the grimy puddles.

English, Lindsey thought. *Manchester*? "Who're you working for? Why are you following me?"

"I don't know what you're on about, I was just—"

Lindsey pushed the tip of the blade a little further into the donut folds of flesh at the back of his neck. "Keep it down, now," he advised. A thin stream of blood pulsed along the cutting edge.

"You people, always fucking things up!" the man said boldly, as Lindsey patted him down. No wallet, no identification. He grabbed hold of the pistol from inside the coat and skidded it across the ground to the far side of the alleyway. "You don't even know what you've done, do you?" the man on the ground gasped. "You want the police on you?"

"And you with a pistol on ye? Ah'd love ta here ye explain tha to the polis."

"I don't have to worry about them."

"Explain that," said Lindsey, thumping his fist in the same bleeding eye. The man's shoulder and head rested against the brick wall of the alley, but he remained seated.

"When they find out," he said, still looking downwards, "your life won't be worth shit."

"Ah'll ask ye again. Who's 'they?' Who're you working for?"

"Fuck you."

It sounded like ill-advised revenge, a civilian out of his depth in a soldiers' world. Well, civilian or no, Lindsay thought, you can't let this kind of thing slide, can't give him a good hiding and leave him be. Or he'll be back. With mates. For two days, Lindsey had been living with the fear that his bosses wanted him out of the picture, on edge for every nuance that might give him a clue as to why. Now, it was clear he was safe on that score at least. And he had a pint waiting inside.

The civilian on the ground struggled, glared at him defiantly through his one good eye.

It had been Lindsey's experience that no one ever believes you'll kill them. But this needed to be done for a good many reasons. Still standing behind him, Lindsey plunged the knife between the neck folds at the back of the man's bald head and let him fall in a heap. Gazing down at him, Lindsey wondered whether people would be more, or less, willing to give you information if they *knew* they were going to die. Still, the shock in their eyes was always disquieting.

He fished a set of keys out of the man's pocket. Maybe there'd be some information inside the car when his boys took it apart in the chop shop. Lindsey wiped the blade on the man's coat and cleaned his hands on the man's trousers. He picked up the gun. Then he made a phone call.

"Is that Mr. Dettol?" he asked. "Clean up on aisle seven, if you please. Jist the one. But mebbe bring a mate. It's a wide load. The wynd behind that hipster bar." He paused to listen, then chuckled. "Naw, nothin like tha. Ah try not ta shit where Ah drink."

3

Imogen's reputation, it seemed, had followed her across the Atlantic, and Ross was still waiting for an answer. At home in the US with a blend of good casework, canny analysis and tenacity, she had tracked down and brought to justice those responsible for conspiring to steal the presidency by manipulating the Electoral College. It was the kind of important case that would have made any other agent's career. But to bring the case, she had exceeded her authority. She had gone outside the FBI, had worked with outside agencies, bypassed proper authority and had used non-FBI staff. She had even gone to the press.

For her efforts, Imogen became the public and photogenic face of the "Faithless Elector" investigation, but an exile within the Bureau. Those who knew that what she'd done was the right thing nevertheless joined the wagon circle against her because she had embarrassed the Bureau, which among careerists was regarded as *the* cardinal sin. What was more, an anonymous agent shouldn't have her picture on the front of the *New York Times* and the *Wall Street Journal*, however good-looking she was.

After all she had achieved and despite the public recognition she received, she found herself sequestered in the Studies in Electoral Integrity office in a non-investigative role, still reviled by many of her colleagues and superiors, still discounted. From the start, her superior at Electoral Integrity had been trying to get rid of her, the FBI's redheaded stepchild.

At their first meeting, he had helpfully suggested that she might enjoy an academic post, away from him and the Bureau. He had tried not to show his elation when she requested leave. She was exhausted, spent. She hadn't made up her mind whether she'd go back to the Bureau after her one-year leave of absence, but she needed to keep her nose clean irrespective of what came next. Whatever this Special Adviser Ian Ross was selling, she wasn't buying.

"Shall we go together?" Ross asked. "The restaurant's about a ten-minute walk from campus on Eldon Street."

"That would be fine, thank you," she agreed. "I'd like to put my laptop away in the office first."

They walked in silence down two flights of stairs. He was waiting for her to respond, she felt, but was giving her space. She knew what she should say—No—but something wasn't letting her do so. She wondered what Duncan would have had to say. He would have been intrigued by the prospect, as she was, but it was a ruinously bad idea.

She had chosen University of Glasgow for her research leave of absence in large part because years earlier, before she and Duncan Calder were together, Duncan had spent a year at Glasgow as a Fulbright Scholar. He had often spoken of his time there, and of Scotland in general, in glowing terms. Coming to Glasgow had felt like a means of staying connected with him. There was a family connection for her, too. The favorite aunt for whom she was named—and from whom she'd inherited her deep, red hair—had emigrated with Imogen's maternal grandparents, the Lochries, from Ayrshire, less than 30 miles to the south and west of Glasgow.

She had wanted time away to heal, to work on some research and maybe a bit of genealogy while she thought about next steps. The idea of doing it somewhere with a connection to Duncan, however tenuous, had been irresistible. She had gone so far as to imagine there might be a kind of ghostly dialogue with him as she worked or took in the sights, like feeling the chill light of a full moon when far from home and knowing that it also shined on a beloved. But a gaze across time—Duncan, younger than when she knew him, walking these streets in the rain.

She had imagined his voice teasing her that first day when she'd gone to the wrong floor looking for her new office—"It's not the metric system, 'Gen," she had heard him say, "but you *do* still have to convert: UK ground floor equals US first floor." Now, as she and Ross trod the wide, metal staircase she imagined Duncan giving an unflattering disquisition on the Brutalist style of the building they were in, the Social and Political Sciences Adam Smith Building:

"I get that 'brutal' comes from the French for raw," she could hear Duncan saying, "but it'd make more sense if it was based on the Italian *'brutto'* – ugly."

She almost nodded in agreement. Squat and gray, it seemed better suited as a bunker than an academic building. "And surely," Duncan's indignant voice continued in her head, "a building named for the author of *Wealth of Nations* and *The Theory of Moral Sentiments* deserves better." It was entirely possible that she was going mad.

The idea of communing with him like this was fraught. No fond memory, no warm thought was free from gut-stabbing regret. Every cheery moment began in her mind's eye with Duncan as he had been, generous yet snarky, bookish but passionate, and it ended where it all ended, with him dead on a slab at the morgue. Although she tried to suppress the memory, it often burst in on her without warning.

As she put her notes and laptop away in the office, she found herself crying bitterly. *Jesus, why now?* she wondered. Fortunately, Ross had stayed in the hallway to make a phone call while she put away her things. He rapped on the doorframe as she collected herself and dabbed at her eyes.

"Ready?" he asked.

Imogen drew a clearing breath. "Yes," she said.

"Well, you've settled in, I see," he said, eyes roving over the office with its well-stocked shelves and a tartan throw over the armchair.

"The only things that are mine are on the desk," she said, her back to him. "The rest belongs to Professor Ogilvy, who's on leave this term. He stops by now and then when he knows I'm not here, to pick up a book or something. He leaves passive-aggressive notes thanking me for keeping it tidy. Cleanliness that I can only assume applies to everyone but him."

She smiled as she turned toward Ross, her eyes still wet. "I'll have to move out of the Druid's quarters and find somewhere else next term."

"The Druid?" he asked, amused.

"That's the nickname." She shrugged as though it couldn't be helped. "A bit like Wee Frankie, I guess. I've never met the Druid in person, though we correspond in snark."

"Snarky runes, eh?" He stared at her as if there was something more he wanted to say. Whatever it was, he let it go and gestured toward the door. "Shall we?"

The rain had stopped. Patches of grass shimmered with icy wet, and there was a cold bite to the air. Light from the streetlamps played and scattered on the pavement and flag-stones as they retraced their steps out of the building, behind the library and down the hill toward Eldon Street.

At the edge of campus, they passed a thick-set man in a leather overcoat. Though he'd sought refuge from the rain under a tree by the Adam Smith Building, he looked sodden, and his bald head glistened. As they continued past him, he left off whatever he was pretending to look at on his phone and fell in behind them, matching their sauntering pace and taking care to keep about thirty yards behind.

Twice, as Imogen passed under one of the streetlights, their damp, trailing admirer snapped her and Ross's picture from his phone. Engrossed in their conversation, they paid him no mind, even if he was one of the few others on the street.

"You're not interested in helping us ferret out any weaknesses then?" Ross asked her finally.

"I'm an FBI Agent, Mr. Ross."

"Call me Ian," he said.

"Even on leave, I'm not allowed to be involved in non-federal cases. I expect someone from MI5 wouldn't be able to work outside the UK."

Ross shrugged.

She thought again of what Duncan would make of this new puzzle. He'd jump at the chance, she was sure, but he was a professor. Well, he had been. He could follow his whims, could take up "interesting questions" because his very job required him to do so. He was also dead because of it.

As they approached the King's Bridge, the bald, beefeater in the leather jacket turned away and headed down a steep side street. When he was out of sight of the bridge, he pulled out his phone and dialed a number. "Can't say," he said into the phone. "Did you see the pictures?"

On the bridge, Ross noted in his lilting accent: "You still haven't said no." He arched his neck to look down over the iron railing into the Kelvin.

"Why me?" she asked again.

"It's delicate," he said, looking behind them for a moment. "Anyone we might use officially would be embedded in or seconded from the Electoral Commission or the Met. Or both. And they would have to make reports. Once that starts, we couldn't be certain whom they were telling or where their directives were coming from—a clusterfuck, if I might borrow a vivid American term—of epic proportions."

Christ, she thought, it sounded a lot like the situation she was running from at the FBI, even if it was delivered in a dulcet Scottish accent.

"You're an outsider," he continued. "One with an astounding track record."

Despite herself, she scoffed. That wasn't the way they saw it back home.

"Am I missing something, Dr. Trager?"

"No," she sighed. "Not really. And please, call me Imogen."

"Well, Imogen, you took on—and took down—the president of the United States."

4

He had been summoned. The view from the Georgian windows of Jefferson Weaver's study in the Chiltern Hills had a reliable and desired effect. Its manicured stateliness unfailingly swelled him with self-satisfaction—how much he had achieved! How far he had come. Today, however, as he stood by the window, he felt no such stirring. He dropped himself into a chair and stared down, not out. Outside, despite his inward thoughts, it was a lovely fall morning, with the sun breaking through high clouds in fleeting, brilliant shafts of light illuminating some feature of a distant hillside or glancing enticingly along the Thames. Wallingford, South Oxfordshire, shimmered comfortably in the distance.

Scotland seemed far away, but not far enough from his thoughts. Like squall clouds in the distance, the storm-in-a-teacup idiocy surrounding the 2014 Independence Referendum bore down on him. Infuriatingly, it was not his mistake that needed correcting. Back in that September, others had panicked, but now it seemed he might somehow pay the price for it. Worse, he reflected, still petulantly ignoring the estate's Gatsby manor charms, this summons interrupted the new work he was beginning—work that he thought would pay off handsomely.

He had been busy planting stories and "thought pieces" about the need—post-Brexit—for a clearly delineated internal market, exhorting the necessity of Britain speaking with a single voice in the marketplace, and questioning the wisdom of devolved powers. His institute was also busy with academic-seeming economic models, forecasts and constitutional questions, preparing the ground for what was to come.

Despite his pretensions to gentry, Weaver, like Imogen, was an American. His confidence, enthusiasm and optimism were formidable—even by American standards. What set him apart was the gregarious cynicism of that energy. He was fond of quoting Rahm Emanuel's dictum that "a crisis is a terrible thing to waste." It had been the making of him.

Not content merely to "move fast and break things," which he regarded as nothing but the illiterate revising of Schumpeter's "gale of creative destruction," he sought to break things *so* that he could move fast. Unions, supply chains and finance, had all been disrupted on purpose. And he had seen his stock (along with that of his companies) rise. But for stock to continue rising, he reflected sourly, there needed to be growth. Weaver had garnered money and connections enough not only to break things but to *create* crises from which he might profit. It would be a waste not to.

The burnished front of the non-partisan think tank, Strategic Choices Institute, held his crown jewel, the Orwellian-named Transparency Project on Government Accountability. Its true purpose was to match its bespoke intellectual property with partisan-funded research, the better to move public opinion and misapprehension by creating and widening divisions. And to garner additional funding.

It all seemed to be going well. Over the years, Transparency's working papers and think pieces had worked their way into the mainstream press. GCHQ and the Foreign Office had found his company's work useful, too, often labeling its findings as "creditable open-source reporting" in their own white papers, when it was nothing of the kind. His work on the Scottish Independence Referendum, he thought, had been masterful; and it should rightly stand out (in the proper, discreet circles of power) as something of a triumph. But because his employers, three men he had nicknamed the "triumvirate," had panicked, there was something of an asterisk next to his efforts.

Now, they had summoned him to account for mistakes *they* had made.

Even before issuing their summons, there had been rumblings of disquiet in London amongst the triumvirate. Suspicion and apprehension attended close at hand in politics generally, but for the group of men financing Weaver's disruptive chicanery, there was an undercurrent of alarm that past mistakes might be compounded. It was a group of men who owed much to their *sub rosa* operations and their ability to sow suspicion and mistrust among others. They came by it naturally. But a talent for low falsehood cuts both ways—having created and provoked mistrust, they imagined it everywhere around them; and they stood to lose all if rumors and suspicions about how they'd gained their place at the table were ever explored.

Two of its members, Undersecretary Nigel Chamberlain and the reliably acerbic Toby Nesbitt, met as if by chance in front of Chamberlain's club. The broad, impeccably swept pavement was sparsely populated, but each nevertheless projected a chance-meeting geniality for the benefit of anyone who might happen along, despite the topic of their conversation.

"I thought these men were reliable," Chamberlain, the cup-bearer to the group, said with a strained smile as the men shook hands.

"They are," Nesbitt replied brightly.

"You're not concerned?"

"Not as yet," said Nesbitt as though considering an interesting point.

"But I hear your man in Dundee didn't check in."

Nesbitt shrugged. "It could mean anything at this early stage."

"I'd say it was getting late, rather. We have to make sure before October 25th."

"Still, the other part seems to be getting underway."

"Should we involve Percy?" Chamberlain persisted.

"Let's see if we can do it without the schoolmarm this time. I've been in touch with Townsend, and he shares my view. Anything else?"

"No," said Chamberlain. "Not as yet." And they parted as genially as they had met.

5

Though it was madness, career suicide, to involve herself in anything like an investigation into possible voting irregularities, next morning, Imogen had opened her laptop and begun her review blithely, automatically, as if she were merely returning to a longstanding task she was eager to continue after a weekend away. Or, as she would reflect later, was it worse, like the long-sober alcoholic who opens the cupboard one day and pours a drink, swallowing before ever taking thought, moved by some self-destructive inward need? It was only now as lunchtime approached that misgivings about the propriety—indeed, the legality—of what she was contemplating began to intrude.

Hoping for some better insight, she stopped by Professor Frank McDougal's office, along the hallway from her own. She paused and knocked at the open door. In repose, or deep in thought as he was now, Wee Frankie had the pinched face and brimstone bearing of a Calvinist minister, but when he looked up and saw who it was, his eyes gleamed and his aspect softened. A genuine look of mischief and fun animated his face.

"Good morning," she said.

"And to you, dear," he said, standing and gesturing eagerly toward a chair next to his desk with that affable condescension only old men can get away with. "I trust my colleagues didn't keep you out too late last night."

"No, not all," she said. "I escaped at about eleven o'clock."

"Wise," he stated, reseating himself. "Are you looking to follow up on our discussion?"

"I'm intrigued," she said equably.

"Did young Ian dazzle you?"

"Not so much him—"

"—Again, very wise," he said.

"More the idea that a vote might have been stolen...And is there something wrong with Ian Ross?" she asked.

"He's an ally, I suppose, and we should take help where it's given, particularly from one so highly placed. Bit full of himself, though." Frankie wrinkled his nose as though detecting unpleasantness in the air. Was it merely a political scientist's general dislike of actual politics and politicians, she wondered, or did Frankie mean something more? "And he talks like he was inoculated wi a gramophone needle. Bit of striver, too."

"I'd regard myself as something of a striver, professor," she retorted.

"Hmm. I would suggest a difference between striving and *being* a striver, Dr. Trager."

"Please, call me Imogen. My friends call me 'Gen."

"Well Genny, there's a difference between passionate pursuit of the truth...or *a* truth," he added evenly, a nod to his political philosophy work, "and striving for personal advantage. Wouldn't you say?"

Only Duncan had called her Genny, but she wasn't bothered about that. She was dismayed that even before she'd admitted to herself that she took this referendum question seriously, she was finding divisions. Not only did officials not trust their own—like the FBI back home—but the people hoping for a second referendum didn't trust each other. And, she thought, wouldn't a highly placed, political operative be a striver?

She didn't want to let on that she'd been a bit impressed with and a little intrigued by Ross, not least because like so many men, Wee Frankie seemed to think all women were pushovers for a pretty face. And Ross was that. Nice smile, too. If she seemed to take Ross's part, she'd be confirming what Wee Frankie probably already thought. She didn't need that. She hadn't been part of an academic department for years, but she knew its lifeblood was gossip and rumor. She'd had enough of that to last a lifetime.

"So," she began, "if I were to begin looking at the past referendum...and possible dirty tricks or malfeasance, what kind of background could you give me? Where would you suggest I start digging?"

"You're taking oor Ian's project on?"

"Not as such. Not yet," she stressed. "I'm not getting involved in someone else's fight," she said. "But I'd be interested to learn more, a little exploration of an interesting question, let's say. Which might allow me to make a determination as to how—indeed, *whether*—to proceed."

"Right enough," he said. He turned to his computer and opened a new tab. "I'll send you what I've been collecting." He began copying bookmarked URL's that he would email her before realizing that he shouldn't be sending her back to her office to open them when he could pique her interest here and now.

He opened a low drawer and pulled out a thick folder of newspaper clippings and copies of official documents. "If I were you...If I had your skills and turn of mind, I'd focus on Dundee and Glasgow. Despite what you said about the difficulty of comparing such rare occurrences as referenda, the Indy-ref had the highest voter turnout in history: 20% higher than the second highest."

"After what?" she asked, leaning in and taking hold of a thick file.

Wee Frankie grinned primly. "You're on the case right enough."

6

From Imogen's high office perch, she gazed north and west toward a far row of hills, called the Campsie Fells, she had learned. She'd been staring out the window (and not at any of the nine open tabs on her computer) for more than half an hour, full of questions. What troubled her weren't the academic's "interesting questions," nor the cop's line of inquiry. Indeed, if she'd thought to name them, they wouldn't have been questions at all, but misgivings. They'd been turning over in her mind long enough for her to have marked the progress of menacing rain clouds as they soldiered toward her under an already gray sky like some conquering army.

"You're on the case, right enough," Wee Frankie had averred earlier in the week, and so she was. Sort of. She felt that she'd figured out a way to hide what she was doing from the bosses back home—rather than study how voting security was processed in another country, as she'd stated in her lecture, she would say she was doing research for a comparison study of voter activation in referenda in the UK, US and Switzerland. But it would still be dangerous. Deadly so for her career if they ever found out. But why did Ian and Frankie want *her*? Why were they acting like a second referendum was simply going to happen? It felt like there was something they weren't telling her.

It was somewhat natural, she figured, that they'd want to make sure the next referendum was on the up-and-up—particularly if there was something amiss in the first one. But now, almost a week into her research, she couldn't find anything, official or otherwise, to suggest a stolen or manipulated vote. And there were enormous obstacles in the way of a second referendum, if it ever came to be.

True, the revolving door at Number 10 argued chaos that ought not to be wasted. And the Scottish National Party, or SNP, had run on a promise that they would hold a second referendum; and they claimed that their majority in the Scottish Parliament was itself a kind of plebiscite for independence. But the first referendum had established the precedent of Westminster *permitting* the vote by having issued its Section 30 order. About a year earlier, the UK Supreme Court had ruled that Scotland could not hold its own referendum. Without such an order for a second vote, Imogen saw, even an advisory referendum wouldn't be legitimate. No permitted vote, no independence. And the Prime Minister, whoever it was that week, had made it clear no Section 30 order would be forthcoming.

The sky grew dark as she watched the inexorable march of storm clouds across the city. Her office grew dimmer. It was also true, she noted, that some quarters of the political sphere said the British government's blunt pledge not to issue a Section 30 order made it a dead certainty that a referendum would take place—like a jealous, possessive lover whose very actions bring about the thing he most fears. But even that conviction, she thought, felt like flabby wishful thinking when you considered the legal and political obstacles, the connections, alliances and more than 300 years of grudging cooperation.

Nuclear submarine bases, Air Force bases, intelligence-gathering outposts, a common currency and the spoils of the North Sea all conspired to make a potential dissolution anything but straightforward, amicable—or certain. As the rain arrived and began smacking against the windows, Imogen wondered how the UK government had ever allowed the first referendum to happen.

Because this time, she realized, there would be more at stake, if it somehow came to be. Since leaving the European

Union, Britons north and south had watched in real time as their sphere of influence, their standing in the world and GDP shrank. The question of the open border between Northern Ireland and Ireland, post-Brexit, remained contentious, with dour political, security and religious repercussions. She wondered how *that* had not been front-and-center of the Brexit negotiations. As she considered it, if Northern Ireland rejoined Ireland, and if Scotland were somehow allowed its independence, Wales wouldn't be far behind. England alone, "set in the silver sea," would indeed be a very "little world."

Looking over what she'd gleaned so far—the obstacles, the entanglements, the very politics of it—Imogen worried that what Ian Ross and Wee Frankie wanted from her had less to do with gathering information to ensure a fair vote a second time (if against all odds it somehow came to be), and more about creating a fulcrum to move public opinion towards ensuring that another referendum took place. Exactly the kind of political intervention that would play disastrously for her back home.

In Dundee, Buff Lindsey was having an equally difficult time understanding what was going on. He had learned nothing about the man he'd killed behind the pub. The search of the dead man's car had yielded only a name, Craig Robertson, and that he was ex-military. Robertson's name didn't line up with any recent victims or villainy on the Madmen's part. Could he have been freelancing, Lindsey wondered, a solid citizen appalled by the free hand (and free pass) Lindsey and his crew seemed to enjoy in the city? Was he gathering information he would later share with the authorities? If so, it would fit with the dead man's belief that the police would be on his side, whatever the truth of the matter.

The dead man's phone was passcode protected, so if he was in communication with anyone else, Buff Lindsey and his Madmen didn't know about it. Just to be safe, Lindsey put it about that everyone needed to be a bit more careful considering recent events. And it never hurt a man in his position for it to be rumored that he'd killed someone who had annoyed him.

* * *

Late Friday afternoon, five days into her review, Imogen stopped by Frankie's office. Ian Ross was there. "Oh," she said, surprised to see Ross. "I stopped by to talk through a few things with you, Frankie, before I called you, Ian."

Ross gave a broad smile. "And I stopped by to talk to him about you."

"Maybe I should make myself scarce," said Frankie. "I've done my office, it seems, bringing you two together. Or," he smiled, "at least, my *office* has..."

"No, this is good. I guess you already know," she said to Ross, though she eyed Frankie warily, "that I've begun looking into this. But if I keep going, if I go forward with this investingation, and the FBI finds out about it, I'll be fired."

"It can be done quietly, Genny. For you, and for us. And it's important," said Frankie. "You're best placed to do it."

"If they do find out, I'll be lucky if they let me back into the country."

"Maybe we're asking too much," said Ross. "I'm surprised you entertained the idea at all."

"It's a peculiar business," she said. "Even if we're only talking about the way the referendum was run. And it's precisely the kind of thing I do. I suppose I've been playing around with it because I felt somehow like I owed it to my old friend and mentor, a professor named Duncan Calder."

"Wait. I know a Duncan Calder!" said Frankie. "Elections specialist. You know Duncan?"

"I *knew* him," she stressed.

"He was here, you know," said Frankie.

"Yes."

"Fine man. About twenty, maybe twenty-five years ago. On a Fulbright," he added for Ross's benefit.

"He's partly why I thought to come here, too," she said. "I started looking into the referendum because I knew that it's what he'd have done...that we'd have jumped at it together. I can hear his voice in my head sometimes, suggesting ways

27

forward with the data, new ideas and perspectives..." She broke off, afraid she would break down in front of them.

"You evidently worked very closely," said Ross.

"We *were* very close."

"I'm sorry," Frankie murmured.

Imogen mastered herself, before adding, "And he'd also say, I think, that when you weigh the high risk—the certainty of my termination at the Bureau—against the uncertainty of whether it'll come to anything, the best thing to do is drop it. As difficult as that is."

"I see that," said Ross. "High risk versus uncertain reward...truth and justice in the balance."

Frankie stared at the top of his desk. "What if," he began. "What if you could be certain there *was* something to find?" He stood up and closed the office door.

"Like proof?" Imogen asked.

"What do you have?" Ross demanded.

"At the moment, nothing. This is difficult," said Frankie, sitting down again. "I swore to keep it secret. To protect a dear friend and his family. But if we can keep it quiet, if I can give him assurances that none but we three—no one else—knows..."

"Who is it?" Ross asked again. "Who are you talking about?"

"He might give us the evidence he saved. I doubt it's the whole picture, but I'll bet it points the way."

"You've been sitting on this for eight years!" Ross exclaimed.

"High risk—certain ruin or jail for a dear friend? Not to mention what might happen to his family? Yes."

"Why now? And who are you talking about?"

"Because now the case is altered. Because now I have a closed circle that might be able to get something done—a high-ranking aide to the First Minister, and a detective with a doctorate who specializes in election fraud. We can get the bastards who stole our referendum, and we can amass the evidence before anyone knows we're doing it. Before anyone official can kill it. I'm counting on you, Ian. Genny, I need to know you'll do it before I try to persuade my friend."

"If it's as you say," she began, "I'm in." She couldn't believe those words had just come out of her mouth.

"Ian?" said Frankie, his eyes burning into the younger man like a hell-and-brimstone preacher.

"Yes," said Ross.

"All right," said Frankie. "I'll get in touch with him, maybe go up to see him this weekend. Let's meet back here Monday morning—nine a.m. I'll have had time to speak with him, and we can make a plan."

7

Ross and Imogen walked down the corridor toward her office.

"Do you think he has something?" Imogen asked.

"He sounds sure." Ross looked at his watch. "Do you fancy something to eat?"

"Yes, that'd be nice." She hoped the shock she felt at his invitation hadn't registered in her face. Had she agreed too quickly? She cursed her impetuousness—first saying she was "in" to Wee Frankie and now yes to dinner. "Let me get my coat and a few things in my office."

"Lovely. I'll meet you outside. I was going to go right back to Edinburgh, so I'll need to make a few quick calls."

"See you in a moment," she said.

He smiled warmly—searingly—and walked away toward the stairs.

In her office, she closed the door, took out her phone and used the selfie camera to fix her hair. She grimaced into the screen, checking her teeth. Teeth were good, she noted, but her hair was a problem. She rested the phone on a bookshelf and continued to use it as a mirror as she pulled her red hair into a simple braid. Lipstick? Bit of eyeliner? No.

For God's sake, no, she scolded herself. It wasn't a date. Couldn't be a date. Sure, an attractive man with a swoon-worthy accent was inviting her to dinner. But they were colleagues, sort of. Would be, if Frankie's efforts panned out. She wasn't sure of the norms for this situation. They couldn't be all that different from the United States, which meant she was thinking much too far ahead. This was nothing more than what it sounded like—dinner, two colleagues. Totally mundane. It didn't necessarily mean anything. But if it did mean something, if it was a date, was it a betrayal of Duncan? Again, no. She wanted to go, she thought with some defiance.

There had been so much pain, such empty loneliness. It had been a long time since Duncan's death. But she still felt connected to him, still felt raw and bitter about the price she and so many others had paid back home. The emotions buffeting her were confounding. He wouldn't want to hold her back now, yet she sometimes felt she couldn't go forward.

Still, as she turned her head from side to side checking her hair, there was a nice color to her cheeks she hadn't seen in a while. Dinner. No expectations. Let's see where it goes, she thought. If it goes anywhere. But maybe a touch of lipstick after all.

They walked through Kelvingrove Park to a steakhouse on Sauchiehall Street, near the Kelvingrove Art Gallery and Museum—three blocks from Imogen's flat on Bentinck Street.

"This is my walk home," Imogen said, as they strolled together in the gathering darkness. She stopped and turned round to face the main building's neo-Gothic tower, looming over the park's trees. "It's almost too dark now, but I love seeing the university from here. I've only seen pictures of Oxford University's 'dreaming spires,' but I think I like these better. There's no dreaming here, but slow-burn energy, dark jets of coal fire poking out over the trees."

"But not after dark," said Ross. "Here, I mean."

"Sure. Sometimes."

"Look," he said, serious, "I know you carry a gun, but—"

"—No, I don't. Back home I do, but I'm a researcher here. Besides..."

"Well then, it's doubly important. You should stay out of here after dark. Truly."

"It's twice as far to walk, if I come home the long way by Argyle Street," she said.

"And probably more than twice as likely that you'll get attacked if you come through the park at night," he rejoined.

"I'm sorry," he added, perhaps realizing that whatever pleasant mood had been evolving was withering. "I'd be seriously remiss if I didn't tell you something that, as a visitor, you might not have known."

"I appreciate your concern."

"And away north like we are here in Scotland, in October, the sunset times change quickly." He paused, searching her face. "You're not going to take my advice, are you?" he said, smiling and shaking his head.

"I will take it under advisement."

"I thought you were the risk/reward lass."

"That I am." She smiled as they resumed their walk. "And," she added, thinking about the old Faithless Elector case, "if Frankie's evidence is as he says, you'll need to be careful, too, Ian."

"Let's not get too far ahead of ourselves," he said. "We haven't seen what Wee Frankie has yet. We don't even know who his friend is."

"All I'm saying is that your position in the government might not protect you. It could even make you a target. You can't always know where the danger will come from. Believe me, I know."

Ross flashed her a curious look. His voice dropped into a different register. "Ah've been in this game a wee while, hen," he said. "Ah think Ah can look after maself."

"At least take what I'm saying under advisement, Ian." She patted his arm warmly, and immediately wished she hadn't.

8

The house along Hyndford Street was still, quiet. And cold. Sandra Alban closed the front door behind her and dropped her purse at the front hall table. "Donald?" she called. She set her suitcase by the stairs and called up again as she removed her gloves. "Donald, it's freezing in here!"

This was the opposite of the warm welcome back she had hoped for after three days away, and she frowned a little as she stalked toward the thermostat in the sitting room. She adjusted the temperature and stood, listening to the house. She heard the furnace kick on, but no other sound.

She stood a moment longer, her face bearing an amused, expectant expression, anticipating that the heat coming on would draw Donald—crossly—out of his lair to investigate. They had been married thirty-five years, and she knew that nothing unseated him quite like someone else fiddling with the heat. Still hearing nothing, she crossed back into the front hall, her sensible shoes rapping smartly on the tile and peered through the front door window toward the garage. His car was there.

She glanced at the case as she began mounting the stairs. Donald could bring it up for her later, she thought to herself with cheery peevishness. Nevertheless, her steps grew tentative. She stopped halfway up and listened again. "Donald!" she called, her voice hollow in the big house. She had pitched her tone to be one of exasperation, but she heard—and felt—a mounting worry. At the top of the stairs, she glanced toward the study. The door was closed. "Donald!" she called, her voice

33

trying to sound stern. She looked back toward their bedroom. The door there was open, and the bed made. She turned and walked quickly toward the study door, knocking and entering in the same movement.

"Donald, I've b—" her voice choked and she recoiled from the body of her husband, suspended from the ceiling. Staring eyes bulged out of a distended purple and brown mask. His tongue had swelled outside his mouth. Sandra felt she was strangling, felt the room pitch. Involuntarily, she reached out and touched a cold hand.

Near the top of the hill, behind the stone wall, blue police lights flickered in the gray light, stabbed through small gaps in the lush privacy trees lining the grounds of Sandra and Donald Alban's very private home. It was private no more. Police roamed across the house and grounds, measuring and taking photographs. The emergency response team arrived. Amid all this activity, Sandra sat mutely in the first-floor hallway in what had once been the designated "telephone chair" next to a small table, where she alternated between sweltering delirium and icy nausea, her mind reeling. The fingers that had touched Donald's hand seemed to have grown cold and lifeless themselves, as if death was a contagion.

The police determined that Donald had done the job the night she left to visit her sister and that he had been dead for two days at least. She remained in the hallway chair, numb, unbelieving. One of the constables poured her a cup of tea from his thermos. She accepted it distractedly, her gaze drawn toward the half-open study door and the policemen still working there. Peering into his study, she felt she could still see Donald's body as she had found him—how long ago?

Her breath came short as she fixated on the spot in his study where she had found him. As she continued to gaze toward the specter hanging in the air, she couldn't help feeling that something was missing. The Detective Inspector on the scene confirmed that it was suicide. "We have a note," he said, "printed from his computer."

"From his computer?" she asked. "Not handwritten?"

The DI shook his head.

They had moved into the house, she and Donald, some 30 years earlier as a young couple. Together, they had brought their three children into the world there, and she assumed she and Donald would die there. But not like this. And why now? What had changed? Donald had a sometimes over-protective care of her and the children. She couldn't fathom him going out now, least of all like this. Their youngest, Jean, wasn't through university yet. With a start, she realized she was thinking aloud.

"I try not to read too much into these things, Mrs. Alban," said the DI. "So much happens that we never know about, could never have known about. Is there someone you'd like to call right now?"

She turned absently to the table next to her, where the old landline phone had not rested for more than ten years.

The official police report that would be filed next morning was perfunctory, confirming the death as a suicide. There was no sign of forced entry, no sign of struggle. The incident report narrative was brief. Donald Alban had been a barrister for much of his life, and the acting returning officer for the Dundee district for some fifteen years. His thoroughness and integrity in the performance of his election duties had been above question. He was a respected ARO, and a well thought of husband and father of three.

His problems, it seemed, had started directly after the 2014 Scottish Independence Referendum. Though there were claims that something was amiss with the vote count in the City of Dundee district, along with that of Glasgow, no whiff of scandal or wrongdoing had clung to him. Allegations were looked into, but they led nowhere and were soon abandoned. Though never implicated, he had resigned soon after, became withdrawn and almost secretive, breaking ties with colleagues and officials with whom he had once been on close terms.

Sandra Alban went downstairs, where she retrieved the phone from her purse and made four calls, the first three to each of her children, to give them the news. The fourth was to Donald's solicitor, his protégé and closest friend, Ewan

Johnston—himself like a fourth child. Where she had been strong for the sake of the children, she was unable to hold together as she spoke with Johnston.

"Ewan, it's Sandra," she began. "There's no way to say this delicately, so I'll just say it: Donald is dead." Her voice was hoarse, and the words came slowly. "I found him an hour or so ago. The police are here, and they're ruling it a suicide...He hanged himself. In his study."

"Oh, Sandy! My God," he said, words sounding hollow. "How...?" he began but trailed off. "I'll be right over."

He rang off and began getting ready. The Alban's three children were spread across the country, the nearest being in Manchester. It was probable that they couldn't get home to Dundee until the next day. He didn't want her to be alone.

Despite his assurance that he'd be right over, he stopped in his preparations and dropped into a chair in the sitting room of his apartment for some minutes, overcome with incomprehension and black despair. He cast his mind back to earlier meetings with Donald and cursed his lack of awareness. If he hadn't been so preoccupied with work, would he have seen the signs? Were there signs?

It had already been a difficult week, and it was only Monday. He called his partner at the firm to let him know what had happened and to say he would not be back to the office right away as he'd promised. That morning they'd discovered that there had been a break-in at their law offices on Ward Street over the weekend, and there was cleanup work to do. Amid his own grief, he began going over in his mind the things he'd need to do—help and be a friend to the Albans; and amid the chaos of his office, begin the work of seeing to Donald's affairs and estate. The break-in was going to make that doubly difficult.

On the face of it, the break-in had seemed like the work of some kids or a less-than-satisfied client. Whoever it was—and he would learn later that CCTV footage showed only four, beefy, hooded figures entering the building—they had ransacked and destroyed the premises. They had spraypainted some vague, illiterate revolutionary slogans, upended and emptied filing cabinets, smashed interior windows and left dog shit in two of the potted schefflera.

The locked cabinet where the firm kept important documents and wills had been broken into as well. The police surmised that the cabinet had been the main objective, since it also held thousands of pounds in ready cash.

But something felt wrong to Johnston. Perversely, the thieves seemed to have expended too much effort in the destructive details. It was one thing to have a bit of anarchic fun on your way to looting the cabinet, but the mayhem had taken time. Why would you take *more* time and risk being caught? Strange, he thought, the break-in had been Friday night, and Donald had killed himself that weekend, perhaps that very night. If bad things happen in threes, as his mother was wont to say, whatever next?

That same morning, arriving on campus for her meeting with Frankie and Ian Ross, the department chair David Reidy stopped Imogen in the concourse as she made for the stairs.

"I know you'd become close with Frankie," he began, his eyes red-rimmed, his expression vacant and staring. He didn't need to finish his sentence. The look of shock and suffering on his face communicated more than words. Imogen recoiled. "He was found dead this morning," he concluded.

She reached for the handrail and sat down on a step, her mind roiling with cold fear. Reidy sat next to her.

"He kept his car at a lot along Cheapside, right under the Kingston Bridge...though I don't expect you know where that is."

Reidy continued talking but Imogen couldn't listen, couldn't focus. Words and phrases intruded. She heard Reidy saying things like "valued colleague," "eminent scholar," "good servant of the university." She nodded at these bromides and lifted herself to a standing position.

"I'll let you know about the memorial," he was saying. "It will be a big affair. We all loved Wee Frankie."

"Yes," she said distantly.

Ian Ross was waiting in the hallway outside her office. His face bore the same stunned pallor as Reidy's. One look at Imogen told him he didn't need to ask if she had heard.

"How could it have happened?" he asked, as she drew near. "What do we really know?"

"That he might have been on to something, and he was killed for it?" he said. He seemed more frightened than despondent.

That was where Imogen's thoughts had led her—she had had far too much experience with such killings. Nevertheless, she felt it was important not to go too far, too quickly. They went inside her office, where Imogen found a televised news report about Frankie's death on her computer.

"The body of Glasgow University professor Francis McDougal," the reporter began, "was found this morning along Cheapside Street by Anderston Quay. Mr. James McManus, a resident of the Glasgow Central Skyline apartments, who was walking his dog, telephoned police."

The news report cut to McManus: "It's an open area, and I sometimes let the dog off the leash," he began. McManus's eyes shifted, a flicker of doubt across his face over whether he should be admitting that. "He found something by the fence on the other side of the street from the parking lot. He was quite excited by it. I couldn't make out what it was because it—the man's body—was on the other side of the fence. That's when I went over and had a look myself."

Imogen and Ross looked at one another with bleak disgust. Frankie's body, it seemed, had been tossed over the high fence like abandoned rubbish. The camera roved over the site, tucked under the Kingston Bridge. It was a weedy, desolate place, surrounded by grim, spare ground.

"Professor McDougal kept a car here under a monthly contract," the reporter continued. "Police have not said whether they have any leads. But they surmise that McDougal was surprised on his way to the car, robbed and killed late Friday night. The car has been stolen, too. We're told that it's been recovered where it was abandoned sometime late Saturday night or early Sunday morning, behind the Possilpark Library."

Ewan Johnston stepped delicately through the wreckage of his office along Ward Street a little outside Dundee's town centre. He had looked in on Sandra and made a few remarks that he wished had conveyed more. But seeing that she had friends and neighbors about her, he left to retrieve Donald Alban's will and to see to the progress of the cleanup.

Johnston paused at the door. He wished he'd changed before coming in, something better suited to a dirty worksite. It was why he had gone home in the first place. He reflected glumly that, as usual, he hadn't thought about it until it was too late to do anything. It was certain that he'd ruin his good suit.

As he made his way in, stepping gingerly through the wreckage of his office, he felt the shameful inevitability of a trip to the cleaners. He had colleagues who could stay crisp and sharp no matter what they were doing, but the cuffs on his pressed shirt always looked dingy and worn after a mere half day of reading a brief and some gentle annotation. He didn't know quite where the dirt came from. Often, catching sight of himself in a bathroom mirror or shop window reflection, he was apt to stare wretchedly at the collar on his starched shirt, the points of which had somehow curled upwards, or at his tie as it roamed across his chest. How long had it been like *that*, he would wonder, and who had seen him?

Two, building-service maintenance staff were sweeping up glass and debris, while his junior partner, clerk and one of their occasional workers were picking up papers and files, sorting them into stacks. The clerk, an eager young man of twenty, was also going through the scattered papers to ascertain any exposure there might have been to clients. He had already noted two current cases where there might have been a breach in confidentiality. These were flagged and waiting for further review on Johnston's desk.

Johnston was mulling what to do about the two possible breaches when the younger of the two maintenance staff paused in his sweeping. A lanky but tough-looking young man of 19 or 20, he stood over the potted plant, looking sourly at the dog mess.

"Here's what Ah'm asking maself," he began, "did they bring the dog with em, and they spent so much time here that the poor wee thing—well, not so wee, eh?—that it had tae go? Twice? Or would ye call it a crime of opportunity, like?"

Johnston gave a helpless shrug. He was a bit annoyed that the mess hadn't been one of the first things disposed of, but then the cleanup crew hadn't been on duty over the weekend. He wondered how much the building management company would bill him for this extra work.

"Ah mean," the maintenance man continued, "Ah'm tryin tae get a mental picture, here. If they didny bring the dog wi them, were they on their way here, and they saw a bit a dog shite and thought tae themselves, 'Aye, perfect. Let's bring *that* tae the party.'" He put a plastic baggie over his hand and picked it up. He looked grimly toward the other plant.

"Did the police say anything about any leads?" Ewan asked the young man.

"Ah wouldney know. Ah don't talk to the polis," he sniffed.

Johnston retrieved Alban's will from the no-longer-locked cabinet. The will appeared to have been opened and stuffed hastily back in its envelope. A quick scan showed that some of the other wills and documents also had their seals slit, but nothing had been removed.

"Just being thorough?" his young clerk offered, looking over his shoulder. "The thieves, I mean."

"But why open these?"

"It doesn't look like we're dealing with Mensa candidates here," the clerk responded, glancing back toward where the maintenance man had extracted the second bit of mess. "Probably, they saw envelopes and wondered if they had money in them."

Johnston nodded. "How much cash did they take?"

"All of it. Three thousand, four hundred and"—here he paused to pick up a loose piece of paper and examine it—"and sixty-two pounds."

As an advocate, Johnston was acquainted with several people whom he wouldn't trust to deliver a take-away, but he knew that it was their business to know each other's business. One such was a young man named Alan Wilson. Perhaps a word with him would be useful. He might be able to find out who had broken into the office.

Wilson was a foot soldier in a local crime "shop," the Madmen, that was part of a larger syndicate. Johnston had come to know him first when he'd been in trouble as a teenager excluded from school. He regarded Wilson not so much as a hardened criminal but as an exploited kid for whom the law of the land was a negotiable abstraction. Now 27, Wilson had largely avoided official notice since coming of age, but his seeming reformation was testament less to turning over a new leaf, and more to his apprenticeship among the Madmen. Johnston had heard that Alan's boss, Buff Lindsey, was keeping a low profile, but Alan wouldn't be hard to find.

"You didn't say anything to anyone?" Ross demanded.

"I don't *know* anyone," Imogen responded.

"So—"

"Before we go down the rabbit hole," she said, "let's take a step back. I mean, Jesus, I'll walk through Kelvingrove Park at night, but even I wouldn't have parked my car in that lot."

"What are you saying?" He sounded indignant. "Are you blaming—?"

"No. But let's take a moment and examine the facts. Let's ascertain whether this isn't just some horrible coincidence. I mean, things like this *do* happen."

"In America, maybe! But this is Scotland. There's homicidal violence, sure: a bar fight? Practically any night of the week. A bit of aggro outside the chip shop? Some thieving or drug dealing? Again, sure. But murder? Robbing someone and murdering him? You're not on."

"You're positive?"

"No," he admitted. "No a hundred percent."

"Can you get the police report?" she asked.

"No, I..." He thought for a moment. "I could, yeah. I'd have to be careful how I phrased my interest."

"Let's start there," she said. "And, yes, we need to be careful. Because if poor Frankie's been killed to keep him quiet, it might draw attention to us."

"I'll do it," he said. "I've been going over it in my mind, and all I can figure is that whoever's running this was monitoring Frankie's friend all this time, and they swept into action when Frankie got in touch with him. Let's hope he never said anything about either of us."

"*If* that's what's going on," she stressed.

9

On the Victoria Embankment near Westminster Bridge, evening was drawing in. Below the pediment atop the fourth floor, light from a lone window shined over a deserted interior courtyard. Calum Percy, Specialist Crime Commander of the Met Police Special Enquiry Team (or SET) was on a tense conference call in his office behind the closed door. Unbeknownst to (or at least discreetly unremarked upon by) most of his colleagues there, Percy was also MI5. His deputy, and younger, fresh-faced cousin in clandestine service, Inspector Jamie Frenz stood across the desk from him, listening in, holding the report that was the occasion for the call.

"A contact in Dundee has reported that the ARO there is dead," said Percy. "Hanged himself."

"And you think it's related somehow?" asked his superior over the phone's speaker.

"I don't know what I'm meant to think," Percy began. "Seems like an awfully convenient development, if it isn't. By that I mean—"

"Quite," said the voice. "See what you can do to get the full police report. Do it quietly, the kind of routine follow-up you might do for any untimely death of a nominally public figure."

"Yes, of course."

"Make it sound more in the line of making sure files are complete than an actual query."

"We're on uncertain ground now, sir, with this...departure." He let that concern hang in the air, hoping for some reassurance, or at least some enlightenment.

"Let me know what you find," was his superior's only reply. Then he hung up.

Percy disconnected, troubled. His superior, an undersecretary named Nigel Chamberlain, hadn't sounded surprised when he hinted at the murder, the "departure."

Percy was a "lifer," in civil service parlance, and he was feeling the years. At 61 years old, his career was nearing its end, and as he had reflected more than once, it was beginning to feel more like a sentence than a calling. He had served as an army officer before joining the Special Enquiry Team, and hierarchy and respect for procedures were second nature to him. He was imposingly tall, and colleagues who chafed at his military adherence to rules claimed that his habit of leaning over people when speaking to them was deliberate intimidation. Only a few realized that the training on Salisbury Plain had left him hard of hearing.

Fastidious and self-assured in starched, white shirt and dark blue uniform, he still looked and acted like a soldier, even if the fighting colors and battle theatre had changed. Even if he sometimes doubted the motives behind the actions he was tasked with carrying out. And, as this evening, he had the soldier's bitter distaste for fighting over the same ground more than once. If that's what was happening. Hadn't the Scottish Question been put to bed? He remained uncertain about his role in the cover-up.

Percy stared at Frenz. "Let's have a look at that police report," he said at last. "And activate the buskers," he continued, referring to their off-the-books surveillance and intelligence gatherers. "For now, just the one each in Glasgow, Edinburgh and Dundee. Same boys as before? We know the sensitive points," Percy mused. "We'll start by monitoring those. Quietly. Surveillance only. And see what—if anything— we find."

In Glasgow next day, the police report Ian Ross had obtained was painful, grim reading, and it was not giving Imogen anything definitive. Frankie had been hit from the back, a rabbit punch, below and behind the left ear, near the base of the skull, with something metal and heavy. He'd have been unconscious instantly, and dead in less than two minutes, the Medical Examiner's report stated. The crime scene pictures were the most difficult for Imogen, her friend's body contorted where it landed after being heaved over the fencing, like an animal run over on the road, its wee body unceremoniously shifted out of the way, where it rested hidden among high weeds.

Imogen sat at her desk as she viewed the report on screen, her arms pressed across her middle. She felt sick to her stomach, her gaze, through welling tears, mesmerized by photos of the body. Thoughts of Duncan, dead at the morgue, crashed in on her. Her breath came sharp and shallow.

"The police don't have any clues about who did it," Ross said over her shoulder. "Is there anything that jumps out at you about whether it looks...professional?"

Imogen scrolled through the coroner's report as she seized hold of herself. "No," she said. "If it's an assassin, he's good. This would've been silent and quick. But it could also be random. The thief wanted Frankie's money and maybe his car. He came up behind Frankie and hit him with something—a metal pipe, maybe? A truncheon?" She found it difficult to separate what she felt from what she needed to do, but she forced herself to look on.

"So, it could be as you said—wrong place at the wrong time. Are there any footprints at the crime scene?"

"But why an upper cut?" she mused, ignoring him and still looking through the report. "Frankie was short. What was he, about five foot, five?"

"Yes, I'd say," Ross rejoined, "something like that."

"If the blow came from above," she continued, "you'd think, sure. That scans. But from below on the left?"

"So, he'd be left-handed, this guy," Ross said. His amateur sleuthing was becoming tiresome.

"Not necessarily," she rejoined, hoping she had kept the irritation out of her voice.

"Maybe," Ross continued, "maybe it was heavy, whatever it was, and—"

"In that case, the killer wouldn't have been able to swing it hard enough or fast enough to do the damage it caused. It struck him here"—she pointed to the sketch on screen—"and it severed his skull from his spinal cord. A single blow – short, quick and very hard."

"So, we can't be sure," he said gloomily.

"No, we can't."

They stared at one another.

"We were a circle of three," Imogen said. "Now it's down to two. Does your chief of staff know about what we're doing?"

"Only in the broadest possible way," he said. "I haven't been able to give her any updates. Things have been happening so quickly."

"Let's keep it that way. Broad, I mean. On the face of it, the evidence points to a robbery gone horribly wrong. Concealing the body the way the killer did could be a panicked, in-the-moment reaction. It's the timing that makes it suspicious. Very suspicious. If it *is* something else, if murder was the intent, the clinical nature of it looks exactly like the kind of thing an assassin might do. Someone well trained."

In Dundee, at his Ward Street law office, still amid piles of paper that needed taming, Ewan Johnston was also having trouble separating what he felt from what he needed to do. He'd pause in his work and stare. The death of anyone close was always hard, but that Alban had taken his own life felt like a double blow. Johnston had forged his way, following in his mentor's footsteps. He had honed in himself those qualities he most admired in Alban, his rectitude and diligence. Johnston was 34 years old, and he looked forward to a wife and family himself one day, to that satisfaction, that unassuming joy. How could all that Alban was—all that he seemed—have ended like this?

His less-than-honest client, Alan Wilson had reported no leads on the break-in. Not a whisper. Which seemed odd—even to Wilson himself: "Ah mean, it had tae've been a local job. Ye'd think there'd be some talk aboot. But nuthin. Ma boss is a bit fashed himsel," he added, referring to Buff Lindsey. The Madmen didn't like freelancing on their patch.

The office phone rang, and his assistant put a call through from Mrs. Alban.

"How are you, Sandra?" he asked, trying to coax a little sunlight into his voice for her benefit. "I'd thought I might drop by after work to see you this evening, if that's all right."

"Yes, Ewan, that would be nice."

There was a long pause on the phone.

"Sandra?"

"Ewan," she asked, "...are we sure about how Donald died?"

"What do you mean?"

"Well, it doesn't seem right. I know a grieving wife would say something like that," she added. "But it just doesn't fit, does it?"

"I'm struggling, too," he offered, his eyes fixed bleakly on the papers still needing to be looked into after the break-in. He looked at the dingy cuffs of his dress shirt.

"His office looks...I don't know. Different. It looks tidy in a way he didn't leave things. I didn't go in there much, it was his domain. But I know my husband. Knew him. Or thought I did."

"Sandra..."

"And today, we received a death announcement for one of his oldest, dearest friends, Frank McDougal."

"Wee Frankie died? When?"

"Was murdered," she said. "Possibly the same night Donald died. I found the report of it in yesterday's evening *Tele*. The police are ruling it a bungled robbery attempt."

Johnston snapped his fingers at his assistant and held the receiver to his chest as he hissed, "bring me the *Tully*, please," he said. "Yesterday's. Do we still have it?" He turned back to the phone and Sandra.

His clerk looked sullen at having been snapped at like a French waiter. He lay the paper on Johnston's desk. Johnston caught the look and mouthed "thank you" elaborately as he reached for the newspaper. He smiled a contrite apology at the clerk's back.

There was the report, page one, below the fold: "Professor Murdered in Car Park Theft." A cold sickness stung him. "Who else have you told, Sandra?" he asked.

"No one. I thought—"

"Say nothing to anyone. I mean no one."

"You agree it's odd? What do you think...?"

"I don't know what I think, Sandra." That was putting it mildly. "I'll be over within the hour."

10

Whatever even-handed posture Imogen had struck concerning Frankie's death, and irrespective of what she'd said about it to Ian Ross, she was certain that he had been murdered for what he knew. But *what* had he known? Imogen was desperate to find out. She felt guilt and anger in equal measure as she set to work in her dim, fusty office, the blinds drawn tight to the side of the window frame in the vain hope of coaxing a little natural light inside. Yet another thing, no doubt, to which the Druid, the permanent office holder, would object. She ran a finger along the side of her desk, leaving a furrow in the accumulated dust. *Her* tidiness? She considered what kind of note she could leave for him, written in the dust for the next time he dropped in for a book, or whatever it was he did when he dropped by unannounced.

Discrepancies and anomalies. Wee Frankie had said his friend, whoever it was, had evidence of both. His death, raw and senseless, seemed to indicate that there was evidence to hide. Imogen's thoughts drifted back to a working lunch she had had with Frankie—was it only a week ago? Outside, that day, it was dismal and wet—"fair dreich," Frankie had pronounced it. Inside, they had slurped the fortifying French onion soup that was the pub's signature dish, while Frankie regaled her with dirt from the 'No' campaign

"No," he had said, "there wasnae much in the papers. I think most inquiries were..." —he searched for the word— "...cauterized before they could become further inflamed."

"And there was a Tory MP who tweeted that she'd *seen* the mail-in ballots and was quoted as saying there was 'nothing to be worried about' regarding the Yes vote?" Imogen had asked.

"Correct."

"But that MP couldn't have—certainly *shouldn't* have—known the results at the time she made the statement. Unless the rules were bent. Or abandoned." She had paused and looked at him.

"Also correct," Frankie had said, "and there was the Queen's statement—very improper."

"What happened exactly?" she asked.

"Just before the election, the queen, who's supposed to be neutral in matters of politics—"

"Wait," she interrupted. "People cared what the Queen thinks?"

He had sighed. "Many do. And in something that smells terribly like a stitch-up, a staged-for-camera moment, the Queen was attending church at Crathie Kirk here in Scotland. A fellow parishioner or a well-wisher asked—very innocently, I'm sure—what Her Majesty thought of the referendum which was then about to take place. The Queen responded that she hoped the Scottish people 'would think carefully about their future'—a bit ominous, don't you think? Four days before the vote. It was trumpeted everywhere."

"It sounds a bit oblique," Imogen had offered. "I mean, maybe she—"

"She'd been the monarch since 1952! She knew what she was doing. Earlier in the week, the PM at the time, David Cameron, had suggested to her private secretary that it would be helpful if, as he put it, the queen 'raised an eyebrow' about the referendum. And then she did! 'Think carefully' – it's a kind of faux impartiality, isn't it? Impartial except that both sides knew it meant: 'vote No'.

"Your own president at the time," he had continued. "Obama! Was prevailed upon by Cameron to give a speech where he said something like, 'we rely upon a *United* Kingdom to help preserve freedom and democracy' or some shite like tha'. The headlines next day read: 'US president says vote No.' Your fucking Bill and Hilary Clinton had already come out against it themselves."

Frankie had put his spoon down and glared at what was left of the soup, as though it tasted of ashes.

"And beyond that," he persisted, "there was an unrelenting fusillade of misinformation from the Tory press about being kicked out of the EU if we voted Yes—rich, that one, now that we've Brexited Europe—and about people losing their pensions if the Yes vote prevailed."

Imogen had been taken aback by his passion. As she'd said at her presentation, some who cry foul over a result are merely angry that they lost.

Now, as she reviewed what Frankie had given her, she noted that it focused on the misinformation campaign. Frankie seemed more concerned with the various and multiple untruths than with what had happened on Election Day. Her world was numbers, votes. She wouldn't be stampeded into this investigation, and she wouldn't risk her career on Wee Frankie's sour grapes. If that's what they were.

Still, she thought, looking at what Frankie had given her, maybe excavating among the trolls and party flaks might help point the way. He had highlighted the "Transparency Project" for special investigation. It sounded cynically opaque enough to be worth looking into. The funding and allegiances were murky, too. Following the money, she thought, might reveal who was involved and could identify the cast of characters she'd need to focus on.

On a sheet of notepaper next to her laptop, she scrawled, "CARLA F BAD," the FBI acronym for Character, Associates, Reputation, Loyalty, Ability; Finances, Bias, Alcohol, Drugs. Carla F Bad was used when vetting known participants, and for security clearances. But turning it the other way round and looking into the financials first might unmask the participants behind the misinformation and anonymous tweeting; might lead to associates; might suggest who was loyal to whom.

Start with the MP who knew too much? she wondered. Politicians were notoriously difficult to assess by looking at character and associates. Their characters tended to be fluid, and it was their business, their lifeblood, to have multiple, intricate associations—particularly ones that led to campaign funding. Looking through Frankie's notes again, she found that a BBC presenter had also said something similar about seeing the mail-in ballots. How did *he* know that? What connected those two?

If she'd been back in the US, and still at her old job with the FBI, there were enough questions, she felt—even before Frankie's death—to open a case file. She wondered how and why there hadn't been one in the UK. It was possible, of course, that the Met office or MI5 had indeed opened a file—only to conclude there was nothing to find. Frankie's notes made abundant mention of a think tank led by an American, Jefferson Weaver, who seemed to be linked with the cloudy Transparency project. It looked like he and his company were engaged in run-of-the-mill dirty tricks and obfuscation. Nevertheless, she'd keep it in mind, a possible connection (or connector) to something bigger.

But she resolved that she'd proceed as she always did. She would let the data lead her, methodically, thoroughly, precisely. All these opening investigative moves—the outrages, the "mights" and "coulds," the dodgy misinformation campaigns, corrupt financing, *mis*feasant leaks—were meant to lead her to the numbers, the data she could analyze.

Numbers. It would be numbers she looked to for the truth; and she hoped to discover, as she often did, her state of grace within that truth, perched on a crowded branch somewhere among innocence, guilt and corruption. Yes, other areas of her messy life could have used the same level of high-minded, disciplined attention and helpful acronyms, but life and love so far had held no prospect of orderliness. Relationships and friendships remained a soggy mess. And people often let you down in the end. Numbers endured.

Starting where she did, amid rumor, whispers and misinformation was a frustrating, if necessary, first step meant to get to the nuts and bolts of how voters acted—what, when, how many. For Imogen, the why was never at issue. In her world, people cheated because they wanted to win, or because they were afraid of losing. Which wasn't always the same thing.

As an official, Ian Ross could provide access to data she'd need, but it would be instructive to speak with a British counterpart, someone who did work similar to her own, who understood the kinds of questions she'd need answered. At the beginning of the school term, David Reidy, the department head, or as Wee Frankie had been fond of calling him—"*the Heid*"—had set up an introduction for Imogen with Marta Serres, a Research Fellow at the European Policies Research Centre at University of Strathclyde, across town.

Serres also held a consultancy role at the Electoral Commission, with a special brief on voter fraud. As fellow professionals, Reidy had thought they should meet, and now Imogen wanted desperately to do so. She reached out to Serres. Replying almost instantly to her email, Serres suggested meeting at a bar near George Square.

Late that afternoon, Imogen strolled into town along Sauchiehall Street toward George Square in an irregular and confounding rain. She stopped three times as she walked, first to take down her umbrella, only to stop again after a few streets and reopen it, and then to repeat the process a little later. Was this "*fair dreich*?" she wondered, looking at the sky and thinking of Frankie, or was it something else? She found it difficult to believe it was "fair" anything.

She stanched her musing and refocused on the meeting ahead. She hoped this Marta Serres could help her start digging into the data. Ross would get her access to official numbers. Frankie had given her good sociological data and a general lay of the land. This Marta Serres, she hoped, would suggest a way in.

The walk was a little over a mile and a half, and despite the rain, Imogen was happy to have a reason to go somewhere.

Alone in a new city, many of her walks around Glasgow, pleasant as they could be, were nothing more than solitary, serendipitous exploration, a matter of setting off in a direction and seeing where curiosity and her feet took her. It had been good for getting to know the city, but it wasn't the same as establishing memories of things done in a place the way she had in D.C., or Seattle. She thought fondly of Philadelphia, too, where she and Duncan had hidden out during the Faithless Elector investigation. In her mind's eye, she saw him that first night they were finally together, stripped to the waist. The play of muscles in his shoulders, across his back, his thighs. And then stripped.

She looked the wrong way as she stepped off the curb and just missed being hit by a Mini.

Collecting herself, and focusing on something less absorbing, she found that Glasgow's appealing grittiness reminded her of Philadelphia. They were both port cities, with strong traditions of shipbuilding. They had both grown rich on trade during the colonial period and again as foundries for the Industrial Revolution. Both wore their working-class identities as badges of honor, and in both that pride and sense of identity had been almost strangled when they fell on hard times.

But how would she get what she needed from this Marta Serres without signaling what she was truly after? It was a skill she was still honing. With her relegation to the Studies in Electoral Integrity office back home in D.C., getting the data she needed had grown trickier. For the Faithless Elector case she had needed to pretend that her requests were for a study she was doing, and not part of a larger investigation. Back then, she had given that smokescreen study the deliberately drowsy title: "The Effect of Super PACs in the Post-*Citizens United* Context, and Differences in Spending Across Region and Party on Voter Mobilization and Suppression: A Structural Equation Model."

That had done the trick. Even her boss didn't want to hear anything more about it—he wasn't sure whether she was giving him the title or the whole paper—and he had left her alone. All well, she thought, but she was nearly there and still not sure what she would say to this Professor Serres. With the death of Wee Frankie, she needed to stay as far below the radar as possible.

In a chilly warehouse on the outskirts of Glasgow, four, massive hard men, each scrupulously bald, as if it were part of the uniform, sat in pairs across from one another at a long, folding table as they sifted through Alban's memoir boxes. Leaning grimly upon the makeshift table, they could have been a former nightclub bouncer, encounter-support group. Imogen and Ian Ross's formerly damp, leather-jacketed admirer was among them. The bouncers' instructions were clear: find anything with "2014" or "independence" written on it.

"This is pointless," said the admirer, as he threw a sheaf of old papers into a box on the floor behind him. "You found anything?" he asked the equally bullet-headed bald man to his right.

"Nothing," Baldy replied.

"Maybe we should be saving more of it?" He reached for the box in the center of the table and looked inside.

"It's not a fucking trick question, is it," a sour, blue-eyed man chimed in. Alone among the support group, he had opted to grow a narrow, "soul patch" beard under his lip that he played with endlessly. "He either had what we're looking for, or he didn't."

"But that lawyer didn't have anything either."

"Which puts us in the clear, doesn't it," said the sour patch.

The bar, off George Square, was below a restaurant, down a set of stairs in a dark and intimate basement. An old, hardwood bar with a zinc top dominated the left-hand side of the room, its curved edges and detailed scrollwork juxtaposed with contemporary tables, chairs and leather banquettes scattered about the room—all in black. The room was bathed in a smoky, Curaçao fugue that seemed to radiate from the wall sconces and behind the bar.

It wasn't a young person's place. Or at least it wasn't one at 5:30 on a Thursday. So close to Strathclyde campus, it looked to be habituated by academics and professionals, who gathered in animated groups at various tables and along the bar. Imogen picked out Serres sitting alone at a table across from the long backlit bar. A waitress tailed her to the table and asked what she would like before she sat down.

"Whisky," said Imogen. "Neat. And a little glass of water?"

The waitress turned to look at the vast array of bottles lining the wall, as if to say, "you're going to need to be a bit more specific."

"Glenlivet," she added. She pointed at Serres's drink. "Another for you?" she asked.

"Yes, thank you. Another Long, Tall, please," she said to the waitress.

"Come here often?" Imogen asked, as she finished removing her coat and sat down.

"Not as often as I'd like, I suppose," said Serres. "This time of day, I'm usually rushing home to take care of kiddies, but when the famous Imogen Trager wants to meet—"

"Infamous, more like," Imogen offered.

"In any case, you tell the hubs he's got the duty, should get some carry-out for dinner and not wait up." She leaned back and smiled. "He says I'm not to allow you to embroil me in any dangerous election fraud cases."

Imogen began to protest, but Serres held up a hand. "If I believed his worry represented a genuine care and concern for my well-being, I'd be touched," she said, "but I suspect he's expressing anxiety about having to fend for himself alone with the children." She smiled and drank deeply as the drinks arrived. She handed the empty to the waitress.

Serres was in her late thirties, Imogen guessed, slightly older than herself. She was slender and long boned, with elegant hands. Her face was long, too, framed by short, auburn hair. She had an easy, languid quality about her in the way she sat, the way she reached for her drink. But there was an able intensity behind her eyes, too. Her accent was polished, though not quite English. Certainly not Scots. Imogen couldn't place it.

"I appreciate your meeting with me, Professor Serres," she began. "And I'm on leave, a sabbatical of sorts. I promise not to embroil you in anything dangerous."

"Pity," said Serres, drinking deeply again. "And call me Marty."

Ewan Johnston met Sandra Alban an hour later, the house as lifeless as a churchyard. And as solemn. Jean, the youngest, home from university, met him at the door, staring and quiet. She ushered him into the well-appointed kitchen. Its polished granite countertops put him in mind of blank headstones. Johnston and Sandra Alban removed to the sitting room, leaving her children to go their silent, aimless ways. A damp, gray light suffused the sitting room from outside. Below, and in the distance beyond the picture window, Johnston could see the Tay River railroad bridge, curving into view. Low clouds and rain obscured the tops of the hills on the other side. Not turning round, he asked her, "Is there anything Donald said that makes you suspicious?"

"No," she said. "It's the lack of any precipitating factor that bothers me. Nothing changed. No news shocks, no dire medical diagnosis, no troubles with the children. We'd had no arguments of any consequence. You've seen that our finances are orderly."

"Yes," he said, still looking toward Wormit on the far side of the river.

"And I've never known him to back down from anything. To just give up," she added. "He wasn't a confrontational man, I'm sure you'd agree. But he was what I call 'effectively stubborn.' Cannily so."

She was crying quietly, and Johnston turned to comfort her. He sat next to her on the sofa, putting an arm around her shoulders. She recovered herself and smiled at him.

"Let's have a look in his study," said Johnston, "if you're up to it."

11

Answering his summons, Jefferson Weaver traveled to Great Shelford, in Cambridgeshire, seated in the back of a black, Jaguar XJ Sentinel. Behind the tinted rear windows as the car hurtled through the countryside, and despite the comfort and style in which he rode, his face bore an expression of beleaguered frustration, tending toward rage.

Outsourcing, he mused acidly. That was the root of the problem. Every middle-management nitwit on the planet touted the virtues and savings of outsourcing, and when idiots were in charge, they took that advice. True, he admitted, it offered distance, misdirection and deniability. But it always ended with a colossal fuck up. Always. Worse, whatever this new crisis was, it was not of the sort he could profit from. He foresaw only losses.

In the fall of 2013, as the Independence Referendum campaign began setting the ground rules, Weaver and his Transparency Project were brought on by the three men he was on his way to meet, the self-appointed leaders of a clandestine, extra-governmental, shadow No campaign. The triumvirate. Weaver and his Project were to be the campaign's Plan A. And his efforts would have succeeded, if his employers hadn't panicked in the end, and brought about their own Plan B. He had known from the beginning that they had a backup plan. And, according to them, the best trained people in the world, men who would do all that was necessary. Ex-military, most of them, they only needed to be pointed in the right direction and turned loose.

It had sounded promising, if ominous, and wise to have a backup. But Weaver's confidence in the effectiveness of his own efforts meant no dire Plan B would be needed. The blithe confidence and credulous simplicity that his employers had for Plan B should have raised a caution flag, Weaver lamented. But he noted with regret that he himself had been too confident, too caught up in the heady rush of playing his own important part. He hoped the men he was rushing to meet wouldn't try to drag him in any further.

The car turned onto Whittlesford Road after gliding through town and passed onto a winding lane that led back into countryside. Presently, a cartoonishly large, modern farmhouse set far back from the road, loomed out of the gathering darkness, its oddly scaled, square segments looking like massive toy blocks abandoned in a field. The car moved toward the house, its daubed whitewash exterior luminous and spectral in the gathering darkness. Turning into the lane, the car rumbled across well-raked gravel, past the largest of the dwelling's white cubes toward an equally substantial garage. Its door rose at the car's approach as if by magic. Two other XJ Sentinels were already parked there—a "shadow" of Jaguars.

Inside the house, the triumvirate had already gathered in the vast, double height living room with its double height windows, its scale and arid uselessness like some contemporary misinterpretation of a Grand Siècle orangerie. Three men lounged across the sofas arranged in a semi-circle facing the story-high rear windows—Sebastian Townsend, Toby Nesbitt and Nigel Chamberlain. Their aides, like his driver, were sequestered in a small house behind the garage. These were men, Weaver recognized, who might not be able to manufacture a crisis (except by misadventure), but they knew how to capitalize on one. And how best to survive one, too. He'd need to be on his toes.

"I don't know that I hold with these crash meetings," a flabby Sebastian Townsend began, as Weaver paused at the threshold to the room. The scale of the room tended to enjoin a kind of whispered, conspiratorial intimacy. Townsend didn't speak so much as murmur. "Could've been handled with a few, quick texts."

Weaver looked about the room for anything out of the ordinary. Townsend reached for something cake-like on the low coffee table in front of him, popped it into his mouth and lounged back. No longer crouched over the table, he continued to radiate a sullen, proprietary interest in its stores, his knees spread to encompass and possess what was laid out.

Weaver always felt an odd shock when he met Townsend face-to-face. Seen on television, he came across as distracted and a little unkempt, but urbane and perhaps thoughtful for all that. In person, he was a doughy, eager-to-please buffoon. A case of arrested development, forestalled (or more likely, held back) somewhere short of the sixth form. He was of a type commonly seen outside any sweetshop near a school in the afternoon, short of breath from roughhousing, a dim, uncertain grin fixed to his face either as a shield against insults or because he rarely understands what's going on around him, a jumper creeping upward over a thick midriff.

There were Public School boys who dressed with equal disregard, and appallingly, but with most it was an unconscious assertion of power; a statement that norms of dress and behavior were for the benefit of other people, and other people didn't matter. This was just thick obliviousness.

His close associate and partner in many unknown crimes, Toby Nesbitt, was by contrast an ascetic dandy, crisp and pressed. No shirttail, no stray, dignified gray hair peeked out anywhere on him. Dressed today in muted, pastel mauves and purples, he looked like the comic book villain, Joker, if the Joker had been an English squire. But Nesbitt lacked even a malignant sense of humor. He had the bearing and terse manner of a former sergeant major (which he never had been), his face sour and haughty, as if someone in the ranks had farted. Where Townsend lay across his couch, protecting his food store, Nesbitt sat bolt upright, knees tight together, at the edge of his.

Ignoring Townsend's whingeing, Weaver addressed him-self to the pair's cupbearer and fixer, Nigel Chamberlain, who stood to greet him; the only one of them who looked like what he was, a high-ranking undersecretary. "What the fuck is going on?" Weaver asked with American bluntness. "Why am I here?"

"Thought it was obvious," said Townsend through a fresh mouthful of food.

"What's not obvious," Weaver began, "is why."

Townsend shrugged, a practiced, couldn't-be-bothered tremor meant to disguise the fact he didn't know either. He glanced at Nesbitt, who was busy glaring at Weaver.

Chamberlain answered patiently, "You know about the upcoming King's Speech to open Parliament on October 25th. And I should say that your work preparing the ground has been exemplary. What you don't know is that we need to guard our flank, so to speak. It's possible that this independence vote—"

"So-called," Nesbitt interjected.

"Yes, er, the possibility of a new referendum—though remote," he hastened to add, "makes us nervous about what might be out there to find, what might link back to those of us in this room."

"I'm not sure I follow," said Weaver.

"Well, you see, we've been able to keep any investigation from digging too deeply. The press was waved off, the official investigation was buried. But can you imagine what would happen if one of the papers decided to do a *full* investigation? If *The National* decided to have a look? Could be a disaster."

"Right," said Weaver. "So, why unbury it?"

"We're not exhuming it," said Chamberlain in a sharp whisper. "We need to make sure it's dead and buried. For good. And before October 25th, when we crush this nonsense once and for all."

"So...?" Weaver wondered.

Nesbitt replied, "We heard through sources that the nationalists were considering opening their own investigation into rumors about a stolen vote. And we have taken steps."

"Rumors?" Weaver asked. "You're jumping at rumors! My stock and trade is rumor, and they're often used to stampede idiots into betraying themselves." He paused before asking, "What steps?"

"I don't think I'm wrong in acknowledging that we acted somewhat hastily last time," Chamberlain interjected, though he colored as he spoke. "And we don't want to repeat mistakes. But everything is in hand to take back sovereignty from the devolved governments. It will be announced as part of this government's legislative agenda, and it will be outlined in the King's Speech in about two weeks' time."

"Right. So...?"

"So, if somehow there were proof of what happened in 'fourteen, that would go a long way toward undercutting our ability to go forward with this government's agenda. Would be very damaging to those of us in this room. It seemed prudent to head that investigation off by getting someone to test it for us, but quietly, unofficially. Which we've begun. That is part of what I mean by 'steps.'"

"Like, get there ahead of them?"

"Precisely," said Chamberlain. "Which will allow us to cover up whatever might be easily found. I must ask you, if there are any activities in which you or your cohort have engaged that could expose our work?"

"You're worried about *me*?" he raged. "As far as anyone can tell, all I did was some opposition research."

"Yes, but your approach was...novel, and I don't think I'm mistaken in saying that the methods by which you effected your messaging and oppo research weren't always above-board."

"Don't worry about me," Weaver began. "*I've* been careful. The Institute is squeaky clean. There's miles of daylight between the Transparency Project and the HCQ- troll farm affiliates. There're dummy- and shell corporations pointing every which way but at me and my work. No direct contact. Your contract for opposition reports with my front company *looks* totally legit from the outside. No formal agreement between the Institute or my Transparency Project and the subcontractor exists."

Weaver paused. He didn't trust them. He didn't feel at all comfortable about where this line of questioning was leading. It struck him with alarm that if it all sounded as though he had it all too well contained, he might be the loose end that was left dangling—or worse, snipped off. Having made his case, he also noted: "I suppose that if someone subpoenaed our financial records, they might be able to put two and two together, but as long as I'm around, I can thwart that sort of thing pretty effectively."

"I see," said Chamberlain with an uncertain tone.

"But I can promise you that I've worked painstakingly not to do anything foolish. Nothing like this stupid idea of stirring the pot to see what jumps out."

"Well, we did," Chamberlain responded.

"And it worked," said Nesbitt, dripping with disdain for the American.

"Yes," Chamberlain hastened to add. "That activity caused them to reveal—"

"*Them*?" Weaver wanted to know.

"Those who might be in a position to do us harm. That's all you need to know," said Nesbitt.

"Sounds like I need to know a bit more before I can feel at all comfortable about this conversation," said Weaver.

Chamberlain looked around at the other two. They both now looked bored. Nesbitt, ramrod straight, stared at the ceiling, his lower lip pressed into a petulant sulk, while Townsend's eyes roved listlessly over the room.

"We now know," Chamberlain began, "that someone in Dundee had evidence, and that he'd told one other person about it."

"Evidence?" Weaver asked. "And you found it?"

"No," Nesbitt spat. He seemed to dislike questions as much as everything else. "But our men are still on it. Only a matter of time."

Weaver looked from person to person. He wished he could have spoken with Chamberlain alone. This had never been a game, and now it was beginning to feel deadly serious. Whom had they found in Dundee, he wondered? Who was the other person? Had they kidnapped them both? Had they bought them off? Or was it far worse?

This was new terrain for Weaver. He was used to the business of politics—opposition research, some dirty tricks, bits and bytes of misinformation; maybe some corporate espionage, character assassination. But it still bore the contours of a contest with a semblance of boundaries, even if his work was meant to push those limits. And it didn't contain any real assassinations.

What these three seemed to be talking about felt more like gangster tactics. And where would that end? Would he end up on some government-redacted casualty list himself? Townsend and Nesbitt were protected and probably couldn't be harmed— "made men," in that sense—but he and Chamberlain might become collateral damage, the human shields behind which the other two cowered and prospered.

Imogen put aside Frankie's research on the "consulting" work done by the independent-seeming arm of the Strategic Choices Institute, relieved to be moving into the realm of numbers. She began this part of the investigation carefully, first with a comparison of what Ian Ross had made available versus what Marta Serres had shared. Ross's and Serres' data were identical, so there was no discrepancy to follow up. She decided to use Serres's data set, which was more complete and "cleaned" in a way that she could more readily use.

Imogen's next step was to look at the demographic information Serres had also provided, together with the opinion polling that led up to the election. There *had* to be an explanation for such a large difference between the opinion polls and the final result, she thought. It could be that the fundamentals of polling had changed, while the mechanics of logging results hadn't. But demographics was a good place to begin looking for discrepancies, Imogen believed, and Frankie's background research had helped give her the lay of the land. And demographics were cleaner, "integerized," less noisy than what she'd been looking at so far.

Preference intensity, or the passion surrounding the vote, would have played an outsized role in the referendum. There was scant middle ground. Leading up to voting day, young voters were strongly in favor of independence, whereas older voters, wary of what might become of their pensions, were strongly in favor of remaining. There might be something she could glean there. There was also something of a North—South divide, too, which might be enlightening, as would the polling data.

She would still need to be wary of the polls. Polling during the 2016 and 2020 elections in the US had been flawed. Inaccuracies had laid bare how anachronistic formerly useful methods had become. For that matter, the Brexit polls in '16 had been off, too, she noted. The fact there hadn't been an exit poll conducted during the referendum loomed conspicuously. Was that the kind of thing someone *decided* not to do for some reason, or was it an oversight, something no one thought *to* do? Was it the first bit of circumstantial evidence that there was something awry? And how had that Tory MP *seen* sealed ballots before they were counted?

Still, polls did tell some of the story. The early polling for Yes, in favor of independence, had started dismally, at around 30 %, but as the date of the referendum drew near, polls showed that it climbed sharply until some news outlets reported that Yes might prevail by a narrow margin. How, then, had it failed by almost 10 percentage points? she wondered. Were standard polls that poor? There couldn't have been that much magical thinking, could there?

The last polls, with one showing 51 % for Yes, were conducted days before the vote. She searched news accounts in the intervening days to see if anything had happened that might have changed people's minds, but short of the Queen's "raised eyebrow," there was nothing. And, as she thought about it, that eyebrow could just as likely have emboldened the Yes vote. But in the end, it wasn't close. So, no single, precipitating factor as yet, even if the dribble of misinformation and fearmongering became a fire hose of cant and half-truths at the end.

In the interest of thoroughness, her next task was to scrutinize the various polls and polling methods, looking for errors or over-weighting something. But after a day and a half of examining their methods, the samplings proved to be well conducted—indeed better than she was used to seeing—as was their seeming accuracy. She took her time with the data. There had been a desperate rush to the Faithless Elector investigation, but now, even if a second referendum was granted, she would have ample time to get things right.

That evening, Imogen met up with Marta Serres at their favored spot to try and get a handle on the data. She was happy to get away from her office. As arid and dull as her office back in the US was, there were others in it. She interacted with people throughout the day and had a staff for which she was responsible. This leave, with its promise of solitude and "pure" research sometimes felt like the dismal product of things one should be careful of wishing for. Dark, stodgy—and cold!—rather like the professor she was borrowing it from, she found herself torn between eagerness to dig deeper, unimpeded and uninterrupted and the need to be among people. She was growing to like Marty.

"I'm making my way in," Imogen noted, as they sat over their drinks. "But I can't square the polling numbers with the results."

"That stood out for us, too," Serres agreed, "obviously. The polling post-mortems showed that we were still operating much as we had in the past, but that new technology, like mobile phones, made it that much more difficult to properly account for and represent the electorate. We put the final result down to a lack of voter activation; that the referendum hadn't been sufficient to move working class voters—particularly in Glasgow and Dundee—to vote."

"Did anyone look further into it?"

"No. The result spoke for itself and the post-mortems were inconclusive."

"Did no one raise the concern officially?" Imogen asked.

"There were *claims* of foul-play," Serres admitted in her languid way, "There were reports of rerouted vans carrying ballot boxes…but they were pretty weak, and of a kind we'd expect in such a preference-intense contest."

"Yes," said Imogen, "that's true for my work, too. I guess I'm interested in how and why preference-intense voters weren't activated, weren't moved to vote. You'd expect the opposite."

"True," said Serres, looking at Imogen cautiously. "It was a high turnout. Which means a lot of people who don't always vote. In the end, though, it seems that many non-voters did what they always do—or *don't do*, I should say—and didn't vote."

"Yes," said Imogen. "I see that possibility. And it may be that the postal ballots, coupled with a lack of activation, made the difference. I'm going to take a look at the breakdown of the mail-in ballots tomorrow. I don't know what that'll show me. I'm still kind of establishing a baseline."

"Sounds like maybe you're looking for something specific?"

Imogen had to be careful here. This was supposed to be a routine, comparative paper. "Not as such," she replied. "But if I'm going to do a comprehensive analysis and comparison, I ought to understand better what I'm looking at, and these are the kinds of questions that always leap out at me."

"Of course," said Serres.

Imogen caught her look. An investigator herself, perhaps Serres had a nose for fellow snoopers, and she had sensed something. A flicker of a deeper understanding she was at pains to conceal flashed across her face. "And I suspect your work leads you to certain assumptions," was all she said, though she continued to eye Imogen carefully.

"Yes. Occupational hazard, I suppose," Imogen replied, trying to sound lighthearted about it.

Ewan Johnston stood in the study of his old friend. He saw what Sandra had meant about it seeming cleaner than normal. In defense of his office, Donald Alban had often quipped that "a messy desk is a sign of genius; and by that reckoning, I must be Einstein!" Folders, books, stray papers and notes taped to the wall, had been the trademarks of his work habits. Still quoting Einstein, he would add: "This seeming chaos is 'merely a pattern that we haven't yet recognized.'"

He used a computer, but he was old enough that little slips of paper were far more useful to him. Notes to self were in handwriting difficult to decipher. He could only edit effectively on paper, and so there were often many marked-up drafts of the same brief or memorandum to be found on his desk. No more. There were no notes taped above his work desk, no dates to be later added to his diary. The top of the desk looked like it might have been dusted. "Have you been in here at all since...since then?" he asked.

"No. I've been like some frightened child, afraid of ghosts. As if I came in by myself something hideous and dangerous would leap out at me." She hazarded a glance above her at where the chandelier had hung, where she had found Alban. "God help me, I can still see him hanging there."

"And the kids?" he asked, as he pulled open a file drawer.

Sandra shook her head, no.

He pushed Alban's chair out of the way and began opening other desk drawers. Though it would have made more sense to sit in the chair, he wasn't sure he could, and he wasn't about to do so with Sandra standing in front of him. As he knelt on the floor, he looked across the desk top toward the open study door. He recalled having seen a stack of boxes tucked in behind that door.

"Well, it's cleaner than I'm used to seeing it. Though I admit, I haven't been in here in a year or more." It wasn't so clean, Johnston noted dismally, that the forearms of his suit jacket weren't already covered in dust.

"Yes," Sandra replied. "I expect the police would say it was part of his...getting ready."

"What about those boxes that used to be behind the door?"

She turned and looked.

"When did he get rid of them?" he asked.

She looked back at him perplexed. "I can't imagine he'd have thrown those out. And I'd have noticed if he had."

"His miscellaneous Returning Officer notes from down the years, wasn't it?"

"For his memoirs, he would say, yes." She smiled at the memory, then looked about to cry again.

Johnston stood up and brushed the dust from the knees of his suit trousers. None of this was yet grounds for going back to the police, but it was worrisome. Not much in itself, of course, but something seemed to be calling to him, a memory or an event he couldn't quite grasp. He stared again at the now-empty spot where the boxes had rested over the years.

Calum Percy was on the phone with Chamberlain.

"Yes," Percy was saying. "A suicide. I've had a quiet word with the lead investigator—as a formality, I told him. And it appears that no one is looking any further." He paused a moment before adding, "I'd like to understand how you knew about this, sir." He paused again. Hoping to give Chamberlain a means of exonerating himself, and thereby absolving his own actions, he added carefully, "It's possible that whoever gave you this information was—"

In Cambridgeshire, standing by the double-height windows, Weaver heard Nigel Chamberlain say into the phone, "—we're monitoring that situation, thank you," before disconnecting. As he put the phone away in his breast pocket he turned to Nesbitt and Townsend and said, "Sounds like that's it. Our man at the Met says the local police are ruling it a suicide."

Weaver felt a chill—they *had* killed someone. But he maintained his hard expression. Perhaps, he thought, there was a Plan C. He wondered if he was part of it, and whether he'd be leaving the way he came.

12

Leaving Cambridgeshire, Jefferson Weaver rolled through the dark countryside. The steady drone of the engine, the comforting whish of the tires as they rolled across damp pavement did nothing to quell his unease. They had killed someone. The fucking idiots had killed someone. Presumably, they wouldn't blanch at killing him either. It was probably, he reflected, that he was still alive only because they feared what might become known if he died. Good, he thought. But now, knowing that the cover-up had entered a deadly phase, he was implicated in it too. Two weeks until Parliament opened, he thought. Two weeks to hold his nerve.

Unable to focus on the messages and emails on his phone, he lay it aside and gazed out the window at the darkness. It was their panic, their use of Plan B that was the root of the present trouble.

Prior to 2014, Townsend and Nesbitt had been nothing more than comfortably wealthy, headline grabbing Colonel Blimpests, he remembered. Perfect for his needs. They were aghast—infuriated—that then-Prime Minister Cameron had acceded to holding a referendum, regardless of promises made. At the time, only Chamberlain had held an actual post, and that had changed often, ebbing and flowing (or was it rising and falling?) with each election or reshuffle. They were all in government now, thanks in large part to his efforts.

Newspapers had become clumsy tools, and their reach was diminishing; television and radio reached more broadly, but they were scattershot—and expensive for all that. Unless they

70

could be directed. Online media, everyone's new darling, promised the world, though for most it remained an inscrutable rat hole. Anyone who could find a way to test or train the rats would have an extraordinary amount of power and influence. He noted smugly from the back of the car that he'd been among the first to seize the potential.

He'd had found a way to deliver bespoke messaging through his "GeoProp" targeting, designed to fracture and alienate demographic groups who might have otherwise coalesced. Balkanizing and moving the electorate in predictable ways was but one leg of the stool. He also strengthened the closed circle of government, press and social media, the better to modulate or amplify the *Sturm und Drang* of popular opinion. A vertically integrated echo chamber of solipsism.

Through various partners, he'd initiated and sustained so-called "butterfly attacks" and keyword "squatting" to amplify his message. And polling agencies weren't the only ones still reacting in old ways to new phenomena. The newspapers were less credulous than the general electorate. But only just. His genius, he noted humbly, was that he'd realized that the goal wasn't to change hearts and minds so much as to ossify positions already held, to give "conscience cover" for ideas and beliefs that couldn't withstand the full light of day.

It had all worked well, and the electorate remained against independence. But, he reflected bitterly, in the eleventh hour the wise men had called Weaver to a crash meeting to explain to them how support for Yes had grown so much, and what could be done about it. He had counseled patience, to hold their nerve; that the polls were blunt, outmoded instruments when compared with his tools.

His polls had still showed a 10 % spread in favor of No, he had said. Moreover, he had always expected the numbers in favor of Yes to grow, but that the vote would still go their way. There was a margin for error, he had admitted—2 to 3 %—but even so, No would prevail handily. But the triumvirate, having initially put their faith in his new analytics and tactics, had panicked. Despite the thoroughly contemporary means of leading the electorate by the nose, Plan B, it turned out, was to steal the election the old-fashioned way.

There was a glimmer of hope that it might all blow over, he reflected as the car drew closer to his Chiltern Hills refuge. As the triumvirate meeting outside Cambridge was breaking up, Chamberlain had taken a second phone call. He had listened intently for about two minutes while Weaver and Nesbitt stared at him silently and Townsend moved some morsels around on the platter looking for something tempting. Finally, Chamberlain had said "thank you" into the phone and closed it.

"More good news," said Chamberlain putting the phone in his pocket. "An interim status report. We don't yet have the evidence that the ARO kept—if there was any. So far, there's nothing obvious, nothing they can easily dig up about the vote. Fortunately, they're stuck on the postal ballots. And those are giving them fits, I hear. I think we'll all sleep better tonight."

Back from the Alban's, Ewan Johnston slouched across a chair staring at the ceiling of his gloomy sitting room. The only light source was a dim floor lamp next to him. Only one of its three light bulbs worked. His overcoat still on, he spoke with a friend at the local Election Commission, Graham Gannett.

"At the moment, Graham," he said into the phone, "I'm trying to help Mrs. Alban find some...*closure*, for want of a better word. I don't imagine there were any fresh investigations that focused on Donald. I mean, he's been out for what, eight or nine years? But I told her I'd follow up."

He listened as Gannett offered condolences and spoke of his respect and admiration for Donald Alban.

"But?" Johnston asked.

"But nothing, Ewan. We were all gutted when he tendered his resignation. There was never a hint of doubt about him or the performance of his duties. Certainly nothing to investigate." He paused a moment before adding, "I don't know if that helps Mrs. Alban or not. There's a part of me that wishes I could give you something, even if it was negative, that explained all this."

Johnston thanked him and rang off.

Donald Alban had cared deeply about his work, yet he had resigned. He had kept notes, reports and correspondence from his years of work stacked in moldering boxes behind the door to his study, but Johnston and Sandra Alban hadn't been able to find them, nor anything in his home office pertaining to it. Nothing. He had been the acting returning officer (ARO) for Dundee, and he hoarded records. They were now missing. If he had thrown them away, why? And when would he have done it that Sandra wouldn't have known about it?

Johnston's legal mind scavenged through events and evidence: Donald seemingly died by his own hand, but there had been no telling, precipitating event to account for why he chose now—no scandal, no investigation, no money trouble, no impending health calamity. There was nothing in his past to suggest he struggled with clinical depression. And why had he *typed* his suicide note? To Alban, the computer was only a slightly more useful typewriter. And he didn't much care for typewriters, come to think of it.

Sandra knew all of this, too. Uncertainty, anger and bewilderment were devouring her from the inside. Johnston wished he could bring her some kind of peace. Wished he could find it himself. His thoughts moved now to the unthinkable: was it possible he was a murder victim? That the records Alban had kept so lovingly, if haphazardly, were proof of something that could get him killed, and that's why they had been removed? Or was he, Ewan, being a coward, grasping at a conspiracy theory to avoid facing an ugly truth? Was he making things worse for Sandra by not only going along with her misgivings but stoking them, entertaining the idea that her husband's death was anything but what it appeared to be?

And yet. The same day that Donald had died, his oldest friend, "Wee Frankie" McDougal had been murdered in what appeared to be a car-theft attempt gone horribly wrong. It seemed a strange coincidence to him, one that had left a dismayed, brooding pall over the Tulloch neighborhood outside Perth where both men had grown up. What could they have been doing together that could get them killed? he wondered.

Donald Alban was a semi-retired barrister and the retired ARO for Dundee, whereas McDougal was a political philosophy professor. Though friends from boyhood who kept in touch, their paths rarely crossed. They worked on very different things in different spheres. Indeed, their opposing views on the Independence question back in 2014 had put a bit of a frost on their friendship. What possible connection between them could explain their untimely deaths?

At that phrase, he sat up and looked toward the old secretary desk at the far side of the room. Like most of the nice pieces of furniture he possessed, he had inherited the desk from his mother. It had settled into its spot against the far wall, promising order and efficiency, but delivering only a sense of one more thing not quite done, not quite where it should be while it stolidly collected papers and a good deal of dust. Unsure of its domestic role, he had pressed the desk into service holding files, memorabilia and odd papers he was equally unsure of. Things he hadn't regarded as important enough to put somewhere else, like in the locked cabinet at work or, if he was honest, had been too lazy to throw away.

He was on his feet automatically, drawn toward the old desk. Over the years he'd put stray documents in it that Donald had given him, along with a great many other things for safekeeping—mostly, as Alban had said, "for my memoirs," his thin, private joke. But now Johnston remembered a different set of papers. Seven or eight years earlier, Alban had pressed them onto him gravely, to be opened, he had said at the time, "only in the event of my untimely demise." Johnston and Alban had been drunk that evening. He had intended to put them together with Alban's will but had never done it. He had forgotten about them until that moment.

If Alban's untidy desk had pointed to unrecognized patterns and unthought-of brilliance, Johnston's filing system in the secretary desk was a study in chaos theory, a disordered cacophony. Finding what he wanted was a long process. The papers he thought he remembered looked like a great many others he'd stuffed away. And he couldn't remember now if they were loose, or inside something. He sat on the floor, still in his coat, for more than half an hour while he pulled everything out of the secretary desk and arrayed them around him on the carpet, his posture and the papers everywhere reminding him of his work after the break-in at his law office.

He paused in his search. On the same weekend, Alban had killed himself, Frankie had been murdered and his law office was broken into. If money hadn't been the motive behind the break-in, it was possible that the papers he was now looking for were precisely what the burglars had hoped to find. The seal on Alban's will had been broken and the contents examined, he now remembered. True, others had been opened too, but none of the others seemed to have been examined. He forced himself to focus as he started burrowing again, hoping he hadn't somehow thrown Alban's papers out during some ill-advised fit of tidying up.

He continued pulling papers and files out, examining them and putting them in ever growing piles in the darkening room. At one point, it had grown so dim that he was squinting. He stood up and turned on the overhead light, finally removing his coat. At the back of the desk, behind a stack of old pop music 'zines, he found what he was looking for inside a thick manila envelope, curled and buried, like an unpublished, abandoned manuscript.

Johnston fetched a chair from the kitchen and sat at the desk for what might have been the first time in his life and opened the envelope. Inside, on the covering page, written in Donald Alban's own hand, were his instructions, and a warning: *"Ewan, if I have died in some manner other than natural causes, it is because I know something the government doesn't want me to share. The Independence Referendum vote was stolen, and whether it was Westminster who initiated it, the way it was done could only have been achieved with high-level government knowledge and its collusion. I'm counting on you to protect Sandra and the children by getting this information out. It's the only hope now. My silence—and thus my implied complicity—has protected them so far. But if I'm dead, then I've failed, and it's probable that they're in danger. You are too. I hope you will forgive me."*

13

Marta Serres stopped by Imogen's office in the Adam Smith Building early in the morning. She knocked on Imogen's open door and walked in, carrying a bulging rucksack. "Sorry," she began, "I hope you don't mind me dropping in on you like this. It's been ages since I've been on campus here, and I didn't want to wait."

"Not at all," said Imogen, genuinely pleased to see her, "come in."

Serres deposited the rucksack on Imogen's desk with a heavy thump. "I don't know what kind of trouble you were having with the postal ballots, but I asked a colleague if he could get them."

"Oh!" Imogen began, "but I didn't mean to—"

"Yes, well. I think I'm getting a little caught up in your tone of intrigue, Gen."

"My tone of—?"

"Let's be honest with one another, 'Gen. You're onto something. Who're you working for—some new Anglo-American, lend-lease arrangement with MI5?"

"No," said Imogen, "of course not."

"Look, from what I've seen, and from the questions you've been asking, it's clear this isn't some drowsy comparison study."

"I'm not sure what you want me to say," Imogen began.

"Then let me start," said Serres. "You're looking into possible malfeasance in the Indy-ref. Though I don't know why. Nevertheless, you're wanting to know why such a reportedly close, preference-intense contest turned out so milquetoast. One: You think the postal ballots were compromised in some way, and two: you're wondering if that alone can explain a ten percent difference."

Imogen stared at her, trying not to betray anything.

"I expect you want to see what the high turnout can tell you," Serres continued. "And I'll bet that you are—or you are about to—begin working to make the districts congruent so you can compare previous elections with the referendum. Yes?" She didn't bother waiting for a response before saying, "I expect by now you've aggregated that data?"

Imogen nodded despite herself.

"Right," said Serres. She opened the rucksack and took out her laptop. She was about to sit down when she walked over and closed the office door. "Have you begun the regression?" she asked, as she sat down and opened her laptop.

Imogen spun her own laptop around and showed Serres what she was working on. Serres spun hers round to face Imogen, a policy-wonk Mexican standoff. Each peered at the other's screen.

"You weren't convinced by my reasoning about non-voters not being activated the last time we spoke," said Serres. "And after thinking about it a bit more, neither was I." She peered again at Imogen's screen. "It looks like you've come up with exactly what I did. You regressed turnout to compare earlier contests with the referendum." She peered again. "I'm assuming the Indy-ref is 'Time two' here." She pointed at the screen.

"Yes," said Imogen.

"And both of our intercepts show that turnout was higher all across the board. The regression line, therefore, moves up." She paused to look at Imogen's screen again. "And it appears we've both concluded that all voting precincts actually came close to or *surpassed* a 20% increase—except Glasgow and Dundee."

Imogen nodded. "The areas that polled the highest preference for Yes."

"So, what suppressed the vote in Glasgow and Dundee?"

"That seems to be the question," Imogen agreed.

Imogen thought carefully. She felt she could trust Marta. She was an investigator, not unlike herself in many ways, devoted to finding the truth. But Wee Frankie was dead, and it was possible that he was silenced because he knew something about what had happened in 2014, though maddeningly she still didn't know what. If he had been killed to keep him quiet, it meant she didn't know where or how information about her investigation was flowing. Or to whom. She couldn't risk expanding the circle, and she couldn't risk getting Marta harmed.

"For my comparison," Imogen began, still holding to her now threadbare ruse, "I wanted to focus on the question of postal ballots. You may know, we had an election overturned back home in North Carolina due to ballot harvesting and falsification."

Marta Serres stared at Imogen, searching her face. Finally, she said: "This is much deeper than that, Imogen. I wish you'd take me into your confidence."

Imogen stared back. Her FBI colleague Nettie Sartain had said almost those exact words during the Faithless Elector investigation. Back then, Imogen had tried to hide what she was doing from her staff and the top brass, too. For their safety. She had finally, reluctantly, brought Nettie in, only to see her shot and almost killed. She didn't want to put Marta in harm's way. She had grown to like and admire her. Which had also been true of Nettie.

If Imogen told Marta, she'd be broadening the circle, which could prove deadly. But if she rebuffed her interest and assistance, if she offended her by not discussing the true scope of the investigation, Imogen ran the risk of Marta continuing her version of the investigation on her own, thereby jeopardizing the integrity of Imogen's, and perhaps inadvertently raising Marta's profile and putting herself in danger. And her family. In the Faithless Elector investigation, the conspirators who tried to suppress information operated like the mafia: first they try to bribe; then they threaten; and if that doesn't work, they threaten your family. And whether you take the bribe or not, they'll still murder you.

"Marty," she began, "it's not that I don't trust you. Far from it. But for the moment, I have to keep this small. And quiet. I've sworn to do so. But if there *is* something going on, I swear to you that you'll be the first one I come to. I need to know that you won't discuss what you've gleaned so far. With anyone."

"My God," she whispered. It was as if until that moment she hadn't let herself believe there might be something amiss. "But why are you involved at all? Why wasn't it handled through the commission? Why hasn't the government...?" Her eyes grew big as she contemplated the full weight of what she suddenly dared not ask.

"There may be a danger," said Imogen. "And I'd hate to run afoul of your husband's wishes about your safety," she added, hoping to lighten the mood, but also deadly serious.

"All right," said Serres. "There's still some work to do on the postal ballots—though they're such a small number I don't see them telling us much. But I think you need to focus here on Glasgow, and on Dundee."

"Yes. I think Dundee and Glasgow are the keys, too. You're OKAY with this as-is?" Imogen asked, uncertain of the answer.

Serres looked at Imogen for a moment. "Yes," she said at last. "For now."

The enclosed sheets that Alban had given to Ewan Johnston, dated 18 September, 2014, the date of the referendum, were handwritten pages denoting rough voter counts from the polling stations in the Dundee area for which Alban, as the ARO, had been responsible. Each page had multiple entries, updated throughout the day. There was a final total on each page, including the number of ballot boxes filled and sealed, and at the bottom of the page, the date, time and Alban's initials.

Each new page carried over the totals from the bottom of the previous page. The last pages were photocopies of a government document listing the number of ballot boxes delivered to the count centre. Below that page, there was the directive from the electoral commission requiring the polling stations to use multiple boxes, "as there would likely be increased voter turnout." It outlined a system for adding in new boxes throughout the day. On the last page, the total number of boxes delivered was underlined, and his signature was circled. He had written "No" next to it. There was also a letter from Alban to one of the presiding officers at the Craigiebarns Primary School poll initiating a substitution of the van drivers. Alban had written "Forged" next to his signature.

Johnston turned back to the final, handwritten sheet, listing the grand total of ballot boxes delivered to the centre. The number of boxes by Alban's handwritten tally was 283 boxes, but the official form read 237. Next to this, he had written "46," for the number of missing boxes.

Johnston stared at the pages. If the sign-off was forged, if the correct box tally was suppressed, it could only have been done by a coordinated, official effort. Which meant government officials were involved. Whom could he tell that wouldn't involve the very people he needed to keep it away from? Who would be able to put things right? What should he tell Sandra, if anything?

When Marta Serres arrived back at her office at Strathclyde. there was a message from Ian Ross, Special Adviser to the Chief of Staff to the First Minister. She was in a hurry to teach her class and didn't respond. When she returned a little more than two hours later, there was another message from him, asking her to please call him. There was an urgency in his voice with the second message, which she found odd. It wasn't as though there were any election results. What could this be about?

"I think we met once," Ross began pleasantly when she reached him on his cell phone. "At some God-awful commission function a year or so ago."

She remembered. Handsome, charming, perfect hair, nice teeth, which he showed frequently because he smiled often, particularly as emphasis on a point he was winning. He was chatty—ingratiatingly so—flighty, self-important. Well, what would you expect of someone in his position? And harmless for all that. Though as she now listened to the oddly assertive undertone in his voice, she also remembered the flicker of a disdaining smile that night when she took her leave a little earlier than most, in order to tuck the children into bed.

"Are you helping Imogen Trager with her comparison study?" he asked.

She felt there was something forced in the way he asked, as though he were still trying to sound chummy, as if this call were something he'd been meaning to do and was now getting round to it. Imogen had mentioned working with someone in the Scottish government but that was all she had said about it. Given the grave tenor of their morning conversation, Marta's antennae were raised.

"I'm not *helping* her," she began, trying for the moment to keep the edge out of her voice. Who did he think she was, a research assistant? "I've provided some data for her to do a comparison study she's working on. The department head over at University of Glasgow, David Reidy, thought we should meet. You know, colleagues engaged in similar work. Fellow professionals." She let that hang there a moment.

"I see," he said.

"Was there something else, Mr. Ross? I need to prepare for lecture and there are quite a lot of other things to get to before the end of the day."

"No," he said. "It's just, well, you requested information about the mail-in ballots for the referendum yesterday. I thought maybe you were looking into something either yourself, or with Imogen...er, Doctor Trager."

Unconsciously, she closed her laptop. She wondered how—and why—a party functionary would know about that. She hadn't phoned the commission archives. This felt odd, and she wasn't sure how to play it. Should she be haughty, as in "who are you to question what I'm doing?" She thought perhaps that might not be the best look. Exasperatingly helpful? No, that tack was liable to lead to further questions—answers to which she was beginning to feel that she might need to lie about. She wondered whether she was she being ridiculous.

Best to keep it chatty and chummy, she decided, and to match the same tone as he'd begun with. "Yes, she had some questions the other day. Called me. I felt a bit sorry for her, if you want to know. She's obviously good at her job over there in America, but she's more than a little out of her depth here. Not that she couldn't get up to speed, mind you, she's clearly intelligent. When we met, I kept trying to pump her for information about that Faithless Elector investigation of hers—you've heard about that, I'm sure. It's a pity, but she wasn't very forthcoming."

"And the postal ballots?" he asked, somewhat impatiently.

"Oh, that. I'm afraid I had to disappoint her on the postal ballots," she lied brightly. "Certainly, I did what I could. She said she was having difficulty, and I said I'd look into it. She was hoping to have them disaggregated from the in-person ballots...but I'm afraid it isn't as simple as she'd hoped. It almost never is, is it?"

She paused a moment and then added conspiratorially, "I feel like I should ask if *you're* working with her?" she quizzed him. "Or perhaps you want to be so? I'm sorry, but your letting slip her Christian name like that does seem to suggest something much more interesting than old postal ballots. Not enough redheads in Scotland for you?" She tossed in a girlish giggle for effect.

"No," he said, without humor, "nothing like that. I know she's working on a comparison study. I was told so—also by Reidy. My chief told me to give her every courtesy. I knew she was interested in the postal ballots, and when I made my request the staff person I spoke with happened to mention that this was the second request in as many days. I wanted to make sure we weren't duplicating work."

"Of course," said Serres. "I see now. And I'm sure you found there was nothing there to help her. As I did. Was there anything else?"

14

Ewan Johnston decided not to reveal anything to Sandra about the notes Alban had left him yet. He needed time to think. The idea that it was a coordinated cover-up seemed far-fetched. He wanted to be certain of his facts, and his next steps before he told her. As shocking—and daunting—as it was, Johnston felt some measure of pride that Alban had chosen him for this task; and far from being angry that he'd been put in potential danger, he welcomed the confidence it showed in him. He wouldn't let Donald down, but he wouldn't put his widow in undue danger either.

Donald Alban had been murdered. And so, probably, had Wee Frankie. They'd been killed to keep quiet that the Independence referendum had been violated. He wasn't for independence himself, nor had Donald been, for that matter. But the whole point of elections was that you abided by their outcome, if they've been arrived at legally. Rather like verdicts.

Growing anger, he found, displaced his initial fear. A man whom he had admired, who had given of himself, who had taught him everything he could; a man who had built a life of integrity and a reputation for impartiality, who observed, enforced and played by the rules, had been murdered for doing so. If he didn't tell someone, the deed would go unpunished. But, he thought, if he were to tell someone, might not he have some convenient accident himself, and there's an end to it? But tell whom? The fact it pertained to the referendum suggested how and why Wee Frankie was involved, too.

The Met might investigate, or MI5, but each would notify those higher up about the investigation, perhaps inadvertently warning those responsible. He could go to the Scottish Government in Holyrood but they'd also run up against official Westminster pettifogging and prevarication. And, if it were taken seriously, the investigation would be remanded to the Met or MI5. So official channels were out.

In theory, getting it to the press might inoculate him from being the victim of any accidents, but that, too, was a minefield. The Tory press wouldn't hear the evidence—and might report him, thereby alerting those he was trying to avoid. The wolf-in-sheep's-clothes lefty press would ignore it or get it wrong as they did most things to do with Scotland; any pro-Independence paper wouldn't be believed outside its charmed circle, and the rest of the Stockholm-syndrome Scottish press couldn't be trusted.

"You should take the train from Queen Street," said the conductor on the train to Edinburgh as he looked at Imogen's ticket. "If you're wanting to be there anytime soon."

She had assumed that Glasgow Central Station was the hub, and that the fast trains would leave from there. It was only now, as they crept across the river and out of town, that she was learning it wasn't the case. "I'm not in a hurry," she said, which was true.

She wasn't meeting Ian there until seven that evening, but she thought it might be pleasant to have a walkabout in Edinburgh. She was hoping for a stroll along Princes Street and maybe a look-in at the National Portrait Gallery. Then, meet Ian for dinner, and...? On the floor next to her was a small suitcase, with a weekend's change of clothes. She had made a reservation for that night at a hotel near Waverly Station. It was a little early to check in, but she could store her bag there while she walked around and took in the sights. *Well, why not?* she thought. Ian had called her the risk/reward lass in that gorgeous accent of his. Bringing the bag was no risk at all.

"Aye, well, it's a good job you're not." The conductor winked at Imogen as he handed her ticket back and continued his gregarious progress through the sparsely populated car.

It was a little before two in the afternoon, and her fellow passengers all seemed to be in the same unhurried state as she. Most were older, pensioners. The conductor kept up his pleasant banter as he moved along. He was old, too, near retirement age himself she guessed, but spry for all that. Slight and wiry, his hair kept in a tight, iron gray crew cut. She thought of Wee Frankie and felt desolate.

"Ah, a cheapo ticket!" the conductor said teasingly to one man. "You'll be wanting the after-six train for the return, then." He started making change for the money the man offered and writing on some kind of official notepad.

Cheapo? she wondered. Was this another time she was mishearing something? Would she have to ask Ian what that meant now, too?

The Scottish accent she heard in most of her colleagues and recent acquaintances was lovely, playful and earthy, with a lilting, singsong quality she enjoyed. But sometimes to her American ears, it could also be unintelligible. Already in her sojourn, she'd found herself staring blankly at a man on Sauchiehall Street who—she was guessing here—was asking for directions to somewhere; and mortifyingly, she'd held up a checkout line because she'd had to ask the saleswoman to repeat herself multiple times before understanding that the saleswoman simply needed a signature for her charge card.

She turned to look out the window at the damp countryside. A misting rain gathered and ran in rivulets across the window. Outside, low hills dotted with sheep stretched away, then flattened and stretched into tilled fields, before the hills swept in close again. The tops of some of the far hills seemed to have tugged a bit of low cloud down to them. Or was it fog rising to join the clouds?

Under the gloom, closer in, it was bright and fecund—greens and yellows, stark against freshly turned earth, a glimpse of riotous purple or fuchsia peeking out over a garden wall.

Here and there as the train rattled past, cattle would congregate, their backsides to the wind, huddled close together as though they were plotting something.

From inside the train at the far end of the car, she heard the conductor declare another "cheapo." She ran through the permutations—jeepo? sheepo? Could it be Gallicized French— *gipeau*?

"Yer no wrong there, and it's no a bad bit extra deal at that," the elderly passenger agreed. "Ah quite like riding in semi-privacy on off-times."

Well, there was one tiny mystery solved. Pensioners paid a reduced fare, and it was further reduced—cheaper—if they traveled at off-peak times. Fair enough. She was glad she wouldn't have to risk looking foolish by asking Ian. But she did have questions for him of a more serious nature.

Why, officially, had the postal ballots been bundled in such a way that they were difficult to un-bundle? It was only luck that Marta's friend and colleague had the data, though it was only a sample. And how, if it was all so secret, had a Tory minister and an ex-government official been able to see them early? Why had there been no exit poll? Why was turnout lowest in precisely the two places—Dundee and Glasgow—that it was expected to be highest?

It all looked odd. The decision not to look at the ballots separately, not to commission an exit poll—these were political decisions, involving multiple agencies. She wasn't ready to claim there was malfeasance, though there was certainly a good bit of *mis*feasance. Ian's answers to her questions might help to allay her misgivings or spark further inquiry. Maybe he could start earning his keep by delving into the decision-making regarding her questions. Who were the decision-makers? What was behind their decisions?

At the moment, all she had were data that raised questions, which couldn't withstand legal scrutiny, much less the withering spotlight of politics. And yet, so far everything pointed in one direction—to some kind of suppression. Now the real work would have to begin. And she'd need to go to Dundee at some point.

Outside, the rain had stopped, and the sun broke through in wide, bright patches. As she looked over the soggy ground, glinting in honey light, she felt a lift in her spirits. A new investigation under way—one with maybe some meat in it—a walk around a new city, dinner with Ian. And maybe...? She shook her head to clear her thoughts. Maybe she could set him looking into the who-and-why of her investigation. Maybe he had some equally interesting information. She hoped he could shed some light on Frankie's research. It was more in his line.

She was glad she'd taken this train, even if it was the slow one. The countryside was lovely, and even the names of towns she passed were heartening, if strange—Cambuslang, Torbothie, Breich. She practiced saying them in a whisper as each town passed by. Her sounding of the "ch" in Breich, she decided, sounded less Scottish and more like German. She'd have to work on that.

Past Addiewell, which wasn't as fun to say as Breich, she looked up and noticed a sign for West Calder. It hit her like a slap in the face. Thoughts of Duncan Calder brought her up sharp, a dog who'd reached the end of her tether and been snapped back. She glared accusingly at the overnight case by her feet and pounded a fist into her thigh with irate frustration, then laid her head against the cold window.

What did she see in Ian? she demanded of herself. Petulantly, she allowed that he was convenient. Also engaging, handsome. Was it him, or the idea of him that she found attractive, like some bland Ken doll she could write her own story on? She'd mourned Duncan and had kept herself to herself. At about the time she had gathered her courage to "put herself out there," Covid-19 struck. Her confinement to barracks stretched endlessly before her, its strangeness and solitude like a prison sentence with no clear end.

She'd leave Scotland in another seven months, back to D.C., or to work somewhere else in the US. Was he the right man for her temporary needs? Was that cruel? she wondered.

Maybe Ian was thinking of her along the same disposable line. He didn't seem the faithful type, if she was honest.

This type of soggy rumination was not her strength, and she grew weary of the uncertainty. Numbers and puzzles were her trade. They were definite, or at least indicative. They told you where to look next, sometimes even what to expect next. If you knew how to read them. And they were infinite. Numbers didn't lie, she thought.

What, after all, would you call a broken promise to love forever? The train had long passed by West Calder, but she continued to think of Duncan. She had thought they would carry on together, forever, but the investigation that brought them together, which had been the midwife of their intimacy, had rent it, too. It had left him dead.

Her phone rang as the train pulled out of Haymarket, the last stop before Waverly Station, Edinburgh. It was Serres. "You around this evening?" she asked. "I thought we might stop together for a quick drink."

"No, I'm sorry, Marty, I'm almost to Edinburgh. I'm meeting with someone tonight."

"About all this?" Serres asked.

"Yes," said Imogen.

"Well, then: I had a strange phone call about you—"

Imogen sat up, alert.

"A man named Ian Ross called me. I think you've met him? He wanted to know about the postal ballots."

"What was he asking?"

"Interrogating, more like," said Serres. "He said you'd asked him about disaggregating the postal and in-person ballots. Did you?"

"Not as such. And why was he calling you?"

"Well, that's just it. He said he was trying to help you out, and that when he made his request on your behalf they happened to mention that I'd made a similar one. He wanted to make sure we weren't duplicating efforts, he said. Only, I'd made no formal request. I happened to mention to a colleague something about it. I suppose things get around, but..."

Imogen reflected for a moment. "I think it's okay," she said. "I did mention to him that I was having difficulty, and he may have taken it on himself to see what he could do. Thank you for letting me know, though."

"May I ask, is he involved with whatever it is you're not officially doing?"

"At the fringes," said Imogen, hedging.

"Well, it's probably a good job I didn't tell him about finding the partial, sampling data from my colleague Brian. I left it as, 'Commission staff unable to help.'"

"Okay...?" The train had passed into a tunnel. Imogen looked at her reflection in the darkened window.

"Maybe I *am* getting too caught up in this," Serres admitted, "but there was something about his tone I didn't like."

"Thank you," Imogen said. "I appreciate the call. And the heads-up. I'll be in touch."

The train broke from darkness into drab, scattered light under the shed roofs of Waverly Station. She looked out across the platform as the slow train trundled in—moving so slowly that it didn't come to a stop so much as cease moving. People were getting up and making for the door as she looked out, still wondering if Ian's call to Marty meant anything. Ian might have been looking to protect her. After what had happened to Frankie, he might want to make sure nothing else happened, that their dangerous, diminishing circle wasn't growing, wasn't encompassing others in harm's way. It would account for his odd tone, wanting to protect her but unable to say why or from what.

Yes, that was probably it.

Unless it wasn't. She moved automatically with the rest of the travelers toward the exit gate at the end of the platform, lost in thought. Only Ian and she had known about Frankie's friend, whoever he was. Only the three of them knew there might be evidence of malfeasance in the referendum. Ian had said "they" must have been watching the friend, and that was how they'd found out about Frankie. It made sense as an explanation, but it was Ian who had supplied that account of events. Now, he was checking on the progress of her work? Why not ask her directly?

Jesus, she was jumping at shadows. She was being paranoid, she told herself. Ian had been forthright about what he wanted and why. He had been helpful in getting data and reports she needed. Unlikely as it felt, Frankie's murder might be a coincidence. And yet she lingered, not taking the Waverly Steps up into the heart of the city. She needed time to think and stopped at a coffee bar for an espresso. She stood at the high, yellow-topped table, sipping her coffee and looked out across the platforms. Even in the middle of the afternoon, there was a pleasing, resolute thrum of people walking through the station. She felt again her foreignness, the strangeness of it all. Notices of trains and platforms updated inexorably on the schedule, announcements droned unintelligibly, but one phrase broke through her reverie: "...train for Dundee leaving..."

She didn't have to be here, she thought. Whatever else might be going on, she had to find out what was behind Frankie's murder. Maybe Ian Ross was what he said he was, insofar as any political operative could be wholly truthful. But if her trust was misplaced... And there'd already been one murder.

Her phone was already in her hand. She inhaled a deep breath and dialed Ross's number. "Ian? It's Imogen. Look, I'm sorry, but I don't think I can get away tonight. I've got a lot going on, most of it going nowhere, and I'd much rather talk when I have something solid. Could I call you in a couple of days?"

"Of course," he said. "Tomorrow then?"

"Well, that's it. I'm scrambling now because I won't be able to work on things *until* tomorrow. There's some Bureau business back home I have to deal with, and prepare for," she lied. "There's a call at three p.m. eastern time, which is eight p.m. here."

"I'm sorry to hear it. I hope everything's all right."

"Yes, no problems, but I'm required to phone in."

"All right," he said, rallying to put a good face on his disappointment. He paused a moment before adding. "Maybe we should prepare ourselves for the possibility that there's nothing to find. We can't rule that out."

"No, indeed," she said. "But I haven't given up yet."

"Good girl," he said.

She held the phone away from her and looked at it, incredulous.

"Sorry," she heard him add hastily as she put the phone back to her ear. "I was just trying to be positive. That kind of slipped out. Sorry. I—"

"I'm going to see that it's all worked out this weekend. I'll call you in a couple days? We'll try again then."

Glasgow and Dundee were the keys. She sipped at the last drip of espresso in her cup. The ARO for Glasgow, she had found, had retired and emigrated to Canada, where he'd dissolved into anonymity in the snowy mists of northern British Columbia. She wanted to have something to impress Ian, something more concrete. He was the one who was going to have to bring the case for stronger safeguards. If he was involved in the way he said he was.

15

On the train to Dundee, she booked a single at a bed and breakfast on Perth Road for two nights. Then she dialed Marty Serres.

"I hope I've caught you before you left work," she said as Serres picked up.

"Yes, you have. Most of us work until five, you know. Not sure what America's like."

"I decided not to stay in Edinburgh. You'd said we should look at Glasgow and Dundee. I'm getting nowhere with Glasgow—the former ARO there's disappeared. So I've booked a B-and-B for two nights in Dundee. I'm on my way there now. Who should I try to talk with?"

"Hang on," said Serres, as she rifled through papers in a box next to her desk. "I was thinking about next steps, too, people who might know something. There's someone...Hang on," she said again. Imogen could hear her rummaging about in her office. "OKAY," she said at last. "Yes. The best person to start with would be the former ARO there. I've met him. A man named Donald Alban. Knows everything. Knows everyone. He's retired now, but he'd point you in the right direction, I'd say. Was on the job for years. I have his personal number here somewhere. Since he's retired, that's probably best." There was another long pause as she looked. "Oh!" she said, "I've got his home address, too. It's on Hyndford Street, in the city proper."

"Thanks." She wrote down the phone number and address on a notepad at her knee.

"Start with him. And you can say that you're working with me. That's fine. It might ease things along that bit more. I don't know him well, but we *have* talked, and he'll know me. How do you think you'll approach it?"

"Good question," said Imogen feeling a little impetuous and foolish. "I guess I'll start with the drowsy, comparison paper angle, talk about some of the things I've found, some of the questions I have about voter activation. Leave it a bit open-ended: What had he noticed? Anything different? Even anecdotal things."

"That sounds like a good beginning," Serres assented.

"Do you think he could hook me up with some party people, like poll watchers?"

"Not him directly. He's meant to be non-partisan. And the tellers—that's what we call them here, not poll watchers—would be party people. If the discussion goes well, he could point you to the right people who could get you in touch with the tellers. Why them?"

"I have a hunch, and the further away from officialdom I can work, the better for me. Funny, it's usually the opposite, isn't it? I mean party people have an agenda. Any sense about this Donald Alban?"

"Straight as they come. And as straightlaced. My only caution for you would be to tread carefully on your follow-on questions after you've started talking about the comparison paper. He's sharp, and he's likely guess what you're really looking for."

"As you did."

"Yes. And if he does, he'll feel duty-bound, retired or not, to notify someone in government of your enquiry."

"I'll tread lightly. Thanks, Marty."

"Are you going to tell me what you think's going on?"

"I'll be back in Glasgow on Sunday night. Can I drop by your office Monday morning?"

"Yes," said Serres. "I'll be back from class after eleven."

"See you then."

Imogen hung up and called up Alban's Hyndford Street address on her phone. It was four blocks from the B-and-B, just off Perth Road.

In Edinburgh, at Saint Andrew's House, Ian Ross knocked at the door to Chief of Staff Janette Ritchie's office. "We have a problem," he said. Not looking up from her computer screen, she motioned him in. He pulled the door closed behind him.

Hearing the door close, she glanced up and asked, "That bad?" She pushed herself back from the desk and sat up straight in her chair with an expression familiar to dentists from their patients that seemed to say, "do your worst, I'm ready."

"I've taken to having drinks with Des Willoughby, from the Conservative party."

"Dizzy?" she scoffed. "That drunken sot, why?"

"Because he's a drunken sot, who says things he should not."

Ritchie's youthful face and open, trusting expression were at odds with her stark, white hair, cropped short and raked back from her forehead. The curated look belied a canny fortitude. She brushed her fingertips along the side of her head, pressed a strand behind her ear. "And?"

"Parliament opens in twelve days' time," he began "Dizzy says that we'll all be mostly out of a job. They're planning to unveil a much more restrictive bill to clarify the Internal Market Act."

Ritchie sat stone-faced.

"The Internal Market Act," he continued, "repatriated—their word—powers that Scotland had ceded to Europe, pre-Brexit. This so-called Clarifying Bill will even claw back bits of Ag and Fish—"

"The fisheries?"

"Yes. And bits of the NHS, Environment, Labour, even some of our tax powers..."

"And the Sewell Convention?" She was reaching for the phone.

"I brought that up, too. He bumptiously reminded me that it's really nothing more than a convention. A political convention. And that's not the worst," he said. She left the phone in its cradle. "We could fight all those things, but the Clarifying Bill would create an extra-judicial Star Chamber for arbitration and the resolution of disputes."

"They'd like to!"

"Also, they'll propose new rules to limit referenda capacity: wherein referenda are only allowed every 30 years or so—"

"That's taking the whole 'generation' bit awfully seriously," she interrupted. "The '98 Northern Ireland Act only sets a limit of seven years!"

"And. It will now need two-thirds majority to pass. No referendum on independence until 2044!"

"And God help us ever getting sixty-seven per cent." She tightened her jaw. "It'll be a grueling fight," she began, "but..."

"That's where the Star Chamber comes in."

"You've confirmed this?" she asked.

"No one will confirm it, but I've spoken with that factotum, Gowrie, and with Proudfoot in Westminster, and their treacly denials—smug for all that—tell me I'm onto something. According to Dizzy, it's to be announced as part of the legislative agenda in the King's Speech from the throne when Parliament opens on October 25."

Ritchie stared bleakly at her desk top. Ross could practically hear the gears turning. He wondered idly if she was venting steam somewhere.

"If I didn't hate them all so much," she said, "I might just admire it. I can see it now: they're merely *clarifying* the substance and responsibility of the Internal Market Act with what they'll spin as the next logical, necessary—for *them*— step. And the Star Chamber will be totally unaccountable but protected—like this Clarifying Act—under the auspices of parliamentary sovereignty." She almost seemed to be talking to herself.

"And it fucks us on a second referendum," he said.

"It does. Will they call it the 'Clarifying Bill,' do you think?"

"No one will confirm that it's even in the works, so I don't know. The 'Make Britain Better Again' Act perhaps? I'm imagining a bunch of red hats, with MBBA emblazoned across the front."

"This is serious, Ian." She drew a deep breath. "Thank you for bringing it to me. The First Minister is due back in about two hours. I'll talk with her, and we'll take steps. And I'll make sure you're included."

"Thank you," he said, and turned to leave. "There is..." He hesitated and turned back round. He would have to be careful. Imogen hadn't turned up anything yet, but the death of Wee Frankie meant there *was* something to find. He'd leave that part—his part in it—out for now. "There is the possibility that the previous referendum was interfered with. I've also heard that someone's investigating it."

"From whom, Dizzy Willoughby?" she asked, incredulous. "That's a dead end, Ian. MI5, the Met, Electoral Commission, they all looked into it. There's no there there."

"But if there *were* something to find?"

"We'd need to have it by at least the Friday before Parliament opens. That's nine days from now." She shook her head. "No, it's battle stations."

In the cab from the station, Imogen called Alban's phone but had to leave a message. Arriving at the bed and breakfast, she stepped out of the cab and made her way up the curving steps to a sturdy, sandstone tenement perched above Perth Road. Before ringing the doorbell, she paused at the entryway and turned to look out over the Tay River. The railroad bridge unfurled across the river to her left. Low clouds stalked the far bank, obscuring the tops of the hills there.

A sinewy woman in her sixties answered the door. "Yes?" She had large, staring eyes. Her short, gray hair lay in stiff, sweat-flattened plaits against the nape of her neck.

"Good afternoon. I'm Imogen Trager. I booked two nights online a little while ago."

"Yes, dear. Come inside." She turned, not holding the door, which Imogen caught and pushed through with her wheelie suitcase.

Imogen's hostess wasn't rude but she was brusque. And perfunctory. It seemed her mind was on needing to be somewhere else. The tour of the premises and amenities amounted to her indicating that the room behind where she stood was the breakfast room and telling Imogen what times breakfast would be served there. She then pointed behind Imogen, indicating the television room and drinks parlor.

"You can have a look in, if you'd like," she said, but Imogen's mind was elsewhere, too.

Alban's voicemail had picked up on the first ring. Did that mean he was screening calls? She trudged up the stairs to her room, unpacked her bag and sat on the bed to call again. Same result.

She flopped back onto the bed, her feet still resting on the floor. *Am I being ridiculous about Ian?* she wondered as she gazed toward the ceiling. If she couldn't reach this Alban, she'd have wasted this impetuous trip. And she'd still want to talk with some of the tellers who had worked the referendum. As someone high up in the party, Ian was well placed to smooth that way for her. Surely, she had to trust him.

In the absence of an exit poll, which she still thought a suspiciously odd omission, her hunch was that the tellers might be able to give her something like the overview of the voting she lacked. Both she and Marta Serres had come to the same conclusion: in Dundee, and in Glasgow, the tallies of voters were lower than everywhere else. But Dundee and Glasgow were precisely where they'd have expected it to be highest.

She lay half on, half off the bed as the sun set and the room grew dark. At a little after six that evening, she roused herself and put on the light next to the bed. She needed food. She disliked the idea of taking a taxi back into town and decided to walk along Perth Road to see what she could find. She'd seen a number of restaurants and pubs on her ride in.

A chilly wind blew as she stepped out, but the rain had stopped. Long strands of hair had come loose from their plaits and blew extravagantly in the wind. She wished she had taken a moment to fix it before heading out. She also wished that she would learn to predict hunger and stop being surprised by it. She was famished. She walked purposefully, not minding the cold, her hands thrust deep into the pockets of her pear-green jacket. As she crossed Hyndford Street, she looked up the road, wondering if she could see Alban's house, and unconsciously brought her phone out to check it. Seeing no change, she put the phone back and continued her food hunt.

Like some ginger Goldilocks, Imogen looked in at a couple of places near the University of Dundee Art School, but none, despite her hunger, were just right. Her first find, the George Orwell pub seemed perfect, but the food options were limited. She was disappointed that the pub had no advertisements for Victory Gin, nor any pork dishes named after Old Major or Snowball. She'd seen a fish and chips place half a block earlier, and she considered getting a fish supper—it would be quick!— and coming back to the Orwell, but she kept walking. Another two blocks on, she found a likely looking pub, the Braes.

On Hyndford Street, though Imogen had already passed by, Ewan Johnston stopped at the Albans' house after work to check in on Sandra, as he had most nights these past two weeks. She greeted him at the door and thrust a phone toward him. "Someone's been calling Donald," she said. "On his phone. The same person, I think. Twice. I..."

She looked at him, not with helplessness, but utter fatigue.

They stood facing one another in the front hallway, both weary with grief. Johnston still hadn't mentioned anything about what he'd found. The weight of that omission left him feeling burdened and guilt-ridden, but he wanted to be certain of next steps before telling her more. He didn't know himself how he wanted to handle it, and so didn't want to answer any questions. He had no idea of next steps, and he didn't want to involve or endanger anyone else until he was sure.

"Whoever it is left a message," she said.

"What was the message?"

"I don't know Donald's pass code," she said.

"I don't know it either, Sandra. I'm sorry."

Nevertheless, she proffered the phone again. He took it and pressed his thumb on the locked screen. A "missed call" notification displayed, along with a number. It wasn't someone in his contacts, Johnston surmised. There was no name attached, but the number was visible. He reached inside his jacket for a pen.

"Could I have a bit of paper?" he asked.

Sandra opened a drawer in the table by the door and took out a notepad.

"It must be someone...some old friend who doesn't know he's gone," she said. "I'm sorry, Ewan, but today I just can't go over that ground again. Can't listen to someone else's new grief. Can't be the bearer of it."

Johnston nodded. He pressed his thumb on the screen again and wrote down the number displayed there. "I'll do it," he said. He let himself out and went to his eager, silver BMW, where he sat, staring.

Seated comfortably in the Braes pub, Imogen was taking care not to drink too much of the cider she'd ordered while she waited for her meat pie to arrive. She was so hungry, her stomach so empty, that if she weren't careful, she'd be drunk before the food arrived. She looked around the pub. It was comfortable, if dark. Warm and buzzing with students on a Friday night.

Then the phone rang.

"Hello," said a voice, "this is Donald Alban's solicitor, Ewan Johnston. I believe you left a message on his telephone earlier today."

"Yes, I did."

"May I ask who's calling? All I have is the call-back number, so I don't know what this pertains to."

"My name is Imogen Trager, I'm an election specialist with the FBI in the United States. Currently, I'm the Alma Guthrie Visiting Fellow at University of Glasgow. I'm writing a UK-US comparison paper on voting norms and behavior. Professor Marta Serres, a friend and colleague at Strathclyde suggested I contact Mr. Alban—they know one another professionally, I believe—because I have some questions about process and procedure."

"I see," said Johnston. "I'm sorry to disappoint you, Ms. Trager—or is it Doctor?—but Donald Alban died recently—"

"When?" she asked.

"About two weeks ago on—"

"On October third?" she interrupted.

"Yes," he said. "The third or fourth."

"Forgive me, but how did he die?"

"He hanged himself, Ms. Trager. Now if that's all—"

"Mr. Johnson..."

"Johns*ton*, Ms. Trager," he said emphasizing the "t."

"Mr. Johnston," she said correctly this time. "Again, I hope you'll forgive the question, but...was he a friend of Francis McDougal?"

There was a long pause on the other end, and Imogen worried she had stepped out of bounds. She cursed herself for seeming so eager in the face of this tragedy. She must seem like a ghoul.

"Yes," said Johnston simply.

"Close?"

"Very," he said. "Maybe not as much lately as in the past. But yes."

"Could I ask—?"

"Ms. Trager, this is the strangest interrogation I've ever been party to. I would like to point out that you're way out of your jurisdiction."

Imogen said, "Are you aware that Wee Frankie died the same night in Glasgow?"

"Yes," he said.

Imogen heard something uncertain in his voice, something that let her know she was maybe onto something. She continued carefully. "Frankie was a colleague of mine at the university. I hadn't known him long. But I count him—count*ed* him—as a friend, and he said he was working on something with an old friend. Something important."

He was quiet for a moment. Then he said, "Ms. Trager, I'm not sure this is something we can discuss at length over the telephone. If you're ever here in Dundee—"

"I'm here now. I'm having dinner at the Braes, over by the Art School."

"I know it," he said. "Would you fancy a bit of company?"

102

16

It would have taken Ewan Johnston less than ten minutes to walk to the Braes pub, but he moved his car closer, parking opposite the pub. He didn't go inside right away. He paused under the canopy of an off-license store to make sure he wasn't rushing into something foolish.

From his phone, he googled "Imogen Trager + FBI." There were countless news stories and photos of her. He paused over a particular picture of her. It wasn't what he'd expected her to look like when she'd said she was with the FBI. He gazed for a moment longer, enlarged the photo. He enlarged it a little further, studying the face. Despite himself, he lingered, looking into her green eyes. All at once he felt odd, guilty. He quickly returned to the original results page.

From the results page, he followed a link to "Faithless Elector investigation." There she was again, but he scrolled past the picture this time and read the text. Yes, she was an elections specialist, a PhD, promoted from the voting integrity office. Another link said she was on a leave of absence at University of Glasgow. Satisfied it wasn't an obvious ruse of some kind on the part of Alban's killers to find out if he knew anything, Johnston wondered again what an FBI agent, an elections fraud inspector, was doing in Scotland. And why on earth would she want to speak with Donald Alban? He was out of ideas for how to bring an investigation into Donald Alban's death and those behind it to justice. Might this Imogen Trager have some insight?

Well, he'd hear what she had to say. He was also determined to let her do all the talking.

He stepped into the pub and scanned the room for Imogen. He saw her in a far corner, not the glamorous, plucky woman in the photos, but hunched over, devouring her Double Beef Pitstop Pie. As he arrived at the table, she looked up at him like a lioness from a fresh kill. There were those startlingly brilliant eyes again. And a big drip of gravy on her chin. Somehow, he thought, she was the more alluring for it.

"Imogen Trager?" he asked. "I'm Ewan Johnston."

She dabbed at her chin with a napkin as she stood up. She swallowed what she was chewing and said, "A pleasure." They shook hands. "Please sit down."

"I'll get a pint first," he said. "What're you having there, cider?"

She nodded, and he walked to the bar.

"Thank you for meeting with me," she began, when he returned with their drinks. "And I'm very sorry to hear about Mr. Alban."

"He was a good friend. It's a great loss."

"I'd grown fond of Wee Frankie, as we called him."

Johnston smiled. "Everyone did," he said. "Everyone liked him."

"I had begun working on something with Frankie," she said. "Something that may have involved Mr. Alban."

"May have?"

"Well, I don't know, you see. Not for sure. But Frankie's death is suspicious."

"Yes. He was murdered. Brutally."

"But maybe not over his car and whatever cash he carried at the time."

"Is that what the police are saying?"

"No," she said. "They're following the theft/car-jacking angle."

"So, it's you who thinks otherwise," he stated rather than asked.

"Yes," she said.

"Excuse me—is it *Agent* Trager?—but why are you investigating anything?"

Imogen stared at him, considering. She'd done some googling of her own while she had waited for Johnston, and her food, to arrive. From what she could glean online, he sounded like what he was, a Dundee solicitor. Did he know anything that could help her? Was he hooked into anything official that could jeopardize her investigation if she showed all her cards?

For his part, Johnston stared back, flat, neutral, waiting.

It was a delicate dance. She hoped she wasn't coming off as some pantomime blustering American rushing about, heedlessly breaking everything in the name of "doing what's right," destroying the village in order to save it. Finally, she said, "Do you believe Donald Alban killed himself?"

"That's what the police have said," he rejoined. "They ruled it a suicide."

"That's not what I asked, Mr. Johnston. I asked if that's what you think."

Johnston leaned forward. "And I asked what you're doing. You have no authority in the UK, no investigatory powers. I'm not fully versed on the structure of American law enforcement, but my understanding is that the FBI is a domestic agency. And not to put too fine a point on it, but you're way off your patch, and we do have our own police force hereabouts."

"Yes," she admitted. "I'm way outside my territory, certainly my comfort zone."

They stared at each other again across the table. He had a nice face, she noted, kind. Strong features, with delicate, long eyelashes. Less smooth than Ian Ross, his imperfections—tie slightly askew, and what was that spot on his shirtfront?—more endearing than off-putting. She needed to keep up the false front, but she also needed to leave enough room for him to divulge something if he had anything to contribute.

"I'm sorry, Mr. Johnston. It's the cop in me rising to the surface, when it should be the academic. Let me back up. I'm on sabbatical from the Bureau this year. Which I think I mentioned. I'm working on a comparison study of UK and US elections. An academic paper that I hope to publish. I was working with Frankie and Marta Serres, a professor at University of Strathclyde. The focus of the paper has to do with referenda—in the US and the UK. Scotland in particular. I'm using Switzerland, where they have a proportionally large number of referenda as a kind of control. So, I was trying to get as much info as I could on the Independence referendum."

"I see."

"Frankie's death hit me hard. The cop in me doesn't like to believe that it could be something as random as a theft gone bad, and I've heard talk that while this kind of thing happens in the US, it's not at all common in the UK."

"That's certainly true," said Johnston, but it was all he offered.

"Anyway, that had me kind of going, and when I heard from you that Alban had also died, the same weekend, if not the same day, as Frankie..."

"Yes, I see."

"I came in charging pretty hard. My apologies."

He waved his hand, dismissing her concerns. "I think I understand now," he said. "What is it you wanted to talk with Donald about? Perhaps I could help."

"Well, the day before he was murdered, Frankie said he had some data—some evidence—I should see. But before he could divulge what it was, he said, he had to see an old friend."

"Which old friend?" Johnston asked.

"Frankie didn't say. And then he was dead."

"How did you hear about Donald?" Johnston asked.

"From Marty Serres at Strathclyde. I told her I wanted to understand a few things better. There was no exit poll on the night of the referendum, you may recall."

"I don't recall that detail," he said vaguely.

"Well, I had hoped for a better angle on some of my questions. The turnout was lower here in Dundee—and in Glasgow—than was expected. I was heading up here anyway—"

"And what, see the sights of Dundee?" He seemed genuinely amused. "We're not on most Americans' list of places to visit, despite the valiant and costly efforts of the Visit Dundee tourism office."

"And yet, here I am," she noted with some defiance.

"You mustn't miss Perth on your way back to Glasgow," he added, ignoring her tone. "I do hope Motherwell's on your itinerary."

"In any case, Marty—that is, Professor Serres—suggested that Mr. Alban might be able to help out."

"He'd been retired for eight years."

"Yes. But Marty said he'd been in the job for a long time, and that he'd be the best person to start with; that he might be able to make some introductions. Things like that."

"And what is it you're looking for?"

"I don't want to bore you with details of my study," she said, "but I'd really like to interview people who worked the polls, maybe even some tellers."

"What are you looking for exactly?"

"If I knew exactly, I wouldn't need to interview people. But I'd like to get a sense from people on the ground, as it were, about how the election was conducted."

It was now Johnston's turn to be careful. "What could you learn from that?"

"Look," she said, "the turnout for the referendum was twenty percent higher overall than any other election. Dundee and Glasgow were the areas that polled the highest in preference for independence before the election, but in the end both cities had statistically lower turnout than other areas. That seems odd. I'm wondering if anyone noticed something, or had some theory..."

"Sounds more like a police investigation than academic research," he observed.

"As I said, it's probably my manner." *Was he buying any of this?* she wondered. "And investigations of any kind are bound to seem similar. They're after the truth."

"It sounds like you think something was amiss," he said, watching her closely.

Imogen demurred. "I have an open mind. I'm pursuing an interesting question. I won't know much until I've had a chance to compare interview material, anecdotal evidence and official data."

Johnston nodded, thinking. "What if you uncovered something illegal?"

"Why?"

"A hypothetical," he said. "But a valid one, given the tone and direction of this conversation, don't you think? Who are you working with officially?"

"No one. Not really. Professor Serres works with the Electoral Commission..."

"Not MI5?" he asked. "The Met?"

Imogen's heartbeat quickened. He knew something!

"Any contacts there?" he asked.

"No, I'm sorry."

"But if you did come across something...untoward, you'd report it."

"Was Mr. Alban involved in something?" she asked.

"Absolutely not! I'm trying to ascertain whether you'd embroil anyone local—"

"I would be completely sure of what I had, and then I'd discuss it with Professor Serres. As you've pointed out, I have no legal standing here. I'd leave it to her to bring it forward if there were anything...untoward." She said it kindly, matter-of-fact, holding her face still, a bland mask. But her eyes were like copper flame. Johnston knew something, she felt, but he was being cautious. There was something he needed to hear from her first. The discussion of a drowsy academic study didn't seem to be working. He kept asking about official involvement. Could he be as frightened as she?

Imogen decided to lay her cards on the table.

"I think you know something about irregularities in the Indy-ref, Mr. Johnston. I think you want to tell me what they are. I think you're trying to find out whether I'm somehow working with the authorities. And you're worried about what might happen to you, if I am working in an official capacity."

He made no reply, his eyes searching her face.

"I've been asked," she continued carefully, "unofficially, to look into charges of voter fraud in the referendum."

"By whom?"

"Wee Frankie. He spoke of an old friend he wanted me to connect with. I think that man is—*was*—Donald Alban."

Imogen and Ewan Johnston drove together to his flat near Dudhope Park. It was a ground floor, two-bedroom flat in a red sandstone, converted infirmary, though to Imogen it looked like an old, nineteenth century warehouse. Or workhouse. The doorframes on the upper floors—now windows—opening onto nothing, she decided erroneously, meant warehouse.

Apart from the apprehension he felt over the documents he was about to show her—and what their revelation could lead to—he was hesitant about letting her see the state of the place. He hadn't invited a woman over in months. This was different, of course, and yet somehow it wasn't. His bachelor home was no showpiece at the best of times, but he hadn't tidied up since the evening when he'd torn apart the secretary desk looking for Alban's papers. That debris could be glossed as work-related, he felt. His thoughts flashed to the kitchen, which was a wreck. Were there still towels on the bathroom floor? He made his mind up to pull the door closed on the bedroom and leave it that way.

"It's been a busy time," he hedged, trying to coax a blithe tone into his voice as he trotted ahead to unlock the front door. The border plantings were ragged, he noted dismally. Empty-headed flower stems lolled across the walk as they made their way to the front steps. Inside, he switched on the sitting room light revealing the paper heap crowding the desk at the far side. "Have a seat there, if you'd like," he said, indicating the couch.

He pulled Donald Alban's papers from a drawer. "This is what he left," he said as he handed them to her. "Can I get you something to drink?"

"No, thank you." She turned to the covering page and read: *"Ewan, if I have died in some manner other than natural causes, it is because I know something the government doesn't want me to share. The Independence Referendum vote was stolen..."*

A shudder ran through her. "On second thought," she said, "what do you have?"

As he disappeared into the kitchen, Imogen looked round. Across from her, dominating the wall, was a tall bookcase, containing an old turntable and amplifier at about chest height. Running in three rows underneath was a record collection, perhaps as many as two hundred albums. The left and right sides of the bookcase were crowded with books. She was considering taking a closer look when Johnston returned. He had unearthed a bottle of Bell's whisky and hastily washed two glasses. She took the drink and sat back with the papers. Realizing he was superfluous to requirements, Johnston took the opportunity to pick up in the other rooms.

After fifteen minutes, she called to him from her perch on the sofa, "Who else has seen this?"

"No one," he said, coming back into the room. "I was getting frantic. I didn't know who I could take it to. Anyone official would alert whoever was responsible—either directly or inadvertently. And I'm for the off, to join Donald. Or maybe something happens to Sandra or the children." It was his turn to shudder.

"Does Mrs. Alban know about this?" she asked, indicating the sheaf of papers.

"No. She suspects there's something else going on. The fact Wee Frankie died at the same time makes her that more suspicious."

"How is it that you have these?"

"Well, if I was a bit more efficient, I wouldn't have. Fortunately, in this case, I'm not. I'd meant to put those papers together with Donald's will, but never got round to it. And then I forgot about them. The same weekend he and Frankie died, my office was broken into."

"Christ," she whispered.

"It was meant to look like a burglary. They smashed up the place, and they prized open the locked cabinet where we keep official documents and the ready cash. They took the cash, but they also ripped open some of the wills and other documents we had in there, Donald's among them. Now, I think the whole break-in was cover for looking to find just this kind of evidence." He pointed at the papers in her hand.

"What does your law partner think?"

"I've not said a word to him about it," said Johnston.

"And why wasn't it with his other papers?"

"My own incompetence. Lethargy's become my strategy, it seems. The last time Donald updated his will was almost twelve years ago. He gave me those papers seven or eight years ago. As I think about it, it was right after he resigned as ARO. He'd dropped by here unannounced one night and we had a drink. Well, quite a few, actually. At the time he gave them to me, he said it was in case of his untimely death. If I'm being honest, I thought he was kidding on. That it was part of what he called his memoirs. His little joke about the mess of papers he kept. He kept everything to do with his ARO work in a pile of boxes in his home office."

"I'd love to have a look at those other papers."

"They're gone too. Sandra and I noticed it the other day. I'm assuming the boxes were taken when they killed him." He frowned as he gestured toward the papers she held. "Is that good evidence in your world?"

"It's good circumstantial evidence."

"That's what I thought. I'd never to go into court with that lot."

"But it's a good base on which to build something stronger, the kind of thing that can't be easily dismissed. Who do you know at the party level?"

17

Jamie Frenz walked into Calum Percy's office and closed the door.

"Our buskers have been keeping an eye on the protégé, Johnston and the widow Alban," he reported. "They're behaving exactly as we'd expect. She stays in the house, receiving visitors. Two of the children have gone back to their work down here in England. Johnston's a workaholic, but he stops by to check on the widow most nights after work. Maybe it'll blow over, eh? Also: there's no one else tailing these two, no one else snooping around," said Frenz.

"Christ, that'd be something wouldn't it? Two sets of heavies stumbling onto one another." Percy shook his head at the thought.

"Dundee: 'where ignorant armies clash by night'," Frenz offered.

Percy gave him a quizzical look.

"At any rate," said Frenz, "they haven't tripped over one another yet. Indeed, our men haven't seen the others at all in Glasgow or Edinburgh either. And, as I say, things may be blowing over. Our busker was on Johnston tonight. After checking in on the widow, he went to a pub. Now, he's brought a woman home from there. So, it's a good night for him. Not the kind of behavior you'd be seeing from someone plotting to dig into the murder of his mentor and friend."

Frenz passed the printed reports to Percy. On top was a photograph of Johnston and Imogen walking to his car. He tapped the picture of Imogen. "Lucky bastard," said Frenz. "Unless there's something else, I'd like to call it a night."

"Yes," said Percy. He looked down at the file as he sent Chamberlain a text: "*No new developments. Ongoing.*" The full, nonevent report could wait until Monday.

"Fancy a pint?" he asked his assistant.

Ewan was having nothing like the kind of night Frenz imagined and envied. His relief at finding someone in whom he could confide, and who might be able to help had given way to a kind of frustration at not being able to readily answer her questions: Was this kind of unofficial notation Alban had kept common among AROs? He thought not but couldn't say for certain. Was there someone else who might have kept a similar accounting? Like whom? he wondered. Who else did Alban trust? Did Ewan know the names of party or election people who would know something useful, and keep it to themselves that someone was asking questions? If he had felt initially that Imogen and her expertise represented a grand stride forward, he was learning that it was not much more than a tentative step in what might be the right direction.

And though she'd apologized for coming off as hard-chargingly American, it did seem to be her natural state. Like the mouthful of food she was chewing when they first met, however, it didn't diminish her allure. He liked that she knew her business. Admired her passion. He hoped he could keep up, and that she didn't regard him as merely a means to an end.

She drank down the first glass of whisky quickly and asked for another. "Where can we have this copied?" she asked.

"My office, if you'd like," he said. "We could go now."

"Are you being watched?"

"No," he said, before adding, "I don't think so."

"Well, if you are, a midnight trip to the office with an unidentified American might look like something worth following up."

"*If* I'm being watched," he said. "And," he added with a mischievous grin, "how would they know you were American if you were unidentified?"

Imogen smiled and shook her head. "People seem to guess it before I've opened my mouth," she said. She paused and gave him a puzzled look. "How is that?"

"Well, I wouldn't know. Though I suspect it's to do with the way you walk—purposefully, impatiently, taking up a little more space on the pavement than is quite necessary."

"Oh, God, do I?" she asked.

He shrugged. "It's no less attractive for that—" He stopped himself short. Prayed he wasn't blushing. "Or you could be from the Highlands, I suppose," he added. "My mother used to joke about how you could spot a transplanted highlander in the city because they lean forward like they're walking intae a gale—whether they are or no."

"So, I could be a Highland lass?" The idea seemed to please her.

"No," he said, his face betraying chagrin at having to communicate an unpleasant truth. "For all your dark suspicions you've a pleasant, open face. Trusting, I'd say. Sunny. Even if you'd rather it not be."

"Are all Scots dark and dour and mistrustful?"

"No more so than any other folk, I suspect. But we don't go smiling into the face a' everyone we meet."

"So friendly and happy is bad?" she wanted to know.

"Not at aw. But it marks you out. Which is what we were discussing."

"I see," she said. "That's a nice, courtroom kind of distinction, isn't it?" The smile faded. "Still, they broke into your office. Do you think anyone's been in here?"

Johnston laughed. "How could I tell?" He glanced around the living room with an amused look. "Are you asking, did I notice anything missing or awry in my meticulous housekeeping?"

Imogen paused to look around again. Her gaze lingered briefly on the bookshelf again. "Well, have you?" she asked.

"No," he said feeling that perhaps a moment had come and gone.

"We should make two copies, and scan them into PDFs. Tomorrow. Where could you keep these originals where they wouldn't be found?"

"I'm not sure. Let me think about it." He had an idea, but he didn't like it.

18

Imogen awoke in the B & B with a start. It was late, and she didn't want to miss breakfast. Looking out the window, the gray, damp morning looked much like she felt, listless and depleted. A full Scottish breakfast would be just the thing, but she'd have to hurry it up. Downstairs in the breakfast room, she gulped her tea and tore into the beans and toast and rashers. She wished there were more black pudding, but consoled her disappointment with real Dundee marmalade heaped onto a second helping of toast. Her teeth tingled pleasingly at its tart-bitter sweetness as she gazed meditatively out the window, across the Tay toward the southern bank and braes beyond. The sun, still low, insinuated itself beneath heavy clouds, stray flashes along the river like golden trout surfacing.

She turned and looked around the room. It was clean, spare and well-lighted. Her fellow diners looked clean and spare, too. They'd risen at a respectable hour and made themselves presentable before coming down to breakfast. Whereas Imogen had stuffed her hair into a ponytail and raced downstairs like a teenager dressed in last night's clothes. She had arrived with fewer than ten minutes to spare before breakfast was over. Was she letting down her home country again, she wondered. Well, what's done is done.

Back upstairs, she cleaned up and called Ewan Johnston. He collected her in front of the B & B an hour later, and they drove into town to scan and make copies of Alban's notes at his office. As they drove, Imogen marveled at how touchingly low-tech it all felt—people keeping tallies with pen and paper and not uploading it anywhere. Dusty things stuffed in drawers. It was like being directed to an old card catalog drawer at a library and finding a helpful, handwritten note about a book you were searching for. The kind of thing Duncan would have loved.

Johnston was dressed less formally than the night before she noticed, in jeans, an old jumper and a windbreaker. She thought it suited him better. In a business suit, as he had been the previous day, he'd looked if not uncomfortable exactly, then perhaps strained. There had been a stiffness about him that wasn't formality or reticence but reminded her of the way some boys, ill-at-ease in their Sunday best, will sit dolefully on the edge of chairs, dull eyes registering their silent, indexed review of fun things they're currently not doing, sourly chafing at clothes they mustn't get dirty, at shoes that pinch. And you can't run in them anyway. Not well. She liked that image of him as a boy who was up for anything, unless it was a bath, and who'd get dusty standing still. She wondered if her picture was accurate.

"What is it?" he asked, taking his eyes from the road for a moment to look at her.

"Sorry?"

"You were smiling just then."

"Oh," she said, caught out, "that's strange. I was thinking that we really need to find someone who can corroborate what we have."

He nodded, eyes fixed on the road again. "There are two people I know of who might be able to help. They were old friends of Donald's. I have their contact information at the office."

The office was empty on a Saturday. While Johnston began copying and scanning the papers, Imogen set up her laptop. With the copy machine going through its first batch of the papers, Johnston turned to his desk and began scrolling through a contact list on his computer.

"I have two people," he said. "Frank Diamond—'Gem' to his friends—and Gerry McTavish. They're both of them counting agents for the SNP here in Dundee. Since they're the party that lost, there's no way they could be involved."

"Makes sense," Imogen agreed.

"And they might lead us to your tellers. Again, party people." He picked up the phone and dialed. "Gem," he began, "it's Ewan. Ewan Johnston. Yes, thank you, it was…yes, a tragic waste." He drew a deep breath. "This is somewhat delicate, but I'm picking up on something Donald had started working on. There's an American professor here, she's doing—" he looked blankly at her.

"A comparison study between UK, Swiss and American referenda."

He repeated it into the phone. "And—"

"And I'm particularly interested in turnout and voter motivation."

"She's…" he began. "Would you speak with her? She's with me now. Thank you." He handed her the phone and went to check on the copying.

"Mr. Diamond?" she said brightly, "thank you for speaking with me. My name is Dr. Imogen Trager. I'm on leave this year at University of Glasgow. My focus, my special brief, is voting and voting behavior. As Mr. Johnston was saying, I'd been in contact with the late Mr. Alban about doing some work involving voter activation," she lied. "I arrived here only to find that Mr. Alban had died tragically. Mr. Johnston was kind enough to offer what assistance he could and to help make some introductions for me more or less on Mr. Alban's behalf."

She listened a moment.

"Yes," she continued, "and I'm particularly interested in the Independence referendum back in 2014. I'm hopeful that you and I could speak in person. I know it's been a long time, but I have some questions relating to the kinds of information—official and unofficial—that you might have. I could certainly arrange to meet with you at your convenience, but I'm here in Dundee now, and I wondered if you were free for an hour or so today or tomorrow." A pause to listen. "It's just background at this point, Mr. Diamond. There wasn't an exit poll on the night, and I was hoping I might—" She paused and looked at her watch. "Dinner?" she asked. "At one?"

"You'd call it 'lunch,'" Johnston whispered, as he snapped a large binder clip on a copy of Alban's papers and placed it on the desk next to her. "Or is it *luncheon*?" he added archly and turned back to the copier.

Imogen nodded. "Yes, I'm sure Ewan—Mr. Johnston—" she corrected herself, "knows where it is. Thank you. And see you then." She wrote down the name of the pub.

Johnston called Gerry McTavish, the second counting agent, and he and Imogen arranged to meet him at another pub at four p.m.

"Gem" Diamond and another man stood up to greet Imogen at a pub a little way off Old Hawkhill near the city center. Diamond was a short, barrel of a man. He looked to be about sixty, with dark, thinning hair combed over and plastered to his skull. He was serious and formal, but there was an amiable, cheerful aspect to him just under the surface.

"This is Liam Gleeson," he said. "Ye'd mentioned you were hoping tae meet with some of the tellers, so Ah brought him along. He's one. Ah hope that's aright."

"Wonderful!" said Imogen, shaking both of their hands in turn.

Gleeson was younger by about twenty years, with a bit more hair on top, though not enough that he didn't also attempt to disguise its absence. Short and stocky, with a patchy, florid complexion, he was well on his way to being as cask-conditioned as his friend. The three of them sat down together as Johnston went to the bar to collect the drinks.

"Whit is it ye want tae know?" Gleeson asked as they sat down.

"Well, as I said, I'm looking for background," Imogen began. She went into what she was trying to glean, noted again that there hadn't been an exit poll, and wondered if there were any official or unofficial records that might help. "For instance," she noted to Diamond, "you watch as the boxes are unsealed and the ballots are placed in the piles?"

"Right enough. And it's a moment where we can get a wee keek at how the various precincts are voting. We stand in front of a table and watch the council employees verify and count the ballots."

"The parties use it as an opportunity to ensure that none of the ballots cast for your ain party are put in the pile for an opposing party," said Gleeson.

"Or No for Yes in the case of the referendum. When that happens, yer permitted tae tell the counter that they've made a mistake."

"Course, if a ballot for an opposing candidate is put in your ain party's pile, ye tend not to say anything." Gleeson gave her a wink.

"Speaking *un*officially!" said Diamond with elaborate rectitude. He gave Gleeson a sharp look. "Ye can also challenge ballots which havna been filled out properly. Though again, when it's just Yes or No for independence, there's no much room for error or interpretation."

"This is helpful," said Imogen. "So, the process is observed by multiple watchers at every stage."

"From the moment the boxes arrive, aye. Parties can argue about disputed ballots before the acting returning officer—Mr. Alban it would be in this case—makes the final call." He smiled impishly and slapped Gleeson on the arm. "Hey, ye ken that time?" he chuckled. "A voter wrote 'legend' next to the name of the SNP candidate. We tried to argue that this should be counted in the candidate's favor, but Alban didn't accept our case."

"Was that a sore point, or a disappointment to you?" she asked.

"Naw, that was just a laugh. Ah mean, Ah don't take kindly ta people messin about wi the vote, no taking it seriously, like, but that was just daft." He paused, becoming a bit more serious. "But ye see, it's also a particularly useful process because each box is counted one-by-one by ward. And it's a guid time ta glean how the different polling stations *within* a council ward voted."

Gleeson laughed in assent. "That is, ye can see that the wee box from the working-class bit of the ward mebee did better than the box from the polling station in the bougie area."

"And so, we stand there and dae a samplin procedure. Try to estimate our percentage a the vote. Per box. But those figures are never recorded officially. As far as Ah know."

"No," Imogen agreed, "I don't believe they are." She paused a moment and then asked, "Do you write that kind of thing down? Your percentage estimates, I mean?"

"Aye, we do."

"And what about postal ballots? Would someone be looking at them?"

"Them too. Ah brought along what Ah wrote out if ye'd like ta see it."

"You kept it?" she asked, trying to keep the hunger out of her voice.

"Right enough. Normally, Ah'd only keep it a wee while, in case there were some questions. But this was historic. It didny go the way we wanted, but it's ma wee way of remembering that Ah participated."

"Ah did as well," said Gleeson. "Wouldye like ta see it?"

"I would indeed," said Imogen.

"Gem," said Johnston, "would you mind if I ran back with these to the office and made copies? I'd return the originals, of course."

Diamond and Gleeson looked dubious.

"I'd be back in half an hour. Mebee less."

"And I could stay behind as hostage until their safe return," Imogen quipped.

"Ah think we're gettin the better part of *that* bargain, Ewan," said Diamond. They passed him their papers, and he walked quickly out of the pub.

"Whit de ye think you'll find?" Gleeson asked.

"I'm not sure," she said. "I'm sorry to be so vague, but I've only made a start. What I'm interested in is voter activation.

You can have an issue or issues that people care strongly about."

"Preference intensity, aye," said Diamond.

"Right. And referenda are often very preference intense. I'm trying to figure out what motivates people to vote. And what keeps them *from* voting."

"Interesting," said Gleeson. "And tha independence vote was polarizing. We seemed tae have a large turnout. Though in the end, turnout was only a little above normal."

"Yes," she said, wanting to be careful. "Just for my notes: there are differences between what I'm used to in the US. I want to make sure I don't make any unwarranted assumptions. For instance, we call tellers poll watchers. In the US, poll watchers are typically people who work for a particular party. People who've lived a long time in the neighborhood. Is that the case here with tellers?"

"It is," said Gleeson.

"In the US, a poll watcher sits outside the polling place, and will typically have a list of registered party members— whether Democrat or Republican—and they cross off names as they come in."

"Aye. Exactly the same."

"And periodically throughout election day someone from the party organization will come by, take down the names of those who may not have shown up, and then have someone at party headquarters give them a call or a text to remind them to vote?"

"That's the way," he said. "Exactly. Ah've been here all ma life. Ah know ninety per cent a' the voters—mebee more. And no only the SNP voters. Ye'll see that Ah kept a wee tally of non-SNP folk as well."

"Interesting," she said. "What do you do with that information?"

"Nothin. No really. It's mair somethin ta pass the time, like."

"Right," Diamond chimed in, "and ye canna say for sure how any ae them voted once they were inside."

"But adding the number of crossed-off SNP voter names to the tally of non-SNPers might give me a close approximation of the total number of people who voted at that polling place, right?"

Diamond looked perplexed. "Well, the *official* tally's the official tally. Accurate. Ah'd go wi that."

"Of course," she said. "Of course. But as a kind of cross-check of my own?"

Diamond tipped his head from side to side, considering it. "Ah s'pose," he said equably. He dug into the pocket of his heavy raincoat and pulled out his phone. "Ah think ye should talk wi a mate ae mine, Gerry McTavish. Ah've got his number here."

"McTavish?" she asked. "I'm meeting with him at four."

"Ah'll let im know you'd like tae see his unofficial tallies as well."

Back at the office that evening after meeting with McTavish, Imogen and Johnston took stock of the piles of papers arrayed across his conference table.

"Christ," said Imogen, her head swimming. "I'm going to need to pace myself if I'm going to keep meeting people in pubs like this." She polished off a bottle of water he had given her.

Johnston smiled. "You want a coffee?"

"God, yes!"

"I've only got espresso. One of those wee, stove-top mocha makers."

"Perfect," she said. "That's what I have at home."

It was a three-cup maker, and he brought her all three cups in a large mug, with a healthy spoonful of sugar.

"Thanks," she said. "This might take a while."

"Have at it. I've preparations to make for Monday anyway."

As he went into his office, Imogen called to him. "Ewan, one or both of us is probably being watched. And if, as Alban's notes say, this is being run from the top, we should be careful about communication."

"Well, I've never had a woman use that excuse not to speak with me before," he quipped. "No, hen, I wasnae ghostin ye. It was a governmental conspiracy, like!"

"No, no," she said, before realizing he was joking. "I meant that we should consider alternate forms. The last big case I worked on, the conspirators were tapping our phones. I still carry a little flip phone with me from back then. Do you think you could get one, something that might not get found out about right away?"

"I have one at my desk. Not all my clients have been...Well, I have one." He tore a slip of paper and wrote out the number. "Give us a call, and then I'll have yours."

She did it, and turned back to her task where she began transferring the tallies to a spreadsheet on her computer, forgetting about the coffee at her elbow. Haphazard and unofficial though they were, the data were good. Once she had the numbers on her spreadsheet and double-checked them, she began running comparisons of them with the data she had from Marty Serres.

They had already tested the 20% increase and found it was evenly distributed, with random fluctuations among voting jurisdictions—some showing an increase of 17 or 18%, while others showed 21%. Ranking the voting jurisdictions from lowest to greatest increase, Dundee and Glasgow stood out. Their reported returns showed barely any increase at all over other elections. Compared with other voting districts, they returned almost 20 % less. It was as if some ballots were missing.

When at last she paused in her work, she realized she hadn't drunk any of the coffee and it had gone cold. She drank it anyway in two, quick gulps. She smiled fondly at Johnston, beavering away at his desk, but he was too engrossed to look up, and she returned to her work.

The official voter tally of ballots cast from the election in Dundee was 118,729. Based on her and Serres's intercept calculations of *expected* voters, she'd have expected to see 142,000 voters casting ballots. Painstakingly, she broke them down further and applied the intercept numbers to the two distinct wards from her meetings with Diamond and McTavish. It seemed that more voters had shown up to vote than could be explained by spoilt ballots—much greater than the official tally of ballots cast, but closer, and crucially, within the margin of error for her expected higher numbers when broken down to the ward level. Also, Gem Diamond had said that there were approximately 350 to 500 ballots in each box. That meant that for both precincts for which she had unofficial numbers, possibly as many as eight boxes per polling center were missing.

What had he said, that there was "total oversight from the moment the boxes arrived" at the count centre? What about *before* they arrived? She turned to her copy of Alban's notes and read again his message to Johnston:

"The Independence Referendum vote was stolen, and whether it was Westminster who initiated it, the way it was done could only have been achieved with government knowledge and its collusion."

19

Jamie Frenz followed Calum Percy into his office first thing Monday morning. Before Percy was settled, Frenz put a file on the desk. "We have a problem," he said and closed the door. "Two actually. First, I kept thinking about the woman Johnston met Friday night at the pub. I couldn't put her out of my head."

Percy looked at him.

"Yes, at first I accused myself of some puerile crush. I mean she's not hard to look at. But that's not why she stuck with me. I realized I'd seen her before."

"And?"

"But I couldn't place it. Until last night. I put together a full dossier on her." He pointed at the thick file on the desk.

"You found all this since last night?"

"That's just the easily skimmed public and official data I found this morning. She's an FBI agent from the US, here on leave. I have scans of her visa documents and entry forms in there too. It's definitely the same woman. And she's a specialist in voting fraud."

Percy's eyes widened as he recognized her now, too. The Faithless Elector case had been all over the news, even in the UK, as had its key investigator, Imogen Trager. He started turning through the pages Frenz had prepared.

"Right," said Frenz. "She's the one whose investigation caused the president to resign."

"And she's talking to Johnston?"

"Yes."

"But the goons who took care of Alban didn't find anything. They broke into Johnston's law office, didn't they?"

"Correct."

"So, *is* there something to find?" Percy wanted to know. "Does Johnston know anything?"

"That I don't know. This is as far as I've come," said Frenz. "But I thought you should know right away."

"Good work. But why is she taking an interest at all? *How* is she taking an interest? How on earth could she have found out?"

"And that's the second part," said Frenz. "Her visa documents say she's a visiting fellow at University of Glasgow in the School of Social and Political Sciences. That's Francis McDougal's department. He was a colleague."

"Was?" asked Percy.

"We didn't have anyone monitoring him," he began. "He'd been graded non-rev since 2017. But our busker in Glasgow found out that he's been murdered. Made to look like a car theft gone wrong. But it happened the same weekend—maybe the same night—that Alban, er, killed himself."

"Fuck!" he spat. He jumped up and began pacing behind his desk. He scratched at the thinning hair on top of his head. "It's just like before. Blundering idiots making things up as they go along—and always making it worse!"

"What should we tell the top floor?" Frenz asked. "I doubt they know about this development."

Percy turned over the file's pages for a few moments. *And what if they knew about it, because they'd ordered it done?* he thought. When he looked up, he stared at Frenz a moment longer before saying, "For now, nothing." He paused again, gauging Frenz's response. "Let's activate the others, working in pairs. Surveillance *only*. For now."

Christ, he thought, if we tell the top floor about this, she might be dead by the end of the day. And then it's an international incident. An FBI agent killed in the UK? He didn't want to think about it.

"But if it comes back at us, sir? That we knew something but did nothing."

"We *did* do something. Let's be clear here. We had incomplete information, and we took steps to ascertain who she was and what, if any, function she *might* have in the ongoing case. And we did it in such a way as to *not* make a bad situation even worse."

Frenz weighed this, his lower lip pursed.

"Which is the truth," Percy continued. "And let's be frank. This could turn into an international incident. But that gate swings both ways. Bad for us if we don't tread carefully, but probably bad for her, too. There's no way she has any authority here. I'm sure that if it came to be known that she was working outside her remit—outside the law, in fact—her superiors in America would recall her. And fire her. I suppose there could even be jail. There are a great many ways to kill an investigation."

Ways, he thought, *without killing someone*.

He continued thumbing through the file. "And look at this: she's the agent who brought one of their Justice Department's biggest cases *ever*. But she's shunted off to the Studies in Electoral Integrity office in a non-investigative role? Sounds like she's already on the naughty step."

Frenz smiled.

"No, if it comes to that, we'll let the American bureaucracy kill her. But let's hold it in reserve."

* * *

Later that day, Imogen and Marta Serres climbed the steep North Portland Street and walked to the back of the Graham Hills Building where Strathclyde's European Policies Research Center, and Serres's office, were housed. The narrow, dark street, tucked between two tall buildings was deserted. Their heel strikes rapped and echoed, a smart tattoo. As they marched along, the whine of a motorcycle engine split their staccato rhythm as rider and machine sped by. The rider stopped at a row of bikes in a motorcycle-only parking zone past the main door and prepared to dismount.

But he didn't. As he seemed to fuss with something on the back of the motorcycle, the busker snapped ten rapid-fire pictures of Imogen and Serres from his phone as they went inside. The photos would be sent to Frenz, along with whatever other information he could glean. When both women were inside, he made a quick call and then sped toward Montrose Street, where he stopped near the footpath to Rottenrow Gardens. It was out of the way but had a good vantage of the Richmond Street door. He began searching EPRC faculty on his phone.

Across town, down the hill from the Adam Smith Building, another man, also dressed to ride a motorbike, in dark jeans, boots and black leather jacket, sat atop his motorcycle, parked along University Gardens. He received the information that Imogen was at Strathclyde, and likely to be there indefinitely. He put the phone in his pocket and walked up the narrow, pedestrian-only lane between the buildings there. As well as his motorcycle kit, he wore a dark, single-strap rucksack slung across his body. As he walked, he kept the helmet on but wore the visor tipped up. There were more people here about than along Richmond Street, but his appearance didn't warrant a second glance. He fit right in.

He climbed the three flights of stairs to Imogen's floor. Reaching the landing, he walked along the deserted hallway to her doorway. It took him less than thirty seconds to work through the lock. Inside, he kept the lights off but put on the phone's flashlight. He began unpacking the listening devices he would plant about the room.

At the Graham Hills Building, Imogen sat silently as Serres reviewed what Imogen had found.

"Jesus, this is serious!" she exclaimed, pushing back from the desk. "I can't find anything wrong with your numbers."

"Is it enough to bring others in?" Imogen asked.

"Like Ian Ross?" Serres asked. "Haven't you done so already?"

"No, I haven't. We've built an excellent circumstantial case. But what are the other angles? How else could this be explained? I've been focused on finding evidence. I've found it. But I don't think it's *proof*. And maybe there's another explanation."

"Yes, I can see us being cross-examined—" she dropped into a pompous monotone "—but surely professor, there are counter examples that explain your little...*theory*? You're saying you would have expected to see certain vote tallies, expected to see a certain number of boxes; and isn't it convenient that you've found precisely what you *expected* to find." She paused. Her mouth twisted bitterly. "Bloody nuisance."

"I think before we reach out to Ian, we should do what we can to disprove what we've found. If we find we can't disprove it, then..."

"Yes, that makes good sense."

"And, Marty, we need to talk about your involvement. What it means. Because when this goes public, it won't just be high-handed, low-minded officials. Ian can protect us somewhat, I think, but when this breaks it'll be the press, it'll be politicians. And their flaks. Social media will turn itself inside out."

"Unionists. Brexiteers," Serres added.

"And. It'll be people in your own organization whom you thought you could trust. It'll be the bad guys, who might come in the guise of high-minded officials. Or even as friends. We'll get this to Ian, which will cover us, but it won't make us safe."

Malcolm Ogilvy, or the Druid within his department, shuffled along the gray hallway to his office on campus, fumbling through his keys in the low light. He needed to retrieve a book, and he had chosen the evening so that he wouldn't encounter the American woman. Almost completely bald on top, he was nevertheless memorably hirsute. His thick, gray mustache flowed abundantly and almost perpendicular to a long, shaggy beard. If he were dressed in robes and carrying a staff, he'd have made a compelling figure in any haunted, Celtic wood.

Inside the office, Percy's operative heard the slow, shuffling footsteps, the jingling of keys in the hallway. He had finished placing the listening devices, but he stopped his signal testing and strained to hear past the door, not sure yet whether the keys were meant for this door. He stuffed the testing device into his rucksack and put the helmet back on.

Outside, the Druid stood a moment in the hall still searching for the correct key. As he put the key in, someone dressed all in black threw the door open. He grabbed Ogilvy, slammed his head into the door and ran past him. Dazed, his scalp bleeding, Ogilvy crawled out to the hallway, but his attacker was gone, bounding down the stairs.

David Reidy, as Department Head, had been called to campus. He met the police and medic-squad in the lobby outside his office. The Druid sat on one of the benches there, a large bandage wrapped across his head. He held an ice bag against it, nursing both the wound and his wrath.

"David!" he shouted as Reidy came near. Ogilvy stood up, clutching the cold pack to his head. "David, this is *just* the sort of thing I worried about when you lent out my office."

"Jesus, Malcolm, are you all right?" Reidy asked, but he looked at the attending paramedic, a young woman with dark hair, rather than at the Druid himself. The paramedic nodded discreetly.

"Yes, but my office has been broken into! Possibly vandalized."

"We've had a bit look round," said the detective sergeant, who had followed Reidy into the building. "It doesn't appear that anything's missing. Computer equipment is still in place. No damage to the interior."

"I surprised him in the act!" the Druid exclaimed. "No telling what he might have taken if I hadn't happened by."

"Well, it's a good job you did," said Reidy. "Did he hit you with something, Malcolm?"

"He surprised me as I opened the door. Slammed my head against it before I knew what was happening. He took off down the stairs. I couldn't see his face. He wore a motorcycle helmet."

The sergeant in charge shook his head. "CCTV can't give us anything."

"This is what happens when you loan out important things, David. How do we know this American didn't leave the door unlocked? That this interloper wasn't just trying doors? Until he found one unlocked."

Reidy began to speak, but he was cut off.

"Have you spoken with her?" the Druid demanded. "I think she should be here to explain herself."

"Malcolm, I should think she's almost as much a victim as you."

"Unless, by her actions, she brought about this very state of affairs."

"Really, Malcolm..." Reidy entreated.

Outside, along the path between the main library and the Adam Smith building, as Reidy attempted to placate the Druid, several students who'd been asked by the police to step outside congregated with others who wanted to see what was going on. They were joined by someone too old to be a student. He was beefy, bald and sharply dressed, looking something like a night-club bouncer. With his thick neck and massive arms, he could easily have been a former rugby player gone to seed, but his smooth head and stiff manner seemed somehow martial, too.

"What's it all about?" he asked two young men, who looked to be graduate students standing at the back of the group.

"A break-in and assault," said one of them, not bothering to turn round. "The Druid surprised someone in his office."

"The Druid?" Rugby asked.

"Professor Malcolm Ogilvy," his compatriot explained. "I thought he was meant to be on leave this term, but I guess he came in for something and surprised a burglar."

"And a clout on the heid for his troubles," said the first grad student.

"Did you see it happen?" asked the man.

"Naw," said the first, "we were working on another floor altogether, but the police asked us to step outside. After making sure of who *we* were," he added.

"Awful," said the man, shaking his head. He walked away. As he turned in the direction of the main gate, he pulled out his cell phone and made a call.

In London, Percy was pounding his desk in fury. Frenz stood at a distance, glad it was now late evening and no one else was around. "We're almost as bad as those other idiots!" he yelled. "How does something like this happen?"

"She's using the office of a Professor Ogilvy, who's on leave this term."

"Obviously not!"

"Yes. Well. I think it was just very bad luck. So far as we can tell, he hasn't been in the office the whole term, and our men confirmed that Trager was at Strathclyde. Nowhere near."

"Have police been notified?"

"Yes," said Frenz. "Regrettably."

"Did *anything* go properly tonight?" asked Percy.

"Yessir," said Frenz, grateful to be able to report something non-culpable, but still uncomfortable about what more he had to deliver. "But it may be worse than we thought. The other woman in the photo...from our man in Glasgow...It looks to be Professor Marta Serres. She works for the European Policies Research Centre at Strathclyde." Here he paused, looked uncertain. "And she consults for the Electoral Commission."

Percy leaned on his desk and put his head in his hands. "I wonder what Trager's on to," he said.

"We might know soon enough," said Frenz. "We've bugged her office and flat."

20

There was a bracing chill in the air as Imogen walked through Kelvingrove Park next morning on her way to campus. The fog was bright and vague as she breathed the damp, metallic air. She slowed her pace, the better to take it all in. The fog seemed about to lift and she fancied that there might be a sunny day in store. She marveled at the luminous intensity of green in this part of the world. Shrubs, bushes—even the grass—fairly glowed. Shimmering with wet, the flora surrounding her bore heavy water droplets, swelling and fecund, like crystal currants. She glanced up and could see the top of the main university spire breaking through the mist. She smiled.

Her phone rang.

"Imogen, it's David Reidy. Could you stop by my office before you head to yours this morning?"

"Sure," she said. "What's up?"

"There was a break-in last night."

"Where?" she asked.

"Your office, the one you share with the Dru—with Professor Ogilvy."

"I'll be there in ten minutes," she said. She glanced longingly at the park before quickening her pace.

Imogen met Reidy in his office. He already had the few books she had brought along in a box, sitting on his desk. "We're moving you," he said.

"Couldn't we just change the locks?" she asked.

"It's a bit more complicated than that. This is difficult. It was your office mate, Malcolm, who discovered the burglary...surprised them, it seems, before they could steal anything. Whoever it was gave him a nice bash on the head for his troubles. And. And, believe me, unless you're somehow dead set against it, I think it makes sense to move you. Better for all concerned. If you're all right with it."

Imogen had never met the Druid, but she could guess what was behind Reidy's difficulties. Besides, they had probably broken in—whoever "they" were—to check on her. It was equally probable that they had planted listening devices and had set up something that might steal or piggyback on her Wi-Fi signal. Which meant they'd probably broken into her flat, too.

It was time to reach out to Ian, she thought. He could get CCTV coverage for her street from the previous night, which might tell her if anyone had been trying to break into her home. She didn't want to go on a bug hunt unless absolutely necessary. Her apartment was as poorly tended as Ewan's. She smiled fondly as she recalled his endearing care and bustling nature.

"Whatever keeps the peace," she said, sighing. "But I thought his was the only space available this term."

Reidy looked positively sick with remorse, and Imogen guessed what he was about to say before he said it. "Well, there is Wee Frankie's office."

Imogen opened the door to Wee Frankie's office. It was exactly as he'd left it, if a bit messier. She wondered if those who'd killed him had searched his office, too.

"Look, I know this is odd," Reidy began.

"It'll be fine," said Imogen.

"Fortunately, you travel light," he said, depositing the box of books on her desk.

That was what Ian Ross had said that first night, Imogen noted. Which reminded her that she needed to call him as soon as Reidy was done apologizing and seeking reassurance that all was well. She'd need to let Ross know that she'd moved, that her office had been broken into. Which meant there was still a breach somewhere. *Another* breach. And he needed to be brought up to date on what she'd found in Dundee. It was time to put him to work as the insider who could maneuver in the halls of power. Their evidence was circumstantial, but it was convincing.

Ross called her cell phone as Reidy was taking his leave.

"Imogen," he asked, "are you at home? I was on campus this morning and I ran into Reidy. He told me about the break-in. I wanted to make sure you were all right."

"Perfectly fine, thanks," she said into the phone. "I'm in the office now."

Reidy was backing out, miming his goodbyes, eager to be gone.

"But I just knocked at the door, and you weren't there," said Ross over the phone.

At the door, Reidy made a thumbs-up as he exited. Imogen smiled her thanks as he turned and went out, leaving the door open.

"He probably forgot to mention that I'd moved offices when you saw him," she said as Reidy disappeared down the hall. "I'm in Wee Frankie's office now."

"On my way to you!" he said brightly and hung up.

The office door was open, and she heard Reidy and Ross meet in the hallway outside. "Good to see you, Ian," she heard Reidy call jovially. "What's it been, three weeks?"

"More," she heard Ross say.

A crack of adrenalin jolted her, and she leapt up to close the door, leaving it ajar about an inch in case there was more to hear. Ross *hadn't* spoken to Reidy already this morning? What reason did he have to lie? She considered locking the door.

The full import came crashing in on her. Maybe he was behind the break-in. Maybe...

Ross rapped at the door and opened it.

"Well, this is macabre," he said. "Frankie's office? Bit of overkill for a campus break-in, wouldn't you say?"

"Yes," she said. "It's odd." She stared at him blankly before mastering herself: "I think the overreaction has more to do with the Druid not wanting to share his space than with what happened last night. It's just a good reason for him to have his office back."

"The office he's never in?"

Imogen shrugged, forced a smile. "He seems pretty territorial. I think he was worried about my putting little, feminine touches in his office. Some paper or paint, a sweet, potted flower perhaps. Now, he can keep it in all its monastic…"

"—Druidic?"

"…charm. Yes."

Her mind was racing ahead. She needed to tell him something about what she had learned. Enough that it would satisfy his curiosity, maybe buy her some time. What could she tell him that wouldn't fully tip her hand?

"Are you here for the day?" she asked.

"I was planning to head back to Edinburgh around two o'clock," he said.

"Meet for lunch? I'm totally scattered right now. I'm not so much flustered by the break-in," she lied, "but I do need to get myself settled. And I need to come to grips with being here. Of all places." She looked around Wee Frankie's office.

"Of course," he said.

"There's a good little place in the lane with a nice French onion soup. Twelve-thirty?"

"I know it. Half twelve it is," he said. Which should have been his exit line. But he tarried. Like the first time they'd met, she had the sense he wanted to say something more. Whatever it was, though, he let it go. "See you then," he said with what seemed to her a forced cheerfulness.

She listened to his footsteps as they faded down the hallway. When she thought she heard him heading down the stairs she peeked out the door to confirm he was gone. Then she closed and locked it. Back at the desk, Imogen lifted the receiver of Frankie's office phone to call Marta Serres and warn her. It was unlikely that his office phone was bugged so soon after she'd moved offices. Ross hadn't even known about the move.

She put the phone down. How had "they" known about Donald Alban? They knew about him from before, probably, when he raised some questions about the referendum vote. No doubt, they had a dossier and a known-associates file on Alban. When Frankie had said he was going to speak with a well-placed friend who had proof the referendum had been stolen, perhaps they'd known exactly whom Frankie meant. And now they probably had a dossier on her, too. Ian Ross had betrayed Frankie, and Alban, to their deaths. That much was clear.

She dialed Marta's office phone rather than the cell phone. "Marty?" she said. "It's Imogen. Things have taken an ugly turn."

"God, what a morning," she said to Ross as she sat down heavily. She wasn't sure, but they seemed to be at the same table she and Frankie had shared some three weeks earlier.

"Do you think this is all related?" he asked.

"It must be. Though I don't know why," she said, beginning her carefully rehearsed speech. "I'm not getting anywhere, Ian. What I have is thin. And it's all circumstantial. Easily dismissed."

She spoke carefully, sticking to Frankie's notes on digital interference. She needed to project that she had no suspicion of Ross or his motives. She needed it to sound as though she'd run into a series of turnings that were all dead ends. And she needed to keep out facts about what she'd found in Dundee; needed to keep back the fact she'd been there. And she should deflect any questions about Marty, she thought. If they came up.

"First, as I told you, the postal ballots can't be dis-aggregated properly. It's probably a non-starter at this point. It seems that there were some ballots up in the north that *were* counted separately. And those were in the eighty percentile for No. That's a red flag because none of the early polls showed anything like that kind of preference."

"Still..." he began.

"I know. And we're only talking about something like a few thousand votes there anyway. We have no idea about the rest of them. I suppose, you, or some proxy, could make a fuss about having the commission separate them and do the count. But there are at least two problems with that. The first, and biggest, is political. A recount like that so long after the fact is bound to look partisan, and the findings disregarded."

Ross nodded. "Yes, I see that," he said.

"And second, if you're trying to do it quietly, there's no way it wouldn't be in every paper in the country. Everyone will know, including those to whom you don't want to tip your hand."

"I see," was all Ross said.

"There are all the surface things—the queen's raised eyebrow, no exit poll, et cetera. But none of it gives us a way in. We're at an impasse," she lied.

"Right..." said Ross, nodding.

"But, the fact that Frankie was killed, that my office was broken into tells me we might be onto something. That there must be something out there to find. We just don't know where to begin looking." She sighed for effect. "I'm sorry, Ian. I thought I could help, but now I feel like I need to turn it back to you. If you can come up with something more, something different, or if there's someone we could interview who had some kind of evidence."

She had to admit that the truth was almost as bleak as she was maintaining it was. It *was* all circumstantial. Ross seemed odd to her, reticent, stiff. He needed to say something. She stopped talking and had a few stringy bites from her soup, waiting.

"It's worse than we thought," Ross began.

It usually is, thought Imogen.

"I have found out from various sources"—here he paused and looked around, but there was no one else near them—"that the government in Westminster plans to gut Scotland's, and others' devolved powers when Parliament opens in under two weeks' time."

"What do you mean?"

He went back over the claw-back of powers, the "clarifying" cover, the unanswerable star chamber that he had outlined to the chief of staff. The new limits on referenda. Imogen listened intently.

"Can they do that?" she asked, when he had finished.

"Certainly, they *can*. They have the votes."

"I mean legally. Constitutionally," she pressed.

"Well, the doctrine of Parliamentary Sovereignty is pretty clear, and establishing an appointed Star Chamber for arbitration takes a good deal of the legal wrangling out of the equation."

"But the SNP will fight it in court."

"Oh, of course, but it'll be an uphill battle. I must tell you, tidying up like this will play well to the Tory base down south...and among some here. The fact it's announced by the King in his speech from the throne, setting the agenda, will make the new bill bullet-proof in their eyes—Make Britain Great Again!"

"Is that what they're calling it?"

"No. Sorry, a little editorializing on my part. I don't know what they're calling it. But it's meant to clarify the Internal Market Act."

"Still..." she began.

"Oh, yes, we can try to tie it up in court...whilst we dust off our resumes. But the appointed star chamber will likely hold sway there."

They stared at one another bleakly across the table.

Finally, he said, "If you were to come up with something *proving* interference, that the previous referendum was stolen. And if you did it *before* they announced their spiteful, chastity belt bill..." He looked at her expectantly. Imogen went silent.

Could she trust him? she wondered. Did he know somehow about her trip to Dundee, and this was some ruse to get her to divulge what she'd learned? Was *any* of what he was saying true? She needed time, she thought. Time, if Ross was telling the truth, that she didn't have.

"If only we could find who Wee Frankie was talking about that day in this office," said Ross.

"Yes," said Imogen. *The man who was also killed by your people*, she thought.

At their favored watering hole on George Street, Serres looked shaken as she drained a Long Tall and signaled for another. For her part, Imogen looked tired, almost resigned.

"Someone broke into your office?" Serres asked, as she traded her empty glass for a full one.

Imogen eyed the waitress and waited for her leave. "Yes," she said. "I expect they've bugged it. Fortunately, they bugged the Druid's office, not my new one. But we have to assume that they also bugged my apartment. And we need to be prepared that they're on our phones and our email. It's possible we're being monitored right now," she added.

"Jesus," Serres whispered. "Is this what the Faithless Elector case was like?"

"A bit, yes," said Imogen. "You don't know who's watching you or who's in on it, so you assume everyone is. Obviously, it can't *be* everyone, but it *could* be anyone. But this is strange. And worse. The Faithless Elector case began as something a researcher stumbled on, and we carried it through. But *I'm* the disease vector this time. I brought this on. And I brought it on you." She reached across the table and patted Marta's hand. "I've been an idiot. I'm very sorry to have implicated you."

Serres nodded. She was listening, but she seemed distracted, too.

"And, if I can believe the source, it's become more complicated." She relayed what Ross had told her about the clarifying bill, the claw-back and new referenda rules. Serres listened intently.

"But you're not sure you can trust the source?" Serres asked.

"No, I think he's working for them...whoever 'them' is. I think he got Frankie killed."

"You're talking about Ian Ross," said Serres.

"Yes."

"So why would you trust anything he says?"

"I'm wondering if there isn't more to it. Like maybe he didn't know they were killers. Here's what I *think* is going on based on what you and I have been able to piece together so far," Imogen continued. "Some group, possibly outside British government, but most likely aligned in some way with UK officials, undertook a systematic effort to steal the Independence referendum. I think that same group is making sure their interference isn't detected this time. It would undermine this new bill they've got coming."

"But you're not sure that what Ross told you is legitimate," Serres noted.

"True," Imogen admitted, "but why even look into it now, unless there's something new afoot. Also: I happened to notice a headline on one of the Red Tops this afternoon: 'Internal Market Rules Need Teeth,' one of them read. I did a quick search. There were similar opinion pieces today in two other right-wing rags. And one yesterday. They were all written by different people, but they all sang from the same score."

Serres wrinkled her nose but shrugged. "That's not illegal."

"No, it isn't," Imogen agreed. "But they each pressed the case for strengthening the Internal Market Act, and they each floated the idea of an extra-judicial body to arbitrate and resolve disputes. I looked back at Wee Frankie's notes, and some of the authors of those recent pieces were names he'd already flagged. Which points at the Transparency Project. They're linked."

"Again, though, 'Gen, not illegal."

"No, indeed, but it suggests to me that since the Transparency Project is anything but; that it was working hard behind the opaque scenes on the first referendum; that they might be looking to protect and strengthen their position with this new Make Britain Great Again initiative."

"Is that what they're calling it?"

"No, sorry. Just a joke...a bad one."

"But this is mad!" said Serres. "Just looking at what you and I can glean, it *may* be that they didn't need to interfere at all in the referendum."

"Well, that's why I'm wondering," Imogen said. "They might well have won fairly. If decidedly underhanded. I think the polls showing that the race was close were wrong. I mean, it's hard to steal ten percent of the vote. And keep it quiet. Nevertheless, whether they *needed* to interfere, it's pretty clear they *did* interfere," said Imogen. "The polls were trending upward for Yes as the vote approached. Maybe they panicked?"

Serres nodded.

"They've been able to keep their involvement and their actions quiet up till now," Imogen continued, "but I think the strong showing by the SNP this past election and the new impetus for a second referendum has them spooked. This time, the polling has started out firmly on the side of Yes. I saw a poll in *The National* that said it was 54 to 46 in favor of independence."

"And they—whoever 'they' are—can't steal eight percent of the vote," Serres added. "They're worried someone will uncover what they did before, on the first one. Which will only make the next vote more likely to be a win for independence."

"Exactly. I think this clarification bill is meant to stop a new referendum from ever happening. Westminster engaged in all kinds of over-the-line, public chicanery, and in preparation for a new vote, their dirty tricks might prod someone to look at what they were doing in the background as well."

"A rearguard action. Find out what *can* be found out. It's not actually stupid," Serres noted.

"No, it's not," Imogen admitted. "And you were right about Ian Ross. He's in this up to his neck, though I still can't see why."

"He's a chancer," Serres offered.

"Yes, a striver, as Wee Frankie said. And *I'm* his patsy. A stalking horse—off the radar, totally deniable. I can examine the data, follow leads, but I don't have to report on anything official. My findings go to him—and through him to whoever he's working for."

"You're sure?" Serres asked.

"I'm open to another explanation if you have one."

Serres shook her head, no.

"If I find something, it gives them early warning. And a chance to bury, misconstrue or distort my findings before they're in the open or can do any real damage. To them." She paused, overcome.

"What do we do?" Serres asked with elaborate calm.

"We can't be sure what Ross and his pack of dogs know about what we've found. I think you should distance yourself from me. We haven't exchanged the data over email. We haven't had long discussions about it over the phone. So that's good for you. I'd say, delete everything you have on this case. Is it backed up on a cloud server?"

Serres nodded.

"Delete it all," said Imogen. "Save it somewhere safe first."

"Will that be enough?" Serres asked.

"Probably not. But it'll give you deniability. If you're questioned—and particularly if somehow it comes up amongst colleagues—you should stick as close to the truth as possible. Yes, we spoke. A number of times. We'd even taken to having drinks from time to time here. You can mention that I'm going to give a talk at Professor Stewart's class at the end of term, and in your class next term. All true. You shared your data sets for a paper I was writing about referenda—a comparison between the US, UK and Switzerland. Also true. Well, true enough. You've helped any number of scholars in that way, you can say. As a public intellectual—"

"I see that," said Serres. "And you think that'll do it?"

"I don't know. But it gets you out of the loop, and it gains you some distance."

"What if that's not what I want? I work with the commission because I care about democracy, about voting integrity."

"This will go fast," Imogen said. "We know *that* they interfered before. And we need to get the information to someone high up, like the First Minister. But we have to figure out how to get it to her without Ian knowing about it. And before October 25th."

Imogen called Ewan's flip phone.

"Testing, testing," he said jocularly, when he picked up. "Read you loud and clear. Over."

"This isn't a test," said Imogen. "They're definitely watching me."

Johnston stood up and shut the door to his office.

"You're sure?" He paused on his way back to the desk and looked out the window.

"They broke into my office last night. And the man who started me on this, Ian Ross, he's not what he says he is. It seems that I was duped. I'm not supposed to be exploring ways to safeguard against future, potential interference, as he said. Ross has run me out to shake the tree a bit. To see if anyone can piece together what they're trying to hide."

"Opposition research?" he said.

"More or less."

"Smart," he allowed.

"That's the second time someone's said that to me today!"

"Sorry, I..."

"I'm sick of this lawyerly sophistry," she spat. "Like we're all playing some game."

Since tumbling to Ross's complicity, she had found herself dragged along in a torrent of alarm and rage, reliving the senseless, bloody deaths of the Faithless Elector case—of colleagues, innocent citizens, Duncan. She saw them all again, felt them all, bleeding, broken, silent. The thought of Marty being targeted, of leaving her children motherless made her breath come sharp and shallow. And why did Ewan—why did *anyone* deserve this?

"A deadly game," Johnston rejoined. "Listen."

Imogen sighed into the phone, the worst of the storm passed, for now. "Sorry, Ewan. I'm not angry with you. This case has brought up a lot of old feelings. And sorry about the 'lawyerly' bit."

"That's hardly the worst I've heard."

"Have you put the originals somewhere safe?" she asked.

"I have. Safe deposit box at the bank."

"Well, that's as good as anything, I guess," she said, not sounding convinced. "But if we *are* dealing with the government, they could get a court order to open it, couldn't they?"

"Not if they want to keep it quiet," he said. "That's where the lawyerly bit might come in right handy, don't you think?"

"I'd like to note in my defense that I said I was sorry. You may refer to the record."

"Let's hope there's no record of this call," he said, before adding, "but yes, the only way they could work around my legal opposition—if it comes to that—is to call it national security, slap a DSMA order on it."

"A gag order?" she asked.

"Right. On me. On you. The press."

"On the press? Wouldn't that make them more rabid for the story, for the truth?"

"What a quaint thought. But no, since you ask. Not so's ye'd notice. The word *quiescent* leaps to mind."

"The newspapers couldn't help?"

"No. All the England-based ones are housebroken and most of the Scotland-based ones are owned from England, so there's not much point. And I can't see the ones that aren't beholden to the conservatives standing up to a D notice. We need allies," he said.

Imogen was silent, trying to think her way through. True, she'd been in trouble for leaking to the press when her superiors dithered about the Faithless Elector case, but the papers had printed it. And, back home, she'd had friends in the Bureau that she could count on. "Do you know anyone in MI5?" she asked.

"No. But I have a different idea."

21

Inside the pub, along Old Hawkhill in Dundee, Ewan Johnston took a seat toward the back at one of the long, communal tables. He sipped at his pint and pored over that day's *Tele*, occasionally glancing toward the door. It was six o'clock and the crowd was shifting, a kind of changing of the guard, as those who had to hurry home to their tea drained their glasses and headed for the door, while others arrived to take their places. The pub was dark and snug.

Alan Wilson stepped inside, looking around as he took off his cap. Johnston looked up. Their eyes met, and he was about to wave when something in Wilson's eyes told him not to. He shook his head ever so slightly and went to the bar. Alarmed, Johnston steeled himself and pretended to go back to his newspaper. After waiting a few moments, he looked up. There was an open space at the bar next to Wilson. Johnston drained his glass and walked over to order another pint. He nodded casually at the man to his left and ordered. As he turned to the right, Wilson nodded though didn't look at him.

"Go tae the Gents in a moment," he said quietly, not looking at Johnston.

Johnston took his pint, placed it back on the table and went to the toilet. The Gents was empty, but he felt odd standing there with no business in hand but to wait for someone else. Wilson walked in a few moments later.

"Fuck's sake," he said as he came into the toilet, "ye cuid at least pretend ye were takin a pee." He unbuttoned and headed over to the side-by-side urinals. Johnston followed suit.

"Yer hotter than ye ken!" Wilson said over the urinal divider. "As a precaution, like, Ah tailed ye frae the office tae here. You were followed. There's one fuck sittin at the far end ae the bar. He's watching you, and waiting tae see if anyone meets ye, Ah'd guess. And there's another ane outside, leaning against a car. Ah'm thinkin he's around tae follow whoever you meet up with."

"Christ," Johnston whispered.

"What's it yer intae?"

"It's governmental. Shady. Corrupt. I've done nothing wrong, but—"

"Ah dinnae need tae know the details," he said. "Ah'm happy tae help, after all ye done for me and mine. But ye did also mention somethin aboot a bit a dosh, Ah think?"

Johnston reached into the inside pocket of his jacket and handed Wilson 300 pounds.

"Another thing," he said. He handed Johnston an old flip phone. "Ah'm thinkin that mebbe the people who done yer office are the same people followin ye. The fact there wasnae a peep on the network tells me that mebbe Ah'm right."

Johnston swallowed hard.

"They might've seen that one old phone in your desk drawer. Take this one just in case. If it's who ye say it is that's following you round—and Ah think yer right—this might buy ye some time."

"I've already called Imogen using the other one," said Johnston.

"Right. Ah'd say, tell yer bird tae get a new one as well. But it'll be difficult. Ah'm sure they're watching her too." He paused, looked hard at Johnston before continuing.

Johnston found himself wondering whether Imogen was anyone's "bird," much less his.

"Look, this is gonnae be hard. Because right now, yer fucked. The wolves are circling. Ah don't know what they're waitin on. But they're no' gonnae wait forever. Ah need tae to go on the attack."

"That sounds ominous, Alan."

"Nothing grand, counselor. All Ah mean is—watch the watchers, mebbe turn the tables on them. And Ah'm mebbe gonnae bring in another man." He turned to the sink to wash his hands. "Keep doin whatever it is you solicitors do. Pretend everything's normal. And keep yer heid doon. Ah'll be in touch in a few days. By that new phone. Now, wash your haunds!"

At Saint Andrew's House early next morning, as Ian Ross worked through his office in-tray his cell phone rang. Seeing who it was on the display, he stood up and closed the door to his office. "Yes?" he said.

"You fucking idiot!" Chamberlain screeched down the line.

"What?"

"What the fuck was she doing in Dundee?" Chamberlain demanded. "I thought you had this in hand!"

"What are you talking about?"

"That American girl. What do you think? This was your grand idea. You set her going, and you were meant to be watching her."

"I am," Ross protested.

"Not well enough it seems."

"She's in Dundee?"

"*Was* in Dundee."

"I saw her two days ago in Glasgow," said Ross, "and I made my report to you that—"

"That she played you," said Chamberlain.

"But she said—"

"Right. She *said*. But she seems to have a left a good bit out. Like how she met with a man named Ewan Johnston, a Dundee solicitor and protégé of our dear, departed friend there. I've only just seen the surveillance photos myself. If you want to make the starting eleven, Ross, you're going to have to find a new gear, my boy. For now, we're taking charge. You're on cleanup duty. Find out how far this has gone and let us know what we need to tie it off. I only hope we're in time."

Ross put down the phone and stared at it. He didn't like the sound of "tie off." And she hadn't told him everything over soup the previous day. Did that mean she didn't trust him? Could he blame her? But *how* did she know? How had it all gone so wrong?

It had been the perfect scenario: earn points with the powers-that-be without having to do anything, meanwhile expanding his casual listening network, as he'd done with Dizzy Willoughby. He had met Chamberlain—deliberately putting himself in the man's way—while in London six months earlier. At a second meeting on that same trip, having sensed what might curry favor, Ross had floated the idea of finding out what could be found about malfeasance or interference in the '14 referendum, with an eye toward putting all the rumors to bed for good—not because he believed there had been any interference, but because, like his boss, Janette Ritchie, he'd been certain there was nothing to find.

He would earn kudos with Chamberlain in Westminster, but not do anything damaging to his party or the government— a win-win. But there *had* been something to find, and now two people had been murdered for it. This wasn't what he had signed on for. Wee Frankie had been murdered after a status update call from him. All Ross had said to Chamberlain the night he and Imogen went out to dinner was that Frankie knew an old friend who said he had proof of some kind, and that he would follow up with more and better intel the following Monday.

He had assumed whatever evidence Frankie's friend had— if he had anything—that it would be similar to the outraged, conspiracy-minded doggerel Frankie had been banging on about for years. Still, in Ross's mind, a win-win. Ross had indeed "been in this game a wee while," and he wasn't foolish enough to believe that someone as twisty as Chamberlain would be openly helpful. But establishing a relationship with an adversary who thinks he has something over you never hurts. Or, it hadn't until now.

If Imogen's research couldn't come through in time, Ross saw, confessing and revealing his part to Ritchie would neither absolve him, nor hinder the MBBA Bill that Chamberlain and his men had in mind for the opening of Parliament. If he were to spill his guts to the chief, he'd be fired, of course; and if the chief was unwise enough to use what he confessed, it was unlikely to be the kind of revelation that would persuade entrenched parties or a divided electorate. Not without something to back it up.

In London, Percy received a similarly shrill phone call. After serving in the military, the hairdryer treatment was nothing new in his experience, and he was already prepared for how he would respond.

"I was unaware that your men were on the case, too," he began, as Chamberlain's harangue ran down. "Our watchers hadn't noticed anyone else tailing them."

"Well, they are now, you can bet!"

"Yes," said Percy. "Quite. As part of my standing brief, I was already engaged in surveillance, as we discussed, to find out what was known, who knows it, and how far it might have gone."

"You broke into her office."

"Yes," he continued patiently. "I took steps. Was that wrong?" he didn't pause long enough for Chamberlain to answer but continued, "I increased the surveillance on her, bugged her office and apartment and started following another person of interest in all this."

"That Spanish woman from the Electoral Commission?"

"Yes. And *is* she Spanish?" he asked.

"Perhaps we're a bit more thorough than you. And yes. Serres is married to a UK citizen, but she's kept her passport. She's Spanish," said Chamberlain. "I want you on their phones, too. All of them—Johnston, Trager and Serres. See if there's anyone else."

"I can do that, but doing so will mean widening the sphere of those involved, and might—"

"I'm authorizing the use!" Chamberlain yelled. "You have two more days to do it your way before we shut down the whole thing."

"Shut it down, sir? How are you—?"

"By any means necessary."

"Sir, I—"

"By any means necessary. That's what the PM said back in 'fourteen. And I intend—"

"With respect, sir, that's *not* what the PM said."

"He didn't have to. And you know it. I think it's time you called the FBI...to let them know one of their own is doing a little illegal snooping."

22

"Divide and rule" is an old adage, and as a tactic, it has a venerable pedigree, rather like those who tend to employ it. Eight years earlier, "Project Fear," as Prime Minister Cameron himself had christened the No-to-Independence campaign, came full circle in its implications, from inspiring it in the electorate to feeling it come to roost in themselves.

First, Jefferson Weaver and his Institute had gone to work seeding mistrust and doubt, amplifying dissent. In the early months of the Independence campaign, his group's efforts were merrily effective at segmenting the populace. Support for the Yes vote—shockingly for the Scottish National Party—began at only 30%.

Over the course of the campaign, however, the polling numbers for Yes climbed. But as Imogen had found out—and as Weaver knew even back in '14—polls were blunt, outdated instruments. Not to be trusted. His own data showed that No still had at least a 10 % lead—whatever official polls said. But his employers, the triumvirate, grew worried. There were panicked, offline meetings. Unbeknownst to Weaver until it was too late, Chamberlain had put Plan B into effect.

Donald Alban's polling station teams were well trained, and Alban had conducted numerous meetings and supervised additional trainings to make sure all would run smoothly. Turnout had been expected to be high, and it was. Unprecedentedly so, the highest turnout since WWII. Election day, for Alban and the polls staff, would happen, as always, in distinct phases, with the most acutely stressful phase taking place between 10pm and 4am, when the boxes were delivered, the count was conducted, and the result was finally released. He and the rest of those working the polls were prepared, and eager for the day.

Throughout Election Day, Alban checked in by phone with the presiding officers at each of the 81 polling places across Dundee's eight wards, issuing judgments, making clarifications, dealing with squabbles. In some cases, he visited those with problems, along with those he'd chosen at random the previous day for inspection. Reported problems were few, beyond keeping up with the number of voters. Staff was under great stress handling the increased turnout, he learned, but they were doing an excellent job. He was pleased.

In most elections, two, 50-liter ballot boxes were sufficient for most polling places, though each had a third or more of the black, plastic boxes to use if necessary. Which was rare. Each box typically held around 500 ballots. The election handbook stipulated a precise course of action for how to deploy a second or even third, should one of the boxes become full, but it was always on an as-needed basis.

Three days before election day, however, Alban had received a directive urging that each polling place should change boxes every four or five hours throughout the day, given the expected increased turnout. The directive had come from his superiors at the electoral commission and Alban thought it a wise precaution. He made sure all polls were provided with multiple boxes. This was an historic vote, and he wanted nothing to stand in the way of a smooth operation.

All through election day, along with the required reporting, Alban made notes to self and kept an unofficial running tally of ballots issued at each location he contacted, along with a tally of the boxes used. Some precincts would fill as many as five ballot boxes on the night, while others used only three. That tally, of course, had nothing to do with the election result. The boxes were sealed. The official *vote* result would come when the ballot boxes were delivered to the count centre after the polls had closed at 10p.m., but he wanted to be sure that none went missing or was left behind.

Presiding officers at each polling place were responsible for delivering their ballots to the count centre, but Alban had long favored a more streamlined approach. As had been the case for years, five separate vans rented for the day would be parked at each of the farthest polling places on the outer west, east and northern edges of the Dundee City district, ready to go well before the polls had opened. Beginning at about 10:15pm, after polls closed, each van would be driven by one of the polling agents from that outlying polling place.

The vans would then make stops at polling places, each along a planned route, ending at the count centre at the Dundee International Sports Centre. Stopping at each polling place along the way, the sealed ballot boxes along with the spent voting slips and marked electoral register—also sealed—would be placed inside the van, and it would move to its next stop. The load-in typically took less than five minutes. If any polling place missed the van's schedule, the Presiding officer at that location would inform Alban by phone and deliver the ballot boxes to the count centre personally.

But there had been a change, one that Alban wasn't to learn of until almost 1:00am that morning. Unbeknownst to him at the time, two men presented themselves at each of the far-flung polling places at 9:45pm—ten men in total. Each pair had paperwork purportedly signed by Alban stating that they, and not the previously designated polling agents, would be delivering the ballot boxes and supporting paperwork.

The man who would now be driving the van said that Alban had thought there would be much to do at the end of the voting day with such a large turnout. Harried presiding officers gratefully accepted the help and handed over the van keys. Each van would have almost 20 stops to make along its route and would typically arrive at the count centre about an hour and a half after the polls had closed. The second man in the van was there not merely to help load, as the letter supposedly from

Alban claimed, but to separate the black, 50-liter ballot boxes and the supporting paperwork.

There was to be one decidedly unscheduled stop.

A sixth van, not rented by Alban, (though identical to the others) sat parked along Granton Terrace, one street off the Kingsway in the north of town, next to a football ground. Along a dark, heavily tree-lined street, it was a world away from the glare and attention of the polls and election count centre. From the five vans making their way to the count centre, a total of 46 boxes were removed and placed in the sixth.

At the count centre, when Alban began what he had meant to be a cursory survey, he found that ballot boxes were missing and that some of the paperwork did not match his own notes. As he began to make enquiries and prepared to lodge a concern, his cell phone rang.

"Mr. Alban," said the voice.

"Yes, I—"

"It would be a mistake for you to make any further note of discrepancies."

"Who is this?"

"This is the voice of God, Mr. Alban. I know all, I see all. I certainly see you."

Alban stopped and looked around frantically.

"For instance," the voice continued, "I know that you think you know something, but it isn't true."

"What?"

"You think there might have been issues with the count. I can assure you that you're in error. I know that you're wrong because it's your signature approving the delivery, and the official tallies match. I also know, because I have a copy of it, that it was your order to replace the presiding officers with special drivers at Lynch Sports Centre, at Northend Social club, Craigiebarns Primary School and elsewhere."

"I never—!"

"The official record contradicts you," God interrupted. "And indeed, if anything *were* to be found amiss, the sin of it would redound unto you."

"I don't understand—" he began.

"Of course you do. But if you'd like to discuss it further, I'm sure I can arrange for you to discuss it with one of my devout followers. He's waiting even now, along Hyndford Street. Waiting for a sign from me."

Waiting outside his house? Alban's breath came short. His wife and daughter Jean were home. He looked around the Leisure Centre counting area, at the throng of activity. He had no idea where, or who the caller was. He felt lightheaded, impotent with fury. How could he have let this happen? What had he missed?

If the box tally matched what the men in the vans had delivered—and those in the vans had made sure that it did—even a full audit might not reveal what had truly happened. And since Alban's forged signature had already certified the box tally, was on the order to replace the drivers, and he had legitimately rented the vans, all blame would stick to him.

He was willing to risk his reputation—even jail. The truth *would* come out eventually. But the threat to Sandra and their daughter Jean was another thing entirely.

"I understand," he had said.

23

"Thank you for coming," said Percy, as Michael Leyser fell into step next to him.

It was a bleak evening, as the two ambled idly along the South Bank promenade towards the Waterloo Bridge. A stinging wind swept across the Thames, stirring tidy whitecaps along its surface. Leyser changed hands and held his umbrella to shield both of them. Though the wind strained the ribs and edges of the umbrella, his expression betrayed concern for nothing more troublesome than a faint drizzle.

Glancing toward the skyline rising above the river, Leyser said by way of greeting: "Like a nocturne in gray and...more gray."

Michael Leyser was listed as a deputy adviser to someone or other in Whitehall for anyone who wondered. But irrespective of his official brief, his work was that he "did things" on behalf of the PM and government. Gaunt and elegant, unruffled even by the battering rain, he strolled contentedly next to Percy. "I suppose the ruse that we're just out for a pleasant stroll is lost somewhat on a night like this," he said.

"Makes you feel that anyone tailing us deserves whatever scoop he gets," Percy observed.

Leyser chuckled.

"I wanted to bring you up to date on this Scottish business," Percy began. "You know—"

"Yes," Leyser said, not eager for any precise detail.

"It appears that, in relation to this business, there've been two...departures."

"Why? I thought you'd kept a lid on all that?"

"*I* did. But apparently, something has happened or is going to happen, and our mutual friends panicked."

"I see," said Leyser. "They seem to do that at the worst possible times, don't they? Can it be proved?"

"It's possible—regrettably—that there are details out there of which I am unaware. Which might brook further investigation *and* might lead to the revelation of wrongdoing. But I can't be sure. You see, what's happening is not happening through my office," said Percy.

"Some rogue, private affair of theirs? Not using official sanction? Sounds like we might be able to let them go to the dogs?"

"Much as I might like to do that, sir, each of them is *in* government now. Indeed, if something came out, it might look like their places at the table were the result of the work they did back in 'fourteen—also more or less rogue." Here he looked sideways at Leyser to gauge his reaction.

"We knew about the Transparency Project," Leyser began, "and that there were probably some things that went along with it that we didn't want to know too much more about. And of course, it was before our time."

Yes, thought Percy, you wanted to use the planning and insight Transparency had gleaned, but you wouldn't have been able to do it if those who were heading it were in prison.

"The PM doesn't like what's going on in the background any more than you do," Leyser continued. "But there are bigger things at stake. For now, keep the lid on, mitigate the damage and we'll see what we can do about offloading them later."

After you have what you want, thought Percy.

"Does that sound mercenary?" Leyser mused as though reading Percy's thoughts. "I suppose it does. They're useful right now, if dangerous. I'm sure you have similar experience with this sort of thing in your world, no?" Hearing no response, he continued: "Play it as you have been, from their score sheet."

With all the attendant danger to me, and the plausible deniability for you, thought Percy. "Very good, sir," was all he said. "I did bring along a file, if you'd care to—"

"No, that won't be necessary."

Well, what had he expected? Back in his office and dry, Percy stared toward the door to his office, rehearsing the reprimand he'd like to give Frenz for going over his head and informing Chamberlain about his, Percy's, wait-and-see approach. It was the only way Chamberlain could have found out. The lambasting he couldn't give. The one wherein he re-assigned Frenz to, say, monitoring campus unrest. In Wales. Or maybe as field man for some abstruse Ministerial study. Driver's pool? He grinned at the thought of it. But it wasn't to be, and certainly not now that Frenz's sneaking about had scored points with Chamberlain.

Calum Percy was not someone possessed of a rich fantasy life, but he often used what little imagination he had as a kind of emotional balm. The invented humiliations or violent ends he conjured for some of his colleagues allowed him to continue working effectively with a great number of them. So, when Frenz knocked and entered, he smiled warmly at his assistant, seeing him as he would have liked to: not entering, but taking his leave for a demotion.

"We're going to need to bring in the Wire Services to tap in and see what Trager *et al* may have," said Percy. "Please make the necessary arrangements. Keep the circle small. I should have the authorization soon." He nodded at Frenz, indicating that was all, and he should be about it. Inwardly he seethed, furious that he'd been directed to call the FBI.

In Dundee, outside Ewan Johnston's office, it was late afternoon. Faint light mused in the pauses between fits of stinging rain. The bleak weather made keeping track of comings and goings that much simpler for the shadow sitting in a battered Skoda in view of the front and back entrances to the building. One of Percy's buskers. The busker's view of the world was binary. People were divided into "targets" of interest, and civilians, or "non-rev;" that is, not relevant to his surveillance duties.

There were few of either stripe about—not even the beefy competition. And those who were out looked as though they wished they weren't. They scurried quickly between awnings and doorways as the busker sat unremarked and unseen, barely a silhouette, behind a calico patchwork of grime and mist-fogged windows. If anyone had cared to look.

Alan Wilson stood out, therefore, a skinny, tough-looking kid, loitering with intent in a doorway on the same side of the street as the specter in the Skoda. Also watching the building. The ghost snapped his picture. When Johnston walked out a few moments later and opened his umbrella, he snapped another picture and turned his attention back toward the man waiting in the doorway. Wilson, as yet unidentified, waited and watched.

"Legal-One has exited the building," he said into the telephone. "Hold a moment."

Wilson looked up and down the street. To the man inside the Skoda, it was obvious that Wilson was making sure Johnston's back was clear before making contact.

Wilson, like Percy's buskers, had found that the watchers employed by Nesbitt & Co. were not accomplished—or thorough. Their tailing was ham-handed, their handoffs clumsy and obvious. Their "front tails" were laughable. And they stood out on the Dundee streets, self-consciously hard, cold-eyed beefeaters, underdressed for the weather.

As Wilson scanned the block, it appeared that he saw nothing to worry him and hurried across the street, head down, hands inside his jacket pockets. On the pavement, he fell in after Johnston, staying almost a full block behind, ambling, seemingly idly, but watching the street in front and behind.

"There's four coming toward you," the silhouette said into his phone. "Legal-One, carrying a dark, blue umbrella: he's almost reached the corner. There're also two non-rev—a man and a woman together under a red umbrella—and somebody new—dark hair, midtwenties, black coat and black Adidas trackies, white trainers, no brully—heading east toward you along Ward Road by Howff cemetery. He's about a full block behind Legal-One. No sign of the competition. I guess they don't come out to play when it rains. Not quite sure what Trackies is up to," he related in hushed tones. "But he's definitely following our man."

In communication the whole time, the busker in the car waited until both Wilson and Johnston had crossed Constitution Road. When his colleague acknowledged falling in behind Wilson on the opposite side of Ward Road, he buttoned his coat and jumped out of the car. He cut across the street and down Constitution Road, where he sprinted east along Euclid in order to be in place to take up the hunt if his quarry walked much more than a few blocks. He came out on Meadowside, a little ahead of them, and found that both men had turned down Reform Street and were now standing together, ostensibly to look at an estate agent's window display. He crossed the street to stand opposite them. When it was clear he hadn't been noticed, he crouched down and took a position between two parked cars. He had a clear view and snapped a series of pictures.

Standing in front of the estate agents', Wilson said to Johnston, "Ah havnae been able to maneuver yet tae get behind your watchers, so Ah don't know anythin about them. Ah'd hoped this walk wouldae given me an opportunity. But they're either really good, and we can't see them. In which case we're both fucked." He looked around, failed to see the two men watching them. "Doubtful. Or they're easy to slip."

"So, I was the tethered goat?"

"We've gottae work this one out. D'ye have a different idea? A plan, like?"

The second busker who'd been tailing them walked by, and as he did so, his compatriot moved out from between the cars and back to a safely neutral position at the intersection. Trackies was a new target. He immediately sent the photos to Jamie Frenz.

They were no nearer breaking the case than they had been two days earlier, Imogen reflected miserably as she stalked through her flat that evening on a "bug hunt." The evidence they had wasn't enough to go to the papers, probably wasn't enough to go to the Scottish authorities. And any overtures to Holyrood would surely alert Ian Ross. She didn't know where to turn. Who could they trust?

Her bug hunt turned up the three listening devices Percy's man had hidden in her flat, one behind the bedside table, one next to the table by the sofa, and another in the dining room. Good spots, she mused. And well disguised. For now, she thought it best to leave them in place. She'd need to make sure she kept her discussions bland and otherwise superficial. As she flopped down on the sofa, her phone rang, a US number.

"Hello?" she said.

"Imogen, it's Jeff Benoit, how are you?"

Her boss, the deputy director of Studies in Electoral Integrity? She disliked speaking to him under the best of circumstances. "Director Benoit," she said blandly. "What a pleasure."

"It may not be, I'm afraid."

"I don't understand, sir," she said brightly, but scowled at the phone.

"We spoke about you keeping your nose clean, Agent, while you were away."

"Yes. I remember our conversation vividly," she said, still trying to keep a chipper tone.

"And, er...are you doing so?"

"Of course. Could you help me out here and tell me what we're talking about? Has something happened?" She wasn't going to make this easy for him. She was playing defense, and the best thing to do was to wait for him to commit, not dive in herself.

"I guess that's what I'm trying to ascertain, Agent Trager."

"I'm unaware of anything I might have done—or am doing—that might be construed as other than what I came here to do: research."

"Yes." He let that hang for some seconds, perhaps playing a bit of defense himself. Finally, he asked, "What are you working on?"

"I'm giving talks, and I'm doing research for a comparative study having to do with voter activation in referenda. I'm looking cross-nationally, at the US, the UK and Switzerland. Referenda are funny things, as I'm sure you're aware. They're touted as 'pure' democracy—direct—but are typically anything but. They—"

"You're not involved with the police at all?" he interrupted.

"Not in the least. I sit up in my office and work. Look, what's this all about?"

"I've had notification that you've involved yourself in a murder case, the murder of one of your colleagues there."

"Oh! That was horrible. His office was a few doors down from mine. He and I had grown close. Friends. Then he was mugged and killed."

"And you investigated."

"How would I do something like that, Director?"

"Well, you couldn't," he blustered.

"Exactly my point," she countered.

"Are you saying that you didn't request an official there, one Ian Ross, to give you the police files on the murder of this man?"

"Shit," she sighed. "No, I did not." She thought of what she had told Marty about interrogations: stay as close to the truth as you can. "But I think I see what's happening, Director Benoit. I know Ian," she began. "We've had dinner a couple of times. He works in the Scottish government and was helping me with data I need for my study. He's also a friend of the dead man, my colleague here, Francis McDougal. A few days after Frankie's murder, he dropped by my office here with the local police report. He asked me to look at it."

"He says you initiated it," said Benoit.

"You've spoken with him?"

"Not him, no. And you shouldn't have—"

"Yes, sir. I know. I could see that he was hurting, looking for something...You're right, I should've put him off in some way. But I didn't. I looked over what he brought me—a cursory look—and said it appeared that the authorities here were doing everything they could. Frankly, I regarded that as a tame way of putting him off. There was no follow-up from me, no inquiries."

"Then why is this coming to me? Why is he saying it was you?"

"I can't be sure, of course. It would be pure conjecture, but it sounds like maybe he was caught over-stepping his bounds? He's a political appointee. Works for the First Minister's chief of staff. He's got nothing to do with the police. But I'm sure someone highly placed like that can pull strings."

"Yes..." said Benoit.

"He probably figured that blaming me for acceding to my request could be seen as a lapse in judgment—maintaining the Special Relationship or whatever the fuck they call it here. He might have his wrists slapped, but nothing major. Whereas his initiating the request might open him up to charges of abuse of authority. I'm going to have to steer clear of him, I guess. It's too bad. I thought he was kinda nice."

"Sounds like you should," said Benoit. "And if you don't mind my saying it, you've had some pretty poor judgment regarding men in the past, and—"

"I do mind your saying it! Deputy director or no. Was there anything else?"

"I..." He cleared his throat. "Agent Trager, it sounds like this is a misunderstanding. But the director himself is aware of this report. I will update him on the details as you've related them to me, of course. Honestly, this feels like one of those the-less-done-or-talked-about-the-better type deals. But be aware, anything further of this nature, or if it becomes clear you were not fully truthful in this conversation—"

"Yes, sir. I understand. Can you tell me who initiated the report?"

"It came through official channels. That's all I have. But having come through official channels, it means that a good many people are aware—on both sides of the Atlantic."

"Good to know," she said. "Thank you, Director Benoit."

Imogen stormed out of her apartment and slammed the door shut. She stalked toward Sauchiehall Street. Though angry, she remained alert for anyone following or observing her. Since they were listening in, they would know she'd been dressed down, so going for a walk to cool off fit the kind of thing she might do. But she didn't want them to see her make the next phone call from her drop phone.

In London, the Wire Service flashed the transcript of Imogen's call with Benoit to Calum Percy at his office.

"Hmm," he mused, reading it on his computer screen. He looked up as Frenz entered, come to hear what was going on and doubtless pass along findings. "Well, I'm not sure he believed her," said Percy, returning his gaze to the screen. "But it sounds like US bureaucrats aren't much different from their UK counterparts—always willing and eager *not* to become involved."

"Maybe you should let the top floor handle it their own way," said Frenz.

"Well, you see, Jamie, this *is* what they wanted. I was content to continue gathering intelligence. If Trager and Serres and Johnston had definitive proof, they'd have revealed it by now, wouldn't they? I mean, what's stopping them? It's possible they're at a dead end, and their findings, such as they are, don't amount to much more than hearsay, conjecture and conspiracy theories. All of which keeps us in the background."

"Yes, but—" Frenz interjected, only to be cut off.

"But now we've shown ourselves a bit. We've confirmed for Trager *et al* that there might be more to find; that someone— someone official—feels the need to protect something. How does it go? 'He that would keep a secret must first keep secret that he has a secret to keep.' And we just flashed our bum!"

"Yes, I see," said Frenz, who had that pessimistic, doubting look of someone who was beginning to wonder whether he should have switched queues at the grocery store.

"And now," Percy continued, "by our own actions, we've proscribed our own range of motion. Not quite Hari Kiri, mind you, but Ian Ross was supposed to be the conduit for information. She was meant to tell us everything because she thought she was helping the other side. Now *that's* been compromised, wouldn't you say?"

"She left him out of the loop about going to Dundee and meeting with Johnston."

"Maybe what Johnston has—if anything—isn't as damaging as we think it is."

Frenz said nothing but stared at a file he held in his hand.

"The top floor approved—and pushed for—this alert to her own people," he continued. "A step that I wanted to hold in reserve. If she goes missing, or turns up dead, the Americans will want to know why. Make sure to tell them that part, too, Jamie. When you make your report."

Frenz all-but blushed. "Sir, I—"

Percy nodded toward the door—interview concluded. But Frenz tarried.

"Actually, sir," he began, "we do have a bit more information. The Dundee team snapped some photos of someone new. He's clearly working with Johnston. We were able to identify him quickly because he has an extensive arrest record. Though no convictions. Which is interesting in itself."

"Why haven't I seen it?"

"You're seeing it now, sir." He handed over a file. Pictures of Wilson and Johnston were clipped to the front.

"After the top floor took a look first?"

"Yessir," Frenz murmured contritely.

"Well?" he demanded, glancing through the photos.

"Someone recognized him, not as an outlaw, but as one of our people."

"Our?"

"He drove one of the vans the night of the referendum."

Percy stared—"Fucking hell. Do they have any other witnesses?"

As she stalked along Sauchiehall Street, Imogen called Marta Serres a second time. She had not picked up on the first try. This time, it was her husband, Michael, who answered.

"Michael?" she asked. "This is Imogen Trager."

"I know who you are."

"I was trying to get hold of Marty."

"We all are. She's been detained by the Home Office. She's to be deported."

"*Deported*?"

"Administrative removal, they call it. But it's deportation."

"I thought—" Imogen began.

"It's a security matter, according to the Home Office."

"The Home Office? What's she been charged with?"

"I don't know. Also a security matter, I gather. And our solicitor informs me that the Home Office has wide latitude in this area. He's inside trying to see her now. I'm outside on my way to pick up the children. I don't know what I'm going to tell them."

"Michael, is there anything I can do?"

"You've done more than enough," he spat. "Whatever you two were into, it's brought this about. If the solicitor can't think of something, she'll be back in Barcelona in less than seventy-two hours. The children may have to go as well!" He hung up.

Imogen stood at the corner of Derby Street and Sauchiehall, dumbfounded. Her breath came sharp and shallow, like she'd been kicked in the stomach. Was she indeed some pantomime blundering American, a Fearless Fosdick simpleton? She'd only make it worse for her friend if she tried to help. That much was clear. But it was all that was clear. It was barely 3 pm, but darkness gathered along the damp street. She crossed the road and sat down at an empty table outside the Ox and Finch restaurant.

Whoever she was fighting, they were playing defense, too. She thought of her high school days and playing basketball.

When on the defensive, it was often enough merely to slow down your opponent, to harry them and wait for them to make a mistake. She certainly felt harried. Above all, on defense, it was crucial not to commit until there was no other option. You don't lunge at your opponent (possibly missing) when they're at half-court. You hold it in reserve until they're in shooting range. The call to her superiors to rein her in, Marty's deportation—it all felt like desperation. Did that mean she was close to the goal? She couldn't see a way through.

Ewan would be in trouble, too.

She dialed his new number.

"Ewan?" she began. "They're definitely on to us. I had a call from my boss at the Bureau, and he's asking why I'm investigating something way out of my jurisdiction."

"It's a fine question," Ewan began jovially. "But how did he know?"

"Someone at MI-Five contacted him."

"Fuck," he said simply.

"And the professor I was working with from the Electoral Commission—Marta Serres—she's being deported by the Home Office."

"Deported?"

"Administrative removal, I think they call it," said Imogen. "I'm sick about it. It's my fault."

"She should be able to fight that," said Johnston. "She's married to a UK citizen?"

"Yes."

"No, it'll be dreadful, but she can get out from under—"

"The Home Office is involved," Imogen interrupted. "They're saying it's a security matter."

"Fuck," he said again.

"I guess we have our confirmation. It's every level of government, including a rat in Holyrood. Ewan, I'm worried about you."

24

Frenz not only passed along Percy's displeasure but also his reaction to there being a witness. That Percy seemed rattled stunned the Triumvirate into silence at the crash meeting Chamberlain called in London. Until now, though they had whinged about his lack of energy and faith, his stolid bearing had also served as a barometer of the true danger level. While he'd dithered (in their estimation) gathering intelligence, reports of his bland recalcitrance had also meant that things probably weren't as bad as they seemed. The revelation that Alan Wilson had been found had shaken Percy. And now them.

A worried silence fell over the cavernous, unfinished 20th floor of the high-rise office building where Chamberlain, Nesbitt, Townsend and Weaver met. Each man looked to the others, wondering what should be done next. Gossamer streams of work site dust undulated across stark rays of light pouring in from the south-facing windows. Quickler than the rest of his cohort, Nesbitt reverted to mean—or rather, angry, breaking the silence.

"He's been wrong at every turn!" Nesbitt fumed. "I've never liked his pompous manner, and I've always been suspicious of his motives. Who is he to question orders?" Nesbitt inspected his suit for concrete dust or fresh paint.

"While I share your concern," Chamberlain answered. "He's done exemplary service thus far."

"Bollocks!" bellowed Townsend.

"Quite," Nesbitt agreed, pressing his lips together tightly. He frowned at his shoes, which were coated in a fine, white dust.

Weaver looked on, quiet.

For his part, as he looked from face to face, Chamberlain saw that the greatest danger was that each might look to minimize the damage to themselves and retreat from the group. They all had something to protect. His own career, for one, Chamberlain mused. But it was the not-so-crack squad of ex-military irregulars recruited by Nesbitt that was the urgent problem. Revelation of their panicked interference, the subsequent cover up and murders would lead back to them all. Mostly, the irregulars were a problem for Nesbitt. Even he knew it. There was no telling what those idiots might do, or say—or whom they might give up—if they were arrested and found themselves facing down a long prison sentence.

Sensing the danger, Chamberlain, uncharacteristically, voiced an opinion: "It might seem like this is the time for every man for himself. But not yet." He eyed his compatriots. "We all have a great deal to lose, but we're nowhere near full time yet. Yes, they have a witness, this Wilson fellow. But what could he say? And what kind of witness could he be? He's a criminal underworld figure. We're not sunk by a long ways." He paused for effect. "We must hang together. If we do not, we shall certainly hang separately."

"You're quoting Ben Franklin right now?" Weaver asked.

"It's not Franklin," said Nesbitt. "I'm sure it's a good old Tommy."

"It's Franklin," Weaver affirmed. "Though *technically*, you're right. Franklin would have been a British subject when he said it. Though not for long. He said it at the signing of the Declaration of Independence."

Nesbitt stared into the middle distance, his brow furrowed in concentration. He seemed to be turning over in his mind whether he wanted to assert that Franklin's Britishness was precisely the point he was getting at. Weaver couldn't keep the bitter distaste for Nesbitt from showing on his face. He wished he could add some other apt Franklin-ism but all that came to mind was *He that lies down with dogs, shall rise up with fleas,* which, though apt, didn't seem helpful at the moment. Townsend frowned, his corpulent lip protruding. For his part, he was finding this renewed talk of independence exceedingly tedious.

Still, no one said a word about what must be done. Each, like Weaver, kept back what he might say. Because without saying it outright, the group was clear about what must be done. But someone would first have to say it out loud. Nesbitt, always happy to say the ugly thing, piped up. "It seems to me that all of them must die."

Weaver frowned while the other two seemed to be waiting for a second to the motion. "No," he said. "The *driver* is the key. This Wilson. Without him, I doubt they have a case. We take care of him and the rest goes away. Trash that lawyer's reputation, send the girl back to DC with her tail between her legs."

Nesbitt replied, "That makes sense. And it's cleaner. He's linked with our underworld contacts. His death could be easily spun."

"How will the local mob feel about us killing one of their own?" Weaver asked.

"Just pay them! That ought to soothe any qualms they might have. Luckily this is Dundee. In Glasgow, we'd have to pay handsomely," Nesbitt quipped.

"And if the others get in the way?" Townsend asked.

"In that case, they're collateral damage," said Weaver. "Percy was worried about what the Feds would do if an American were killed. If she was somehow caught in the crossfire of an underworld gang war—or however we spin it— and dies, that's pretty cut-and-dry. Not much to follow up there."

"Then we're agreed," said Chamberlain. "And it needs to be soon."

* * * *

Eight years earlier, Alan Wilson had been 19 years old, never mind what his driving license said. The Madmen crime boss Buff Lindsey had called Wilson and five other apprentice felons to a meeting at a converted warehouse along West Henderson's Wynd, behind a pub, the syndicate's hiring hall.

"Yous gonnae dae a job fir me, boys," he said expansively. "An hour and a half, mebbe two hours at most. Fifty pound tae each of you."

The young men nodded their assent. Each liked the sound of £50.

"Yer gonnae drive a wee van and be directed by someone not from our group who will ride with yese in between stops on your route."

"What is it we're transporting, Buff?" one of them asked.

"Not yer job tae ken. Yer tae stay in the van at all times, and dae whit yer telt."

Nesbitt's irregulars had needed additional manpower. And they needed people who wouldn't ask questions, who could keep their mouths shut after the job was done, which was where Buff and the Madmen group came in. Ideally (for Nesbitt's men), they'd be people with no political affiliation or understanding. Wilson and the five other young men Buff Lindsey loaned out—for a fee—fit the bill perfectly.

The Madmen syndicate, of which Buff Lindsey was the self-proclaimed shop steward for the Dundee local, acted in many ways like a workers' union, albeit with a twist. Or a bend. They brought on and brought along, young men, training them up, giving them increasingly more responsible, and deplorable, work. They would start as lookouts, drivers and low-level drug distributors. Their ranks and feeder arms came from the upper echelon, if that's the word for it, of Dundee's street gangs. They'd do some collecting, too. Some couldn't hack it, some showed a talent for violence or thieving, some fell to the wayside. Still others were arrested. Indeed, getting nicked was the only certainty in their lives. Which was why, to survive as an organization, they had to be bringing on and grooming the next generation, whose career life expectancy seemed about that of a fruit fly.

Wilson had always been a kind of odd man out. His lack of roots meant he'd never been attached to any of the district gangs in any permanent fashion. This might have led to his not being trusted by those who'd been recruited from those ranks, but his native intelligence, his drive and his affability meant he often seemed able to stand above it all. And he had friends from most of the various street gangs.

The irregulars' deal was straightforward. Lindsey saw there wasn't much upside to trying to horn in on whatever it was these Londoners were after. It wasn't drugs, it wasn't a murder-for-hire, and they didn't appear to be looking to expand territory. It seemed governmental. And corrupt as hell. He wondered idly whether there were any blackmail possibilities in it for him. It never hurt to have something to dangle over an official or a politician.

He knew it had to do with the election and that they were moving something, thus the vans. But that was about the extent of what he knew. The rest he could guess, though he couldn't be certain. This lack of knowledge sat uncomfortably. In what economists call an asymmetrical information environment, he was accustomed to being the one who knew what cards the other players held. But he was blind on this hand. Lindsey approved of the irregulars' careful planning and timing of the various rendezvous, even as the whole thing seemed to be coming together on the fly. That caution would protect him and his boys, but it didn't leave room for much else, or for him to take advantage of.

For the opening of their dealings, he'd decided to appear helpful, maybe a little awed by their southern splendor. They looked like the kind of toffs who'd appreciate that sort of thing. Meanwhile, later, he'd get information from the boys. His boys were to be drivers only, and their ignorance was their insurance, though it occluded his look-in.

"Ah doubt even one ae them's registered tae vote," Lindsey noted cheerfully to his contact. "If that's whit yer worried aboot."

Alan Wilson, unbeknownst even to himself, was to be the key.

The irregulars carried the paperwork forged with Alban's signature, giving them the duty of delivering the ballots. Just as compatriots did across Glasgow. In Dundee, five Ford Transit cargo vans would leave their respective polling places beginning right after the polls closed at 10pm, stopping to pick up ballots at polling places along the way as they headed toward the count centre at Dundee International Sports Centre. But each had one unscheduled stop.

In each of the five vans, as one of the apprentice felons drove, the other man worked feverishly in the back to separate the ballot boxes and update the paperwork so that it would all match when they arrived at the count centre. There was a thin dividing wall between the driver and cargo area, which was all to the good for the irregulars' purpose. Wilson was in a sixth cargo van, and he was meant to wait along Granton Terrace, near Graham Street, less than a mile from the count centre, but in terms of activity, a world away.

Granton Terrace was a quiet street, off East Kingsway, invitingly dark, with an open football ground on one side, and terrace flats on the other. The flat buildings stood back from the street, facing inward at a car park. Not a single window looked toward the street. Tall trees provided good cover on the football pitch side. A high fence surrounded the ground, which meant that Wilson had the place to himself. Election night, Wilson pulled the van under the trees and onto the grass verge on the football ground side a little after 10:30pm, where he turned off the lights. And waited.

Across the country, ballot boxes began arriving at count centres. Across Dundee, the five other vans began weaving their way from polling place to polling place, picking up boxes and setting certain ones to one side in the back. Blind to what was going on, all any of the young drivers would be able to report was that they would arrive at a school or a sports centre, and someone would meet them in the car park. That person would hand over a stack of plastic boxes to the one who rode in back. Once all the boxes were inside the man in back would close the cargo doors and then pound on the divider to move on. They were rarely stopped for more than three minutes before pushing on to the next. Whatever was happening in back, it ran like clockwork.

At 11:15pm the first of the delivery vans arrived at Granton Terrace. It cut its lights as it glided past Wilson before it reversed, putting the vans back-to-back on the verge. Wilson started to get out to help but was told to stay in the van. The first surprise was that unlike the other five vans, Wilson's had no divider. He could see the men loading plastic boxes into the back, though it was dark and he had no idea what the boxes were or what they held. He assumed it was drugs or stolen goods, which was the kind of thing they were used to moving.

"Face forward!" one of them hissed, as Wilson looked backward that first time.

Wilson heard them whispering sharply to one another. "How the fuck did this happen? It exposes everything!" said one.

"Calm down. Let's do the job," said the other. "He doesn't know anything."

Wilson caught the second man's eyes in the rearview mirror. There was a hardness in them that impressed Wilson, who was used to getting the better of those who regarded themselves as hard men. He focused on the road ahead and checked to the sides to make sure no walkers were coming their way. But he never looked back again.

The scenario replayed itself four more times. On the last, one of the men told Wilson to move to the passenger side. He would drive. They sped off toward the center of town. Moments later, as they came to a halt in front of the Maryfield Medical Centre on Clepington Road, the man who was driving said, "Get out. And remember: we know who you are, but you don't know who we are. Keep your mouth shut."

Wilson hopped out. As he slammed the door, he gave the driver a middle finger. The van was gone so fast he couldn't be sure if his valediction had registered. The other boys loitered against a stone wall, some smoking.

"Aye, well that's that," said one of them, pushing himself off the wall.

"Whit de ye think that was all aboot?" Wilson asked.

"Fuck if Ah know. Denna care, either," said Brodie Adair over his shoulder for the benefit of the rest of the group. He made no attempt to hide that he regarded himself as the leader. "Shall we go see Buff, tell him job done? Ah'd like to collect ma fifty pound."

He was a big lad, taller than Wilson, but like him still not grown into his full frame.

"AW-fly decent of you chaps to hang about like this for me," said Wilson in a cod, upper class English accent as he fell in alongside Adair, leading the group. "Warms the cockles, chaps."

They tried to put a bit of swagger into their ambling dander, taking up the entire pavement. But there was no one about to force off the pavement and into the road, so that was a bust. One of them started whistling, and Adair gave him a sharp look. He stopped whistling.

"We were telt tae wait on ye, Alan, and no tae turn up withoot the whole group," said the boy who was no longer whistling. The group menaced aimlessly toward the hiring hall in silence.

As they drew within a few blocks of the hiring hall, Wilson paused and spoke to Adair.

"Does that no seem odd tae ye, Brodie?"

"What?"

"Having to show up all together like this."

Adair shrugged.

"They were all on about how we're no supposed to know anything—the fucks we was driving fae—shouldnae breath a word, like," Wilson pressed.

"Aye."

"Well, who doesnae breath a word? Who tells no tales, Brodie?"

"Dead men!" said one of the boys at the back of the group. He seemed pleased to have given a rare correct answer.

Adair looked at Wilson. "What're you saying?" he asked. "That Buff's is gonnae dae fer us?"

"Ah'm sayin it's odd. Ah'm sayin mebbe we shouldna go in all at once. Mebbe recce the place, like. To be sure."

Adair seemed to want to be angry, insulted on Lindsey's behalf, but he had stopped walking, perhaps not accomplished at doing more than one thing at a time. The whole scruffy gang stopped. They looked back and forth between Wilson and Adair.

"What about this?" Wilson proposed. "As we get there and head doon the wynd tae the back door, we separate into two groups of three. We keep aboot forty or fifty feet apart. The first group walks in and leaves the door open. Buff or someone'll say 'shut the fucking door!' but you or me, or whoever's in the first group will say, 'the others are comin noo.' Wan ae them could make to look out the door. If all seems well inside, the guy wi his heid oot the door says 'Hurry up!' If not, he gives a sign and everyone in that first group scatters. And the rest of you too."

Adair nodded, thinking.

"It might make sense tae have one a yous in the second group hang back and watch the street. Make sure they don't come in behind us. Once we're doon the wynd there's nowhere tae go."

"You really think Buff would—?"

"Ah donnae ken, me. It seems odd, Brodie. Dunnit? Where's the harm in being safe, watching oor backs?"

"Right," Adair said. "Who's in the first group then?"

"Ah'll go. It's me that's worried." Wilson turned to the other boys: "Lexie, Beansie, you wi me?"

"Aye, fair enough," said Beansie, answering for both.

The walk down the wynd to the back room behind the pub seemed to take an age. When they arrived at the door, Wilson looked back at Adair's half of the crew tarrying near the street. He knocked. Alec, the monster who guarded the door opened it and admitted them without a word. Wilson saw that Lindsey was alone, except for his silent, massive high chamberlain. It seemed safe enough, and he felt a little foolish.

"Ah said come all together!" Lindsey roared, seeing only three of them.

"They're comin the noo," said Wilson. "Beansie, tell them tae hurry it up, eh?"

The boss paid them, and offered pints all round, delivered from the pub through a low window in the back wall. Lindsey interviewed each of them separately to glean information, but all he learned were the various routes and times. Later, he seemed to talk a long time with Brodie Adair. An hour later when Wilson made to leave, the boss called him over, indicating he should seat himself at the table across from him.

The boss leaned in conspiratorially and said, "So ye don't trust me, is that it, Alan?"

"It's no that so much, but..."

"Mebbe Ah have ma reasons for wanting things done a certain way. Ye ever think a tha'?"

"Ah did, Buff. And Ah wasnae sure yer reasons and ma reasons weren't in...conflict, shall we say?"

The boss furrowed his brow and looked hard at Wilson.

"Look," Wilson went on, "Ah had a bad feeling aboot whoever that was tonight. They felt like the kinda people who tie off loose ends the hard way."

"And ye thought Ah was in on it?" asked the boss.

"Well..." He wasn't sure how to answer. Wasn't sure whether he was in danger now. But Lindsey leaned back in his chair, breaking the tension. He studied Wilson.

"Never mind the insult, lad," he said after a moment, though it was clear Lindsey wasn't the kind to let a second insult pass. "That's good thinking, that. Yer given an order on a strange, one-off joab, and ye look to yer mates and yerself and try tae see a way out."

"*And* still get paid," Wilson affirmed as he drained the last of his pint.

Lindsey roared with laughter.

Far from being his demise, that night had been the making of Alan Wilson. Adair had been the rising star from their cohort, the natural leader—bigger, harder than anyone else and not bothered about a bit of aggro. But thereafter, jobs leading the line came to Wilson and Adair in equal measure. They had passed their apprenticeships. There could have been a kind of camaraderie between them, having come up together, but Wilson knew that his conversation with Buff Lindsey that night could have gone differently indeed, and he knew Adair was the one who'd shopped him.

Lindsey, for his part, felt a vague dissatisfaction with the night's work. He'd gained nothing but a bit of spare change. He didn't mind it if someone thought of him as a for-hire service. As the local leader of a larger syndicate, he was used to being underestimated. He could often turn it to his further advantage. He had pieced together what had gone on, that it had to do with the Independence referendum, but he wasn't quite sure whom he could extort. He'd learn nothing further out of that night's transaction, and he agreed with young Wilson's assessment that they seemed able and willing to tie off loose ends "the hard way." Wilson remembered that night well, as did Adair, but each in their own way, and for different reasons. Adair had hoped to cut Wilson out, an able, canny rival. But now in the boss's eyes, he was a bit of a grass.

Wilson had long since stopped thinking about what might have been in those boxes he saw away back in 2014. In the long list of things he'd moved, removed, or "liberated" in the intervening years it registered as barely a ripple in his memory. He'd have been stunned to find out that Nesbitt and the irregulars had kept him under surveillance for months after election night. Indeed, until two days earlier, when he'd been photographed with Ewan Johnston, he'd been graded "non-rev."

25

"There was another break-in at my office," Johnston said to Imogen over the phone. "Much more subtle than the first time. The only reason we know is that it looks like a couple of files that were locked away were left out."

"Maybe your clerk forgot?" She tried to coax a hopeful tone into her voice.

"No. He doesn't make mistakes like that. I might have considered his carelessness as a possibility, but it looks like they broke into our computer. I'm worried they planted something there."

"Jesus, Ewan," said Imogen. She sat in Wee Frankie's cramped office, the door open, alert to every sound from the hallway.

"I'm worried about you," he said.

"You're worried about me?"

"I am. I'm fine. I switched out the hard-drive after the first break-in, so if they've planted something there to discredit me or make it look like I've done something illegal, I can prove it wasn't on there as of October 9th. But I have that drive here at my house. Alan said they were circling, and that they wouldn't circle forever. I think they're preparing for something."

"What do you have in mind, Ewan?"

"We need to go somewhere we can think. Somewhere that we're not always looking over our shoulders, where you and I can have a full review of the evidence and think about how to present it."

"Sure," she said. "But where?"

181

"My parents had a wee house up in Alyth, north of here. My brother and I still hold title to it. It's two bedrooms," he added quickly. "I'm not suggesting..."

"No, of course," she stammered.

"Not like a getaway," he added, still pressing the point. "But a place to, you know, get away. Have a think, withoot the wolves circling."

"Sounds like a good idea. But how do I get there?"

"Ah'd fetch ye," he said.

"Come to Glasgow?"

"I don't see how you could get here without showing our hand," he said. "I thought about you mebbe taking the train and getting off in Perth. But I don't think it could work. I'll come collect you, and then we go north back to Alyth."

"I've never heard of Alyth," said Imogen.

"No, you wouldn't have, probably, it's wee. Unless you're a fan of the poet James Young Geddes, lover and lasher of Dundee?"

"Wait," she said, "that horrible poet who's so bad he's good?"

"That's William McGonagall. Another Dundonian."

"Then I'm not familiar," Imogen began.

"But you *do* know McGonagall?" he asked, incredulous.

"Only by er, reputation," she rejoined.

"'The Spectre Clock of Alyth' by Geddes?" he asked. "Nothing? Well, we've a copy at the house. It'll be required reading."

"If McGonagall was required reading, I might take my chances with the bad guys," she quipped.

"Lovely. Okay, we'll meet up tomorrow morning. I'm thinking Alan could run interference here, so's I can get away. I'll make like I'm going to work, lose them—God help me—and then come for you. You lose whatever watchers you've got by no later than 8:30, 'cause after I make a run for it, they'll be on you right quick."

"Got it," she said. "And you'll have that hard drive with you?"

"Aye. Call me when you're somewhere safe. Somewhere you can wait for an hour or more. It'll take me 90 minutes to get to you. And you should work out a Plan 'B' in case I fail."

The thought of a Plan B, and what it implied chilled Imogen. If Ewan felt protective of her, she certainly felt that way about him. People she cared for ended up casualties in her skirmishes. Marta Serres was the latest. It still wasn't clear whether Marta would be deported or not. Marta's husband had warned her off, and as she considered the situation she saw the sense in it. She couldn't do anything but make it worse.

She collected her things and went home, where she double-checked everything she'd need. She saved the election data from her laptop onto two thumb drives, one for her trouser pocket, one she would wind into her hair bun the next morning. The first backup, in her pocket, might serve as a decoy if she was captured and searched. She stuffed a couple pairs of undies into the bottom of her messenger bag.

In Dundee, Johnston prepared himself, though he took care not to be seen carrying anything out of the ordinary. He had the data—the scant evidence—on his laptop and on a thumb drive. All in the shoulder bag he carried everywhere.

He put in a call to Wilson.

"If we're lucky, Ah expect tomorrow will go as it has the last few days," said Wilson. "Ah hate getting surprises. Though Ah don't mind giving them."

"I'll drive up Ward Road like I always do," Johnston began, "and park across the street from my office right there in front of the Dundee Baptist Church."

"Aye," said Wilson.

"And I'll go straight in."

"Fine," said Wilson. "Do everythin as you would on a normal day. And if the watchers work tae form, they'll arrive two minutes or so behind ye, see ye goin in. And they'll park a wee bit past your car, taking up a position a little farther down the road, the better to follow ye when ye leave."

"And they're always there?"

"Aye, even when you use that private car park on Rattray Street, cause they know it's one-way around that "U" of streets behind yer building."

"And they stay there all day?" Johnston asked.

"Naw, they'll get spelled after about two hours. Another car'll park and the first one will leave."

"Are they ever there together?"

"Ah've never seen em together. Except at the handoff. That could make things difficult. Putting it lightly," he added. "But in any case, that never happens until ten o'clock or so. And Ah'll be waiting and watching everything in a van down by Howff Cemetery. As soon as the watchers take up their position, Ah'll move forward and park where Ah can block them later when you come out and head for the hills."

"Good," said Johnston.

"Hey. Do ye think Ah should plow intae em? A wee fender-bender, like? Ah'd love tae have a go at them." He chuckled down the line. "Or would ye counsel against it?"

Johnston laughed himself. "Yes, that's exactly the legal advice I'd give you."

Next morning, in Glasgow, Imogen stepped through a misting rain on her well-worn, if sodden, path through Kelvingrove Park to the university. Her tail, one of Percy's buskers, maintained a distance that allowed him to keep her in view, but far enough away as to be indistinct himself, an intermittent form in a shifting mist. She knew he was there, which was enough. She didn't bother to look back, even as she strained to hear any quickening of his pace.

Her FBI training served her well, and she also paid attention to what was happening in front of her. Too often, agents worried about what was behind them, to the exclusion of what might lie ahead. It wouldn't do to worry so much about what was happening behind that she ran blindly into a trap. Today of all days.

From past experience and observation, Imogen knew that the man who followed her through Kelvingrove had a partner, already at the building. The partner generally waited in a car along Bute Gardens on the east side of the Adam Smith Building, a narrow road with parking spaces reserved for handicap licenses. If things went typically, the one who had tailed her from the park would get into the car to warm up, and they would drive around to the north side of the building together, to the parking spots on the west side.

During which time, she'd have two minutes. Maybe. She reached campus and hurried toward the building.

Inside the building, she paused on the stairs, pretending to look for something in her bag. From the corner of her eye, as she pretended to dig through her bag, she saw her watcher come into view and then walk out of sight, presumably toward where his partner waited in the car. Though she couldn't see what was happening, it seemed that their routine was playing itself out.

With her pursuer now out of sight, she turned and walked down the stairs. As she did so, she pulled an olive-drab rain shawl from her pack, and dragged it on over her head and coat. She tucked her red hair into the hood and pushed through the glass doors. The two watchers in the car would be headed away from her momentarily, before coming around the building from the north, to the very side she was coming out of now. As she stepped through the glass doors onto the wet pavement, she steeled herself not to look back. If they were already rounding the north side of the building, that might give her away.

She darted to the steps, her anorak flapping after her, and headed down along the path that led toward a narrow lane running between the Queen Margaret Union and the Sir Alexander Stone building. She took a clearing breath as she approached it and quickened her pace as she stepped into the lane, a confined space with high walls to either side. There was no one else about. If they were onto her, this would be the perfect place to take her. It felt like a damned cattle chute. She broke into a run.

Having reached the far end of the chute with no visible damage, she slowed her pace again and continued down to University Gardens, made her way along Ashton Lane and out toward Byres Road and the Hillhead Subway stop. It was 8:25am, and she was prepared to ride the loop for as long as it took. She knew that a complete circuit took 24 minutes. She was going to be down there a while, and she made sure that she changed from the inner to the outer circle from time to time, making sure to stay clear of Hillhead station. She'd looked at Ewan's probable route from Dundee to Glasgow, and when he called she could offer to meet him at either St George's Cross or Cowcadden stations. If he called. She was supposed to have a Plan B, but where else could she go that wouldn't alert the conspirators? To leave the island, she'd have to show her passport, which would give her away. Renting a car was also out. She hoped that Ewan would deliver.

But Ewan Johnston's escape went anything but smoothly. Ward Road was an old street, with sandstone buildings pressed close to the road. And it was deserted at this time of morning.

At 8:20, Alan Wilson and his big white van, on loan from Buff Lindsey, pulled into a parking space next to Howff Cemetery. He left the engine idling. Idle was how he felt, and he hated that feeling. His blood was up, too. He hoped that these bampots tried something. He was more than ready. He'd made his name in the Madmen syndicate through his intelligence, subtlety and patience. But that patience had a limit. He hated all this sneaking around, and he was frustrated that he hadn't been able to turn the tables on them. The solicitor deserved better from him.

A cellphone rested on his thigh, connected with Johnston. "Ah'm there," he said aloud.

"I'm on my way now," he heard Johnston reply.

Seven minutes later, Johnston's silver BMW glided by and pulled into a parking spot a hundred yards or so past where Wilson had set up. Wilson watched Johnston get out and cross the street to his building. Less than two minutes later the dark blue Skoda the watchers used rolled by and took up its place in the parking strip a little past the BMW.

"They've arrived," said Wilson. "And it's the regular two, Sausage and Egg," he added, giving the nicknames he had for

Nesbitt's pair of irregulars. Eggy was driving. Wilson put the van in gear and inched forward to a new spot closer to where he could block in the Skoda when the time came.

There were parked cars between him and the Skoda, but Wilson could see them well enough from his high vantage point in the van. Idiots, he thought. He had seen these two multiple times on past forays while he watched Johnston's back, mundane, always paired together in the morning. They were porcine thick, and not half so clever. It was a good job the street was pretty much deserted at this time of day, or they'd have been made easily.

They just *looked* like they were up to no good. There was something about the curve of the shoulders, the downcast glare that seethed menace. Wilson would never have accepted this level of obvious malicious intent from someone working for him, he thought. Where was a cop when you needed one? As he stared forward, hating and pitying them in equal measure, it almost seemed like they were looking back at him.

"You're good tae go," Wilson said into the phone resting on his lap. A moment later, Johnston popped out of his office and jogged across the road to his car. Though he looked back at Wilson, he made no sign. To the men in the Skoda, it would have looked like he was checking traffic.

Inside the Skoda, Wilson saw activity as they prepared to follow Johnston. He put the van in gear. As Johnston put on his turn signal and moved into traffic, Wilson also pulled out, gathering speed so he could block the Skoda as Johnston passed it. Johnston's car drew away as Wilson came up next to the watchers.

Right before Wilson came level with them, the Skoda turned hard out of the parking space and rammed into the side of the van, ahead of his front left tire. Sausage, on the passenger-side, began lumbering out. Now, so did the driver. Who reached for the locked door of the van, as another van rammed Wilson from behind, on the right, in front of the tire, wedging him between them.

Wilson's impression of the next twenty seconds—and that's all there would be—was of time slowing down, of a noiseless calm. He realized with dismay that somehow *he* was the target and not Johnston. And that he was pinned down and outnumbered. Ahead of him, he saw Johnston's BMW driving away and turning a corner. Well, good for him at least.

Wilson hit the accelerator hard, turning the wheel one way and then the other. But the two cars holding him didn't budge. In quick succession Sausage bashed a hammer against Wilson's passenger side window, while someone from the van that had rammed into his back also struck his driver's side window with a hammer. Glass exploded over him.

To his left, Sausage was about to open his passenger side door, while next to him someone stood on the running board step and reached in for him. With his left hand, Wilson flicked open a switchblade. He reached across himself and stabbed the blade into the eye of the man trying to open his door. He fell backward into the street, clutching his face and bleeding mightily, just as the passenger door opened and Sausage clambered across the seat toward him. Wilson lunged at him stabbing him under the armpit. The knife broke off inside him.

Which meant he'd disarmed himself. Wilson could see the man screaming, could see pain and fear on his face. But he heard nothing. Blood gushed across the seat and onto the floor, but he heard nothing. In his bloody hand, Wilson thought the nub of the broken blade made it look like he held a carpet cutter knife. Well, those still work for something.

A new face showed itself in the broken window next to him, and he stabbed what was left of the blade into its cheek. He raked it across his face as the man twisted away, slicing through his ear. On the passenger side, Eggy was having difficulty dragging Sausage's bulk out of the way so he could climb in, and the one he'd cut had recovered and was opening the driver's side door.

Wilson kicked his heel into the door, knocking Scarface onto his back in the road. He twisted and jumped out, making sure both feet landed on him. In one quick motion, he gave

Scarface a swift kick under the chin as he skipped away to prepare for whatever came next.

Which was: Eggy hopping between the car and van to rush Wilson, while at the same time the driver of the van that had smashed into him climbed out the passenger door. There was a gun in his hand. He thought to grab Eggy and use him as a shield. But how long would that last? After the first shot, how long could he hold up that bag of guts?

As Alan moved toward Eggy, Johnston's car came roaring out of the side street. He braked hard and threw the wheel over, his back end fishtailing into the van driver, crushing him between the car and van.

Eggy froze, stunned, as Johnston sped toward Wilson, narrowly missing the two bodies on the ground. Johnston screeched to a halt and threw open the door. Wilson dived in, and they were off.

"Well fuck *that*!" Wilson roared as he pulled the door fully closed and gathered himself in the seat. "Thanks, pal. Ah saw ye turning and thought, 'Well, at least *he* got away.' But you turned down Rattray Street, eh? Made the loop in record time."

"Ah looked in the rearview," said Johnston, "and saw aw that carry on. I couldna leave ye there, now, could Ah?"

Wilson gave Johnston a friendly tap on the shoulder with his fist. "Right, slow down now, counselor. We're away. Let's not draw any undue attention."

"Right," said Johnston. He looked in the rearview mirror as he took a deep breath and eased up on the accelerator. Clear behind them. He flexed and opened his hands around the steering wheel.

"Turn here," Wilson instructed. "We're gonnae have tae ditch this car. Ah'm sure it's been seen, and Ah think ye've lost the left rear fender. We wouldney make it two miles. Slow now," he repeated soothingly. "Take yer time. Turn here, and then a quick left."

"Do you think I killed him?" Johnston asked. "The one I hit?"

"Ah fuckin hope so!" said Wilson. He paused, realizing how shaken Johnston seemed. "But ye canny be sure ae they things. He was holdin a gun, and he meant ta kill me."

Johnston nodded.

"Ah feel like Ah've seen him before, the one wi the pistol," said Wilson. "Ugly pus, that one."

"Probably during your surveillance?" said Johnston absently.

"Mebbe. But Ah denna think so." His voice trailed off. "Turn here, down this wee road. Very slow. Right, tap yer horn four times quick."

They were now in a part of Dundee Johnston hadn't been to in ages. Was he still *in* Dundee? He didn't recognize the streets, and he'd been so distracted he couldn't have said how they'd arrived there. Ahead of them, a low, brick building with a metal roll door stood directly in front as they glided down a narrow street between two seemingly derelict warehouses,

"Four quick taps," Wilson reminded him.

He did so. "Where are we?"

"Chop shop. Ah'll get ye a good price for the Beemer."

"What?"

"Ah'm only kiddin on," he laughed.

Johnston realized he was bathed in sweat.

"But it *is* a chop shop, counselor."

The roll door opened and a young man with wild ginger hair about Wilson's age looked quizzically at the car. Wilson rolled down his window and leaned his head out. "Just me, Lexie," he said. He threw a quick look at Johnston sitting dismally in the driver's seat and added jocularly, "And guest."

26

It was a metaphor for her life, she thought bleakly as she sat in the subway underneath Glasgow. Round and round, never getting anywhere. Meaningless stops, haphazard breakdowns. Her fellow riders seemed to feel it too, gazing downward, or staring a little over someone's head—no eye contact—rushing to God-knew-what, their thoughts inward. The subway cars themselves reminded her a bit of the Seattle Monorail, their designs nodding toward an aspirational 'sixties aesthetic, created for a bright and orderly future that had never been. Like the Monorail, the short trains with their blunted heads looked like caterpillars. You half expected to see them undulate into the station.

But remembering Seattle brought back thoughts of Duncan Calder, and their future that had never been. Had it been a mistake to resurrect him like this, trying to feel somehow closer to him by sharing the city with his ghost?

She should never have become involved, she accused herself. Damn Ian Ross! It was her misplaced fidelity to Duncan, she reasoned more soberly, that had brought this all on: but for her snooping, Wee Frankie would still be alive, as would Donald Alban. Marta Serres would be doing research and taking care of her children, rather than fretting over her—and their—future. Yes, Marta's husband was right. She'd done more than enough. And now here she was again, grappling with something bigger than her, something elusive that she couldn't pin down. And she was once again about to go into hiding.

Ewan Johnston was a bright spot in her thoughts. He seemed an open book but difficult to read for all that, written in a language in which she wasn't quite fluent. He was doing what he thought was right for the memory of his friend and mentor, but he kept his other emotions close. It worried her how deeply she cared about his safety.

In the chop shop, Wilson asked Johnston to wait in the office while he took care of a little business. "And, counselor, try not to notice anything," he said with a wink.

"I couldn't even tell you how we got here," he replied.

"That's the way," affirmed Wilson. "Ah'm sure there's some whisky about, d'ye fancy a wee bit? You look like you could use a brace-up."

Johnston shook his head, no. "Water?"

Wilson pushed some chairs out of the way and bent down to open a small, square fridge, full of Tennent's lager cans. One, battered plastic bottle of water rested in the door rack. Wilson opened it and sniffed it carefully before passing it to Johnston. Then took his leave.

Johnston pulled out his phone and stared at it. He needed to call Imogen, needed to let her know there'd been a setback, and that he'd be late. A "setback?" Is that what he'd tell her had happened? Two men—at least—were probably dead. There were three crashed vehicles, the car and two vans, blocking Ward Road. He'd had to swerve to avoid running over one of them. The city would need a fire brigade truck to hose away all the blood. He'd driven through it like it was puddle, and he shuddered now, remembering the viscous, glaur-like splatters along the lower left side of his car when he'd stepped out.

Those men were after Alan. Why him? None of it made sense.

He hoped she was safe. The quickest way to find out, of course, was to call, but he tarried, staring at the phone. Was she alive? Dead? Captured? After what had happened in front of his office, he feared the worst. Making the call would reveal all, but still he sat, paralyzed in a Schrodinger's dilemma.

Wilson had sneaked over to the hiring hall to let Lindsey know what had happened. Lindsey was incandescent with rage—less that some of the attackers might have died, and more that one of his own had been a target.

"Boss, it was self-defense. Ah swear. It'd all come out, but frankly, Ah'd never make it to the trial. Somehow, some government thingy Ah've been helping ma old solicitor with— on ma own time," he added quickly—"has turned deadly."

"Whit kind of governmental *thingy*?" the boss wanted to know.

"Ah didny ask, and he hasny said. He was bein followed, and he didny know who it was."

"Did ye find out?"

"No."

Lindsey wanted all the details up to that point, and Wilson told what he knew, about the break-in at Johnston's office, how there hadn't been a peep about it through any of his contacts; about the surveillance, the second, quiet break-in. And now the attack.

"And yer sure they were after you?" he asked when Wilson was done.

"No question in ma mind. And there's somethin else. Ah'd swear Ah'd seen one before."

"Like another outfit?"

"No. Somethin else." He stared off, trying to fix it in his mind, but nothing would come.

"How many dead?" the boss wanted to know.

"Two by me, and a third by the solicitor."

Lindsey smiled. "Yer gonnae need a new solicitor, Ah think. Sounds like he'll need one an all."

"Honestly, Buff, the way this is playin out, we'd never make it to trial. We'd be murdered in the cells."

Throughout Wilson's story, Lindsey had been tasking some of the others around him to gather information corroborating Wilson's story. Now, a man walked up to him and shook his head. He handed Lindsey his phone. "Ye might be right aboot it bein a governmental thingy," Lindsey said to

Wilson. "As bloody as you say, but there's naught about it anywhere?" He turned the phone to face Wilson. "The only news from Ward Road's a report about a fender-bender incident that turned intae a fracas. The drivers were aw taken ta hospital."

"Ah don't think it's another outfit."

"Ah'm inclined tae agree wi ye, Alan."

Johnston had mastered his fear and made the phone call.

"You nearby?" Imogen asked brightly.

"I'm no'. Ah'm that sorry, Imogen."

"What's happened? Are you all right?"

"For now, yes," he said, his calm returning. It was good to hear her voice. "Are you somewhere safe?"

"I guess," she said. "I've spent the last hour in the Glasgow subway."

"Jesus, wumman, Ah asked if ye were somewheres *safe*!" he said playfully. More seriously, he told her what had happened.

"Jesus," she whispered. "Why Alan, though?"

"We're all wondering. Alan included. It makes no sense. Anyway, I think we stick to plan. Alan's talking with his boss right now. I'm going to suggest he come along. We all need to be lost for a while. I'll call from the road. Where do you want to meet?"

"I'd thought somewhere near either the St George's Cross or Cowcadden stations. I looked at the map, and that looks like the easiest place for you—you can jump off and then straight back on the highway."

"St. George's Cross then," he said. "Not Cowcadden."

"Bad area?"

"No. Just kinda exposed. Wide streets, no cafs—not near the station anyway. There's some pubs and cafes along Great Western Road near St. George's though. Pick one and stay there. Call and tell me which one you're at."

"Okay," she said. "I'll stay down here till I hear you're on the road, and then I'll head out. I'll call you back when I'm settled someplace."

In London, Jamie Frenz delivered the report of the botched snatch-and-grab to Percy and only then transmitted the details to Chamberlain.

"I put a radio silence order over all of it," said Frenz. "I hope that was correct."

"Well done," said Percy. "I'll get on to the DI in charge."

"Here are his details," Frenz noted efficiently. "I figured that was the next step."

"Excellent," said Percy. He scanned the report, astonished. "What about our boys, the buskers?"

"Per orders, they were observing, hanging back when it all started. They were able to rush in and control the scene. It's locked down pretty well. The story for the Dundee police is that it was an MI5 smash-and-grab that went awry—counter-terrorism. Details on a need-to-know basis, and the local cops'll know they don't rank. For the papers, we've put it out that it's a fender-bender that went bad."

"Fine," Percy said. "And our witness, the driver—he got away?"

"He did."

"Any thoughts on where? Did our men see anything?"

"Nothing, sir. Their first priority was containment."

"Of course, of course."

"I thought these men were professionals!" Chamberlain thundered.

"They …were." Nesbitt began.

"How many dead?" asked Chamberlain.

"Three out of five," said Nesbitt bleakly. "He had help," he added, as though that explained everything. "Wilson killed two outright and knocked our leader out of commission for a few days, maybe longer. The solicitor he was protecting doubled back and took out another."

"Good God!" said Townsend, who looked like he thought he should make a contribution.

"And the FBI Agent has vanished, too?" asked Weaver.

"Yes," said Chamberlain. "I suggest we recall the boys in Glasgow and have them recombine with what's left of our assets in Dundee. We'll still be short a man, won't we? And we've lost the element of surprise."

"One of our men seems to have died instantly," Nesbitt carried on, still focused on the deaths of their operatives. "The other two bled out at the scene."

"How do we know so much?" asked Weaver.

"Percy's men were first on the scene," said Chamberlain.

"And didn't help!" Nesbitt hissed.

"They were meant to be observers," Chamberlain said, "and they had no foreknowledge of what your men were going to do."

"Our men!" Nesbitt emphasized, needing to hang together rather than separately.

"Yes, quite," said Chamberlain. "*Our* men. According to Percy's buskers as he calls them, and your own man, it was over in less than a minute." He handed Weaver his phone. "If we get another chance, it'll have to be heavy."

Weaver scrolled through images from the scene, taken by Percy's men. "It's a good job they were there," he offered, "or we'd have never gained control of the narrative."

"Indeed," Chamberlain said.

"Will that hold?" Weaver asked, as he passed the phone to Nesbitt, who didn't look but thrust it toward Townsend. "Two stories—one for the cops and one for the press?"

"I think so," Chamberlain averred.

"Gad, what a mess!" Townsend commented, though it wasn't clear whether he referred to the operation in general or to the sticky job public works would have reopening the Ward Road.

It had been simple to convince Wilson to come along. He didn't show it, but he was rattled. He'd done any number of illegal things, but he'd never killed anyone before. As they rolled down the M-9 south of Stirling through intermittent sun breaks, Johnston had called Imogen. She met them along the Great Western Road, piled into the car and they retraced their steps through low-slung countryside as far as Perth before turning north toward Alyth.

"So, d'ye have a gun wi ye right now?" Wilson asked straightaway when she climbed in. He was driving, and she had seated herself in the back, behind Ewan.

"No," she replied, clicking her seatbelt, "I don't carry a gun. Back home I'm required to carry it all times, but here I'm not allowed."

Imogen had thought it was merely a prudent question, given the circumstances, but it turned out to be the first salvo in a barrage of questions about the FBI and America. As they drove, Imogen feigned an enthusiastic preoccupation with the view, but Wilson wouldn't be deterred. He seemed to have stored a lifetime's worth of questions. The stunning green of the lowlands, running from horizon to horizon under sullen skies, was beautiful and gave her something to think about in between Wilson's interrogation. For his part, Johnston sat quietly in the front passenger seat.

"Does everyone carry a gun in America?"

"No," she said. "The large numbers you hear about are because many of those who do own them have multiple guns."

"So, what does the FBI do?" he wanted to know. "Ah mean, ye've got sheriffs—which is brilliant!" he laughed. "Ye've go the polis..."

"And State Police," added Imogen, still looking out the window.

"But yese're at the top, like. The FBI, Ah mean."

"We like to think so," she chuckled.

"Whit does that mean?"

From the corner of her eye, she could see Ewan growing fidgety at all the questions from Wilson.

"There are multiple jurisdictions within the United States..." she began.

"So, like those films where the bad guy runs across a bridge intae another state to get away from some lawman, that's real?"

"No," she said. "Typically, jurisdictions that abut one another have pursuit and arrest agreements in place to avoid that sort of thing."

"Pity," said Wilson. "But whit d'ye mean the FBI's not at the top?"

"Alan, for fuck's sake, give it a rest, would ye?" said Johnston.

"Aye, fine," he said. Looking quickly back at Imogen, he raised his eyebrows and indicated Johnston with a flick of his head, as if to say, "some people, eh?"

Johnston glowered out the side window.

The sky grew darker, and though the fields reaching out to either side of the road seemed flat, Imogen couldn't shake the feeling that they were headed inexorably uphill. She was sorry that they would come to Alyth in darkness. She was intrigued to see the place Ewan came from, to see his house. She wondered how much of the town she'd be able to see, wondered how long they'd be safe there. It was Ewan's parents' home they were going to. He had said that he and his brother still owned it together. Which was the kind of detail that those who were after them—whoever they were exactly—would look for. And if they were in government, they'd certainly have access to tax records.

After some miles of silence, Wilson caught Imogen's eye in the rearview mirror.

"What's a Pop-Tart anyway?" he asked.

27

They arrived in Alyth a little after 4:30 that afternoon.

"Slow," said Johnston, as they approached the village center. "And now real slow, here, right onto David Street."

Imogen was a little unnerved. David Street was narrow, like something out of the eighteenth century, with low houses wedged against each other. Her mind flashed back to the alleyway she'd had to pass through on campus. This felt only slightly less like a kill chute. She glanced out the rear window and up at the dark windows in the houses crowding the road.

"Pull over here," said Johnston. "Park on top of the curb."

Wilson pulled over.

"No," said Johnston. "*On* the curb, or no other cars will be able tae pass." Wilson dutifully drove the two right wheels over the curb onto the pavement. "That's us there," he said, pointing at a house across from them. They climbed out, and Imogen stood in the road as Johnston and Wilson pulled some things from the boot of the car. The air was cold and damp. She could feel the fog growing thicker around her.

Johnston turned and looked up and down the street. Nothing moved. "I belong to the things of yesterday," he said to Imogen.

"What?"

"From the first stanza of the poem," he explained.

"Oh," she replied, distracted, trying to sight the exits should that become necessary.

Wilson slammed the boot shut.

"The Spectre Clock poem," Johnston continued. "It enjoins the citizens of Alyth to wake up and realize it's the end of the nineteenth century; that they're living in the past." Johnston looked round again. "I think we still might be." He flashed that kooky grin he had, and Imogen smiled back. Wilson caught their exchange and smiled at something himself.

They trooped across to his family home.

"That's all ye brought, hen?" Wilson asked Imogen, as Johnston closed and locked the door behind them.

"I have the things I need," she said. "And I didn't want to make it look like I was planning on going away."

He nodded.

"You can have my parents' old room," Johnston said to her. "It's through here," he said indicating the way. "Alan and I'll share my and my brother's old room."

"Don't worry about me, counselor," Wilson began, amused. "If you and—"

"No, that's fine," Johnston interrupted. "Nothing like that, Alan. Through here, Imogen," he said, blushing.

It was a small house, dark, a bit drab and quiet, the kind of silence where you expected to be able to hear a clock ticking on another floor. A standard two-up, two-down configuration. The back room was a tiny, tidy kitchen, and the front, where they stood, was a combined dining and sitting room. Imogen tried to imagine Ewan's parents, living out their lives here. Looking at the small space she tried to imagine what it would have been like sharing it with two sons rampaging about. Did Ewan rampage, she wondered? A television so old it might be a museum piece rested on a low bookcase against one wall.

Imogen followed him upstairs, a little disappointed she wouldn't be sleeping in Ewan's old room. She felt it might give her that bit more insight into him. She told herself she'd have to take a look at some point. Would there be movie posters on the wall, pop stars? Or maybe a few football heroes she wouldn't recognize.

They each took a few moments to go upstairs and drop whatever they'd brought and get settled. When Imogen returned to the sitting room, she found Wilson and Johnston sitting quietly. Both gazed toward the windows.

"There's a pretty good chip shop about three blocks away," Johnston said finally. "Anyone *not* fancy a fish supper?" he asked. "Alan, would you make some tea? Everything's in the kitchen."

"I'd be happy to make the tea," said Imogen.

Ewan and Alan exchanged a doubtful look. "Ah'm on it," said Alan, as Ewan made for the door.

Sensing a rebuke, Imogen shouted at Johnson, "And see if you can find any Pop Tarts for breakfast while you're out."

He paused and turned back round. "I was hoping you'd come with me," he said.

As they walked up the main road in gathering darkness, Imogen looked back. "It's like the fog's following us," she said. "Is there a river near here?"

"That's the Alyth Burn running behind the house," he said. "No river, but the fog rises off it and seeps up through the streets. This won't be a thick one," he added, looking about and gauging the air. "It's too cold out."

"It looks like a cozy place to grow up," she said, glancing around as they reached the High Street.

"It was that. My school was over there." He pointed across the road. "My mother was a teacher there." As an afterthought, he added, "Sometimes a little too cozy, if you know what I mean."

"I do. Everyone knows everything about you. It's hard to grow. People see you as one thing, and that's all you'll ever be in their eyes."

"Sounds like you know it pretty well," he said.

"I'm from a small town myself. Ripley, Ohio—just across the Ohio River from Kentucky."

Johnston chuckled. "The mighty Ohio? Well, our shallow rill may be somewhat disappointing."

They walked along in silence for some time. Presently, shining out of the fog, the chip shop came into view.

"They do a fried Mars bar here, served with ice cream," he said. "Have you had it?"

"Like battered and deep fried?" she asked.

"Exactly."

"And it's good?"

"You've no lived till ye've tried it."

"All right," said Imogen gamely.

Seen through the glass front, the stout woman in her late forties with the small, hard mouth and bobbed, salt-and-pepper hair didn't so much greet Imogen as deign to acknowledge her. Her expression, flat, to the point, looked as though she wished she could tell Imogen that they were closed. But her aspect softened at the sight of Johnston.

"Ewan Johnston!" she exclaimed. "Where've you been keeping yourself? How long's it been?"

"Too long, Jenny," said Johnston. "This is a friend, Imogen Trager. Imogen, this is Jenny Dixon. Imogen's all the way from America to try your wares," he announced.

"Ah didn't know we were on the tourism circuit," she responded. "But it explains the hundreds and hundreds of orders we're sending out now." She looked back at the pass-through window where the kid manning the fryer leaned against a back wall and studied his phone. Feeling everyone staring at him, he looked up. His mouth twisted, but it seemed he couldn't be bothered with making a grimace. He returned to whatever was happening on his phone.

"The works, Jen," said Johnston lavishly. "Three fish suppers and three fried Mars bars. With ice-cream, if you please."

"It's your money, Ewan," said Jenny ruefully, "but Ah don't see this one even finishing one whole supper." She looked Imogen up and down, not unkindly. "Ah mean, where would she put it? And here you are ordering *three*? Is your wee brother here as well?"

"Naw," he said, "it's jist another pal ae mine up from Dundee. We're only biding for a day or two."

As they walked back to the house, steam rising from the damp bag mingled with the thickening fog. Imogen was worried about how much she'd be able to eat. She didn't want to give offense. But Jenny hadn't been wrong. She'd seen the portions as they were heaped into the containers.

"We're going to have to be careful," she said. "Everyone knows you. If those thugs learn about the house through tax records or something, they won't have to case it to see if we're here. They'll ask 'Seen Ewan lately?' at the chip shop or the grocery store, or the bakery...or the gas station."

"Yer no wrong there. Ah just thought a day or two to gather ourselves. Think our way through, ye know."

Imogen nodded.

"And we need to understand why they tried to kill—or at least kidnap—Alan."

"Yeah," she said. "What's his story?"

"I've known him for some time. Seven, eight years. Maybe a little more."

"Like a family friend?"

"No," said Johnston smiling. "As a client."

"I see."

"He's hooked in with the Madmen syndicate, but he'd done—or had been *accused* of doing," Johnston added judiciously—"a little fencing of stolen goods."

"But he was innocent?" she asked.

"The jury found him not guilty. Yes."

"You're being lawyerly again," she observed.

"And young Alan has reason to thank me for it."

"Someone might say he's a petty thief?"

"Petty's hardly the word for it. For someone so young, he's in charge of a lot. Allegedly," he added with a grin.

"You do work for this Madmen gang?"

"No. Never," he said. "I'd done some work for a mate of Alan's, and on that mate's recommendation Alan called me up when he was nicked. I'm assuming he was freelancing because none of the attorneys on retainer to the Madmen—we all know who they are—were engaged for him."

"So did he do it?"

"My job is to give my client the best possible defense. Which I did."

"You didn't ask," said Imogen.

"I didn't ask. I liked him," Johnston offered. "He seemed the kind of bright, enterprising young person we're always told that we should be on the lookout for. In a good way." Johnston went quiet for a moment before continuing: "He's no sociopath. I expect he's done some pretty sordid things, but I have the feeling there's more to him than all that. He came up pretty hard. No father around, his mother was a drug addict. Died of an overdose when he was 14."

"Jesus."

"I expect Buff Lindsey—the local chapter crime boss—is the closest thing to a father he's had. Sort of a Fagin character."

"And he's Oliver Twist?"

"Maybe more Charley Bates, the Artful Dodger's mate," Johnston reflected.

"And who are you to him, some kindly, wealthy relative, who arrives late in the story and fixes everything?"

"I'm afraid the metaphor rather breaks down there," he said before adding, "And Ah'm skint intae the bargain."

Imogen nodded, though she had only a vague idea what he meant.

"How does this work, Ewan?" she asked. "There seem to be a couple of Scottish accents."

"More than a couple," he averred.

"I mean, most of the time I understand you completely. But other times, I really don't know what you're saying."

Johnston smiled and shrugged.

"You speak like most of my colleagues at the university," she continued. "There's a definite brogue or whatever you call it, and maybe some words I'm unfamiliar with. But when I listen to Alan..."

"Right, he's Dundee through-and-through. Very similar to Gem Diamond and tha' McTavish we interviewed," he said. "D'ye want me tae start subtitling for you?"

Imogen laughed. "It's that sometimes you sound like them, too."

"The different registers, you mean?"

"If that's what you call it."

"There's a sort of home-and-friends way of talking," said Johnston, "and then there's professional. And class can have something to do with it as well."

"Is that what you mean about 'more than couple accents?'"

"Well, not only that. You're probably used to hearing the Glasgow and West of Scotland accent where you've been living. But anyone from Dundee knows Ah'm not fae Dundee the second Ah open ma mouth." He winked. "Or from the west for that matter. And certainly not Edinburgh."

"And every town has its own accent?"

"Sometimes neighborhoods have their own. It's the same down south—Yorkshire, Geordie, Scouse...all different. All of them mark you."

"Mark you?" she asked.

"As either in or out."

They had turned onto David Street, almost back to the house, when she stopped. "How sordid, Ewan?" she asked. "You said you thought Alan had done his share of sordid, illegal things. I want to understand who we're relying on. Murder?"

Johnston shook his head. "I doubt it, but I don't know."

"And why would the government want him out of the way?"

"Let's hope he can tell us," said Johnston.

With the ranks of irregulars depleted by the failed attack, Chamberlain instructed Calum Percy to redirect his buskers to Dundee. Together, with the irregulars moved up from Glasgow, they would make an assault force of six. Though as yet they had no idea where to strike. On the phone, Percy demanded that he be allowed to supervise operations.

"I thought you already were," hissed Chamberlain.

"Not of your men," he countered.

"There is to be no question of your countermanding or diluting orders. If I agree, you must understand that they have standing orders."

"Yes," said Percy. "But I can offer strategic nous and direction to make sure this doesn't get any further out of hand." He paused a moment before continuing. "I would never countermand standing orders, but I *can* make sure they're carried out effectively."

"Percy—" Chamberlain began, trying to regain the high ground, but he was interrupted.

"—Our targets knew they were being watched, sir. I don't know much about America's FBI, but I do know that they're well trained and not stupid. They probably knew about our phone taps. They'd clearly cottoned on to your men's surveillance, which is how she—and they—were able to escape. In Dundee, your men were so ham-handed that they almost gave away everything. Can you *imagine* the difficulty if they'd been arrested?"

"Yes, I see," was all Chamberlain said in response.

"Which is what would have happened if my men hadn't been on hand, acting properly under strict orders."

"Yes—"

"And if this Spanish woman is deported, she'll be outside our purview and free to make any kind of accusations she wants."

"What do you propose?" Chamberlain asked.

"Stand your men down—at least until I can meet them all," he added. "I suspect—though I don't know—that they're itching for a little payback."

"Understandable," Chamberlain interjected.

"Indeed. But counter-productive. People like this have to be *directed*. Instructed."

"All right. But what about sending your deputy, Frenz? Wouldn't that work the way you want it to?"

Percy shook his head in disbelief. An idea seemed to occur to him. "If that's what has to happen to contain this mess," he said at last.

"Anything else?"

"Yes," Percy began. "You need to get on to whoever's managing this disaster at Home Office. Once this Serres woman is deported, you've lost all leverage, and whatever story she has to tell starts leaking out."

"Yes, I see," said Chamberlain.

"Have someone stay her deportation. Say that her case is under review or something...say it's humanitarian reasons, if you have to say anything at all. But draw the whole thing out a few more days."

"What if we don't find them in another few days? What then?"

"Sir, this is damage control. I'm thinking on my feet, trying to buy time, to create room in which to operate. We're in this situation first because your men—or some version of them—panicked at the rising poll numbers."

"You don't have to remind me," said Chamberlain.

"Good. But back then, the best course was to do nothing. I'm not saying we do nothing now, but let's at least have a *plan* for what we're going to do."

"Very good," he said, sounding more confident, almost relieved.

"And sir, I'm going to need an order from you sending young Jamie to Scotland. He can't operate there without some kind of cover."

"I understand. I'll have it over to you right away."

"Thank you, sir. I've checked, and there's a plane leaving in a little less than two hours. I'll need the orders and the contact information for your men before that. I'll direct my men to meet up with him and your men in Dundee tonight."

Percy hung up and turned to Frenz. "Looks like you're going to get some field work," he said. "I'm trusting you. You've heard all I said. You and I are both on the line here. We need to start looking for somewhere they might go. I doubt they'd flash their bums like this, but we need to check their credit cards, bank withdrawal locations. I'll check on that. Maybe there's a pattern. Also: do the Madmen have a safe house we might know about? Does this solicitor own a summer cottage or something where he might go to ground? Has the American woman taken a vacation somewhere out of the way that might be a good place to hide?"

"Very good," Frenz said.

"We won't do anything further with regard to this FBI agent or the solicitor. I don't want there to be anything pointing back to us if this all blows up—and if we try again to discredit her and she somehow turns up dead..."

"I understand, sir."

"And I need your assurance that you're working for *this service*, Jamie. You and I are in deep if this doesn't work out. And it will be a very black eye for the service. We've allowed these idiots to operate a bit too freely because we didn't want to know. And this is where it's got us."

"I'm fully aware. You can count on me."

"All information flows through me."

"Count on it, Commander."

In Alyth, along David Street, they spread their fish suppers across the table. Johnston insisted that they use plates and cutlery. Wilson smiled quizzically as Johnston handed him a plate. He opened the carrier container and put it on top of the plate, looking unsure as to what could be gained from doing so. The cutlery sat untouched to either side of the plate, except for the spoon, which he deployed first, shoveling the Mars bar and ice cream into his mouth.

"Ah hate it when the ice cream melts," he said between gulps. He peered into the carrier bag. "No sauce, eh?" He ate rapidly, hunched over his food like someone afraid it would all be taken away if he didn't get it in quickly.

"Alan," she began. "Can you think of any reason the people who were tailing Ewan would want to kidnap you?"

"None," he said through a mouth full of chips. He swallowed. "Ah've been tryin tae think of the why maself, and Ah'm gettin nowhere." He shook his head. "There is one thing: one ae them that attacked me—Ah've seen him before."

"Where?" she asked.

"That's the sticky bit. Ah don't remember."

"Was he with Buff Lindsey?" Johnston asked.

"Naw. Somethin else. Like on a joab."

"I have to ask, Alan," Johnston began, leaning in, "if you're still on good terms with Buff. If you're not, maybe he was—"

"We're fine, counselor. Nae bother there. Ah'm one ae his best boays."

Johnston sat back, holding up a hand to say he didn't need to hear anymore.

Imogen picked at her supper. Jen at the chippy hadn't been wrong about the portions, nor how little of it she could actually eat. But Alan looked a likely candidate for taking whatever she couldn't finish.

After supper, Wilson stepped out to smoke a cigarette, while Imogen and Johnston sat down to try to figure out next steps, facing each other across a coffee table in the tiny front room. Imogen opened her laptop.

"Is there Wi-Fi here?" she asked.

"No. Damn it. Hadn't thought of that. Ah just wanted somewhere away."

"It might be for the best," she said, trying to sound like she was making the best of things. It was good to be away, to stop looking over her shoulder for a while. But she knew it was temporary. She stared at her screen, willing the data to suggest something new and useful.

"Could we get into see the First Minister, do you think?"

"That's probably our best bet," Imogen sighed. "But I don't see us getting in without Ian Ross. I don't know about him. Is he a victim, too? If I'm wrong, then his bosses—his *real* bosses—will know what we're up to."

"Right," he said.

"And there's the problem of it being circumstantial."

Wilson opened the door, flicking his cigarette butt into the street as he did so. "Christ, it got cold, didn't it? Fucking Baltic, that is." He closed the door.

"Right," said Johnston, staring at Imogen. "We don't know or have any proof of who tried to steal the election."

"Or how those ballot boxes were stolen—*if* the ballot boxes were stolen."

"Fucking Christ!" said Wilson, causing both Imogen and Johnston to look up. "Whit does a ballot box look like?"

"You know..." Johnston began before realizing Wilson didn't know. "It's a black, plastic box with a lid on it. About so big." Here his hands described a box roughly one-and-a-half or two feet by two feet, and about that tall. "There's a wee slit in the lid for putting the ballot in."

"Ah fucking know where Ah saw that bastard from this morning."

At the Met office, Percy got to work while Frenz made ready to leave. Frenz gathered files, notes, flash drives and the order from Chamberlain. He broke out a heavy coat and grabbed an extra jumper, too. He was, after all going to Scotland. He hadn't been north of Liverpool in ages.

They all had something to lose, and Percy was no exception. In 2014, Percy and Frenz's investigation of the referendum had uncovered the election interference only days after the referendum. But they'd been persuaded to keep what they'd learned hidden, in the national interest, because it hadn't affected the outcome. The No vote, against independence, had prevailed by 10 %. In his under-secretary capacity, Chamberlain argued that revealing the interference after the fact was not in the national interest, and Percy, to his growing regret, had acquiesced, distasteful though it had been. In a long career it wasn't any more unpleasant than some of the other things he'd done "in the national interest."

Percy felt he was now beginning to glimpse how much deeper the corruption went. The referendum result had strengthened Chamberlain's position, and it had brought Townsend and Nesbitt into government, and wielding power. Which had fed their hunger for more control. Worst, his lassitude made him culpable. "Just following orders" hadn't been any kind of defense for more than 75 years.

Though Percy didn't know it at the time, and still could only guess at the outlines of how far the corruption went, the referendum conspiracy had begun as the triumvirate's

Manichean reflex against what they held to be a ludicrous, unconstitutional—not to mention ungrateful—political maneuver by Scottish nationalists. But it had come to stand for more than itself. The triumvirate saw that its successful defeat might also be a way to strengthen their hand, and to persuade the PM to sanction a Leave the EU vote—a move which they would promise (falsely) to work just as hard at defeating, all the while gathering strength, data and allies to ensure just the opposite.

And the PM had been receptive to the idea, not guessing what lay behind it. He'd had some success keeping the Eurosceptics and Euro-curious in his own party at bay—and ostensibly within the party—by *seeming* to talk about a Leave the EU vote that he had no intention of holding. But he couldn't dodge it forever. With Weaver's Transparency Project in the mix, Chamberlain had shown him a potential sure thing. He could accede to the Eurosceptics' demands for a Leave the EU vote while ensuring that the referendum vote went the way he wanted it to go. To win the argument would simultaneously silence his critics and put the Euro question to bed for a year or two more at least, the PM calculated at the time.

But first, the Independence referendum had to fail. It would be the key to everything that would follow.

Frenz left for the airport and Percy set to work checking for any patterns or hiding places. That he saw imperfectly what lay behind the cover-up he had thus far stage-managed effectively only increased his sense of unease about letting Frenz take charge on his own. He'd already gone freelance once. The job required tactics and subtlety. The irregulars didn't have it, that much was certain. Percy felt that Frenz did have subtlety, but could he be trusted? Moreover, if events grew more difficult, which way would he jump?

A moral compass. In the clandestine service, it was vital to keep your *own* moral compass. Was Frenz's in good nick? Percy wondered. Which way did it point? How, he accused himself, had he not noticed the wavering in his own? Too easily, what officials wanted could be mistaken for what official government required. Officials bestowed advancement and reward, and that attraction could come to seem like true north. Now, there were two murders on their hands.

As he continued working out where Wilson, Trager and Johnston were, he remained distracted, uneasy. Percy had seen firsthand how little care or regard Chamberlain's group had for democratic norms, for electoral integrity or the rule of law. And yet they still seemed to believe they were entitled to the respect and prerogatives conferred by norms and the rule of law. What, he wondered, did they think would protect them—or anyone?—once the dogs were let fully off the leash? He worried particularly about what kind of men Frenz would meet in Dundee that night, wondered how you trusted or managed people who'd spent years tearing away at the very edifice you had sworn to protect.

In Alyth, Wilson told the whole thing as Imogen took notes. About the van waiting on Granton Street, how a series of black plastic boxes had been delivered by five other vans and piled into the sixth, the one in which he waited. How none of the apprentice-felons had any sense of what it was all about. How, like him, the events of that night barely registered.

"How many boxes were in the van when it was done?" Imogen asked.

"Ah couldna say. They were very specific aboot us not havin even a wee keek at what was there. Need-to-know, like. An we didnae."

"Okay," she said. "And the man you say you recognized. What was his name?"

"No names. Barely even faces. Everything was done in the dark."

"How did you *see* the man you recognized?" Johnston asked, trying to nail the cross-exam to make sure the story held.

"He was the one that drove me to meet wi ma mates. Ah sat next tae him in the front."

"Would Buff be able to help us with names?" Imogen asked.

"Naw." Wilson shook his head. "Ah mean, he might know, but he won't help."

"Even if it was clear they tried to kill you because of it?" she asked. "Organized crime isn't my area, but I can't imagine a man like that would stand for anyone trying to take out one of his...boys."

Johnston looked expectantly at Wilson, who had a bit of a think. Finally, Wilson replied, "Naw, that's not his way. He'd deal wi it himsel."

Imogen nodded gravely.

Wilson suddenly brightened. "But he wouldney have tae, would he? Buff, Ah mean. The counselor's already done fae that bastard." He smiled widely and tapped Johnston on the shoulder with his fist.

Imogen's face darkened. "Done fae him?"

"Oor Ewan here came flying oot the side street and does a fishtail right intae him. Crushed that fuck between the rear fender of his no-longer-pristine Beemer and ma van. Hard!" he added with relish.

"Dead?" Imogen asked.

"Ah fuckin hope so!" said Wilson.

At the airport, as Frenz's flight was being called to board, Percy telephoned with an update:

"Nothing on the cell phones," Percy said. "They're turned off, it seems. We're still working on the credit cards for patterns. Nothing there yet, either. But we've had what may be a hit," he said. "Johnston holds title to his parents' home in a tiny town north of Dundee called Alyth. I'm sending one of the buskers to check it out. Quietly."

"Excellent," said Frenz.

"What's wi the telly?" Alan Wilson asked.

"Oh," said Johnston, "I don't think it works. It's an old one, and it only ever received three channels anyway."

"Fucking Christ! An no Wifi either?"

Imogen closed her laptop. "I want to go over our escape if they find us," she said. "Is there no way out the back?"

"The front's the best bet," said Johnston, "but we could definitely go out the back window, oot through the back and between ma da's shed and the neighbor's garage. Like when Ah was a boy."

"Can you show us?" she asked.

Ian Ross was sick to his stomach as he sleepwalked along the glaringly bright, antiseptic hallway to Janette Ritchie's office. She had something "delicate" to discuss, she had said on the phone, and "could he spare a moment?" That last phrase meaning, "drop whatever you're doing and see me immediately." He feared the worst.

Maybe it was all out in the open now, his collaboration, his crime. It wasn't a long walk, but he took it as slowly as he could, a gallows march. Far from working out how to get back into Chamberlain's starting eleven, Ian Ross was contemplating a transfer. But did he have the courage? What could he say to his boss, Ritchie, in his own defense? he wondered. Was there any way—even telling his side of the story—in which he didn't look like the villain?

The truth was squalid enough. On a trip to London, he'd had a kind of reconnaissance chat with Nigel Chamberlain. They had met for drinks, he could say, quite innocently chatting about all manner of things, touching on the game of politics and so-called higher loyalties. They had gossiped, too. The real currency of government functionaries. And toward the end, they even spoke vaguely, amiably about the possibility of a second referendum. Surveying the landscape of their conversation, Ross had seen a chance to create an "in" at Westminster, access in his back pocket that he might later trade on. He did that kind of thing all the time. It was how he'd found out about the Clarifying Bill they were all so worried about. That kind of wool gathering didn't sound innocent, he allowed, but it didn't sound particularly sinister either.

But at their second meeting a few days later, a dinner, it seemed that the referendum was Chamberlain's real agenda. Amidst the low light, sparkling glasses and very good wine Ross had sought to make himself useful—and maybe gain something from Chamberlain in return. Over brandy, Ross had floated the idea that he might find someone outside of government to have a quiet look at the results, a kind of flushing spaniel (he thought Chamberlain would like that image). He had suggested looking into it, he would stress to his boss Ritchie, because, like her, he had been sure there was nothing to find— no there there, as she herself had said recently. Something for nothing.

The murder of Wee Frankie and Donald Alban had shocked him. Implicated him. No brassy spaniel, he, but a cur. He had unearthed them so they could be killed. He had reached Ritchie's office. Ross stood in mute terror at the threshold and rapped on the doorframe.

"Oh, Ian," the chief of staff said as though surprised to see him, maintaining the fiction that it wasn't an urgent matter. "I need you to take a look at something." She tossed a file across her desk and gestured that he should seat himself. "The Home Office is deporting a professor from Strathclyde, a Marta Serres. They're saying it's a home office security issue, so there isn't much background. I wonder if you could look into it."

"Of course," said Ross, feeling no relief that his execution had been postponed.

"She also consults on the Electoral Commission, so I'd like to understand everything we can—official and any backchannel intelligence."

Well, he wanted to say, for one, she's collateral damage from the forces I set in motion. Though again, he didn't know how or why exactly. He said nothing other than, "And how's the other thing coming? I'd be happy to help on that."

"We're working on that, thank you. There may be some things I need from you, but for the moment, I'd like you to focus on this Professor Serres. There may be a useful PR angle there. Who knows," she added, returning her attention to the papers on her desk, "maybe we can link the two somehow. And please close the door on your way out."

As he pulled the door closed, he looked balefully at the top of the chief's white head. Ignored, discounted. Again. It struck him that Imogen must know about his collusion, or she'd have already contacted him about Marta Serres. He needed a way to fight back. Had Imogen found nothing? he wondered. Would she trust him with the information if she had? They were running out of time.

Percy dispatched a busker to Alyth that night.

He arrived in darkness on his motorcycle and coasted quietly down David Street. Lights were on inside at the address he'd been given. Though he couldn't spend much time at it, he was sure he could see shadows moving around inside. He checked the license plate numbers of the five cars parked on the curb. Looking at the first two digits on the license plate, four were local, representing Blairgowrie/Alyth. But one began with the two-number Dundee code.

He rode back to the main road, Airlie Street, and pulled over to make his report to Percy.

"They're here, sir," he said into the phone. "I don't have one hundred percent ID, but there are lights on and people moving about inside. One of the cars parked at the curb has a Dundee license plate. All the others are local."

"Did you *see* them inside?"

"No, I didn't want to go that close. I'd hate to spook them, and me the only one here."

"You did the right thing," said Percy. "Can you sit tight on them, keep them in view?"

"No. This is a small town," he said glancing around, "and I already have people looking at me strangely. I'll make a pass by every hour or so, but I won't be able to keep them under total surveillance."

Next morning, Percy's busker happened to be rolling by the house when Alan Wilson stepped out for a smoke with his morning tea. He didn't stop to photograph Wilson, but he recognized him from the digital files he'd been sent. He sped down Smythe Street and stopped at the main road again where he called to make his report.

Unbeknownst to him, Wilson was making a call—and a kind of report—of his own to Buff Lindsey. Cigarette in hand, he set his teacup on the ground next to the front door and walked across the footbridge at the bottom of David Street, where he sauntered carelessly across the playing fields and children's playground there. The air was chilly and damp but invigorating all the same. Inside the house, while Wilson smoked and dandered, Imogen and Ewan Johnston were going over the same ground.

"You don't have any connections in Edinburgh?" she asked. "I'm worried about using Ian. It may be that he didn't know what the bad guys were planning. But he's likely to betray us. Isn't there someone you know with access to Holyrood? Someone who could get us in to see the First Minister? Or at least her chief, Janette Ritchie?"

"I thought Ritchie was Ross's boss," said Johnston.

"She is."

"Doesn't that make her kind of suspect?"

"It means we should be careful, but if the chief of staff is working for the bad guys, I don't think we have a chance..." She paused a moment before adding. "I think we have to trust her."

"But walk me through the last bit," said Johnston. "They *didn't* steal the election?"

"They *interfered* with the election. We have strong circumstantial evidence and an eyewitness to the ballot removal. The theft."

"Right," he said.

"But the crazy thing is that they didn't need to do it. Marty and I are pretty sure, based on our findings, that even without the interference, 'No' would've prevailed. Even with all their resources, they couldn't have engineered as big a win as they had. Certainly, they wouldn't have been able to keep it quiet. Their interference—what they did—was the kind of thing you do when the margins are tight. But based on our analysis, it wasn't that tight."

"So...?"

"So, they're covering up their interference," she said.

"Not the crime but the cover-up."

"Exactly. They duped me into chasing down what could be found so that they could make sure it stayed buried. Frankie's work has turned out to be helpful. At first—maybe it's ugly to admit—I discounted much of what he'd done. It was all outrage and conspiracy stuff. Nothing I thought I could work with. But he did a good job of drawing links that point to the Transparency Project on Government Accountability. It's part of the Strategic Choices Institute, a non-profit think tank."

"How would they be involved, if they're non-governmental and non-partisan?"

"That's the thing. According to Frankie's research and what I've been able to glean, they're nothing of the kind. Nigel Chamberlain who does something in the Home Office and the institute's owner, an American named Jefferson Weaver who's involved with Transparency, seem to be chummy. The government often takes white papers or other kinds of research published through the institute and cites them as "open source" intelligence in all kinds of areas. But always—conveniently— in support of things the government already wants to do."

"Aye, well, that's..."

"You were going to say it's 'smarmy but not illegal,'" Imogen offered.

"If Ah knew what smarmy meant. Though I get the gist, now."

"And according to Frankie's snooping, Weaver's institute is aligned with some pretty awful characters online. Hackers, troll farms. There's one that calls itself HCQ, short for Hydroxychloroquine, which Frankie seems to think used to be called Ursa Gummae."

"Gummie bears?"

"Weaver's other company does behind-the-scenes political work in Third World countries, too. I'm guessing now, but I think Weaver and Chamberlain are behind what's going on now. Either they're covering up for someone else, or they're the ones who interfered with the Indy-ref. I've been so focused on whether, and then *how* it was interfered with that I'm only now getting to whom. Either way, these two—at least these two—have blood on their hands. They've killed two people. And I don't think they meant to kidnap Alan."

Imogen pushed away from the laptop and sat back in the chair. She stared toward the hazy window, her eyes watering. A bleak emptiness filled her. "I got two people—and almost a third—killed."

"You didn't know," he said tenderly.

"I could've said no."

Johnston reached across and patted her knee consolingly. "I don't think that's your way," he said. Their eyes met. Each looked as if they needed to say something. Johnston was the first to retreat. He drew back his hand, worried that he'd overstepped his bounds.

"The problem," Imogen began, leaning toward him, "isn't only that we don't know how to get the information to Ritchie, but that it's still largely circumstantial."

Johnston gazed at her, transfixed. It was as though he was both inside this moment, and outside, watching it. He heard what she was saying, felt the fear and anger in her voice, an edge with which he was familiar, too; but he also felt his longing for her, imagined the heat of her body, the touch of her skin. He seemed to see himself draw her gently toward him, taking her face in his hands and kissing away the damp tears. He wanted to, he needed to.

"Ewan?" she said, looking into his face.

For her part, Imogen was imagining nothing like the calm, deliberate caresses that Johnston envisaged, but saw herself pouncing across the table at him, sweeping the laptop and papers off the table and...

"Not proven," he said, breaking her reverie.

"What?" The flush of her imagined pounce faded.

"Scottish law has three verdicts in a trial, not two. There's guilty, not guilty. And not proven."

"I don't understand," she said.

"Anglo-American law has two verdicts. Scottish law permits a third: Not Proven. The 'bastard verdict,' Sir Walter Scott called it. These days, 'Not Proven' means that the jury thinks the accused is probably guilty, but they don't feel that the prosecution has demonstrated its case against the accused well enough; that they don't find the proofs sufficient for a conviction."

"So can they try you again if the case is not proved?" she asked.

"No. It's an acquittal."

"So, it's the same as not guilty," she said.

"Yes, and no. Yes, it's an acquittal, as I said, but no one regards it as a vindication. The jury, or the judge in a summary case, didn't say you were not guilty. They said the case was not proven."

29

In Dundee, Jamie Frenz received the news that their targets were in Alyth, just as he was about to meet with the four remaining irregulars and two of his buskers in the snug room of a pub off the King's Way. He decided to continue with his planned talk about strategy and the rules of engagement. This lot would need it. Only after he'd gone over everything he thought they needed to know would he tell them of this new development.

The irregulars sat in rows facing him, their squared forearms crossed ponderously in front of them like hams at a butcher's. As he gazed over the group, he understood why he and Percy didn't know any of them. Ex-military, they didn't look anything like the kind of men the clandestine services would have tapped for further use. Smug, over-fed and over-confident, each radiated a kind of petulant, undifferentiated anger. These were men who thought of themselves first, last and only; who had grievances, held grudges, settled scores—and there were grievances against many of them, too. Indeed, a quick review of the files Chamberlain had sent him revealed that three of them hadn't retired from military service so much as were required to leave it.

If Nesbitt was no good at recognizing good soldiers, Frenz thought, it was perhaps fortunate that he had chosen these aggrieved military has-beens or never-weres. Better soldiers might have rebelled at their shallow, thick orders. But anyone who understood soldiers would have regarded this group as dangerous and unpredictable. Like ill-trained attack dogs, you couldn't be sure from moment to moment where their aggression would be expressed, nor against whom. The two buskers present were conscientious, adroit and thorough. There was nothing subtle about the irregulars. Neither doubt nor conscience had ever nibbled at their infantile, bully serenity.

As Frenz closed the door to the snug room, he decided that the best way to get these irregulars onside was to flatter that checkered military background, to insinuate that he knew what they were about, that they shared important secrets, were players at the forefront of a noble, dangerous game, and that he approved of them; that he was expecting great things. Their military careers, he guessed (such as they were), had been the only happy or fulfilling aspect of their lives. He would trade on that.

"Pipe down, you bunch of heathens!" Frenz began, with an approving smile. "Eyes on me. By now, you've received word from your handler that I'll be directing things here. Any questions? Good!" he barked, without allowing them to ask anything.

"You are now under MI5 auspices and regulation. I'm the group commander. What's my name? Well, we've all been here before, haven't we? You can call me 'Captain.' There will be no slip-ups, no going rogue on my watch." He looked across the room, saw some vague nodding. He needed them pumped up, full of confidence, but not wound too tight.

"We're going to get another bite at the apple, boys," he said after a moment. "And we must be ready for anything. That little shit, Alan Wilson turns out to be a bit more formidable than we thought. He's the main target, and we'll get our own back there. The woman's an American FBI agent.

"Now, I'm *required* to say this next bit," he began, as though burdened by foolish superiors, "but Upstairs would very much like it if you'd try *not* to kill her. Don't want an international incident for something that's our own dirty pants. Right?" He paused a moment.

"Having duly communicated to you that we're meant to be careful of her, I would also stress that you should not endanger yourself or any member of the team by not taking her out...should that become necessary. But don't let taking her out be your first impulse. Right?

"The solicitor, Ewan Johnston," he continued, "is a bit of a wild card. Frankly, I'd have thought he'd have folded by now. And my team tells me he did some nice defensive driving to get away a few days ago. We won't want to underestimate him either." He let that sink in before continuing.

"I think I know what many of you must be feeling right now. You've lost comrades, friends. You need it to mean something. I'm here to give you the chance to make their sacrifices stand for something. But we'll do it the smart way. My way. Or we risk losing it all. And don't worry: we're going in heavy."

In Alyth, Alan Wilson knocked and came in the front door. Imogen and Ewan sipped reflectively at their tea across the coffee table.

"Christ, it's a fuckin mausoleum oot there!" said Wilson as he closed and locked the door. "Naebody about. Ah took a dander over that wee bridge tae the kids park. It's clean an all!" His tone suggested that this was a drawback.

Johnston smiled. An idea seemed to come to him. "I know one person who might be able to help," he said. "She's..." he looked at Imogen. "She's an old friend. We're not together anymore," he added hastily. "So, I don't know what kind of reception she'd give us..."

"Where does she work?"

"Now, she's in the office of the Edinburgh Lord Provost. A bit like the mayor's office in the US," he said.

"That's local government, though."

"Look, how long are we gonnae bide here?" Wilson wanted to know.

"I'm not sure," said Johnston.

"Ah mean, no offense tae yer home town and yer mither's hoose an that, but Christ it's dull. Nae telly, nae Wi-Fi. Streets are deid."

"Well, since the alternative is being dead ourselves, Alan..."

"Aye, fine," said Wilson dismally. "If Ah'd known, Ah'dve said we could hunker doon in Edinburgh or Glasgow...Aberdeen, even. Ah've got mates all over. Mebbe their accommodations are no as tidy as this, but safe." No one seemed to be listening to him. "Is there still tea on?" he asked as he walked to the kitchen.

For Imogen, it all seemed forbiddingly familiar, a step backward: an open-ended, albeit temporary lockdown, sheltering in place to avoid harm. The very air carried a threat, miasmas, dangerous agues. *We* belong to the things of yesterday, she thought, thinking of Geddes' poem again. When would it end? *How* would it end? Johnston watched Wilson go before returning his attention to Imogen.

"Yes," he said, "it's local, but it *is* government. And it's Edinburgh. She's likely to know how to get in touch with Janette Ritchie."

"What's her name?" Imogen asked.

"Sharon," said Johnston. "Sharon McAllister."

"Still have her number?"

"...yes," he said. Johnston thought he detected a tone of something. Though he couldn't swear to it, he felt as though somehow there were two conversation threads going simultaneously, neither of which seemed to be doing him much credit.

"Well, give her a call," she said. "Find out if she can get us access. She'd probably think to go through Ian Ross, so make sure you're clear that we can't do that."

"Right," he said.

"I expect the mayor—"

"Lord Provost," he corrected.

"...that the Lord Provost doesn't have much to do with Holyrood, but it's possible he or she may have a direct line. Ritchie's personal cell would be optimal."

In Dundee, Frenz made a great show of having newly received information about where their targets had gone to ground. "We had intel from one of our office staff, and I sent one of my men to chase it down," he announced. "It's paid off! We have confirmation. They're in a small town north of here, called Alyth."

The whole room perked up.

"We have eyes on them now," Percy continued. "If they move, we'll know. We're going to put together maps and details of the neighborhood. And right quick! We need to know every entrance to the house, where each street leads. We need to know what kind of vantage any potential pain-in-arse witnesses might have, too. We can't have a repeat of the failed smash-and-grab in Dundee. Who's done some map reconnaissance?"

Two men raised their hands.

"Good. You two will assist Gray whilst I and you two"— he pointed at the remaining irregulars—"get equipment squared away."

Sunday morning, in Alyth, Johnston left a message with Sharon in the Lord Provost's office. And waited.

"What can we do if they find us?" asked Imogen. "The bad guys, I mean. According to Alan here, only one of them was armed with a gun."

Wilson nodded.

"I don't expect they'll make that same mistake again," she added. "Are you armed, Alan?"

He reached into a pocket and pulled out a knife. Imogen sighed.

"I've been thinking about that, too," Johnston replied. He stood up and walked to a closet door by the stairs. "My father liked to hunt," he said opening it. "This was his pride and joy," he said, turning around and showing them a gleaming deer rifle. "It's a Sauer Two-O-Two. He bought it second-hand." He reached in and pulled out another rifle. "This is a Sako. The only one he let me use." He smiled wistfully.

"I thought Brits couldn't own firearms," Imogen began.

"Course we can! We don't just hand them around like something you'd win at bingo, like you lot. These are fully registered—to me and my brother, now. For hunting." He paused and turned again. "There's also this. For birds."

"Whit is that?" asked Wilson. "A shotgun?"

"Course it is," Johnston replied. "Why?"

"Ah've jist never seen one that long before." He winked at Imogen.

"Yes," said Johnston tartly, "that would be because you don't need to conceal it under a coat for the pheasants."

Imogen took hold of the Sauer rifle. She checked the action, verified it wasn't loaded and looked into the barrel. "Bolt action," she said. "One shot at a time."

Johnston shrugged. "Typically, the game isn't firing back," he said.

"Ammunition?" she asked.

"Couple of boxes of Winchester two-forty-three bullets," said Johnston. "About twenty shotgun shells."

"How old are the bullets and shells?" she asked.

"Four or five years," said Johnston.

"Fuck," Wilson muttered.

"No," Imogen interjected. "If they were stored properly, they could easily last eight to ten years." She peered into the closet and looked up and down and into the corners for any hint of mold or mildew. It was dry and clean. "Anywhere we might clean the guns?" she asked. "If they've been sitting that long, even in good conditions..."

"The kit's out in the back shed," said Johnston.

All three traipsed across the back garden to the late Mr. Johnston's shed, a moss covered, slapped-up affair. They stepped inside and Johnston put on the light. Inside, at odds with its outer appearance, the shed was clean and spare. And cold. Tidy bins and coffee cans arranged around the walls held well-labeled tools, screws, nails and solvents. A workbench dominated the center of the room, with a proper vise grip and padded jaws to hold a gun steady, along with various sized bore brushes. Imogen nodded approvingly. She handed Johnston the Sauer rifle.

"No, you go ahead," he said, smiling. "My father never thought I did a good job."

She put the first rifle in the grips and tightened them.

"I'll make some tea," he said. "It's about the only thing that'll keep you warm in here." And he turned to leave.

"Can ye walk me through that?" Wilson asked, as she set to work. "Ah've never had tae clean one, and Ah think mebbe Ah should ken how."

"...sure," said Imogen, pretty certain that along with investigating outside her jurisdiction, training criminals in the proper care and cleaning of firearms was also something an FBI agent shouldn't be doing. But she needed him on her side. Was this the kind of hair-splitting, moment-to-moment, best-worst-choice thinking that undercover work required? she wondered.

In London, Nesbitt took a telephone call from Sausage, who told him that the targets had been "reacquired."

"Good. What's the plan?" Nesbitt asked.

"It's being developed right now."

"Jesus! *Developed*? Get some weapons and head in. You know what to do! Take them out, and let those others clean up. That seems to be what *they're* good at."

"Yessir," the Para said into the phone, "but we're reconnoitering the area and—"

"—For what? You know where they are! Go after them!" he spat.

"We need guns and ammunition," he said to Nesbitt. "Everything we had was collected and impounded by the police in Dundee when they cleared up the accident scene."

"You're *in* Dundee, for God's sake! Use that idiot from before...Lindsey. He'll be happy to sell you some guns. I'll put in a call to his superior."

"Yes, on the face of it, that makes sense—" he began, but Nesbitt had hung up.

Imogen and Wilson returned with the freshly cleaned guns. She placed one next to the front door and put a box of bullets on the floor by it. Next, she trotted upstairs and placed the second rifle at the back window, on the landing of the stairs. She put the other box of bullets next to it. Wilson put the shotgun and shells next to the front window and sat on the arm of old Mr. Johnston's favored chair at the window so he could look out.

Ewan Johnston, sitting with the laptop at the sitting room table regarded their preparations nervously. He looked at the rifle by the front door. "Ah've heard of planting rosemary for fertility," he said. "And that Italians put a wee broom by the front door for witches. Apparently, they cannae resist riding away. Ah'm dubious of both practices. And Ah can't say *this* carry-on inspires much confidence."

Wilson grinned.

Imogen, returned from upstairs. She stood at the base of the stairs, contemplating the room and its defenses. "Ye look like ye cannae decide where the new settee should go," Johnston quipped.

"I suppose it lends a sort of *frontier* hominess," she said.

"More like Mafioso feng shui," mused Wilson.

Imogen and Ewan looked at him in surprise.

"Ah had a bird used to bang on aboot that," he said by way of explanation.

The walls of the house were stone, and thick. Unless they came with Howitzers or mortars, they could shelter against the walls, she noted. Would they come like SWAT, like cops? she wondered. Would they *be* cops? A Molotov cocktail or teargas grenade through any window could force them out. She pulled on her jacket and went outside. Wilson slid off the chair arm and followed her. Outside, he lit a cigarette and zipped his puffy coat over his track suit.

"Ah don't know," he said, glancing up and down the road.

David Street was a sweet, narrow lane, with low, two-story houses crowded against one another like pebble-dashed Philadelphia row houses. The street formed the head of a "T." It dead-ended for cars a few doors down from the Johnston's, but there was an outlet mid-block, via Smythe Street. At the dead-end, a pedestrian footbridge over the Alyth Burn led into the playground. It felt mad to be reconnoitering such a lovely, tranquil spot.

If Wilson didn't know, Imogen didn't either. If the attackers flushed them out of the house, where could they go? she wondered. "Let's check the street behind," she said to Wilson. They crossed the footbridge and walked north along the burn at the edge of the playground to the James Street footbridge, where they crossed back and had a look at the rear of the Johnston's house.

She called up the street plan on Google maps using Wilson's phone.

"Mebbe if we went out the back windae like the counselor said?" Wilson began.

Imogen shook her head. "They'd have someone waiting, don't you think?" She showed him the map on her phone. Even some of the structures were outlined. "*We'd* cover back and front," she noted, the "we" in that sentence meaning the FBI. "I imagine they're studying this map, too. They'd see it as an option before they even set up. And look," she said, pointing at the back of the house, "we'd be in single file going between Ewan's father's shed and that garage there."

"Ooch, sitting ducks," he said, before adding, "If they're coming."

"Let's keep looking," she said. "Might as well make a full tour."

"I've been going over what we have so far," Johnston said to her as she and Wilson came back in. "I'm getting it into shape that will make sense to the government's lawyers."

"Good," said Imogen, and she sat down next to him to look at the laptop.

"I'm organizing it like a Statement of Findings report." He pointed at the laptop screen: "Title: Official Interference in the 2014 Scottish Independence Referendum. Our names, witness list. I'm including Wee Frankie and Donald along with Alan Wilson. I've listed Marta Serres, too. She consults with the

Electoral Commission, so she'll have some standing. And, it might help keep her in the country. Scottish government is bound to be aware of her impending removal. And this is the beginning of the summary, with notes and links to relevant data."

Imogen read it over. "Good," she said. "Leading with Alan as a witness to ballot boxes being stolen...Summary, with link to Alban's saved papers noting how the theft was effected. Donald Alban's apparent suicide. Could I tweak the language here regarding Marty's and my methodology and findings?"

He pushed the laptop toward her, and she began typing, clarifying how the intercept numbers were arrived at, how the lower-than-expected turnout was a close match with the number of votes removed. She added language and figures to bolster that finding, referenced other tables.

"And while we have better data, as well as a witness to the vote theft in Dundee," she continued, typing and reading aloud as she went, "the missing vote amount in Glasgow is consistent with what we've outlined in detail in Dundee."

When she'd finished, she pushed it back to him, saying, "Do you think some of Frankie's research into links between Jefferson Weaver and Nigel Chamberlain should come earlier?"

"I note it here briefly," he said, pointing, "and it's part of the narrative: 'Donald Alban was coerced in some unknown manner into concealing the fact that votes in Dundee had been stolen and letting the result of the referendum stand.' Here, I go on to talk about the inability to find the former ARO for Glasgow... Then the death of Donald, the murder of Wee Frankie, the break-in at my law office; that the burglars were particularly interested in Donald's will...the break-in at your office, the bugs you found in your apartment." He looked over the screen at Wilson: "Alan, can you text me the pictures you took of the people you were watching—the ones who were watching me."

Wilson nodded and opened his phone.

"Good," she said.

"That's the key," Johnston continued, pointing at another portion of the narrative section. "The numbers you and Professor Serres crunched are largely circumstantial, but I think I can make a strong case that if they weren't related, *why* was there such a significant, concerted effort to silence those involved in finding out about the stolen votes? That'll be the most damning," he said. "And, the administrative removal—the deportation—of Marta Serres supports that theory. *And* it means there are UK government officials complicit in the effort to quash this investigation. I'll maybe soft-pedal the bit about the guys who were following me since it's likely some of them are dead now."

"But that's another part ae it, counselor," said Wilson. "How, why—and *by whom*—was the attack outside yer office organized and authorized? There's been naught in the papers or on the telly about a bloody fight on Ward Road...or anywhere. The fact it's been tidied away and zipped shut means someone official is in on it—or MI5 like."

"I suppose I could reference it by talking about 'wounded' operatives," said Johnston. "We don't know for a fact they were all killed."

"Ah think we can be pretty sure..." Wilson began.

"Yes, but for this presentation, we can acknowledge that possibility—but only on something like a cross-examination. And if we were acknowledging such, it would be *them* sticking their necks out, confirming for us that it even happened." He stared hard at his screen before adding, "I wish we knew who, specifically, *they* are."

In the frustrated silence that filled the room, Johnston's phone rang.

"Hi Sharon," he said brightly.

Imogen stood and walked to the front window by Alan. Marty might be in Barcelona already, she thought. How were her children holding up? Had Ewan and Alan really killed some of the men who attacked them?

"Yes, long time..." Johnston was saying.

This had to mean something, Imogen vowed: Marty, Wee Frankie, Donald Alban. There would have to be a reckoning. And they were running out of time. If Ian Ross had been telling the truth about the new parliamentary agenda, their findings, such as they were, would be moot as of next week—dead and buried. She'd need to make certain Ewan, Alan and she weren't dead and buried, too.

"I realize that," he was saying, "but we're—" Johnston looked in Imogen's direction, her back to him as she gazed out the window. "er, some colleagues and I..."

Wilson, who had caught the look, and Johnston's discomfort, smiled to himself. He glanced sideways at Imogen, but she seemed miles away. As she reviewed their options, she noted that they would have to leave. The house was indefensible. It had bought them some time, but not much.

Johnston was listening. Finally, he said, "Well, thank you for looking into it anyways, Sharon. Yes. I can't go into it, but I think it's important not to involve Ian Ross. It has to do with proper hierarchy, with having a full hearing....Yes, it is a shame, I suppose...Absolutely, I'll make sure to look you up next time I'm in Edinburgh. And don't be a stranger in Dundee. Thanks again for trying." He hung up.

Imogen turned round. "It was a long shot," she said dispassionately. "Maybe we need to think about Ian again."

"He can't be trusted," said Johnston.

"It's possible he's as much a dupe as I am.

"Or, he's a stone-cold killer," said Wilson.

30

Next morning in Dundee, three men ducked under the heavily graffitied garage door of Buff Lindsey's chop shop. Alan's ginger friend Lexie, leaning under the weight of a black Thule ski bag, switched on the work lights as Buff walked in and the roll door came down again behind him.

"Fucking hell!" Buff Lindsey roared as the lights flickered on across the work bay. "You two." He pointed accusingly at Lexie and a taciturn, young man called Beansie. "Cover that fuckin thing up!" He pointed at Johnston's damaged BMW. Lexie and his silent colleague scampered across the garage and set to work adjusting the tarp over Johnston's car.

"Christ, *that* could give up the gemme, eh," said Lindsey when they'd finished. "Make sure it stays on. But jist tae be sure, wu'll dae this transaction in the office." He made a quick survey of the bay, looking at angles. The office was the best place to conduct the business, quiet, apart. But it also had windows into the work bay. "Awright," he said, when he'd finished having a look round, "I want yese to get to work takin the front fender off ae that Benz there in the corner."

"We only just got it on," Lexie protested.

"And now ye'll take it off, so yese can put it back on again." He reached into a zippered compartment at the top of the ski bag and handed each a pistol. "Ah need yese tae keep a sharp eye. Everything should go straight with these...clients...but ye cannae be too careful, like."

Disconcerted, both held the guns awkwardly at first.

"Ye'll both be working in the far corner on that fender, but ye can see intae the office from there. Put the gun on the ground—out of sight—in front of ye while you work. If anythin goes wrong..."

Outside, someone pounded on the garage door.

"It'll be fine, boays," he said. "Ah'm thinkin this is jist a straight transaction, but these are the fucks that tried to dae fir oor Alan."

Lexie colored deeply. "Buff, why don't we jist take them here, noo? Ah'm up fir it."

Lindsey patted Lexie on the shoulder. Lexie was indeed ready. Beansie didn't say a word, but he was no longer holding the gun gingerly as he took the safety off and aimed it at the door. It's the silent ones you have to watch out for, Lindsey reflected.

"Ah'd love tae, lads," said Lindsay. He placed his hand on Beansie's forearm, gently forcing him to lower the weapon. "But these fucks are tied intae something bigger, and until we know whit that is, we'd only be cutting oor ain throats...and Alan nae safer intae the bargain."

Outside, there was more urgent pounding.

"Impatient little fuck, isn't he?" Lindsey observed with a grin. With a flick of his head, he told them to take up their places at the car in the far corner.

Sausage's thick, bland face met Lindsey as he raised the door to let the clients in. "I was told that you were expecting us," said Sausage. Lindsey nodded and gestured toward the office. He looked past them out to the road as he pulled the door down once more. Lexie and Beansie paused in their work to watch Sausage and two others as they walked into the office.

Lindsey's garage office, normally strewn with spare parts, crushed beer cans and half-drunk coffee cups transformed into a dystopic armory. One by one, he laid out the weapons. To outfit the six men who would go after Wilson, Johnston and Imogen there were four HK416 assault rifles, two, stubby MP5 submachine guns, four 9mm pistols and a Remington sniper rifle, along with extra magazines, ammunition and a well-used red, Sigma "Enforcer" battering ram.

"Yous said ye wanted all assault rifles, but Ah couldnae swing it on such short notice. The MP-five's will dae yous jist fine. Think ye'll want that sniper rifle? Same price as discussed."

Sausage nodded. "This'll do," he said. "We'll take the lot." He shoved the money bag across the table toward Lindsey. The irregular began stuffing the assault rifles back into the ski bag. "We'll definitely have a good chance of getting our own back with this lot."

"Ah wasnae told," Lindsey began, "are you looking for information, too? Am I supposed tae give you manpower? Not a local job, I hope?"

Sausage said nothing as he checked the action on one of the MP5s.

"Fine by me," Buff continued blandly. "Ah'd jist hate to get crossed up—me and mine going in heavy on something you'd already decided ta dae. Tha's bad fir business, that."

"Not your jurisdiction, mate." Sausage winked. "Out in the country. Never-you-mind *where*. We tracked down his car, and we're going in well-equipped thanks to you." He handed the last submachine gun to a thick-set, bald man.

In London, Percy strolled across the Millennium Bridge. The sky threatened a dreary rain. About mid-span, Leyser, elegant as always, fell into step alongside him.

"Events are in motion again," said Percy, looking out over a slate gray river, away from Leyser. "My second-in-command is leading the line up north. Our people are there, too. But I'm worried about the irregulars, as I call them—not ours—at his disposal. I'd hate for this to get out of control." He stopped and leaned against the rail.

Leyser stopped, too, some six feet past him. "Containment is of paramount importance," he said, looking upriver. "Whatever must be done, must be done thoroughly and quietly. Less than a week from today, whatever's happened won't matter, but anything that might trip us up before October 25th *must* be resisted."

"Which is why I thought we might do well to have a chat," said Percy. "I know what I can count on from my men—and I have every confidence in them. But I'm worried about the others embroiled here, the irregulars."

"Their loyalty?"

"Their *ability*," Percy stressed. "Their effectiveness, and their ability—or willingness—to follow orders."

"There's nothing I can offer you at the moment. Unless it's some advice. Now is not the time for uncertainty or half-measures. There's no prize for second best."

"Are you authorizing—?"

"—I'm not *doing* anything," Leyser interrupted. "I'm not here. This meeting isn't in my diary, no one in Cabinet or the PM's office will be briefed..."

"You're a ghost, then, and I'm on my own?"

"Think of me as your conscience," Leyser said. "The angel on your shoulder."

"The *angel*?"

"Yes," he emphasized, catching Percy's doubtful tone. "And if you prevail by whatever means you feel are necessary, we can see about mending and smoothing over certain things—as well as giving out honors and rewards. It all comes down to this."

* * *

In Alyth, Johnston had revised the Statement of Findings report, making the case for electoral interference—and murder—with all the legalese of an opening statement, backed up with links to evidence sources, Imogen's data and Wilson's statement. Johnston wrote it so that there was a record if the worst happened, and to help keep Wilson focused if he was deposed or cross-examined.

"Right, get ma story straight. Ah ken all aboot that," he said.

"Yes," said Johnston uncomfortably, "but in this sense, you're going to need to give the *whole* truth Alan."

"Whit should Ah say aboot ma working fir Buff an tha? Am no bringing him intae this shite."

"Yes, I see."

"Ah suppose Ah could say Ah kent a boy who kent a boy who said there was an offer ta dae some driving—nae questions asked. And be coy and confused as to who it might hae been."

"I suppose it'll have to do," said Johnston. "Fair enough."

"Everybody's got something tae hide, eh?"

Imogen perked up her head from the laptop at this but didn't say anything. Who had something to hide among those he had identified? she wondered. It might point to who was behind it all. Jefferson Weaver and Nigel Chamberlain seemed likely to be involved. Maybe one or both could be made to do some singing.

She wondered how she might keep her FBI job after this; how she might keep her part in all this hidden. It was a fruitless exercise. She was fucked. So be it, she thought as she returned to her review of the statements of finding, her methodology for the missing votes. She wanted it to be clear enough for even a journalist to follow, should that become necessary. Still, they were no nearer to having anyone to whom they could give it. The gray, stifled light seeping through the front curtains enforced her sense of dismal isolation and defeat.

"All dressed up with nowhere to go," Imogen sighed as she closed the laptop and leaned back from a fourth, compulsive reading. A moment later, she reopened the laptop and began sorting through Wee Frankie's notes again. She needed to get those in order as well.

Imogen turned from the document to thoughts of escape. Their tour around the houses showed that they were trapped. Should they move the car up Smythe Street? she wondered. It would make for an easier getaway. If they'd had automatic weapons—or more than one shot apiece—she might have liked their chances of going on the offensive. Instead of cowering in the house, they'd shoot their way out and take the fight right at those goons. She stood up and looked out the window at the street. If there had been hedges or bushes, they might hide outside in those, pick the bastards off as they attacked the front. She saw two, low stone walls that had good shooting positions, but anyone inside either of the homes behind those fences was bound to see them. And there at the window, those innocent bystanders might become more collateral damage, more bodies in her tally.

Best to be gone, she thought. The sooner the better. But where?

Amid the silent waiting, Wilson's phone rang. "Lexie!" he said, pleased to have someone other than Imogen and Ewan to talk with. He listened intently for some moments. "Right, ta," he said and hung up. "They're coming," he said to Imogen and Ewan. "They know where we are. They've tracked the car, too." He looked out the window. "Ah shoulda thought—the license starts wi the Dundee designation. Sticks right oot."

"They're coming now?" Imogen asked.

"As soon as they can," said Wilson flatly.

"And how does this Lexie know?" she asked.

"Buff sold them the guns for their attack."

"Why would he do that?" Johnston asked, "but still tell you?"

"He'd been told ta dae it by someone higher up in the organization—though Ah don't ken who. Buff had tae." Wilson shrugged as if it all made perfect sense. "Chain a command. But he could also warn me. Or he could tell Lexie to dae it. On his own initiative, like."

"Well, that's something," said Imogen. "How long ago?"

"They left about a quarter of an hour ago."

"It's only a little over half an hour from Dundee to here," said Johnston.

"So, they could be here any minute," said Imogen.

"I doubt it," Wilson began. "They were only two men, Lexie said, but they were outfitting for six. They'd have tae get back wi their mates an that." He checked the time on his phone.

"It's two o'clock more-or-less," he observed. "Ah'd reckon they'd want a bit of dark."

"Right," said Imogen. "If they came around three-thirty or four, they'd have some darkness, and be here before most people were back home from work. Fewer witnesses."

"And they're coming with assault rifles and submachine guns," Wilson added.

"Fucking hell," Johnston whispered.

"I thought Britain had draconian gun control laws," said Imogen.

"For the right price," said Wilson, "anything's possible. Anywhere."

In London, Percy's phone rang. "Jamie?" he said. "You're ready?"

"Yes," said Frenz. "We're loaded. Leaving within the hour."

"And you have them under control?" Percy asked, meaning Nesbitt's irregulars.

"Yes," said Frenz confidently. Then, "We'll see. I've paired one of ours with one of theirs every place I could. And I'll be on site, too."

"Good work. And be careful. Keep me apprised." He hung up.

Percy rested his elbows on the desktop and clasped his hands tightly together, like praying with fists. He rested his chin against his fists, staring at the computer screen, at the map of Alyth, the Streetview photos of the area. It was a good plan to pair buskers with the irregulars, he thought, but would it work? He considered where the various teams should set up, and he felt confident that Frenz's plan involved exactly what he'd have done—cover the back from the street behind, cover the exit to the park over the footbridge and attack from the front door with the battering ram, the "big red key."

If anything were routine about the pinch, he'd have felt that the odds favored Frenz's crew. On paper, the lineups and game plan were good for his team. The operation looked to be quick, surgical. Maybe a bit of tidying up with the local police afterwards, but that wouldn't be difficult. Still, this Alan Wilson had fought like a mad dog, the solicitor ran over one of the irregulars without so much as a pause. And those two were led by an FBI agent who'd fought and outsmarted a corrupted US government. As he thought more about it, she was very much the kind of person he'd have wanted on his side; was sorry that they were on opposite sides. Would *she* have acquiesced to Chamberlain's view back in '14?

He cleared his head and reached for the phone, calling an Edinburgh team that had been en route to Dundee. He hoped they wouldn't have to dirty their hands, but he needed backup. Leyser was right: now was not the time for half-measures. "It's near time," he said into the phone. "Status?"

"We're almost to station in Dundee," said the team leader.

"Don't stop. Continue to Alyth. The timing has moved up, I'm afraid. Team one will engage there in about an hour. I want you to be there to catch them if they fall. You understand the delicacy. If the worst happens, you have all the details."

Ian Ross wasn't finding anything helpful about Marta Serres through official channels. Decidedly unhelpful. National security meant that no one would say anything on the record, except to grudgingly acknowledge that it was happening. The back-channel discussions he'd been able to have were odd, though. And maddeningly incomplete. Pieced together by him, they told a story of confusion and indecision; of a rushed judgment and total secrecy with quick, unacknowledged administrative moves regarding repatriating Serres—only to have the process pause when orders were reversed.

Ross couldn't get through to Imogen, though he had tried several times. It seemed her phone was turned off. Or worse, he thought. He knew Serres had done some work with Imogen, but he didn't know the extent to which Imogen had taken her into confidence. She hadn't told *him* anything. So it was with empty hands that he knocked and entered Janette Ritchie's office that afternoon to give his non-status report.

"I can't get any official information on Professor Serres," he began, "only that it seems whatever process was working has stopped. She'd have been due to be repatriated by now, but she's still in the UK, in a detention centre...though no one will say where exactly."

Ritchie listened impassively.

"Have *you* heard anything more?" he asked. "She has young children here, is a well-respected scholar and she does consultative work for the electoral commission. There might be a PR angle there, though raising a public stink about it might make matters worse."

"Yes..." said Ritchie nebulously.

"I haven't seen or heard anything about the King's Speech and the Parliamentary agenda," he began.

"That's being handled behind the scenes. If we can get them not to go ahead with it, or only with some part of it, we need for it *not* to be known. Once it's known, it becomes harder to backtrack."

"*Are* they backtracking?"

"No. They're not even negotiating." She dropped her eyes back to her computer screen. Meeting concluded.

"You remember," he began tentatively, "I mentioned an unofficial investigation into voting fraud in the 'fourteen referendum? I can't find anyone to speak with me, but I think this Professor Serres may have been involved in it...if only partially."

Ritchie looked up again. "How did you hear that?"

Because I set it all up, he wished he had the courage to say. *Because it's all my fault*.

"Anything concrete?" she asked sharply. She searched his face, trying to figure out if this was a productive line of inquiry, or merely her communications adviser trying to make himself seem important. She went back to her work, deciding it was the latter. "Because I need evidence, Ian. Facts, figures. A trail. Do you have anything like that?"

"No," he said.

"Stay on this Serres case, Ian. For the time being, we still have jobs. Let's do them. See if there's anything that *can* be done. We're about to walk into a buzz-saw."

31

"Alan," Imogen asked, "you said you had a mate in Edinburgh?"

"Aye."

"Could we all stay there for a day or two?"

"Aye, but ye'd no like it. It's a cold flat wi beds on the floor, an tha. A toilet doon the stair. Mair a flophouse, like. Aberdeen would be farther oot the way..." he offered.

"No, we need to be close to Edinburgh if we have any hope of getting this information out. Is it safe?" she asked.

"Safe as houses...or tenements, I should say." He grinned.

"Is it some derelict building?" she wanted to know. "Would three people moving in not look suspicious? Not a shooting gallery or anything?"

"Not at aw," Wilson replied. "The front's respectable. It's a four-floor tenement. The lower floors are an Airbnb, like. All kinds of people comin and goin. Naebody looks at ye twice. But the top floor was never renovated."

"It's owned by the Madmen?"

"Aye. Even the Airbnb part."

"Would yer mate feel bound tae tell Buff aboot it?" asked Johnston.

"Naw..." he began and then reflected. "Ah donnae see why."

"Call him," she said. "Find out if we can stay there tonight and tomorrow. At least."

Alan got on the phone as Imogen zipped her laptop into its case and stuffed it into her bag. "The car's a problem," she muttered. She stood and walked to the stairs as Johnston put his laptop away. He took out his burner phone.

When she returned from collecting her things from the upstairs bedroom, Wilson flashed Imogen a thumbs-up. Johnston was on the phone, too.

"Right. An emergency, Mairtin," Johnston was saying. "Ye ken a wouldnae ask otherwise..." a pause to listen, then—"right, son, that's the *nature* of an emergency."

Imogen caught his eye, looked at him quizzically. Johnston smiled uncertainly at her, made a see-saw gesture with his free hand that seemed to suggest that whatever he was discussing could go either way. His face brightened: "Yer a star, you are, Mairtin! Ah'm tha' grateful." He gave Imogen a thumbs-up as well, though as yet she hadn't a clue why.

"Right, right," he was saying. "Ah know where you keep it. *Very* careful. Right, Ah promise." He hung up. "Ma auld school chum Mairtin's gonnae lend us a car from his garage. He works on old cars and gets them up tae snuff before selling them on. We could go noo." He looked at his watch. "We *should* go noo."

"Wait," said Imogen. "They're watching the house. Otherwise, how would they know about the car, like your friend Lexie told you," she said to Wilson.

"Right enough," he said.

"How far away is it?" Imogen asked Johnston. "The garage, I mean?"

The first silver delivery van pulled to a quick stop on James Street behind the Johnston house.

"James Street in place," said the passenger into his radio as he clambered into the back alongside his partner and readied his rifle. At the same moment, the busker who'd been watching the house stepped off his motorcycle on the opposite side of the footbridge.

"Parkside's in place," he said. "I can see that the car hasn't moved." Moments later, the main delivery van, driven by Frenz, sped past Wilson's car and pulled to a sharp stop blocking the exit to Smythe Street. Two of his men jumped out the sliding door and scampered toward the house. The lead man carried the "red key" and his partner an assault rifle.

"Look sharp, everyone," he said. "Here we go!"

The man with the key stopped at the front door and set his feet. He heaved the bosher against the front door. The door gave way, and he and his partner swarmed into the sitting room. Over the radio, Frenz heard Walker say, "front room clear." Frenz stepped out of the van and began walking toward the house. "James Street?" he said into the radio, "anything?"

"Nothing yet," the James Street team reported.

About this time a faded white Jaguar XF in need of some aesthetic attention sped southwesterly between fields along the A-94/Forfar Road. "Legend," Wilson whispered contentedly, settling back in his seat. Blueberry fields blurred past on either side.

"Oh!" said Imogen, "Blueberries."

"We're no stoppin," said Alan.

"No one asked tae, Alan," Ewan spat.

Twenty minutes earlier, they'd scarpered out the back door, squeezed through the space between the shed and the back neighbors' garage and they'd begun walking up James Street. She had nearly jumped out of her skin when a passing car on the main road honked at them, but it turned out only to be someone who knew Ewan.

In the car as they trundled southward, Alan Wilson turned around in the passenger seat to look at Imogen. "That's the way, eh?" he said to her. "None ae this macho shite aboot goin through brick walls, standin yer ground an that. Just scarper!" He nodded in appreciation. "Live tae fight another day, eh? Work smarter, no harder." He was about to turn back round in his seat when he added conspiratorially, "Hey, Ah'd love tae be a fly on the wall back there right aboot now"—his voice dropped into something approximating a Yorkshire accent— 'Oooh, where are they, de ye think? Foock if I know.' Wankers."

In Johnston's parents' house, Frenz spoke to Percy by phone as he stalked through the house. He kept his dismay—and fear for himself—masked behind a stern, angry expression. "The back door is open," he said. "But it's still warm in here. I doubt they've been gone long." Something caught his eye by the back window and he stepped toward it.

"Fuck," he said over the phone. "There's an empty box of Winchester two-forty-three cartridges. They're probably armed." He stood in the middle of the sitting room and turned round, taking it all in, the mask falling. "How did they *know*?"

"Fall back to Dundee for now," said Percy. "I'm going to look into it."

"Traveling in style," Wilson whispered, making himself comfortable in the car. "Ah'm thinkin aboot where we're goin and Ah'll be honest, counselor, Ah feel like Ah'm lettin the side down with the accommodations we'll be enjoying fae Edinburgh. Mebbe Ah should put in fir an upgrade to the penthouse suite. Ah'll learn tae crook ma wee finger."

The immediate danger rapidly diminishing behind them, Imogen almost felt something like the explorer-tourist she had hoped to be when this sabbatical had started. Ewan navigated the traffic confidently, Alan chattered inconsequentially as he blew cigarette smoke through a crack in his window, and she looked out the window taking it all in. Even the smoke didn't bother her, though she thought it was kind the way Ewan checked on her in the rearview from mirror time to time to see that she wasn't bothered about it.

Looking round as they thrummed along, it all looked so safe to her, so prosperous and tidy. But it was a lie. They weren't safe. They'd bought some time. But they still had no idea how to end this.

In London, Nesbitt did not take the news of his irregulars' failure well. They were falling back to Dundee, he had learned, to regroup. For what? he wondered. He had put in an angry call to Chamberlain, which caused him to call Percy. Some might have regarded it as chain-of-command. Percy thought it was merely an attempt to displace blame—ending with him. He did little to hide his irritation at being interrupted at a crucial time.

"I'm looking into it," said Percy. "They knew we were coming. Now, not only are they in the wind so to speak, but it seems that they're armed, and we don't know what car they're driving. *If* they're driving. The solicitor is from Alyth. Maybe he found someone else's house—some friend—to hide out with. It's possible they're still there."

"So, you know nothing?" said Chamberlain, his annoyance grating on Percy. "And why did you have them fall back to Dundee then?"

"What would you propose, a house-to-house search? We know they were tipped off," Percy rejoined. "I learned too late that you were outfitting the strike force through the Madmen."

"They didn't know why our men needed those things. Didn't need to," he declared.

"I expect they could guess," Percy offered, barely masking his own exasperation. "A quick tip-off to our witness? Why wouldn't they?"

"Because we made a deal!"

Percy stifled a laugh. *When you stop playing by the rules, so will everyone else*, he thought. He wondered idly about honor among thieves, noting that at least some of the Madmen seemed to have working moral compasses.

Patiently he said, "Even if they were wrong about why we needed their...equipment there's no harm—from their perspective—in giving their boy a heads-up. But now, sir, as I say, they're in the wind. They know we're after them. And it's probable they have at least one rifle."

"We've lost, then? Is that your defeatist attitude?"

"Far from it. I'm not defeatist, but a realist, looking at the situation coldly—*really*—and making a proper assessment of what's wanted. I have one or two ideas, and I need to get on them. So that's what I shall do. Unless you'd like me to give up. Sir." He hung up and walked to the door of his office, where he called to the Wire Services' head snooper, Catherine Hernes.

"Cathy," he began, his tone decidedly more dulcet than he'd just left off with, "could you come in for a moment? I'd like to follow up on one or two things."

* * *

Imogen stared out at the countryside. "Ewan," she began. "I think we need to talk with Ian Ross."

"You said—" he began.

"I know. And it's risky."

"Deadly so," he rejoined.

"But this needs to be dealt with at a high level," she pressed. "We don't know anyone that we could call and set a meeting. If we were to call the chief of staff directly, she'd put the security services on us first, even if she half-believed us. She'd regard it as maybe some kind of double-fake, misinformation...something designed to make her and the government look bad."

"And Ah don't fancy hangin aboot waitin tae have an accident while we cooled off in the cells or one ae they interview rooms," said Wilson. He rolled the window down a bit farther and flicked his cigarette at the countryside.

"Will he believe us?" Johnston wanted to know. "Will he help us?"

"I think," Imogen began carefully.

"How can we be sure we can trust him?" Johnston interrupted. "How do we—"

"We paint *him* into a corner," she said. "Alan, can I have your phone?"

Wilson looked at Johnston, who thought for a moment. Finally, he nodded to Wilson, who handed her his phone.

In his office, Percy asked Catherine Hernes to have a seat. She was young, and earnest, a bit awed to be in the office alone with Percy. This was the inner sanctum. Only Jamie Frenz spent any time here. Percy seated himself next to her in front of the desk.

249

"You've been doing a good job, Cathy," Percy began, "but I wonder if we could go a bit deeper. Have you been monitoring the irregulars who are attached to Jamie's detail?"

"Yes, I have, as instructed. I'm afraid there haven't been any new calls—only the ones I reported to you. And there hasn't been a peep...not even a blip from Trager or Johnston. It appears their phones are off and have been so for days now. We have no idea where they are."

"Yes," said Percy. "But about the irregulars..."

"And you are aware that a number of calls have gone from the irregulars to someone at the Home Office and to a Cabinet Minister?" she said.

"Yes."

"We aren't allowed to snoop on those, of course, and there's no open inquiry regarding them."

"No, there wouldn't be, would there," he noted.

"Without further, explicit instruction from superiors..."

"I understand that loud and clear." He smiled with what he hoped conveyed an avuncular warmth. "Wouldn't have it any other way. But you identified them, I think, by isolating their numbers from proximity to Jamie. Is that correct?"

"We did. Geo-fencing, it's called. We don't know names, but we can track the phones."

"Yes, good. I'm wondering if you could perhaps identify any new numbers in proximity to one or a number of the irregulars' phone signatures. Could you work up a sort of tracking timeline for today?"

"Certainly, sir."

"How long would that take you?"

"If you put Ned on my overwatch duties, and I worked only on that...an hour, maybe an hour and a half?"

"Lovely," said Percy. "Send Ned in, and please get right to work."

As the car left Perth, Imogen put in a call to Ian Ross. He didn't pick up, and Imogen left a message, telling him to call back at the new number.

"What if they're watching his phone?" said Johnston. "What if he gives us up? They can track us as soon as they know the number."

"Right," said Imogen. The phone started ringing. "We'll turn this one off as soon as we've conducted the business."

"Imogen!" Ross said down the line. "You're all right?"

"Yes, for now."

"Where are you?" he asked.

"We have evidence," she began, ignoring the question, "that the First Minister, or at least your boss, should see. There *was* interference in the election, and we have strong circumstantial evidence that—"

"Circumstantial?"

"Very strong. And we have a witness to the theft of ballot boxes in Dundee back in 2014. The murder of Wee Frankie and the apparent suicide of the ARO in Dundee, Donald Alban, makes that case all the stronger."

"My God! Where can we meet?"

"We can't. Not yet. Here's what you're going to do."

32

In London, Cathy Hernes was back in Percy's office. "I've sent you the tracking readout for the phone search you requested," she began. "If you could call it up on your screen, I could walk you through it."

Percy brought it up, a signal-tracking timeline set against a map that showed the movement of each of the phones they were watching. He turned his screen sideways so she could see as she stood at the side of his desk.

"The timestamp is there at the bottom left," she said. "This is from today, beginning at 0:01 this morning and carrying through until about 20 minutes ago. If I may..." She pressed 'play' onscreen, and the phones and their timelines leapt to life. "Not much going on from midnight until about 08:25 when we begin to see some activity."

They ran through the display at ten times the normal speed.

"As you can see," she continued, "not much activity. But a little after noon, as you can see here, two of the signals separate from the group." Hernes slowed the playback.

This is what Percy had wanted. Two signals from the irregulars' phones came into proximity with three unknown signals in northwest Dundee. They were at tight quarters, most likely inside, not meeting out of doors. Percy surmised it was the gun buy. He clicked pause.

"I wonder if you could look into these three new signals for me," he began.

Hernes grinned at him. "I've already done so, sir," she said. She handed him a piece of paper. "I wonder, sir, if you'd mind

252

signing the order to track those three. It's backdated to earlier this morning."

"With pleasure," he said with admiration.

"And...well, I went ahead and added all three into the rest of the search. Based on your...*earlier* request. The one you just signed."

"Thank you, Cathy. This is fine work. I think I can take if from here. Relieve Ned and resume your overwatch duties. Though I may have some questions when I've worked through all this. All right?"

"Of course," she said. She turned smartly on her heel and walked out.

Watching her go pertly back to her desk, Percy thought young Frenz had some strong, new competition. Of course, he reflected, if he didn't bring this case to a close Cathy might have *his* job, never mind Jamie's. The new phones, he found, weren't properly registered either—no real names attached to them— but he could still watch their progress. There wasn't much. The three new people remained behind for much of the day after the irregulars left. But less than ten minutes after they left, there was a call to yet another new number. In Alyth.

In Alyth, he saw, there were no other signals around the new number, perhaps that of Alan Wilson. Hernes had said she believed that Johnston and Trager had their phones off. He enlarged the frame to look closer at where in Alyth the signal was coming from. It corresponded with the location of the address they had. Letting the playback continue at quadruple time, he saw Wilson's phone move off from the house. Smart of Cathy to "follow" him now as well. He took his eyes off the screen to review the order he had signed. Bless her, the number attached to Wilson was included in the permissions. If he was going to fail and have the book thrown at him, he'd like it known that it was the book he'd always gone by the letter of. Mostly.

It was probable they were all together. And yet, his man, Davidson, had seen only Wilson during his surveillance of the house. Could this be some sort of misdirection on Trager's part?

She was canny, true, but could she be that clever while on the run? And they *were* running. After the call alerting Wilson, he'd placed a call to someone in Edinburgh, and then to someone there in Alyth. Quickly thereafter, the signal moved away from the house, about a quarter of an hour before Frenz and his merry band arrived there. They seemed to be on foot, because later the signal moved quickly away from Alyth down the A94 toward Perth, and presumably on to Edinburgh. A few miles short of Perth, and just before the playback ended, he saw a phone call from Wilson's phone to someone in St. Andrew's House in Edinburgh.

Percy walked to Hernes's desk. "That traveling signal down the A94 at the end of the playback," he said, "what more do you have on it?"

"Nothing, sir. I'm sorry. We lost the signal right around Perth. I think it's been turned off, too."

They crossed the new Forth Bridge and headed into the city along the Queensferry Road, through the Meadows and suddenly they had arrived at Bernard Terrace. Imogen stepped out of the car and stretched, astonished to be looking down the road right at the pommel of King Arthur's Seat.

"Beautiful!" she said. "Where's the castle?" she asked, turning round.

Wilson shrugged as he walked across the street to the building, one of many aging terrace facades mottled with new, fortifying white sandstone perched amidst the weathered stone.

Ewan pointed vaguely northward. "But you can't see it from here," he said.

Already at the dull, battered door, Wilson worked the key code.

"This is an Airbnb?" she asked.

"More accommodation rooms, like," said Wilson. "There are a coupla swanky apartments on the third floor, but they're no fer the likes of us." He grinned.

The front door opened onto a Stygian hallway, its walls and ceiling a dispiriting putty color. If the shade had been chosen for its dirt-hiding properties, it had failed. In the dim light, large stains loomed. Candy wrappers and torn bits of newspaper congregated along the sides. At the end of the hall, the entry to the stairs leading down to the basement was covered in yellow caution tape. Past the tape, there was nothing but a ghostly outline etched in the wall where a staircase had formally been.

"Jesus," Imogen breathed.

Wilson, hearing her, looked back over his shoulder as he mounted the steps to the fourth floor: "Temporarily closed for renovations," he quipped. "Pardon our mess!" he sang.

Percy charged Catherine Hernes with finding the identity of the person Wilson had phoned at St. Andrew's House, the Scottish government offices. Then he drew what files he had on the Madmen. As an MI5 officer, he had access to files on the Madmen's key players, but because organized crime wasn't his area, the information he had on the files contained few details regarding their holdings and operations. To involve MI5 further in his mess, he'd be inviting a wider interest. Which he could ill afford. But he held a double role, as MI5 officer and as commander of the Special Enquiry Team in the Met Police. So, it was to his Met Police opposite number in the Specialist Crime & Operations (SC&O) Organised Crime Project Team that he now turned, Simon Mundry.

After dispensing with pleasantries and a quick catch-up, he turned to the real reason for his call. "Simon, I'm wondering if I could get a look-in at what you might have concerning the Madmen syndicate's operations. Specifically, real estate they might control in and around Edinburgh. We have a witness in a delicate case, and he may be hiding in something like a safe house run by them. I realize it's an imposition, and I'd be happy to send someone round to do the digging, if you'd point her in the right direction..."

"Ye-ess," said Mundry. "I'm sure we can make some accommodation."

"Thank you," said Percy, though he noted that Mundry's tone didn't sound anything like accommodating.

"But there may be some difficulties, Calum. Delicate in nature. Having to do with exposure. You see, there may be a good many chargeable things we know about, but that we're allowing to continue in the hope of it leading to something bigger or at having a wider view of their enterprise. The worst thing we can do is to let it be known *what* we know. I'm sure you understand."

"Yes, I see," said Percy. He had been prepared for reluctance. "I can assure you that we'd make no move on the property in question—if indeed we can find it—but rather take the witness some ways apart from said property. Officially, if it comes to that, we'd say we received a tip-off."

"Ye-ess...It might help me, Calum, if I understood the nature of your investigation."

"I regret that I'm not able to divulge details. My other hat, shall we say?"

"And you need to keep things under it?"

"Yes, rather. But. As a brother-in-arms I can tell *you* that it concerns a witness to—and possibly a perpetrator *in*—an attack against some occasional laborers I use in...my other capacity. No hint of your intelligence gathering will make it into any report. Unless, upon consultation with you, you find that it would be advantageous that it did. In which case, I can also be accommodating."

There was a long pause. Finally, he said, "Send your man round. I'll make sure we point him in the right direction. But I will require him to stay within the confines you and I have just discussed. Who is it, Frenz?"

"Thank you," said Percy, "but today it'll be Catherine Hernes. New girl. Very keen. Jamie's in the field just now."

Hernes herself was waiting outside the closed office door. Hanging up, he beckoned her in.

Closing the door behind her, she said, "The number you asked about at St. Andrew's House belongs to the communications adviser. An Ian Ross."

When Imogen had told Ian Ross what he needed to do, it contained all that he had feared it would: full admission, full disclosure, including who had recruited him; dates of phone calls and meetings, subjects discussed. He had also written his resignation. It would mean being on the outside again. But the inner circles of power were dismayingly corrupt, and he might himself end up a casualty if he didn't come clean now.

He had spent some time that afternoon putting it into a coherent form. His first meetings with Chamberlain in London, their discussions surrounding possible interference in the referendum, and most damning, the date and time of his call regarding Wee Frankie and the information that he had a friend who had proof. Further, he detailed the surveillance Chamberlain had more-or-less admitted to regarding Imogen's trip to Dundee. His upbraiding for not being more thorough.

Imogen didn't trust him, *and why should she?* he thought. She had told him that he was to see Janette Ritchie, to make a full disclosure of his activities. Then he was to relate what Imogen had told him; that she had proof, a witness, and could deliver more.

But the only way she would trust that he had done all that, was if Ritchie and Ross both "met" virtually with Imogen over Facetime, conducted through Ritchie's personal phone. Imogen had demanded the number. Ritchie would hear their findings, and they would arrange next steps and how to transmit it all to her. He was standing up, detailed report and resignation in hand, when his phone rang.

"She called you?" Chamberlain shouted over the phone. "And you didn't tell us!"

"I was about to call you," he said. "The chief's been in my office every ten minutes this whole afternoon," he lied. "There's something big happening, though I don't know what it is. Something to do with Parliament."

"Yes," said Chamberlain. "Is the chief there now? May I have your report?" His voice dripped sarcasm.

"Yes, of course. Though there's not much to tell. She's scared. She called about two hours ago from somewhere on the road. She said she had information about the referendum. But she wouldn't tell me more. She wouldn't say where she was or where she was going. She said she'd me call back when it was safe."

"And that's how you left it?" Chamberlain asked.

"I had to. She'll get me the information when she feels safe."

"And you'll get it to me."

"Of course," said Ross.

"And make sure you set up a place to meet. Our people will be there, too."

"Sounds ominous," said Ross.

"Yes. For them. And for you, if you can't deliver. But you may still come out to the good. With advantage. Hold your nerve."

"Very good, sir." Ross disconnected. Ominous for all of them. He'd begun to field questions from journalists about what he might have heard about whisperings of a bold new direction for the opening of Parliament come Monday. Not one of those who called knew anything worthwhile, but the Westminster PR machine was ginning up. He drew a deep breath and turned to the final page of his statement. In the blank space at the bottom, he wrote the date, checked his watch and wrote the time. And then wrote a précis of the discussion he and Chamberlain had just concluded. He phoned through to Janette Ritchie.

"Not now!" she said by way of greeting. "Only matters of life and death—"

"—That's precisely the matter I'm calling about," he interrupted.

Percy texted Hernes, asking for a status report. She responded that she might be on to something, before adding that she had already thought that on two earlier occasions. She ended her text with a frowny face emoji. He texted Frenz and the back-up detail on station in Dundee. The message to both was the same: *Move to the capitol. Targets somewhere in Edinburgh. Need to be ready. Details to follow.*

When there were any.

Johnston had suggested the café around the corner from Blackwell's bookstore, across from Old College on South Bridge for Imogen's talk with the chief of staff. It was about a ten-minute walk from where they were staying, and it had Wi-Fi. Imogen would be able to keep her phone signal masked—in airplane mode—but still use the Wi-Fi for her Facetime call with Ritchie. All three hurried down the dark stairs of their tenement and headed north, walking briskly toward Blackwell's.

In St. Andrew's House, Janette Ritchie was red-faced with fury. "For fuck's sake, Ian! What were you thinking?" She read over the disclosure again.

"I..." he faltered. He checked his watch. "She may be calling anytime now. Facetime."

"And who is she again? Why is an American even involved?"

Ross gave the short explanation: that she was on sabbatical at University of Glasgow; that she was the one who'd broken the Faithless Elector case. He'd thought to enlist her because she was outside the mainstream. And since he didn't think there was anything to turn up, it seemed...

"Wise? Is that what you're going to say? It seemed like the *smart* thing, the *right* thing to do? Fucking hell!"

"Obviously," he proffered a piece of paper, "you can have my resignation."

She took it from him, held it in the air. The resignation was signed and dated, with a line for her to sign and date. She started to hand it back to him. "I'm not going to fire you, Ian." She stopped and drew back the paper. "Not yet anyway."

Catherine Hernes had come through. She had identified four separate places that might fit the bill as safe houses for Madmen operatives. She texted the addresses to Percy and headed back. Percy's men were about to leave Dundee when he forwarded the texted addresses to them. Frenz texted back that he would divide the men into four groups and set up outside each place.

Percy stressed delicacy, as he had personally promised it in return for the information. Frenz let it be known that allowing for travel time and getting secured, they would be staked out in no more than two-and-a-half hours. Percy acknowledged the text and went outside to see if Ned on overwatch had seen any developments.

"Nothing, I'm afraid," he said.

Janette Ritchie's phone made the characteristic, insistent Facetime ring. "Well," she said to Ross, "you'd better come stand by me, so she knows we're together." Ross moved around the desk as she accepted the call.

"This is Imogen Trager," she began, sitting in a corner of the Blackwell's café. "I'm here with my associates." She rotated the phone as she said, "This is Ewan Johnston, solicitor, and friend, to the former Dundee ARO Donald Alban." Johnston nodded gravely. "And this is our witness to the ballot theft in Dundee, Alan Wilson." Wilson tossed his head back slightly, chin up, an East Coast wave. Imogen brought the phone back to herself, while Johnston and Wilson went back to monitoring the room and activity outside the front window.

"And I'm Chief of Staff to the First Minister, Janette Ritchie. Ian Ross, I think you know. I've heard a good deal about what Ian's been mixed up in, but he also said you had proof."

"I can send you the documents right now, if you'd like," said Imogen.

"That would be helpful. Time is of the essence. I don't know if Ian's told you..."

"He has," Imogen interrupted. "Your email address?"

Ritchie gave it and Imogen sent the statement of findings report, with backup, including the scanned sheets of Alban's notes from the night along with scans of the handwritten sheets from tellers Gem Diamond and Gerry McTavish, her and Marta Serres' work; Wee Frankie's surmises about Nigel Chamberlain and Jefferson Weaver; and Wilson's statement of what happened the night of the referendum.

Through the phone, Imogen watched Ritchie open the file and begin reading. "Are you somewhere safe right now?" Ritchie asked.

"Yes," said Imogen. "For now, it seems."

Ross leaned down toward the camera lens. "They're tracking whatever phone you used last, 'Gen," he said. "I had a call from Chamberlain about you. He knew that you'd called me."

Imogen was shaken. Out of reflex, she looked around the café. She quickly gathered herself and asked, "and what did you tell him?"

"That you were worried about safety; that you hadn't told me where you were or where you were going, but that you'd be in touch as soon as you felt it was safe."

"Good. Okay," she said absently.

Ritchie was still reading from her screen, but her eyes were wide.

"You'll see that while it is largely circumstantial..." Imogen began.

Ritchie cut her off. "This is astonishing, Ms. Trager. There's much to digest and consider. We have the documents, but we need you, too. *Are* you three safe for now? We could bring you in..."

Across the table from her Wilson was shaking his head, no. She glanced at Johnston who was doing the same thing. "Anyone official," Wilson said in a hissing whisper as he pointed at the phone, "could be working with they boays we're tryin tae avoid. Not her, obviously, but who's workin fir her? We wouldney last the night."

"We're fine for now, I think," Imogen stated as confidently as she could muster.

Onscreen, she saw Ross lean down and whisper something into Ritchie's ear. Was he talking about her as the risk-reward lass? she wondered.

In her political role, Ritchie was concerned with controlling that which *could* be controlled—political messaging, line votes—and taking opportunities—breaking news, scandal, fortuitous gossip—when they presented themselves. It was rarely ideal to smother opportunities, or immediately wrest what was useful from them. Such things had to be handled, not controlled. Like Weaver and his calamity projects, a crisis *was* a terrible thing to waste.

This was new to her, containing a great many moving parts. Her institutional instinct told her to bring them in. Now. And to keep them safe, under her control. But what they had brought her was highly charged, dangerous. The three involved—along with the detained Strathclyde professor, Serres—were themselves highly volatile, like a downed power line; and you don't go grabbing hold of something like that before taking thought. She considered for a moment longer before saying, "I understand your concerns. I'm not sure I share them. We have good people here. But your instincts have kept you alive and kicking so far, so let's go with that."

"Do we need to come in at all?" Imogen asked.

"Yes," said Ritchie. "I'm going to have a team up all night going through this—attorneys, political people, election specialists like yourself. And we'll have questions for each of you on the record. The testimony you'll give in response, in addition to what you've already provided, is the only way you'll be truly safe."

Imogen looked across at Wilson and Johnston. They seemed to agree, though Wilson was mouthing the word "testimony" with dismay and not a little distaste. On her phone, she saw Ross lean down and whisper something else to Ritchie, who nodded and said, "Be at St. Andrew's House at eight tomorrow morning?" said Ritchie. "Bring all the documents you've just emailed me with you. I'll make sure your arrival is public—but safe—and that you're *seen* delivering something important directly to me. We'll meet outside—me, Ian and possibly some others—before coming inside." She paused a moment before continuing: "Thank you for bringing this to us. It couldn't have been easy, and your bravery and commitment to truth are greatly appreciated. See you in the morning."

Imogen disconnected and sat back with a lingering sense of dissatisfaction. It was always like that, she reflected. Lingering. No single, gestalt moment of done.

"Ah could murder a kebab right aboot noo," said Wilson. "Let's get some food and run along hame."

Imogen nodded. "Ewan, could you order me a large, black coffee to-go? I'm going to want something first thing tomorrow."

"I didn't see a hob or microwave in the flat."

"Cold will be fine." She reached for her wallet.

Johnston waved at her to keep her money as he stood up. "Alan?" he asked.

"Aye, why not? Ta."

Imogen called up email. The top message hit her like a slap in the face: "IMMEDIATE RETURN – Disciplinary Hearing" it read. A cold jolt hit her. It was from her boss, Benoit, copy to the FBI director's office, attorney general's office, the director of personnel, and an FBIAA union representative. Well, she thought, it had finally happened. The email was dated today.

With an odd feeling of resignation, she scanned it. Phrases like "superseding authority" and "illegal investigation" leapt out at her. She was to "return to the US to answer charges relating to..." She stopped reading. She was to be on a plane by no later than Tuesday of the following week. Today was Wednesday. Tomorrow she, Ewan and Alan would deliver the fruit of her illegal investigation to the Scottish authorities. By Monday, something would be happening. And Tuesday, she'd have to leave.

Her heart pounded in her chest. She had hoped to postpone a decision about her working future until near the end of her leave. Which had roughly seven months to go. Her face flushed, her mouth set grimly, she composed a number of responses in her head. Most of them, she realized, could be reduced to "Fuck you." Best to leave it as seemingly unread until after tomorrow at least. She might need allies—even ones, like the FBI, who might assist in order to avert Bureau embarrassment. Johnston, returning with the coffees for the morning, stopped short of the table.

"All right?" he asked her.

Imogen nodded.

33

There was little talking going on amongst the assembled "team" members nestled between the Indian silver greywood panels of the fourth floor conference room. The divider had been opened and Ritchie's burrowers had spread out across the two rooms. Heads down, four men and four women, each with a particular specialty, peered into their laptops, reviewing the part they had been assigned. They typed notes, concerns and questions that would be gathered and edited into a broader document for the morning.

Ian Ross's phone rang and he stepped out to take a call from Nigel Chamberlain. Ritchie followed him out.

"Anything?" Chamberlain demanded.

"Nothing," said Ross. "Jesus, I thought it was her just now."

"Can't you call you her?"

"No," said Ross. "That's the problem. She's spooked. Look, what's happened? She can't have put it together about Wee Frankie"—he gave a sideways glance toward Ritchie. She looked on with growing anticipation.

"Not unless *you* let something slip," Chamberlain rejoined.

"But I don't know anything. Maybe it's time I did. I might be more useful."

"You couldn't be much less useful." Chamberlain hung up.

"Not very damning," Ritchie observed.

In London, Chamberlain was with Weaver, Nesbitt and Townsend. There couldn't be any group texts or calls going between them at this late date. As he hung up, he turned to them and said: "No news...which is good news. Time is on *our* side. And, as I mentioned earlier, Percy may have a line on them."

"This waiting is agonizing," said Townsend.

"The main outline of our original plan is still in force: if we can get to him, a criminal underworld figure like Wilson gunned down—and the other two, regrettably, caught in a crossfire—might still benefit our cause. Even if they've somehow transmitted *some* of what they know, there's not much use in a non-existent witness. If he could be killed and organized crime smeared for it, it might undercut whatever hearsay Johnson and Trager have come up with. We must hold our nerve."

Settling nerves was more what concerned the three fugitives as they lay down on their beds in the cold flat on the top floor. It was only ten o'clock, but with nothing to do but wait until morning they had decided to turn in early. Imogen scooted and shifted under the duvet cover, shivering herself warm. She punched her pillow a couple of times, with no visible effect nor enhancement of comfort. Well, she thought, it was just one night. Would it really be all over soon? Would those who were so intent on kidnapping or killing Alan catch up with them? Ian had said they were tracing their phones. Which increased the likelihood that it was someone in government. That probably meant MI5 or the Met Police. Or both. Was there even more here than she had been able to find out?

What she'd done was enough, she told herself—enough to put her in danger and to get her fired when she went back to the United States. Could this Janette Ritchie go deeper? Expose whatever lay behind it? Whoever "they" were, perhaps they had to be sure their unnecessary interference in the referendum remained hidden, not only because it would undercut the power grab set for Monday, but because it might implicate something they had done during the Remain or Leave campaign.

In the documents she had sent to Ritchie, she had flagged the names Chamberlain and Weaver, because they had also figured largely in Frankie's notes concerning Brexit disinformation. In the dim light seeping through the windows, she saw Johnston shift one way and another as he also tried to get comfortable, and then seemed to drift off to sleep. For his part, Wilson lay on top of his duvet, playing some game that had come with his phone—one that didn't need Wi-Fi.

The whole case was like this room, she thought: dark, hard-to-see outlines; you could guess at what else was there, but you couldn't know. Rash decisions and bloody-minded stubbornness had led her step-by-step to this gray, freezing room. Even her diminished role at the Bureau now seemed untenable. She thought of her friends in the Bureau, Amanda Vega and Nettie Sartain. They were effective, respected, admired. Promoted. They achieved things without pissing people off and suffering the enduring enmity of their superiors. Why was she like this? She had risked all twice and had paid a heavy price—personally and professionally. So had others. She might yet pay the ultimate price. So might Alan and Ewan.

The cover pulled up to her nose, Imogen idly watched Wilson at the far side of the room until some ten minutes later when, bored by the game, he switched it off and put the phone on the floor by the bed, extinguishing the sole light source in the room. He rolled over and scooted under his covers. Imogen looked toward Ewan, quiet, unmoving. As she stared at him, his breathing didn't sound like someone who was sleeping, lacked the evenness and depth of slumber. He was lying on his back. Were his eyes open? In the dark, she couldn't be certain. For perhaps a quarter of an hour more she stared toward him. Still, he didn't move, still, he seemed to be staring at the ceiling.

"Ewan," she whispered.

She saw his head turn toward her. She glanced toward Wilson, who did seem to be asleep. She rose, wrapping the duvet around her. The cold, bare floor stabbed at her stocking feet as she toddled over to him. "Scoot over," she whispered. "If you'd like to."

He moved to one side of the narrow bed and pulled the cover back. She climbed in and he dropped the cover over her.

"Tell the truth, noo, hen," he whispered as he took her face gently in his hands and kissed her. "Yer only here tae get warm, aren't you?"

She worked herself a little closer to him, put her arms around his neck and kissed him. "Not only," she said playfully. "I mean..." she put a hand on his chest and stroked it. "I've been thinking about you. And me. Maybe an us. Am I wrong to think you...?"

"*An us*?" he asked playfully. "Where *do* you Americans learn your grammar?" More seriously, he added, "No, you're not wrong," he said.

She laid her head on his chest. "It looks like the FBI is going to fire me," she said. "Someone has gotten to them." She raised her head to look in his eyes again. "Whatever happens tomorrow or after...I don't want us to just go separate ways." She brushed a strand of hair from his face as she looked into his eyes. "I wanted to be close." She glanced over her shoulder toward where Wilson slept before adding. "But tonight, I don't think—"

"Och, dae whit ye wull!" said Wilson from his side of the room as he made a big show of turning his back on them. "Ah wouldney watch, or anything, but it'd nice tae know *something* good's happenin in this dirty world..."

Outside, in a parking space along Bernard Terrace, it was even colder. Jamie Frenz sat watch in a car, as his compatriots did at three other locations across the city. To stay ahead of police patrols, which might notice and question someone sitting idly in a car late at night, a total of five cars rotated through the city on a two-hour timetable between the four locations across the city—always one car spare. Frenz took status reports throughout the night from the others and relayed them to Percy in London.

Chamberlain's tête-à-tête had broken up, and each had gone his separate way. Across the south, in London, in Cambridge and in the Chiltern Hills, the four men who had sown this bit of chaos in the hope of grabbing more power kept vigil, too. Apprehensive of what the day might bring, Jefferson Weaver's dream of digital kingmaker felt stillborn now, a nightmare of regret and dashed hopes. Separately, Nesbitt fretted while Townsend dozed fitfully, both anxious that their standing might diminish, that their prospect of a sovereign Britain, a government beholden to them, might fade. Chamberlain sat in his study, two cell phones charging, the overnight news running muted on the television in front of him.

In contrast to the impatient silence of the triumvirate and their servants, at St. Andrew's House, Ritchie's team continued their feverish work to cull a coherent narrative and timeline. With Ian Ross's statement—and there had been some bitter, angry stares directed his way—they were able to add in more details—most notably that Nigel Chamberlain was a confirmed actor in this drama. If not the leader, he was at least high up. The fact that "official channels" had been used to try and warn off Trager, strongly suggested MI5 or Met involvement. As a precaution, though perhaps tardily so, since the documents Trager had sent had been disseminated via email, Ritchie instructed the diggers to turn off their WIFI connections. Only one computer would have access.

They brought out a large whiteboard on an easel and were busy drafting a visual representation of the conspiracy. Chamberlain's name went at the top on the right-hand side of the board, circled with lines radiating outward. Above his name were question marks.

"Who's directing him?" Ritchie called out. "That eager little shit"—here she tapped Chamberlain's name on the board—"wouldn't go to the toilet without someone else's say-so." At the end of one of the short, radiating lines away from Chamberlain's name, she wrote "MI5/Met-?" She pointed at the one person with a laptop still tied to Wi-Fi: "Gavin," she called, "who's head of Met's Special Enquiry Team? They'd have investigated—and possibly covered up—this mess."

At the top left on the board, Weaver's name. A solid line stretched across the top connecting Weaver and Chamberlain. Gavin, quarantined at the far end of the room, called out Percy's name. Ritchie duly wrote "Calum Percy/SET Commander" directly under MI5.

In London, alone in his office, Percy worried too. He had sent his new righthand man, Catherine Hernes, home for the evening; and he couldn't shake the notion that he had done it partially to avoid damaging her good opinion of him if Frenz's operation miscarried. The sting he felt at disappointing a promising young officer like Hernes caused him to wonder again why he had originally acquiesced to this cover up, why he had ignored his own compass. Which inevitably brought him to thoughts of Imogen Trager. He turned to the file Frenz had prepared on her. Was it only two weeks ago?

He had read the file often enough that most things in it were familiar to him. He turned quickly through the pages, picking at the scab of his conscience. Her dogged pursuit of those behind the Faithless Elector case in the US stood out to him like a rebuke. Those in command had waved her off, dismissed her concerns and finally demoted her for her actions—even though they were the right ones. She'd have never taken this devil's deal, he thought. Never have faltered in her lust to expose the truth.

Whereas, Percy accused himself, he had concealed interference in an election. Further, by his inaction, he had helped to conceal Frank McDougal's murder and that of Donald Alban. Marta Serres was cooling in a detention center near Luton Airfield, in legal limbo and stateless. They had tried to kill the young villain, Alan Wilson (and would try again if they had the chance in the morning). He knew that once the shooting started, there would be no way to save Trager or the solicitor. And he would have to throw a National Security blanket over that, too. What more might happen that he would need to keep concealed? How much farther away from true north would he stray?

Next morning, Imogen brushed her teeth and wrangled her hair into something close to presentable in the cold bathroom at the top of the stairs while Johnston and Wilson dressed inside the flat. Johnston brushed at the dirt on his trousers, frowned at the wrinkled shirt he was meant to put on. Wilson fired up a cigarette and drank deeply from the cold coffee.

Imogen came back into the room and walked over to kiss Johnston. As they embraced, Wilson observed: "Ye know, Ah couldae done wi' a bit cuddle maself last night," his smile crooked around the cigarette end. She walked over to him, and despite the smoke gave him a warm hug.

"You gonnae let me drive this morning, counselor?" he asked.

"Aye, why not," said Johnston. He tossed him the keys to the Jaguar.

Outside, a bleary watcher, one of Nesbitt's irregulars, took the call that his replacement was en route, and he should be ready to trade parking spaces and move along. "I'll be ready," he said. "It'll be nice to have a few hours rest."

"By all means rest," came the reply from Frenz, "but stay sharp."

The man in the car frowned uncertainly as he contemplated how he might sleep sharply. "Fucking officers," he muttered, shaking his head. "What *do* they think with?"

Inside the tenement, Imogen was also counseling that they remain sharp. "This feels like the end," she was saying, "but until we're inside St. Andrew's House—and maybe not even then—this isn't over."

Wilson nodded. Johnston took a deep breath, almost forgetting to exhale.

"They've gone to a lot of trouble to find us. They found Alan's phone somehow. There's no telling what other tools they have to locate us. Maybe they know the car, too. We have to be on our guard."

"Maybe I should drive," said Johnston.

Wilson held out the keys as though handing them over, before he quickly snatched them back. "Naw," he said, grinning. Johnston grasped playfully at Wilson's hand.

"Guys," she said. "Focus."

At St. Andrew's House, the overnight scramble had left the double conference room strewn with coffee cups, empty plates and stray papers. A second whiteboard had been unearthed and placed next to the first. It pieced together the timeline of the conspiracy events—dates, actions, and likely perpetrators. Janette Ritchie was stalking through the room, checking the progress of each person, when Ross tapped her on the shoulder.

"It's getting near time," he said. "They'll be on their way. Maybe already. If they're somehow early, it wouldn't do to—"

"Yes," she said sharply. "Have you tried calling her?" she asked as they moved toward the stairs.

"Twice," he said. "No joy."

"Is security in place? Did you drop some hints in the right journalistic corners?" "Everything's ready."

On Bernard Terrace, the man who was looking forward to a sharp rest saw his fellow operative come into the rearview mirror. He started the engine and made to pull out of the spot. The new watcher, glided slowly along the street. He watched the man he was replacing pull away. He drew up, ready to reverse into the open parking spot when he realized that another car, a tiny Honda Jazz, had been following him closely and was now stopped next to the open space, blocking his ability to pull in.

"Fucksake!" he hissed. He looked out the grimy back window and motioned the other car around. The figure inside the Honda made a helpless gesture with his hands. Or was it her hands? It was difficult to see. Irrespective of who was inside, the Honda stayed where it was. The relief driver pointed elaborately at the space he wanted into and signaled again that the other car should go round.

Across the street and down the block from where this urban dumb show unfolded, Imogen, Johnston and Wilson walked out the front door and made purposefully for the car, unseen by the relief driver, who had finally made his intentions clear to the driver in the Honda. The car backed up, however, rather than go round. He reversed slowly into the space while the Honda waited.

As he pulled forward to straighten himself against the curb, the Honda drew level, stopped, and the middle-aged woman inside started gesticulating angrily about something or other. The relief man peered through his window at her incredulously as he killed the engine. His quarry had reached their car, and it was only the flash of red hair that caught his eye as Imogen clambered into the back. The Jaguar started the pull out and he saw Imogen and Johnston clearly through the side windows. But the relief man was caught in the parking space.

"Fuck!" he screamed and started the car. He laid on the horn, a constant bellow, but the Honda, and its driver, remained unmoved. It was her turn to look incredulous. Over the car horn, he said into the radio: "This is Ed-4, on station at Bertrand Terrace. Targets are here. Together. They've just left in a white Jaguar XF."

"Are you in pursuit?" asked Frenz.

"I'm stuck in the parking space by some madwoman!"

"What?"

"Will advise." He clicked off his safety belt and opened the car door. As he unfolded his bulk from the car, the Honda sped away. He closed the door and pulled out after them, speeding round the Honda.

"In pursuit now," he said. "Turning left—North—onto St. Leonard's."

"Watch yourself," Frenz admonished, "you're going to drive right by a police station."

The relief driver eased off on the accelerator. "Copy," he said. "They're a ways ahead, but I have eyes on them."

"Keep your radio on," said Frenz. "We'll use the signal to converge. But take them if you can. Cars are converging on your route."

"With pleasure." The relief driver dropped the radio on the seat next to him. He heard Frenz telling others to gather. As he passed beyond the police station he pressed hard on the accelerator, closing the distance.

Inside the Jaguar, Wilson swore. "Ah think we've got someone on our tail."

Imogen turned around and looked out the back. She could see a dark blue car speeding up on them. "I only see a single driver," she said. "No one else in the car."

"Right, we'll have to watch ahead, too," said Wilson.

"They've seen me," said the relief driver. "They're accelerating."

"Stay with them," he heard Frenz say on the radio next to him.

The dark blue relief car continued closing the distance, coming right on the back of the Jaguar. Wilson's eyes were fixed on the road ahead. Johnston turned to look out the back. "Faster, Alan. Faster!"

"Ah'm bringin him in." Wilson had noticed something.

"You're what?" Imogen and Johnston asked in unison.

"Talk tae me, Goose," said Alan.

Johnston and Imogen exchanged a confused look as the relief car smashed into the back of the Jaguar. They approached a wide spot—Deaconness Garden on the left, and Brown Street to the right. Inside the Jaguar they could feel the back end break sideways with the force of the pursuit car.

Wilson made two quick adjustments: he turned slightly to the right and accelerated. The relief car matched his speed. Then Wilson turned sharply left. The pursuit car, hard on their bumper, slid off the back and rammed at full speed into some dumpsters corralled between a set of metal bollards. The right rear wheel of the Jaguar clipped the curb, but the pursuit car crumpled and twisted with the force of the impact. The Jaguar, back in its lane, roared up Pleasance.

"Splash one!" yelled Wilson. He caught Johnston's look out of the corner of his eye. "*Top Gun*," he said. "The film? Och, c'mon!"

"And you're Maverick?" asked Imogen.

"Aye. Only Ah'm taller than Tom Cruise. Just."

A minute later, Wilson sped through the Cowgate intersection and onto the cobblestone of the St. Mary's Street hill. The car rattled and bounced. Johnston put his hand to the ceiling to help hold him in his seat. He glanced nervously about the car, wondering how well his pal Mairtin had put the car back together. Imogen, wondering if they'd run a red light at Cowgate looked out the back and saw a new car slide around the corner and speed toward them. "Mig-2 on your ass, Mav!" she said.

Johnston gave her look that asked, "Why are you encouraging this?"

The street grew narrow and cars flashed by in the opposite lane. Wilson put on the emergency flashers and started laying onto the horn. The car bounced and shimmied across the cobblestone. Imogen reached down by her feet and unzipped the gun case. She drew out the shotgun, cracked it to make sure it was loaded and reached for the rifle. She set both across her lap.

"Turn here!" yelled Johnston, as Wilson ran the light and turned hard onto the Cannongate, blissfully tarmacked and a downhill slope. Wilson sped up—he was loving the Jaguar—leaving Mig-2, a green VW Golf in the distance. Wilson narrowed his eyes.

"He's no comin on," Wilson observed. "Bet he's a spotter. Watch ahead counselor and keep an eye oot at the crossings." The car continued at 50 miles per hour between sooty, stone buildings.

In Mig-2, the driver radioed that they were heading for the Scottish Parliament Building. Frenz ordered the cars to converge there. One would make it.

As the Jaguar flew toward the roundabout at the base of the street, a Skoda surged out of the Horse Wynd road, narrowly missing them. Wilson again made two, deft turns, downshifted and growled up Abbey Hill Road. Inches behind him, the Skoda missed the mangled rear bumper of the Jaguar and lurched sideways into the curb before righting itself and continuing pursuit.

The Skoda's left rear-wheel axle had bent. The engine whined and shook, champing to rejoin the chase, but it slowed, like running with a dead leg. The Jaguar surged ahead up the hill. Over the chunk and thud of the damaged wheel, the driver radioed that their quarry was headed up Abbey Hill Road, just as Mig-2 overtook it and roared up the hill. Ahead, Wilson's eyes flicked toward the rearview mirror. "Mig-two's back," he said.

He accelerated, pressing his advantage. Inside the car, the green blur of the park gave way to a haze of gray, dun and red sandstone.

Near the top of the hill, as they approached Regent's Terrace, Wilson's instinct to climb took him through the stop light where he aimed the car toward Carlton Terrace. "No, Alan—left!" Johnston shouted. "Hard left!" The Jaguar's tires groaned and juddered as he braked and threw the wheel over. The car came almost to a dead stop.

Imogen looked out the window down the hill, saw Mig-2 coming fast up Abbey Mount. Wilson saw it, too. He jammed the car into gear and lurched onto Regent's Road. To the left, Salisbury Crags, to the right, high, privet hedge. As the car surged to forty and fifty miles per hour, Wilson slalomed between cars.

Imogen looked out the rear window. Mig-2 had made the turn and was coming on. Wilson caught her eye in the rearview mirror. "He'll no catch us now!"

Ahead, two cars that had been too far away to meet them at the parliament building now scrambled to stop them along Regent's Road. Just down from the Burns monument, they both stopped dead and turned sideways, nose to nose, across the road, creating a roadblock. Wilson, rounding a curve, saw them take up position. "Fuck," he whispered as he let his foot off the accelerator.

Behind, Imogen could see Mig-2 gaining.

Wilson's eyes flicked left and right, looking for a way through. He shook his head slowly, then accelerated. "Tell yer mate, Mairtin, Ah'm sorry," he said and aimed for a three-foot gap between the two cars. Inside the car, Imogen and Ewan pressed themselves into their seats as the roadblock loomed closer.

The sound was shocking as Alan slammed between the two cars, sending glass and debris flying. Both cars spun with the glancing blow. Inside the Jaguar, Imogen felt weightless. There was an unholy crunch of metal and gears. The Jaguar sailed past the crash site, still traveling at high speed.

For a moment.

That speed, it quickly became apparent, was due almost solely to momentum. The Jaguar groaned and grinded as Mig-2 neared the two demolished cars. The Jaguar continued to lose speed and Wilson began coaxing it to "come on, come on ya bastard!"

Behind them, Mig-2 shot the gap between the two demolished cars and drew nearer to them from behind. Glancing back and seeing how close the other car was, Imogen yelled: "Ewan!" She handed over the rifle.

"Fuck!" Wilson hissed as the tried to keep the car moving.

"Roll down your window," she yelled at Johnston over the screaming engine. "If he catches us, I'm going out. When I've fired both barrels, I'm gonna need you to hand me the rifle."

Johnston nodded, his face white. He rolled down the window.

Imogen gauged the area, not many people around. Good. She'd fire the first barrel at close range, take out a front tire. The second she'd aim at the driver. Then she'd take the rifle for whatever came next. "Ready?" she asked.

"Wait!" Wilson yelled as the car rounded the bend, St. Andrew's House now in view less than 300 feet away. "Put that fucking gun away!" A red police car stood at the top of a security entryway. The crash some two hundred yards down the road had brought the people Ross had gathered to the front pavement of St. Andrew's House. A security officer stood next to his car, looking intently at the damaged Jaguar. Imogen could see he was saying something into the radio at his shoulder.

Ahead of them, another security car, a red and yellow Volvo Cross Country, zoomed toward them, a game of chicken.

Ewan let the rifle drop to the floor and crammed it against the seat with his heel as Imogen dropped hers. Security officers were pouring out of the near side of the building, rushing across the grass front as Wilson turned into the outlet for the front of the building.

Imogen looked behind. Saw the other car slow and come to a full stop. It reversed and turned round, speeding back the way it came. The Jaguar limped through the driveway toward the front. Four security guards, hands on guns stood in the road and signaled for them to stop.

"Haunds on the dash, counselor. Imogen, let them see yours, too."

She grabbed Ewan's headrest.

Johnston's window was down and he stated as calmly as he could muster: "We have an appointment with Janette Ritchie. I'm Ewan Johnston. These are my compatriots, FBI Agent Imogen Trager and Alan Wilson. We have vital information for the chief of staff."

"Slowly," said the guard nearest the open window. "Hands where I can see them."

A photographer ran toward the Jaguar, clicking pictures as he came on. Janette Ritchie and Ian Ross came quickly, too. The guard's partner held up a hand to them, telling them to stay away.

Across from this activity, at Calton Hill Road, Frenz's car, a silver Volkswagen standing alone at the intersection, also drew scrutiny from security staff, who began moving toward it. Inside, Frenz's radio was blaring. Scottish police, he heard, had surrounded and pulled over Mig-2. More police were swarming toward the two, disabled cars. Someone else was braying for fallback instructions.

Still in view of security officers, Frenz didn't want to pick up his radio. He fixed a look of frustration to his face—for their benefit—as though he was there by chance, having gambled on a shortcut that hadn't worked out. Which in many ways, was true. He turned the car and crept slowly away down the hill to Calton Road.

As Johnston, Wilson and Imogen stepped out of the Jaguar, hands open and away from their bodies, the lead guard's eyes grew wide as he saw the rifles on the floor.

"Gun!" he shouted, and pulled his service weapon. The squad surrounding the car did likewise. Ross, Ritchie and the photographer, who had slowed down rather than stopped at the guard's earlier signal, now stopped.

"Back up!" he commanded them.

Ritchie and the photographer started backing away, but Ross remained rooted to the spot. He saw it all ending here. Images of the January Sixth attack in Washington flashed through his mind. Could he trust that these officers weren't somehow complicit? One guard was leading the three away while another barked sharply into his radio wondering where the hell the bomb squad was. The shattered and smoking car, the guns—it *did* look like a botched bomb attempt. Around him, other security officers were talking into their radios.

Ross turned to Ritchie, who was still taking tentative, backward steps. He beckoned her forward to him.

"Jesus," she said as she drew close, "I wanted—"

"If they think it's a bomb," he interrupted, whispering harshly, "that means terrorists. Which means MI5. Which means we lose control of the situation; that *they* regain it and this was all for nothing." He looked apprehensively toward Calton Hill rising above them.

Ritchie squared her shoulders and stepped forward. "Captain," she began, "by all means do what's necessary to secure this situation, but we *invited* these three people, and *they're* part of what we need to protect right now."

She was next to the guard captain by this point, and she glanced around, up the road and down it. Her gaze fell on the steep, leafy bank across from them. "In fact," she said, lowering her voice, "we're very exposed right now. I'd like your men to surround them for protection and escort them inside. They have vital information which someone has gone to great lengths to prevent them from giving." Ritchie turned to the three, still standing by the car and held out her hands. "You have something for me, I think," she said.

Imogen opened her rucksack to reveal its contents—files, loose papers, and a laptop—for the benefit of the police and the nearby photographer. Ritchie took the bag, closed the top and slung it over her shoulder.

34

In London, Catherine Hernes was organizing her desk for the day ahead as Percy took the call from Frenz. "A bloody shambles, Calum," he said. Percy regarded the phone with some concern. Frenz had never used his Christian name before. "Scottish police are all over it. Three of Nesbitt's men have been taken. One is dead. The ranking MI5 officer has called me in. I'm on my way there now."

"And our buskers?" Percy asked.

"I left them out on this one. Told them to be ready, but that the first team would handle it."

"I see," said Percy. Under less tense circumstances he might have pointed out that the buskers should be regarded as the first team, but it was clear now to Percy that Frenz was taking his orders directly from Chamberlain and his cabal. Perhaps he had always done so. And they both knew that the irregulars could be counted on to kill everyone, which was probably why Frenz wanted only those thugs involved. Nevertheless, he was relieved that his men hadn't been involved. That, at least, was something. "Say nothing, during the interview, Jamie. Refer them to me."

"Yes, thank you," said Frenz.

Percy rang off with a promise to be in touch again as soon as possible and put in a call to Nigel Chamberlain.

"Yes," said Chamberlain, his voice far away. "It's been on the news. Something happening at government house in Edinburgh."

Percy relayed the details.

"Still," Chamberlain began, "no one knows what happened, or what it means. Certainly, they're not saying anything. There might yet be something in that, mightn't there? One of your MI5 brethren might be able..?"

"I shall try, sir, but I wouldn't put too much stock in that. I think it's damage control now."

"Every man for himself, then?" said Chamberlain.

In saying so, Chamberlain was reflecting on how he'd been able to hold his group together once, and how none of that seemed possible a second time. But Percy heard something else. He received what Chamberlain said as confirming much of what had been worrying him since the murder of Frank McDougall; that he'd been wrong to believe that he was protecting a secret that was damaging to the nation. In fact, it was damaging only to a few, well-placed people and those who were parasitic on them, like the PM's man, Michael Leyser. As he had for much of the night, Percy rehearsed the blows to legitimacy, good government and accountability that he had abetted. And the devil takes the hindmost.

"I'm still trying to figure a way out," said Percy equivocally. "Give me an hour or so?"

Seeing that that her boss was now off the phone, Hernes knocked and popped her cheerful head inside. "Anything burning you need me for?" she asked.

"No," said Percy, reflecting dismally on her choice of words. "But do stay close by."

The chief of staff had wanted a public scene of something important being delivered to the Scottish government. She got it. And if the fourth floor of St. Andrew's House had been a quiet hive of diligent activity overnight, the whole building now buzzed. The frantic, caffeinated energy of Ritchie's team seemed to transmit itself throughout, even as details of what was happening remained vague. Those not in the know greatly outnumbered those in. But not knowing in no way hindered conjecture. Throughout the building, large groups clustered together in offices and office doorways while the main business continued behind closed doors.

Who were the three people brought inside? Had they delivered something? In the tight gatherings throughout the building, rumor and speculation reigned, fed by a panorama of contradictory certainties. It was clear the three were now being grilled and sweated by counter-terrorism agents. Someone had said so. The view that they had survived an attack and were being debriefed for vital information was as confidently posed. Perhaps plans for an attack were what they'd delivered in that rucksack. Or, had they *foiled* an attack, and if so, how? Though the police had made arrests outside, it was significant that no one was talking about those developments either, on or off the record.

Someone had heard that the red-haired woman wasn't even British! Was this an international incident? Also: the chief of staff and First Minister were nowhere to be found. Were they in protective custody? Did the building remain in danger? Should they all be sheltering somewhere? Someone had heard from someone else that the First Minister was preparing to contact the Prime Minister.

Away from the tumult of buzz and gossip, Imogen, Johnston and Wilson had been placed into separate conference rooms to give their statements on the record. Two, bleary-eyed team members sat with each of them, recording them and asking pointed questions. For the record, each recapitulated details of the conspiracy, as they knew it, those recording them checking and confirming particulars.

On the second floor, two young assistants from Ross's communications department were hastily conscripted to begin work on what they were told was to be a draft of some final document. They looked dismayed and exhilarated in equal measure as—now among the elect—they were led past suddenly restrained knots of confused conversation, following Ross to the fourth floor. He walked them to the door of the double conference room. Taking leave of them, he instructed them to give every assistance to the Permanent Secretary, who had been briefed that morning and would bring them up to speed.

It was time for Ross to go to work. He felt that the best way to contain what they needed to conceal was to give events of that morning a drab patina of truth. He began the press conference with a bored, pompous tone, noting in his official drone that it was still unclear what was behind the events and that it could turn out to be as routine as a drunk driving spree. But the fact it had taken place near St. Andrew's House and in full view of the police and guards meant that every avenue needed to be explored.

Rebuffing questions, he read a statement from the First Minister (which he had written and which she had not seen) praising the quick work of the guard and singling out for special commendation, Captain Sunderland, whose alert thinking and quick action kept the incident from developing into something potentially worse.

"We are all trying to get to the bottom of what's happened here," he concluded, "and I must ask you all to refrain from making more of this than may be warranted."

In response to a reporter's question about guns being found inside the Jaguar, Ross said he "hadn't heard that," and he stressed again that, "we let the police do their job before jumping to conclusions or fanning rumors." He stepped off the speaker podium hoping that some other calamity or shiny object might draw their attention and hunger. He had few illusions that his thin gruel had satisfied them, but it would, he hoped, buy some time.

35

By late afternoon of a day that began so violently, Imogen and Ewan awoke in a cheery, expensive hotel room to a blissful sense of calm and relative quiet. And each other. (Imogen and Ewan had caused a bit of a stir on arriving, when they insisted on sharing a room at the hotel where they were taken a little after lunchtime. While Wilson grinned and shook his head, the officer in charge considered a moment and shrugged. It would make guarding them simpler. Behind the locked door, with a guard at the end of the hall, they had all three immediately fallen asleep.)

Ewan and Imogen tried, without much success, to keep their lovemaking quiet. As they lay resting in each other's arms getting their breath back, Imogen observed, "if it's not someone in the room, it's someone directly outside the room. Maybe one day you and I will be truly alone together." The remnants of a clear, brilliant sun scattered among high cirrus clouds outside their window. Unbeknownst to them, even if they'd been able to care, Wilson, in his own room across the hall, for once with all the Wi-Fi and telly he could use, slept soundly on.

The white sheets gleamed in the winter light, Imogen's hair lustrous and deep in contrast. It was a massive bed, and Johnston was feeling expansive. "These four corners," he declaimed, spreading his arms to include the whole mattress, "have seceded from the Union. Henceforth, no longer the UK, nor Scotland, this shall hereafter be known as Johnston-Trageria. Proclaim it through my host!"

She rolled on top of him and sat up, her hands pressed into his chest. "I think I'd like to hear you proclaim something else. You were sounding awfully religious just a little while ago..."

In Ritchie's office, as she and her team strategized, an email popped up on Ritchie's screen.

"That's alarming," she said, turning the screen so that others could see. "From MI5. Bet they're going to try and put a muzzle on us." Her hand hesitated over the mouse. "If I don't open it, could I say it didn't arrive in time?"

Ross peered at the screen. "It's from the SET Commander, Calum Percy."

They all looked at one another.

In London, Percy stared at his own screen, wondering what would happen next. Whatever it was, it would do so without him. He printed out his resignation and signed it. In the details about the cover-up he had sent to Janette Ritchie, he had initially tried to keep Jamie Frenz's name out, but he had learned from his counterpart in Edinburgh, that CCTV showed Frenz as the driver of the car on Calton Hill Road. His counterpart had wanted to know what action Frenz had been directing, and how it had all gone so wrong.

That evening, while eating room service dinner, all three gathered in Wilson's room to watch the news. There were few facts and none of the fireworks they had expected. There were news reports that the men in the two cars who had tried to block their final run were in custody, as was the driver of Mig-2, but there wasn't as yet any clear indication regarding how they were related or what they had hoped to accomplish by their actions. Further, there was speculation that a one-car crash near Deaconness Garden might also be related. But revelation of the conspiracy and the actors remained obscure.

The First Minister had missed some early appointment that day, but Ian Ross, communications adviser, noted that there was no relationship between events, "other than that the tumult and surprise of the initial investigation had thrown her schedule into something of an upheaval...as you can well imagine." Talking heads pondered how, and in what way—indeed if—they were all related. For the moment it remained a mystery.

In London, behind closed Cabinet doors, there was no mystery. The documents and allegations transmitted to the PM's office laid bare the case for interference in the 2014 referendum and its subsequent cover-up.

The PM and select Cabinet members were in rapt, private consultation. Michael Leyser, cast in the role of Prefect, was dispatched to convene a disciplinary tribunal for Chamberlain, Townsend and Nesbitt meant to convey the Head Boy's displeasure, assign blame and mete punishment. Jefferson Weaver, not one of them—not even British—would be dealt with separately.

* * *

As pleasant as it was to feel safe and be together, the next few days began to feel like imprisonment. Kept at bay with superficial reports of work and negotiations meant to show progress—but no details—it was not until late Sunday, the 24th, that Ian Ross turned up to inform them about what was happening.

"You've done excellent work. All of you," he began. "Imogen, this is a copy of the official notice that was sent from MI5 to the FBI, with profuse apologies for the mix-up about your involvement, and that discipline surrounding the cock-up is being handled internally." He handed her a two-page memo. "The First Minister appended a personal note commending your help —your perfectly *legal* help, of course—in a small, unrelated matter."

"A *small* matter? I—"

Ross held up a hand, asking her to wait. "Also, Professor Serres is in the process of being let go. She'll be reunited with her family as soon as possible tonight." He paused to smile at his own job well done, but Imogen, Johnston and Wilson looked concerned.

"For tomorrow morning's opening of Parliament," Ross continued, "the language about the Tories' power grab is gone. A dead letter. And as part of the King's Speech, he will announce that Scotland will be granted a second independence referendum. Parliament will grant the Section 30 order, and the referendum will be held in six months' time."

"And then what?" Johnston demanded, aghast at what he was hearing. "Job done, smiles all round? What about the murderers? The *murder* of my dear friend is officially received as a suicide! The family are bereft."

"They killed Wee Frankie," Imogen interjected. "*You're* complicit in it, Ian!"

"Yes," said Ross. "Though I had no *idea* what they would do. I was merely giving a status update—one...again, that I had no idea would—"

"And MI5 was involved!" she shouted. "The Met investigation into allegations of voting interference was suppressed. Probably internally."

"May I continue?" Ross asked pleasantly.

Imogen stared ferociously across the room. She seemed ready to burst into flame.

"As part of this arrangement," he continued, "those responsible for the murders of Francis McDougal and Donald Alban will be brought to justice."

"On what charge?" asked Johnston. "If you're suppressing the fact that the referendum was interfered with, what possible motive could they have?"

"Theft, in Wee Frankie's case, and a home invasion in Alban's."

"Thin," said Johnston.

"But enough," Ross countered.

"You're going to ruin *another* fuckin patsy's life?" demanded Wilson.

"No," said Ross. "These are no patsies. The killer of Frankie and the killer of Alban—the *actual* killers—will be brought up on charges and tried. They'll plead guilty."

"How're yese gonnae keep them two quiet?" Wilson wanted to know.

"I'm given to understand that certain arrangements for family and so on have been arranged on their behalf. Though not by us."

"Fuck, Ah thought *we* were mercenary," Wilson observed. "And when're we getting oot ae here?"

"And Chamberlain?" Imogen hissed. "Weaver, and whoever the fuck else was involved—they get a pass?"

"As part of agreeing to drop the Make Britain Better Again—"

"Is *that* what they were calling it?" Johnston asked.

"No," said Ross. "But as part of retracting their claws and issuing the Section 30 order...and bringing to justice those who committed the murders, we've agreed to let them handle their own housekeeping."

"So, nothing public?" Imogen asked.

"I'm afraid not."

"Where's the accountability?" she demanded.

"In the referendum," Ross replied, his tone that of a teacher to a bright student who isn't applying herself.

Imogen wondered what kind of whitewash deal she could get if she strangled Ross right there.

"One last bit of housekeeping," said Ross, piercing a menacing silence. He passed out three pieces of paper. "Standard, non-disclosure agreements," he explained.

"I have some housekeeping as well," Johnston said. "That destroyed Jaguar was a loner from a friend. I need you to stipulate that His Majesty's government—not Scotland—will pay to have it replaced."

"I can't speak for His Majesty's government," said Ross, "but I'll do what I can."

"You'll do it," said Johnston firmly.

Ross drew a pen from his inside jacket pocket. "I'll just jot something on the back of your ND form, then, shall I? Would you mind signing it first?"

"And if we don't sign?" asked Johnston, already reading his.

"Well...there is the matter of your striking and killing a man in the street in Dundee, Mr. Johnston—from which accident, you fled. Aggravated assault and unlawful death for Mr. Wilson here. There's a firearms charge..."

"This is MI5 paperwork!" Imogen exclaimed. "How do we know—"

"The Met's Special Enquiry Team commander has resigned, and his second-in-command is in custody. He will be charged with something or other. From a close, internal source," he continued, though he wouldn't name Calum Percy, "we have files detailing who was involved. Changes will be made. For starters, too many people are wearing too many different hats." He drew another pen from his inside jacket pocket and handed it to Imogen. She ignored it and continued reading.

Wilson turned to Johnston and asked in a low whisper, "You're my solicitor. What would you advise me to do?"

Johnston took the pen from Ross and signed at the bottom. With a sour, resigned expression, he handed it to Wilson, who duly signed the document. Imogen sat back in the couch, arms folded.

"It's for the best, Imogen," said Ross. "No one likes this, but it's the best that can be done."

"*This* is the best?" she spat.

Johnston put his hand on her thigh. He shook his head.

Imogen sat forward and hurriedly signed the document. Ross flashed his 100-watt smile and placed the signed forms in his portfolio as he stood up. "Thank you," he said. "Check out time is 3 pm tomorrow. We'll have drivers to take you wherever you want to go. Your cell phones and laptops will be returned to you shortly before then."

He clapped the binder shut and put it in a leather satchel. "You've done a great service. And your work will usher in great changes. Even if it doesn't feel like it right now." He looked at Imogen for a moment longer, as though there were something more he wanted to say just to her. But, as on their first meeting, whatever it was he wanted to say, he let it go and walked out. The policeman outside the door pulled the door shut.

"This is bullshit!" Imogen raged.

"It is," Johnston agreed.

"Am Ah the only one who was glaikit enough tae believe that government was meant tae be *better* than a pack of thieves?" Wilson demanded.

"Well," Johnston began, "there *are* rules..."

"Aye, an they've aw been broken, haven't they? Rule of law? That's jist fuckin words."

"Whether the punishment fits the crime is always a bit of a crapshoot, but it *seems* that everyone who had a dirty hand in it is being dealt with," said Johnston. "This whole thing feels like a pretrial plea agreement."

Wilson considered a moment, then nodded, understanding. For her part, Imogen either didn't, or didn't want, to understand. She was also finding Ewan's reasonable tone infuriating. "A plea bargain?" she asked bitterly.

"Before a case gets to court," Johnston continued, "the parties have latitude, options. At trial, both parties are constrained..."

"Oh, I understand *why* they did it this way," she said. "A full fight in the open—threads leading everywhere, political parties staking out ground, maybe some backstabbing from the backbench."

"And in a public trial, you can't predict the outcome," said Ewan.

"We're settling for the bastard verdict," she said.

James McCrone is the author of the Faithless Elector series—
Faithless Elector, *Dark Network*, and *Emergency Powers*—
"taut" and "gripping" political thrillers about a stolen presidency, which also feature FBI Agent Imogen Trager. *Bastard
Verdict* is his fourth novel. You can find the other Imogen
Trager novels at your local, independent bookstore, or wherever
you buy books.

To get the details right for this novel, he drew on his boyhood
living in Scotland, and he scouted the locations for scenes in the
book while attending Bloody Scotland in 2019 and again in '22.
His short stories have appeared in *Rock and a Hard Place*;
Retreats from Oblivion: The Journal of NoirCon, and in the
short-story anthology *Low Down Dirty Vote, vols.2 & 3*.

He's a member of Mystery Writers of America, Int'l Assoc. of
Crime Writers, Philadelphia Dramatists' Center, and he's the
vice-president of the Delaware Valley Sisters in Crime chapter.
A Pacific Northwest native (mostly), he lives in South Philadelphia with his wife and three children. James has an MFA
from the University of Washington, in Seattle.

You can follow James on Mastadon-@JMcCone@mastodon.scot,
Facebook-@FaithlessElector) and (at least of this writing) on
Twitter -@jamesmccrone4.

www.ingramcontent.com/pod-product-compliance
Lightning Source LLC
Chambersburg PA
CBHW010509100726
47902CB00011B/2143